# *A Fancy Man*

Sue McCauley lives in Christchurch with her husband, Pat Hammond. Her first novel, Other Halves, won the Wattie Book of the Year Award and the New Zealand Book Award for Fiction and was made into a feature film. Her other novels are Then Again and Bad Music. Her short stories have been published in anthologies and magazines. She also writes for film, television and radio.

SUE MCCAULEY

# A FANCY MAN

𝒱

VINTAGE

My thanks to the New Zealand Arts Council and the University of Canterbury for their support and financial assistance. This book was completed with the assistance of the University of Canterbury Writer-in-Residence Fellowship. Thanks also to Anna Rogers.

Random House New Zealand Ltd
(An imprint of the Random House Group)

18 Poland Road
Glenfield
Auckland.10
NEW ZEALAND

Sydney   New York   Toronto
London   Auckland   Johannesburg
and agencies throughout the world

First published   1996

Printed in Malaysia
ISBN 1 86941 283 4

For my excellent friends Norman Crosson and Karen Robinson, whose lives I have, in this book, borrowed from, reinvented and generally played fast and loose with. So that, while this book is indeed fiction, they are still there in the heart of it. With thanks and love.

The material quoted on page 119–20 and page 122 is from *My Country* by Dorothea MacKellar, courtesy of Curtis Brown (Aust) Pty Ltd; on page 40 is from *The Kroonbit Boys* by Lex McLennan; on page 184 is from *The Never-Never Land* by Henry Lawson.

# PART ONE

C H A **1** T E R

SHE LOOKED DOWN at the plate he set before her. Grey flesh sliding from delicate bones, rounds of carrots sawn like logs, unravelled leeks. She didn't look at him or at the girl sitting across from her. They watched her furtively, heads down. Aware of their own breathing.

Suddenly her hand shot out and she knocked the plate forward with the heel of her open palm. It cleared a trail across the discoloured formica. The plastic salt dispenser toppled into the girl's meal, a pile of salt dissolving in the gravy.

The door slammed behind her and from the bedroom the baby gave a waking cry.

Frank watched the girl as she carefully edged her knife under the transparent salt. He tried to come up with some fast remark to ease her thin face into a smile, but this time they were beyond all that. The girl knew it. Frank knew it. Perhaps even Lisa herself knew it.

The baby's crying persisted. Frank went through and lifted it from the cardboard box that was its crib. Lisa's clothes were spread about the floor and the blankets on their double mattress lay in a sour-smelling lump. She had stayed in bed most of the day. Just lying there, eyes moving from wall to ceiling.

Frank carried the baby back to the kitchen and held it on his knee while he ate one-handed. He could feel dampness seeping through to his thighs. The girl reached out a finger for the baby to clasp. She left it there encased in his small hand.

'Your dinner'll get cold,' Frank warned. 'Even hot it wasn't such a big success.' Grinned to himself.

The girl disengaged her finger and returned to eating. The baby began to grizzle. Frank jiggled him half-heartedly.

'Reckon it's because of this fella,' he told the girl. 'Sometimes it happens like that. I had a mare once, good little mare, but after

3

she dropped her foal you just couldn't get near her. Wouldn't have a bar of anything, not even her own foal. Had to bottle rear it. After a bit she came right, though.'

The girl chewed on it. 'Was she like that when I was born?'

'You'd have to ask her. Unless you can remember?'

'If I could remember I wouldn't've asked.'

Frank grinned fair enough.

'I can remember lots of things,' the girl said softly.

Frank looked at her. Bet you can, you poor little bastard. She looked away as if she'd heard him.

Just before dark he found Lisa crouched up beneath the pine trees. The baby's crying drifted from the house, now an enraged bellow of hunger. Frank stopped beneath the outer branches and waited until she raised her head. Even then he didn't speak because of the anger. Couldn't she hear her own baby? Why in God's name had he landed himself with this unnatural woman?

'That was opossum,' she hissed. 'You're disgusting.'

'You'd sooner we all went hungry?'

'What about rats? There's plenty of them about. Are rats on the menu?'

'People've lived on rats. In fact —'

'Oh Jesus! Yeah, I saw the movie. They were prisoners-of-war, for Chrissake.' She dragged herself to her feet. 'Whereas I'm just a prisoner.'

'That's right,' he said, 'that's what you are — a prisoner of your own bloody self-pity. Doesn't it matter to you — poor little sod, hungry as buggery, crying his heart out?'

'I've got no milk.' She rubbed her breasts. 'They're not even tight. There's nothing there.'

'You don't eat. 'What do y' expect?'

'There's nothing round here that's fit to eat.'

'Your daughter eats it,' he said. 'She's got some sense.'

Lisa suddenly bent down, searching for missiles. 'I hate you,' she hissed. 'Hate you.'

Frank deflected a bleached jaw bone with his hand. He grabbed her by the wrist. She tried to twist free.

'I wish to God I'd never met you.'

'Me too,' he said. 'Should've run you down, I surely should've.'

He'd dropped his mate, Rumbo, off in Campsie and was

heading back into town. She'd run in front of the car, heading straight for it. He'd stopped within an inch of her, every loose bit of junk in the Holden nose-diving forward. He'd felt suddenly sober and praiseworthy, but she was leaning on the bonnet hammering with a closed fist.

'Run me down,' she demanded. 'Run me down. You won't regret it.'

Her glazed eyes pleaded through the windscreen. Ridiculous. He wound down his window.

'Okay,' he said. 'You just stand there, and I'll back up a bit so I get a decent run.'

'So laugh at me,' she screamed. 'Why not? I'm fuckin' ridiculous. Laugh at me. But do it.'

He leant over and opened the passenger door. 'Hop in.'

'Why?'

''Cause I'm not in the mood for running someone down.'

'Where'd we go?'

'Where do you wanna go?'

'Hell,' she said, then reconsidered. 'No, I'm there now. In the ground, that's where I wanna go. The nothing place.'

He pretended to give it serious thought. She was moving slowly towards the opened door.

'Up to you,' he said. 'Only I wouldn't recommend it.'

'Why not?' Not so much a question as a playing out of the melodrama.

'Because,' he said, 'it gets very crowded this time of year.'

He watched her grin fight its way out. She heaved herself in beside him.

'Okay,' she said. 'Be it on your own head.'

THE BABY'S CRYING was eating into him, breaking him up. But he was still stronger than her. He twisted her right arm up behind her back and propelled her towards the house.

The girl was standing in their bedroom, hands clasped behind her, looking down at the baby. Frank let go his grip on the mother's arm.

'Feed him,' he said.

Lisa glanced at the baby's face, clenched with rage like a moving fist. She ducked her head.

'I can't.' She dropped onto the mattress that was their bed.

'You have to.' Shouting over the baby's unremitting wail. The girl staring from one to the other. 'Out,' Frank told her. 'You can start the dishes.'

Lisa was dragging her shirt from the waist of her jeans, pulling it right up to stare at her unengorged breasts. 'There. See. Blood from a stone.'

He snatched the infant up, hurrying to lay him against that exposed flesh but she whipped her shirt down and rolled away from them.

He lent the baby his thumb for a moment's silence. Lisa's shoulders were heaving. With effort Frank softened his voice.

'Look,' he tried. 'Poor little bastard's famished.'

'So you feed him.' Her voice muffled by bedding and tears.

'Ha ha.'

She raised her head so her voice would be clearer. 'There's that milk in the safe.'

'Cow's milk. You can't give him cow's milk. Don't you know anything?'

'No,' she said, still not looking at Frank or the baby. 'I know nothing.'

'And we don't have a bottle.'

She turned her head far enough to give him a look of contempt. 'That's a joke,' she said. 'That's a great joke.'

'Yeah. Okay. But we don't have a teat.'

The baby was disillusioned with Frank's thumb. Pulled his mouth away. Lisa kept her eyes on Frank's face.

'So grow one,' she said. 'You're so shit hot remarkable. Grow one.'

In the woolshed Frank fumbled around in the dark. If he put the lights on the manager would see it from those vast living room windows and be down like a shot, asking questions. He lit matches to identify the dried milk, hard as a rock of salt, and locate the beer bottles lined on a greasy shelf. The bottles all wore teats, a gang of bank robbers in balaclavas. Frank unmasked them one by one, slipping the teats into his pocket. He left the bottles on the shelf — there were newer, cleaner bottles under their house.

The girl eyed the teats as they revolved in the boiling water. 'One's falling apart,' she said. 'And they're too big.'

'They'll have to do.' He jollied her. 'He might grow wool. All those little brown tufts might curl up into a decent kind of fleece. He'd be the black sheep in the family.'

She refused to find him entertaining. 'Shall I take this off now?' The milk.

'Leave it a bit. If we boil the shit out of it it has to be safe.'

Exhausted by outrage, the baby had fallen asleep.

'He's supposed to have orange juice and stuff too,' said the girl.

Frank stared at her. 'You're right. I reckon you're right. How come you know that?'

'They had a couple of babies at the home.'

Frank glowered at the wall. Through boards and greasy wallpaper to the bedroom where she wallowed. 'They told her all that stuff at the hospital. Complete rundown, she said. Fat lotta use.'

Glancing at the girl, he saw her closing off. Tried to make amends.

'You'll be a good mother, Rube. Some day. Can just see you with the nappies all flapping on the line and the lino polished, tossing together some fancy casserole for dinner.'

She smiled out of the side of her mouth, not looking at him. He wished they could have spared her this reminder of maternal neglect.

IT WAS ONLY when she fell pregnant that Lisa had bothered to mention that she had a daughter. They were living, then, at Gundagai where Frank was halfway through a fencing contract. Her daughter, Lisa informed him one day, was in a welfare home in Dubbo. Frank had suggested they go up to visit. He wasn't thinking about the kid so much as Lisa — had the idea that the child might somehow jolt her life into alignment.

His mates in Sydney — Ken, the young guy he was flatting with at the time, and Rumbo — had strongly advised Frank to shake her off.

'She looks good, but she's loopy, Franko. Dangerous.'

But to Frank she'd seemed more okay than not. A firm rein, a calm and steady voice, sensible feeding was all it would take. Anyway, back then he'd enjoyed her unpredictability. Each day was like climbing behind a wheel and going wherever the road took you. It took a while to dawn on him that he was just the passenger in that car. Too late, though, to bail out. He'd bought into the mood swings, the irrationality, the adrenalin. By then she was carrying his child.

Ruby. On the drive to Dubbo he'd dribbled the name around in his mind, seeing a robust kid with rosy cheeks and her mother's smooth solid limbs. But this Ruby was a thin, white child with wispy hair tied back so tight her eyes popped. Bloodless lips and a chin you could have planted seedlings with.

'You come to get me?' Her voice so full of longing it fenced off all their possible exits.

It took another three months. The welfare authorities visited Frank and Lisa in their rented Gundagai home to assure themselves that the mother was now a fit and suitable person in a stable relationship. Frank, imprisoned between the wall and the kitchen table, vouched confidence in Lisa and the future for all three — all *four* — of them as a happy family unit. Even when the woman revealed how Ruby had been put into care — found alone in a flat two days after Lisa had gone out to buy Coco Pops and got sidetracked — Frank kept a confident face.

He knew he was painting himself into a corner. Heard himself inflating small particles of truth and presenting them as a varnished and wildly optimistic whole. But only had to remember that small brittle face and *You come to get me?* to know this was the only tenable course of action.

THE TEAT KEPT clamping shut, having to be removed, unclenched, replaced — but the baby persevered. Contentment spread from belly to limbs; he stretched out his legs and splayed his toes. The girl laughed.

Frank changed the nappies, slowly, carefully. His fingers were weather-rough and calloused. The baby watched him through half-closed eyes. Frank dangled the soiled nappy in the toilet bowl and pulled the chain. He tossed the sodden yellowed bundle into the bucket beneath the wash-house tub.

Lisa lay, still, among the dishevelled bedclothes. Asleep or pretending to be. As Frank bent to place the baby in his box he remembered Rumbo's yellow bitch Bridie with the mangled remains of her once-lively litter.

He carried the box and the baby out to the kitchen and placed them beside the woodbox.

'Reckon he'd like to have company,' he told the girl.

He went out, then, to feed the dogs. While they were crunching their biscuits he reached into Sal's kennel and pulled out the half-empty flagon of port. He unscrewed the cap and gulped down a few quick mouthfuls, one eye on the wash-house window, the only part of the house he could be seen from. The liquid oiled his bones. He took another couple of swigs, still watching the house, and edged the flagon back inside the kennel. Took tobacco from his pocket and rolled a smoke.

She wasn't against drink, not as a rule. It was just the way they were placed right now with his lousy wage, and the paraphernalia they'd needed for the baby, and the money they owed Frank's sister Helen.

Yet they were getting by, he was putting food on the table. Nothing wrong with opossum, he'd eaten it often enough in the past. If Samuels wasn't such a tight-arsed bastard they'd be eating hogget or maybe beef, as they should be.

For the price of the port — refill gut-rot, unnamed because no vineyard would be prepared to admit to it — he could have bought a baby's bottle and handful of teats. If he'd known.

ON THE THURSDAY Win Samuels, the manager's wife, offered Lisa and the baby a ride into Windsor to do the shopping. There was a message in that but Frank wasn't sure how to read it. Up till then he'd been borrowing the station's Landrover — to get Lisa to the hospital and to bring her and the baby home, and a couple of Friday nights to cash his pay cheque and buy groceries. Each time Jack Samuels had flinched as he handed over the keys.

'You'd've thought,' Frank said behind the wheel, 'I was asking the miserable bastard to lend me his wife.' Frank and Win Samuels — gotta be joking.

If Win was providing transport did it mean that use of the Landrover had been withdrawn? Frank would have to wait and see.

They drew up a list. Including a baby's bottle and teat, though Lisa had been cheerful for the last few days and her milk had returned in modest supply.

The port flagon was long empty but even if Lisa was willing it wasn't the kind of advertisement Frank needed, not just now. He could manage without. Had before and could again.

'See the doctor,' he told Lisa. 'I think you should.'

'What doctor?'

'Any doctor. The one that delivered you.'

'Delivered me from where?'

'Y'know what I mean.'

'I wouldn't know him again if I went down on him.' She slid her eyes to watch his face and laughed. 'Oooh.' She slapped herself on the wrist. 'You filthy bitch, you.'

He took no notice. 'Thought you were supposed to go back for a check-up? You and the boy?'

'You're so prim,' she told him. 'You're like some dried-up old spinster, you know that?'

'I didn't say a bloody thing.'

'Didn't have to.'

'A check-up,' he repeated.

'Even if I was s'posed to go, they don't check your brain. Only check me from the waist down, so that's no good to you, is it?'

'Please,' he said, and it wasn't a word he used freely. 'Cash the cheque, buy what you need and try and get to a doctor.'

She smiled at him as she stuffed clean napkins into a plastic bag. 'Pills aren't what I need,' she said. 'A life is what I need. I hate this bloody country.' She picked up the baby. 'Dunno why we came here.'

Frank scooped his tobacco from the table and jammed it in the pocket of his oilskin. He allowed himself an image of his hands around her neck just above the little gold chain with her zodiac symbol (Capricorn) and looked down to see his fingers and thumbs curling in like chicken feet.


THAT DAY HE was moving cattle from the eastern ridge. A sharp southerly wind making the beasts obstinate, the dogs reluctant, Maguilla edgy. The stallion danced up and down the narrow sheep tracks, his tail swishing like a cat's. All day Frank was telling himself things would work out, things never were as bad as they seemed.

It was because of Lisa — *only* because of Lisa — they'd crossed the Tasman. Not long after they'd requisitioned Ruby a couple of well-dressed Asian men had come to the house looking for 'a friend'. They rolled off various names she could be using, Lisa Adams among them, but Frank was onto them, acted friendly but bemused. He walked them to their car, talking all the while about Aussies having to put the past behind them, the RSL having it all wrong. Was still talking when they drove off.

Lisa had an explanation. The year before she'd been picked up for dealing speed but never charged. In her circles that was reason for suspicion. Lisa knew she had to get away, and did. A few weeks later Frank was kind enough to refuse to run her over. And, well, yes, okay, she had done a deal with the cops, but a harmless one. As agreed, she'd enrolled at a drug rehab centre and, as agreed, they dropped the charges.

'Must've struck some good sorta coppers,' said Frank. It wasn't exactly disbelief. Right or wrong he was on her side now. And she was in danger.

Frank took credit, back then, for the fact that Lisa was no longer eager to die. And there was the unborn baby, his baby. And Ruby, who didn't deserve to have her newfound mother slaughtered so soon after re-acquaintance.

'You'll like New Zealand,' he promised them. He'd never been there himself. It had seemed a little tame, like stepping out your back door, but he liked New Zealanders, the ones he'd met. Had found them low on bullshit.

THE GIRL WAS waiting by the steps when Frank and the dogs got back to the house. He knew by her face that something was wrong, something more than usual, but the wind whipped their voices away.

He slid from the saddle and flipped the reins over the stallion's head. Ruby backed up the steps as they approached. Horses made her fearful.

'She's gone.'

He put his hand on her thin hair. 'S'okay. They went to town with the boss's wife. Must've got held up.' He turned to unbuckle the surcingle.

'No,' said Ruby flatly. 'She came back.'

Frank slid the saddle and saddle cloth from the horse's back. The dark brown coat retained the damp outline of the saddle. An Australian saddle with knee pads, Jack Samuels coveted it. Frank stood with the saddle on one arm as the girl unclenched her fingers and handed him a crushed scrap of brown paper.

'She said give you this.'

*See you in hell, L.*

There were grease stains on the paper. He rolled it into a ball.

'She was here when you got home from school?'

Ruby nodded.

'So how did she go?'

'Just walked.'

'What? Carrying the baby?'

'He's here.'

In the bedroom Frank peered down at his son. His eyes were open, they were no longer blue.

'So when was this?' he asked the girl. 'How long ago?'

'Just after I got home.'

Two hours at the most.

'Mind the baby,' he told Ruby. 'I might be a while. If you get scared call Sal in to keep you company.'

MAGUILLA HAD NEVER yet let him down. Even after a full day's work they reached the saddle through the hills in no more than twenty minutes. From there they could see, in the fading light, the road snaking across across the flats towards the town. No ant-sized figure crawling along the verge, but she could be on the down slope of the hill and temporarily out of view. He waited in the gusting wind and watched, but the light was fading quickly. One solitary vehicle wound its way up the hills. He saw its lights come on as it rounded a bend and he watched the beam for a while as it slid over grass or gorse, first on one side, then the other. Never lighting upon a solidly built young woman with aching breasts trudging into the darkening distance.

Had she managed to thumb a lift? Or arranged for one? Nothing, with Lisa, could really surprise him. Good riddance, he told himself, but there was the girl to consider, and the baby.

She'd be back. *See you in hell.*

'What do you reckon?' he said to the horse. 'She's probably back at home already. Probably shot up to the big house. Bloody hell, would've spent the whole day bawling on Win Samuels' shoulder telling her God only knows. Poor Lisa stuck out in the wops with a hopeless old bastard. What do you reckon Maguilla, old mate? Wild goose chase? Turn around?'

The ute passed them as they headed back home. It went by slowly and pulled over just round the next bend where the road widened. The woman wound down the window. Frank steered Maguilla to where he could see her face in the almost-dark.

'Hi,' she said. 'You're the new shepherd at Titahi Station.'

'Right,' he said cautiously. The terminology made him cringe. *Shepherd*! But priorities were different here. Besides, she was from Yorkshire or thereabouts and wouldn't know any better.

'I recognised the horse,' she said, 'from description.'

'Jack Samuels been complaining?'

She laughed. 'I run the local pony club. Leila comes from time to time. Besides, small place. You know.'

Frank slid from the saddle and moved closer to the window.

'What else,' he asked the woman, 'have you been told about me?'

'Nothing you need to worry about.'

'That's a relief.'

She laughed politely. 'It wasn't just the horse, impressive though he is — you look like an Aussie.'

'The hat.' He pushed it back.

'That too.' Her hand reached out. 'Judy Gordon.'

'Frank Ward,' he said, but she was looking past him at Maguilla.

'Uncut. Has he got papers?'

'No. But I can tell you his lineage.' He unwrapped his tobacco and tugged a tissue loose, holding it with the corner of his mouth while he pinched out a ration of tobacco.

'The stud fee?'

He rolled the cigarette between his fingers and thumbs and ran his tongue along the glued edge. 'Truth is, I don't know what a fair rate is over here. You could come and see me and we'll talk about it.'

'I will,' she told him. Forty, not much more, blond hair, or grey, tied back. A good face. Sensible.

'Can I ring you?'

'No phone. You could leave a message with the Samuels.'

'Good. Nice to meet you.' Winding up her window.

'You didn't happen to . . . pass anyone . . . hitching?' Jabbed his thumb at the road behind them.

She shook her head. He could see the questions forming but she wasn't the type who'd ask. A kind face, for a moment he was tempted to tell. My woman's left us. Us is me, a baby so tiny he

*13*

could sleep in a decent-sized baking dish and a scrawny bantam of a girl. She's left us with a half-filled bag of groceries and no money till next pay day.

Help me!

But Lisa would be waiting for him back at the house, coaxed in from some ridiculous hiding place by the lure of electricity. The unspent money still in her pocket.

Frank took a step back, gathering up the reins, and the woman finished winding up her window and slid the gear lever.

THE GIRL WAS cooking fat pale pancakes. She looked hopefully at Frank's face as he came in the door then turned back to the stove.

'Rube, you're a treasure,' he said. 'I got a whiff of those three miles up the road and it kept me going.'

'Did not!'

But he saw he'd pleased her.

'Not a sign. Not a bloody sign.' He unzipped his boots and kicked them away. Went through to the bedroom to check the baby. Asleep in dry nappies. The girl came and stood at the door, whispering.

'I made up the milk like it said and he drank it all and I bent him over for the wind.'

They went back to the kitchen. 'You're a nanny *par excellance*.'

'What does that mean?'

'Buggered if I know.' He flipped a smoking circle of dough onto its back. 'No. It's French for fantastic.'

She was a glutton for food and compliments, but never anything to show for either.

'Am I useful?' she asked, as they were eating.

He let her wait while he chewed and swallowed, took another bite, chewed and swallowed it.

'Rube,' he said finally, 'I'd say you're as useful as hind legs are to a dog.'

She considered. Looked down at the table, rocking gently back and forwards in her chair. He took it to mean she was pleased. Then she resumed eating. Frank reached out and put a hand on her skinny shoulder.

'We'll be okay,' he said. 'We'll be just fine. You and me and the babe and Maguilla and old Mac and Sally. We'll all of us look after each other.'

14

# C H A 2 T E R

BETTER A STRAIGHTJACKET or hacking his veins with a blunt nail. In his forty-five years Frank had never felt so humiliated.

He stood in the Samuels' kitchen where everything gleamed red and white beneath a fierce bulb and explained. The Samuels kids drifted in, drawn from the television by a whiff of real drama. They propped themselves at the open door. Two boys and a girl, all of them fleshy and freckled like their mother.

'So what happens now?' snapped Jack Samuels. As if life was a soap opera and Frank was privy to forthcoming episodes.

'She gave no hint,' said Win. 'None at all. Not to me. You'd've thought . . . Did she take her clothes?'

Win thought he'd done Lisa in. Her dismembered body stacked in the hot-water cupboard or jammed beneath floorboards. The moment Frank left, Win would ring the police.

'Some,' he said. 'According to Ruby.'

No one had asked him to sit down. No one had said, 'You poor bastard,' or offered him a drink. Frank standing in the Samuels' shiny remodelled kitchen beside a casserole dish with the remains of an apple sponge pudding at his elbow. *Wayne's birthday* ringed and arrowed on the calendar and the TV twittering from the lounge. It all felt, at that moment, so desirable. So unattainable.

'So what,' nagged Samuels, 'do you plan to do?'

Frank could only shrug. 'Buggered if I know.'

He'd washed up and put on clean clothes before coming up. Win would be seeing that as evidence of a murderer's guilt.

'One thing's for sure. I can't herd cattle and mind a brand-new baby at the same time.'

'Then you better get someone to mind it for you.'

Frank had punched men in the mouth for using just that tone of voice.

'By tomorrow?' He tried not to make it derisive.

'Take tomorrow off if you have to.' The offer dragged out of him. *You bastard. You miserable arsehole swine. I hope some day life drops you in some great bloody unexpected hole and you have to crawl on your hairy belly and beg from strangers.*

'She took my pay.' Frank looked at Win, who was, after all, a mother. 'I won't have money to pay anyone until my next pay day.' Two weeks away.

No one spoke. The clock behind Frank ticked him off, and from the other room the TV chorused *Are your McLeans showing?*

'He could call in the Welfare people,' said the girl, Leila. 'They'd look after the baby. And Ruby.'

'Bugger that — they'd take them away. Nah. Never.' Frank glared around in case Jack was inclined to favour this solution. Unexpectedly, Leila gave him a smile.

'We could talk about the money,' offered Samuels, heavily. 'An advance.'

Frank looked at Win. 'Where would I find someone? By tomorrow!'

Samuels was also looking at Win. She lowered her eyes and heaved a resentful sigh.

'One week.' She raised one hefty finger in case Frank was deaf. 'For one week I'll mind your baby during the day. You can bring him over in the morning and take him home when you knock off. In that week you sort something out.'

Frank looked at Win's kids, strapping great things. Surely that was what counted, she knew how to raise them sound of limb. As for the rest, how much harm could anyone do in a week?

'Thanks,' he said. He glanced at Samuels, who had made no move to reach for a wallet or chequebook; obviously Win's offer was deemed to have cancelled out Frank's need of funds.

FOUR DAYS INTO that week and Frank had done nothing about finding a baby-minder. Where to start? He had no phone and knew no one in the district. Besides, he felt paralysed by the possibility of Lisa returning. The tobacco had run out and the port in Sal's kennel was just a soulful memory. Frank and Ruby spent the evenings pegging out and bringing in nappies. Nights were a stumbling cycle of ruptured dreams and fractious awakenings.

He would remind himself that one day all this calamity would be a memory. A yarn to tell on a summer night. Highlighting the funny bits. There were bound to be some.

On that fourth day, when he walked home from the Samuels' place holding the baby to him with blood-splattered hands, he found Leila there with Ruby. She jumped up as Frank walked inside.

'Can I take him?' Shoving out her arms. 'I think he's just gorgeous.'

Frank passed the baby over. He saw the girl's eyes move from his caked and blackened hands to his blood-smeared shirt.

'I just killed your dinner,' he said. Including her in his anger.

She pushed her cheek against the soft baby cheek and rocked the boy. Ruby caught Frank's eye then looked away. Frank peeled off his offensive shirt. The Samuels girl was making dovey sounds. Ruby put down the potato she was peeling and left the room.

'Found someone to mind him yet?'

Frank grunted no. Filled the kettle.

'School holidays start next week.'

'Rube never mentioned.'

'Only for secondary. Hers start the week after.' Leila was still goo-gooing at the baby. 'I could mind him.'

He put the kettle on the only element that worked and took a good look at her. 'How old are you?'

'Old enough.' Her eyes skittered over his face then away. 'Fifteen. Old enough to mind a baby.'

At fifteen Frank was a working man. He had his own dogs, his own horse, a saddle and a sex life. Cora Watson, twenty-two and divorced.

'Have you asked your folks? So ask them.'

'How much'll you pay?'

'Ask your parents. Then we'll see. Wouldn't be much — you know how I'm placed.'

When he got out of the shower she'd gone. Ruby was back with the potatoes.

'You don't like her,' he said.

Ruby sniffed. 'She's alright, I s'pose.'

'You're allowed not to like people, Rube.'

'I said she's alright.'

'Came down to keep you company, did she?'

'To have a nose, more like.'

'She offered to mind the baby during her holidays.'

'Why?'

'To earn some money I guess.'

'S'pose you said yes?'

'Have to get someone, don't I?'

'Only 'till my holidays.'

'Rube,' he said, 'you're a cracker of a kid, but you're only nine.'

JUDY GORDON TURNED up on the Sunday to talk about stud fees. Frank was shamefully pleased to see her. They were both of them foreigners in this miserable place. He knew that in different circumstances he'd find merit in the district — in the lie of the land, the circumspection of the people.

As Ruby hunched watchfully over her social studies book, turning no pages, Frank brought in the baby. Showing him off, why not? Each day the infant grew more appealing. Judy Gordon smiled but didn't reach out to hold him.

'What's his name?'

Frank had to think. He and Ruby made do with 'baby'. The name had been a matter of dispute. He'd favoured Arthur, after his maternal grandfather. Another drinker, it was in the genes, but a good man nevertheless. Made a fortune then gave it away to strangers during the Depression. Frank's mother had thought her father a drunk and a fool.

'Ben,' said Ruby, for Frank.

'Babies seem so fragile,' said Judy 'Make me nervous.'

Frank snuffed out an emerging hope.

'Seems he made his mother nervous. She pissed off on us.'

He knew how it would seem to a woman.

If Win Samuels had told the coppers they'd never bothered to call on Frank. He had the feeling Win might now know more about Lisa's whereabouts than she was letting on. But nothing that had improved her opinion of Frank. Each time he dropped off or collected the baby he could read the headlines on her face: 'Mysterious Disappearance of Young Woman' had been replaced by 'Young Wife Abandons Children to Escape From Cruel and Improvident Husband'.

Maybe she was partly right. Like everything else, it depended on how you looked at it.

Judy had taken her time. 'So how are you managing?'

Frank looked at the girl. 'How are we managing?'

'Potatoes,' she said. 'And your boring damper stuff.'

'She took my pay with her.' Did he seem to be whining?

'I imagine that was no great sum anyway?'

'You'd be right.'

The baby gave Frank a smile. A baby with a smile like that deserved the best life had to give. Frank smiled back.

'I imagine you can shoe horses?'

Fool of a question, but he saw what she was thinking. On the other hand his back was dodgy — he'd done it in eight years ago at a rodeo, too much in need of the prize money. Shoeing Maguilla and the station horses was already more strain than he needed. Back pain could turn you overnight into an old man.

His mouth was saying, 'I've yet to meet the horse I can't slap a shoe on.'

He saw Rube's eyes head for the ceiling. She'd lived with his backache complaints. Also she favoured humility. He caught her eye and sent her a wink. Their luck was turning.

# C H A P T E R 3

A FLY WAS trapped at the window. Intermittent buzzing anger and then it would rest. The fly was Jess, but had a better view. From her desk Jess could see only a slice of hills, sun already sliding from them. The same sun that lay in narrow rectangles across the floor and slithered onto Mrs Whittaker's brown cardigan. A pattern like a picket fence around the bottom of the cardigan with glimpses of an olive-green blouse showing through. Same on the sleeves.

The sun bathed Gavin Cawley's black shoes, impeccably nuggeted. His legs stuck out beneath the desk. Curling hair, fine and golden in the sunlight. Gavin Cawley had kissed Jess on Monday in the gym equipment room, his tongue like raw liver jammed against her epiglottis. An urge to retch — disappointing, when they'd taken so long to get around to it. But Jess had told Janine it was fabulous.

Janine was big on kissing. She had a list pinned beneath the lid of her desk: encoded names and how they rated. One of them, who drove trucks for McGovern Transport, was twenty-five and married. A five-star kisser — as good as they got. Janine said people had the wrong idea about kissing. They thought of it as something you did before you started in on the other, but really kissing was the important bit. The other stuff was just transference of bodily matter. To kiss was to merge your soul and his.

Gavin Cawley's parents were religious. They mentioned God with a casual intimacy, as if he slept in their back bedroom, though they were only Presbyterians. The Cawley children went to great lengths to avoid any mention of God — as though he did indeed sleep in the back bedroom but was embarrassingly loopy.

Where did Gavin stand on the merging of his soul and Jess's?

Gavin had told Jess to ask her parents if she could go with him to the movies on a Saturday night during the holidays. Jess reported back that she wasn't allowed. It seemed the kindest way out. Gavin's parents would have had to drive them the twenty miles to Windsor and bring them home afterwards and that would be too embarrassing to bear. Better to wait till he got his licence.

Jess had known Gavin for years. Right through Curvey's Creek primary school where Jess's father taught them both — and every other child in Curvey's Creek — with painstaking fairness.

Gavin was not on Janine's kissing list. 'Scout's honour,' she said. 'Swear on m' mother's grave.' Her mother, in fact, was still above ground, working three days a week at the Windsor Four Square checkout.

Jess couldn't understand why Gavin had decided on her to look at and stick his tongue into. Her life was full of things she didn't understand — like the point of spending fine days in a classroom.

Still there. The fly. But sitting quietly. Seething or defeated.

The sun creeping up onto the blackboard. Chalk scrawl from the English teacher: *essays not yet handed in — Jessica Bennington, Keith Chapple, David Kake . . .* Jess's essay in her desk, still uncompleted. 'The Best Day of My Life'.

'What's wrong with that?' Marion, Jess's mother. 'Or hasn't there been even one good day in your fourteen years of suffering?'

In the end Jess wrote about her ninth and best birthday when she got her pony. 'The Day I got Lucky'. After the title nothing came. It was like that with writing. Feelings refusing to narrow down, lose their noise and colour and dribble out in the drabness of words. The storm of disappointment when she first saw the little grey Welsh pony. A horse, her father had said. She'd envisaged black and permanently rearing. Or white and brittle like her nine china horses, each of them standing in a different yet perfect pose. Until the breakages.

Four still good as new, three with legs Octopus glued, two raised toi-toi tails restuck (one slightly off-centre). And one with plasticine prosthesis — all four legs. Her brother's work when he was perhaps too young to know better. To their mother's distress, and Jess's, the original legs were never found.

Up until Lucky's arrival those nine white horses had run untamed in Curvey's Creek, racing cars and trucks along the road verges, jostling to drink beneath the bridges, stamping and rolling their eyes. After Lucky they shrank back into china ornaments.

Lucky was malicious; she bit, she kicked, she bucked. When all those tactics failed she would refuse to move, standing motionless except for her grinding teeth while Jess lashed the grey rump with willow sticks. And then, when finally she condescended to budge, Lucky would disregard Jess's instructions, clamp the bit between her teeth and go wherever she pleased at whatever speed she fancied. Rushing under low-hanging branches to sweep Jess off, cantering close to barbed wire fences to rip Jess's leg, bolting — then stopping dead in front of huge Scotch thistles or rivers so that Jess would fly over her head. The pony would watch with pleasure as Jess removed clinging prickles or climbed sodden onto the river bank.

But Jess grew larger and stronger and meaner. She became Lucky's match. The pony grew more obliging, but never entirely obedient. Always thinking up some new malevolent act.

These days Jess rode Lucky only now and again, as a favour. Lucky was too old and too small. But, irrationally, the girl loved the grey pony more than she loved her sister or brother, more than she loved her parents. Loved her much more than Pedro, the horse she now rode, who was kindly and eager to please. Assuming, that is, that love was a certain aching glow beneath your rib cage. Loved the pony for her dogged intractability.

Mrs Whittaker's patterned arm catching the sunlight as she gestured. 'In 1960 Lin Piao began to use the People's Liberation Army as a Maoist propaganda machine. Now what do we know about propaganda?'

Linda Quigley waving her arm. Janine looking up from her love comic, catching Jess's eye. Jess biting back a laugh though nothing was funny. The second to last day of term. Sun shining. Sitting like battery chooks while Mrs Whittaker tossed them the history of China, handfuls of yellow wheat. Hardly anyone bothering to nibble, or even make closer inspection.

Mr Whittaker killed himself in his brand-new Skyline garage. Blocked up the holes and ran the car in neutral, as if he'd had the garage installed for just that purpose. He was a Scout master so people jumped to conclusions. Mrs Whittaker's history lessons weren't nearly as interesting as her own life, about which she said nothing. Year after year her students stared at her serviceable serge skirts, her subdued cardigans and saw Mr Whittaker slumped in his car, blue-faced and bulging-eyed, the fly buttons on his khaki shorts undone.

It seemed to Jess that Mrs Whittaker must know this was so. Why didn't she leave Windsor? Did it give her secret pleasure that her husband's manner of dying had lifted her out of anonymity?

Jess, too, was anonymous. The teacher's daughter who sat in the middle of the classroom, keeping quiet. Neither clever enough nor dumb enough to merit special attention. A girl whose childhood golden curls had darkened and lengthened into a coppery ponytail with chewed ends. Freckled skin and three warts in that little cove of flesh between finger and thumb on her left hand. (She's tried the milk from dandelion stalks and rubbing them with a coin but each morning they're still there.)

Jess's stars in the *Windsor Express* on Wednesday said, *Your emotions are under control, reflecting a more analytical phase in your life.*

Janine poked Jess with her ballpoint pen. Gavin Cawley was looking around at them. Janine grinned at Jess. Janine and Jess were best friends, everyone knew, but Jess liked being with Pedro more than she liked being with Janine. Did that make her odd?

IT USED TO be that Leila Samuels was Jess's best friend. Their last years of primary school and into the third form at Windsor High. Because they each had a horse but also because the Bennington kids and the Samuels kids didn't fit in at Curvey's Creek the way other kids did.

Curvey's Creek is farming land. Sheep and cattle. Two, three, four generations of farming families — including the Curveys — on blocks of land bought or swindled from the Maori and sub-divided over the years to accommodate sons. So everyone living in Curvey's Creek is a farmer, a farmer's wife or a farmer's child. Everyone except for the Benningtons, the Samuels and, more recently, Judy Gordon.

Owen Bennington is the schoolteacher while his wife Marion commutes to Windsor in her red Toyota Corolla to sell real estate for Barker Hanley Realtors Ltd. Jack Samuels is a farm manager. Titahi Station, backing up into the ranges is, in 1982, the largest property in the area. The owner lives in England. Jack Samuels is a farmer like everyone else's father, but it's not the same.

23

'Manager,' the kids would say in the school playground, in the kind of voice they'd use for a shearing-shed 'rousie' or 'janitor'. If Jess could hear it in their voices so could Leila. Though maybe Leila didn't care.

Jess had never trusted Leila any more than she'd trusted Lucky. Couldn't be sure, now, that she'd even *liked* Leila. But back then they sat together in school and rode together out of school. Made a jumping ring which Lucky balked at and Johnny, Leila's pensioned-off stock horse, knocked down. And they raced — neck and neck, stirrups short and noses pressed to the mane like real jockeys. Johnny should have won these races but Lucky would swerve in, yellow teeth flailing, and unnerve him into second place.

In Curvey's Creek there was everywhere yet nowhere for two girls to ride. Up and down the roads, because Leila liked to be seen, but there was only the main road with three minor roads branching off. Two of these were no exit, ending at gates with private property signs, and the third was nothing more than a detour. Even the main road went nowhere much; tarseal gave way to shingle just beyond Titahi Station, after which it snaked up over the ranges to come out eventually on the coast. A handful of rough holiday shacks clinging to the rocks above stony coves littered with seaweed. Waves dumping and churning so hard you always had to shout. Nothing to make it worth driving there.

So the girls rode to the gravel pit many times. They rode to the top of Thompson's Saddle and back. They rode to old Mr Thornley's to get the horses shod. They built their jumps in the horse paddock that Owen leased for Jess. A barrel jump, two brush jumps, a log jump. In summer they rode to river holes and forced the horses in to swim. Each year the river holes would alter. The horses would splash up and down river beds looking for the slowest and deepest holes gouged by winter floods.

If Curvey's Creek bordered a highway, traffic and life would pulse through it. Shops and service stations would spring up, people would move faster and laugh more often. Young men would have pulled up and leant out the windows of Ford Falcons and offered Leila and Jess cans of beer and cigarettes.

There was one other road, long disused, that linked Turnbull Road with the main road. Jess liked it best for riding, but it didn't suit Leila. On a road like that she would never be seen.

Before the school house was built the Benningtons lived in the rabbiter's cottage down Turnbull Road. It was built by the Rabbit Board in the days when men were employed by the government to shoot rabbits. The second and last rabbiter to live there turned his rifle around one night and shot himself in the temple. His dog went bush and his horse drank the trough dry before Rick Chaney, his neighbour, found the rabbiter's body. A few years later the Education Department bought the house, cleaned it up and added a patio with french doors.

Jess spent her first seven years in that house. She watched frogs raft on green slime in the old water trough, she climbed the scratchy old macrocarpas and built stockades and villages around their roots. She explored Turnbull Road and discovered rutted wheel tracks, encroached upon by scrub just across from the Turnbulls' rural delivery box. A secret road that everyone else was too busy to notice.

The Benningtons lived for almost eight years in the Turnbull Road house but still people called it the rabbiter's cottage.

'So IN 1963 a limited test ban treaty was signed in Moscow.' Mrs Whittaker paused to let this sink in. The sun had moved to the blackboard, a collapsing rectangle.

'China refused to sign. Do we know why?'

Linda Quigley's arm shooting up. Linda knew why. Clever Linda.

Janine still intent on her comic book, chewing her hair.

JESS HAD WANTED to ride on the hard wet sand. To look behind and see beach receding mile after mile and only her horse's hoofprints. She wanted to ride into waves, slide from the glistening back and float with her fingers entwined in tail or mane. Leila just wanted adventure.

They'd set off on a Sunday morning, not so early that questions would be asked. An early autumn day. Jess took two apples, six buttered slices of bread and her swimming togs. She was riding Pedro, newly on loan from Judy Gordon. They waited for Leila at the station gate.

Leila was only a little late. She had a packet of Chocolate Wheatens and a bottle of home brew she'd stolen from the wash-house. Just before the Cawleys' loading bay the cap blew off the bottle with a sound like rifleshot. Johnny leapt all over the road with beer foaming down his flanks. Leila managed to stay on, just. She was cursing and kicking at Johnny. Then she took the bottle out of her sodden bag, drained the sediment and spat it out with disgust. She hurled the bottle at a rock on the road. It shattered. Jagged spires of amber glass.

'We'll pick it up,' said Jess.

'What for?'

'You know —' Soft hooves, the frogs gouged and shredded.

Leila gathered up her reins and slapped them against Johnny's neck. 'You can if you want.' Over her shoulder.

Jess looked down at the base of the bottle. Largest, most lethal. Johnny was leaving and Pedro was anxious. They left the glass on the road.

By four that afternoon they were over the ranges but still couldn't see the ocean.

'Let's go back,' said Jess. 'It'll be dark before we're even halfway up the hill. And look.' Clouds that would block off the moonlight. The horses feeling their way on treacherous roads. Their families phoning each other, phoning Judy.

Leila wanted to go on. They went, Jess still thinking of virgin sand and Pedro's hoofprints, back feet slightly pigeon-toed.

Jack Samuels pulled over in his Landrover as they were looking down at a rocky cove. He was a hard man, Leila's father. Hard body, short cropped hair, angry face. An especially angry face. He had to find an occupied bach, a phone, somewhere to leave the horses overnight. Bundle the girls and their horse gear into the Landrover and drive them home.

They sat in the back, nervous, in trouble, trying hard not to giggle. Just past the Cawley farm Jack Samuels got a flat tyre and changed the wheel, cursing and muttering, while Leila stood holding the torch, its batteries almost flat.

That was adventure in Curvey's Creek. The worst trouble Jess had been in. The next worst was rabbit-punching Sheenagh, who asked for it, but was two years younger than Jess so everyone took her side.

Jess's parents blamed Judy Gordon for Jess and Leila's ride to the coast. They didn't say so, but Jess could tell. Owen rang Judy and asked to borrow her horse float, told her why. Judy offered to go herself the next morning and collect the horses.

The girls, she said, could spend the next weekend bagging horse dung.

'You owe me,' she told the two of them. Jess knew that already. She's owed Judy since the first time they met.

Jess was in Form One when Judy Gordon bought the fifty acres that Charlie Bradford had been forced to sell after he overspent in replacing the old family home with a sprawling brick mansion. Indoor swimming pool, heated conservatory, covered parking for five vehicles. People would take a drive while the builders were still at work, just to park on the grass verge and smirk.

They guffawed when the Dalgety's sale sign went up on Charlie's topside block. But Charlie Bradford got his own back — he turned down Gap Thompson's offer in favour of a middle-aged single woman with no connection or claim to Curvey's Creek.

As soon as the deal went through Judy parked a caravan beneath the blue gums and moved in. Lived in the caravan for eight months while she put in fences and built her house. Sometimes she could be seen working alone, other times she had helpers. Tents would go up alongside the caravan. Neither Judy nor her friends mixed with the locals. There was nowhere at Curvey's Creek for people to meet. Not a store, a pub, a petrol station or community hall. Not even a phone box. The school, a rugged eight-hole golf course and the cemetery — that was Curvey's Creek.

Judy Gordon had no children, didn't play golf and had no one to visit in the cemetery.

No matter how things may have changed in the rest of the world women didn't live alone in Curvey's Creek. Widows lived with their children or retired to easy-care houses in Windsor. Girls who couldn't find a husband in the district went off to train as nurses and teachers and secretaries.

The house Judy built was even sillier than Charlie Bradford's mansion, though barely one-tenth the size. It looked like something a child might draw with a first compass and set-square. Glass where there should have been corrugated iron, angles where it should have been straight.

By then she'd already raised the fences and brought in stock. Horses. Everyday-looking hacks, a tribe of underfed ponies, a handful of Shetlands. Judy Gordon was a horse farmer. Not a stud

27

farm, not even a specialist breeder. She outbid the pet-food men for younger horses, then prettied and trained them up to sell as riding hacks.

What a joke! Watch her come a cropper.

Horses were out of fashion in Curvey's Creek. On all but the steepest farms at the west end of the valley horses had been replaced by farm bikes and four-wheel drives. Some kids had ponies but half of these didn't get ridden after the novelty wore off. Their parents were glad to give the ponies away and buy the kids pushbikes. Raleigh 20s didn't need to be fed, or shod, or groomed; they didn't get ill and lose condition or overeat until they foundered. They didn't bolt or buck or open gates; they didn't need covering in winter and watering every day. They didn't need bridles and saddles and saddle blankets and girths and surcingles and hoof picks and brushes and curry combs.

Judy Gordon started up a pony club. Once a fortnight. Eight kids went, including Jess and Leila. No matter what they thought of Judy Gordon, the parents approved of pony club. Imagined their offspring aspiring, progressing, competing. A pony club made sense of the inconvenience and expense of keeping the animal.

Marion was one of those parents. Before the club, Marion would ask absurd things like, 'But what do you *do* at the gravel pit?'

At the first meeting Judy Gordon whacked Lucky on the flank and called her a wicked old tart, said Jess deserved better. The following month Judy tried Jess out on Pedro, offered him to her on loan.

Pedro was obliging and a decent size but Jess was prepared to forgo him if her parents insisted on selling Lucky or giving her away. She tried to get Sheenagh interested in riding. That was a rabbit-punching occasion; Sheenagh had a pushbike with eight gears. Then Jess tried Corin, but he'd seen Lucky's bared teeth at close enough range for the memory to last him a lifetime.

Her father let her have both horses. Marion wouldn't have. 'Got you curled right round her little finger,' she said to Jess's father in front of Jess. Anger like tiny shards of metal in her voice.

GAVIN IN THE back of the school bus where the boys sat. Jess

28

second seat from the front, reliving the feel of his tongue in her mouth. Might it have felt less horrible than she'd thought?

Leila Samuels pushing in front of Annette Chaney to talk to Jess, though they were no longer friends.

'One more shit day. Gotta job? For the holidays?'

Leila had, or she wouldn't have asked.

'You?' said Jess obediently.

'Nanny. A laugh, eh?'

'That's good,' said Jess. 'I s'pose.'

They hadn't fallen out, Jess and Leila. Just gone into different classes and in different directions. Leila hanging out with the rough kids from the north end of town. Weekends Johnny stayed in the paddock while Leila squeezed into noisy Cortinas and went off to live a life that Jess didn't want yet sorely envied.

Compared with Leila, Jess was still a kid playing with horses.

'Yeah good,' said Leila. 'Easy.'

'Who for? The married man?' That's what he was called. A farm worker if he was single, or else a *married man*. Nancy Bradford went off to Massey College and became a farm worker, but no one would hire her, not in Curvey's Creek.

'He might do you in,' said Annette Chaney hopefully, her voice muffled against Leila's side. 'Like his wife.'

'Ha ha! Anyway she's not dead,' said Leila. 'Julian Curvey's father picked her up just past the bridge.' Back to Jess. 'He's paying me and all. Only I might do a deal. You seen his horse? You'd go crazy for it. You'd give anything for a horse like that. Well, I might do a deal. 'Stead of he pays me I'll take the horse.'

Leila was like that. Mixed bullshit in with fact and shoved it in your face, so you either had to call her a liar or turn away. And if you turned away it was as though, somehow, she'd scored a point. But Jess turned away. Jess was the kind who turned away. And Leila was the kind who believed that making Jess turn away meant Leila was winning.

# CHAPTER 4

'YOU'VE GOTTA LAY down the law,' Ruby had said after the first time.

'Lay down the law.' He imagined sliding it from his shoulders and setting it on the floor among the bottles — his relief, his visitors' indifference.

'Right,' he said. 'Yup, you're right. That's what I gotta do.'

But the taste was still in his mouth, its essence of well-being, and the debris from their visit only reminded him that he had been lonely.

So the next time they arrived — a Saturday night — with the easy confidence of old friends, bottles clinking in their crate and something bubbly for the girls, Ruby fixed them with her fiercest magpie stare. Glaring at Frank when her disapproval went unnoticed. He knew she was right, but a frosted bottle was already in his hand and open.

Leila's friends. The first time, they'd been there when he got in from work. Waiting like a tour party, so he knew young Leila had painted him as a curiosity. Ruby was skulking in the bedroom. Frank had read that as shyness. Her dislike of Leila had been substantially modified by assorted trinkets which Leila presumably no longer needed. Ruby kept them in an empty chocolate box, also provided by Leila, and would examine and rearrange them in a way that Frank found hugely depressing. Ruby's school holidays had now started. This meant spending her days with Leila, like it or not, and the older girl was, quite sensibly, bribing her way into acceptance.

Frank was grateful to Leila. She kept his baby warm and clean and fed. She kept the wetback fire burning and was company for Ruby. Yet he was paying her for all this, rather too much, it seemed to him, without ever getting to feel like her employer. The kid was shrewd, in an ignorant kind of way. She never let Frank forget she was his boss's daughter.

And the three young men and the pink-cheeked girl were the boss's daughter's friends. So that, even when Leila reluctantly left her friends and set off up the paddock to the big house and Frank turned the mutton-flap stew into soup for six with hot damper, he felt the need to keep an eye on himself.

Later Leila had crept back to join them and she and the boy called Jason had spent quite some time together in the bathroom. He tackled her afterwards.

'You trying to get me in the shit?'

Leila had smiled at him. 'Don't worry, Frankie, I'm not a virgin.'

The others were watching, waiting on his response.

'That's your concern, not mine. Keeping my job is my concern. You get the picture?' But he felt skewered, ridiculous, and Leila just went on smiling.

He could see her life mapped out in that smile. At thirty-five a brick house, swimming pool, mobile barbecue, sales rep husband and three kids. Gin and tonic in one hand, her girlfriend's husband in the other. Living on the Gold Coast, where her type migrated from all over to nest and preen.

Her mates were town kids and not very shrewd at all. They'd never met anyone like Frank. Told him so repeatedly.

'You're somethink else, Frank. You're really somethink else.'

Who was he to argue?

'Wouldn't take you for an old bloke, Frank. It's in your head — the way you look at life. Is, eh?'

Forty-five. Not exactly old, not exactly young. But Frank had observed that the more a man owned, the faster he seemed to age.

They were okay kids, after all. Just wanted to get drunk and stoned and sit around listening to Frank's life the way he remembered it. He was glad Ruby had stomped off to bed because she'd heard most of his stories a couple of times or so, and would try to head him off by chipping in with the end when he'd barely got started.

THE NEXT SATURDAY night they arrived all dressed up. Girls in pantyhose and little skirts, and spidering eyelashes. Boys with pastel-coloured shirts beneath their windbreakers. Leila was with them. They'd formally collected her from her front door in the pretext of attending the high-school netball social, then they'd parked down by the culvert just before the station driveway and sneaked around the fenceline, boys lugging the bottles, girls clutching their frail party shoes.

They boasted about this and still he let them stay. Was, in truth, pleased to see them. Saturday night had never, for Frank, quite lost the echo of promise and pleasure. Besides, he had a terrible thirst.

Ruby went to bed in disgust while Frank was still setting out saucers for ashtrays, apologising for the lack of seats. This time there was another girl and one less boy and Frank made an effort over names. There was Jason, who had been with Leila in the bathroom, and Ian, who obviously hoped to be the next favoured. There was the pink-cheeked Lynette, who kept a proprietory hand on Ian even while dandling Frank's baby. And there was Carol, who periodically laughed aloud, then, having gained all attention, smiled to imply some deep reservoir of private amusement.

At some point Frank dropped off to sleep and woke fighting for breath, Leila's mouth clamped on his, her arm locked around his shoulder. Much merriment as he fought his way free. Explanatory fingers pointed at the floor where an empty brown bottle lay pointed his way. Frank wiped his mouth with the back of his arm.

'Your turn, Frankie.'

A fast inventory of the liquor. It was almost cut.

'Not me,' he said. 'I'm buggered. Have to be up in the morning. Crack of dawn.'

Carol gave one of her disconnected chuckles as he heaved himself up from the mattress that served as a sofa.

Having nudged the baby awake, Frank messed about in the kitchen, hoping they'd get the message and depart. Ian, the owner of the car hidden down by the culvert,was scarcely capable of standing, but Frank had driven in that kind of state. In worse states. The night was done, he wanted them out.

The baby kept falling asleep on the job. Meant he'd be yelling in an hour or two. The baby as an instrument of torture . . . How long had Frank slept? . . . How long had he not slept? . . .

Through the wall they were whooping and thumping like Red Indians on celluloid.

Carol came in, walking at a list, Leila a few steps behind.

'My turn now. It was pointing through the wall.'

Carol draping her thin arms around him. The movement disturbing the baby into feverish sucking. Frank looking down at his son. The girl moving her lips down the side of his face and onto his neck. It stirred him. He thought of Lisa. Pain, anger, longing, all tangled together.

He stood up to shake the girl off. The baby made a sound of protest and Frank reinserted the teat. Carol's hands had simply repositioned themselves. Leila was watching from the doorway.

'Take her away,' he said to her. 'Take them all away.'

It sounded plaintive. Not laying down but begging. Ruby would cringe.

Leila pouted, kicked the door with a red satin shoe. 'Now the booze is finished . . .' Her jaw dropped into a mocking smile, top lip drawn tight.

Carol's tongue ran down Frank's neck like a rapid slug. He pushed her away.

'I need sleep,' he said. 'Sleep. And I got trouble enough as it is.'

'Don't worry,' said Leila, suddenly kind. 'No one'd tell.' Smiling. 'They think I'm staying the night at Lynette's.'

She went to the sink and filled the kettle, put it on the wood stove. Carol was whining and rubbing the funny-bone she'd banged on Frank's chair.

Leila spoke carefully and clearly. 'I could say anything about you, Frank. Anything at all and people would believe me.'

Frank carried the baby into his own bedroom, into his own bed. The boy holding his finger and staring unblinking at Frank or perhaps the lightbulb. A crease in each chubby thigh just below bunched nappies. No logic to the things that could suddenly bring you happiness.

Next morning his visitors were still there. Frank stood looking down at them — a bunch of kids huddled together beneath one rug and a couple of coats. Harmless.

He was pouring himself a cup of tea when Ruby got up. He heard her padding into the room next door, pausing to take it in. She came into the kitchen, wearing a jersey of Lisa's over her pyjamas.

'I told them,' he said to her. 'I did, Rube. I laid down the law. And they laid right down on top of it.'

She didn't even crack a smile, but backed out, closing the door behind her. He opened it and went after her. Couldn't stand her disapproval. She was in the next room, kicking at the sleeping teenagers with her bare feet. 'Get up. Get up. Go now. Go.'

He left her to it.

JESS TAKING THE old forgotten road, though it took longer that way. Taking it not just because she has time — so much time she's suspended in it, thrashing about, will be almost glad to get back to school — but because she has foolish, flighty Pearl on a lead rope. On the old road there are no tractors or heavy trucks to throw Pearl into a trembling, white-eyed frenzy.

Taking Pearl as a favour to Judy Gordon. Judy making it sound that way, as if Jess had every right to say no, it didn't suit her, Pearl on a rope was too much of a hassle. At home Jess objects to much. Hears herself sometimes. 'How come I always have to?' Her father trotting out the same old tired reasons. Her mother's chisel voice, *'Because!'*

Because you're mine. Because I said so. Because I know what's best.

But a girl needs a mother, and Jess has chosen Judy Gordon. Who (possibly) was forced to give Jess up for adoption to strangers in a distant country, but eventually tracked them, and her long-lost daughter, to a rural district of New Zealand. On finding the adoptive parents were reasonably decent kind of people, Judy bought land in order to live close to the daughter without disrupting the family she has become accustomed to living among, and has grown to resemble.

Judy Gordon has said nothing to disprove this possibility. In fact she is secretive about her past, deflecting questions and giving nothing to feed the curiosity of the locals and garner sympathy or respect. She seems indifferent to local opinion or, at most, faintly amused by it. The people who matter to her live in other towns, cities . . . other countries.

Judy is proof that Curvey's Creek is just another small rural district, no more interesting or important than any other. Her existence cuts the place down to size and thus offends the local residents. It offends Jess a little, too, but also excites her. Judy Gordon reduces even Windsor to a place you could leave without looking back.

Everyone said that Judy ran her place at a loss, it couldn't be otherwise. Must have a private income she was prepared to fritter away. Buying horses destined for the knacker's yard, feeding them, working them, training them for stock work or show ring or child riders. It didn't make sense. Except to Jess and, surely, to the horses.

To Pedro trotting, neat and obliging as a bank clerk, when he could have been at this minute passing through a couple of dozen checkout counters in cans. Who maybe knows this and channels his undying gratitude into obedience. Or is just naturally boring.

Judy has suggested Jess swap Pedro for Solly when Solly's leg heals.

Along Turnbull Road, past the rabbiter's cottage, long since bought from the Education Board by Leila's second cousin who has one glass eye and, according to Leila, a windbreak of curling hair running all the way down his spine. Kevin Samuels, who works for the Windsor County Council and his wife who works for the Bank of New Zealand. Commuting each day in their green Ford Fairlane; another non-farming family, although (according to Leila) Kevin is saving up for a farm.

The house looks neglected. Broken glass outside the front door sends out signals of sunlight, grass creeps through a pile of boards and dead branches. The Fairlane is parked outside with its boot open but no one's in sight.

Coming up to the Webster driveway, Pearl has a panic attack. Nothing in sight to explain her terror — a stand of gum trees, a woolshed, a rural delivery box. Jess slides from Pedro and talks Pearl round, humouring her in a soft and constant voice.

'You stupid, scatty, half-witted drongo. Grow up, Pearly, get it together, dear.' But turning the words into creamy endearments. And when the skin stops twitching and shivering, she strokes Pearl's white neck, rubs the base of her ears.

Jess can calm horses out of their terror, can catch horses that don't intend to be caught. Has done it. Knows she can do it, maybe not always but mostly. Talking to them without words, bridging the space between her and them, slowly, slowly. *So what?*

No one uses the abandoned road except Jess. Well, hardly ever. Sometimes in a dry summer she'll see tyre marks from a tractor or fourwheel drive in the sand at the river banks.

The road fords the river in three places, and over the years the river has altered so that the concrete slabs laid at each of the crossings are no longer a guide as to where it is easiest or safest to cross. Carts and buggies have travelled this road, wooden spokes churning, children stretching hands out to the flying water.

Once a house stood between the second and third fords. Now all that remains is the bottom section of a brick chimney and some perverse and knobbled rose and gooseberry bushes. The native bush that fringes the river encroaches on the house, vines arch and tangle.

Each time she visits, or even rides past, the old house site, it fills Jess with a feeling she has no words for.

*TITAHI STATION.* THE wooden sign, barely legible, arches drunkenly above the cattle stop, causing Pearl major alarm. Jess has to dismount and talk the mare through the small side gate behind Pedro. Just inside the gate Pedro, with nice timing, casts his left hind shoe.

It's almost two years since Jess last came here, as Leila's friend. Nothing has changed, except now Jess hopes not to be seen by the Samuels. Even though she and Leila never fell out, it makes Jess feel odd being back here. Not heading up to the big house but taking the gate that leads down to the 'quarters', where Leila and Jess used to spy on weedy Lew Sparrow — one of a succession of single men to work for Jack Samuels.

The rutted clay road changing shape beneath the horses' feet, taking them down and across the side of the hill. All around, that soft country silence that isn't a silence at all but a mossy background blending of birds, newborn lambs, cows and somewhere a distant car. Much closer a horse whinnies in greeting.

Jess turns to see the dark horse rise up over the ridge and come hurtling towards them. He skids to a stop just short of the fence. Pedro's neck slamming up to vertical, Pearl surprisingly unconcerned.

The big dark horse rears up and paws at the air; his eyes are planets, white-circled. His haunches rise as his front feet hit the ground, showing off. He rears again and takes a few steps on his back legs. Pedro steps back ramming into Pearl, his skin rippling like a beaten rug. Automatically Jess has laid a placating hand on his neck but she has no words for him, the stallion has taken her breath away. Not his magnificence, but his familiarity. She knows this horse, has always known him.

FRANK, SITTING ON the steps rolling a cigarette, heard Maguilla getting excited. Frank's sigh blew the tobacco from the frail paper. He needed the money, God knows, he was grateful to the Gordon woman, but shoeing was a bastard. He'd already done two ponies that morning for a couple of girls no older than Ruby. The mother of one had come along. Must have dribbled all the way behind the girls in first gear. She bumped down the track from the Samuels' driveway in her green Mercedes and informed Frank that he should have a sign telling people to leave their cars at the gate. He told her anyone with half a brain did just that. Thought for a moment she would drag her girls away then and there. But there was no easy way of turning that car and getting back up the track so she stayed.

Stood around, her head swivelling in case there was something she'd missed — a glimpse of Ruby at the window, some item of clothing on the washing line, Mac lifting his leg against the tankstand.

Frank didn't bother talking to her. He chatted a bit to the girls when his mouth was free of nails, and he murmured to their ponies in a comforting dentist tone.

Finally the woman threw herself into the car and slammed the door. He'd almost relented and asked Ruby to make her a cup of tea but was glad he hadn't when she winced at the price, tugging the note out of her purse like a soiled sheet from a bed.

He'd watched her trying to get her car facing the track without either ramming the fence or sliding down the hill and never offered so much as a whoa-up or a signalling hand. They wouldn't come back. He was a fool to himself. Wondered how much Ruby had seen, what she would say.

Now he saw the girl riding down the track on a good-looking bay, with a piebald pony beside them. He saw the black riding cap, the blue jeans, the raincoat strapped at her knee, the clipped mane, the neat, easy way she sat in the saddle, and he thought, Oh Gawd, another one! Squatter's daughter, that's what he thought, and felt angry at himself for not having foreseen that this is how this country would be. As bad, if not worse, than Britain, where the nobs had commandeered the horse and turned it into

37

an accessory, a servant, a status symbol. In New Zealand, Frank had thought, watching Jess ride towards him, a man could become ashamed to call himself a horseman.

Later, much later, he would remember the thought and tell her, 'I had you figured for a spoilt uppity little wench.'

JESS SAW FRANK sitting on the step in his hat (though clouds had long before blocked out the sun) and his checked bush shirt and she looked at the face beneath the hat for signs of unhappiness such as you would expect from a man whose wife had run off and left him. She thought he looked a bit grumpy and it seemed, under the circumstances, an insufficient emotion.

Later she would tell him this and he would give it some thought and inform her that Lisa was an insufficient wife.

C H A **5** T E R

HE'D MISSED OUT on so much sleep he'd forgotten how to do it, like a reptile whose legs had shrivelled away from lack of use. You'd think walking and sleep were things you didn't need to learn — watch a brand-new foal rise and stagger on spindly shanks, awkward but able. Yet the baby had as yet found nothing better to do with his feet than stick them in his mouth, at the same time robbing Frank of the knack of sleep.

Lacking sleep, his brain spun. Not thinking straight. How could he? A drink or two would get him to sleep. Soon. Soon. He'd slipped the money to young Ian (the one with the car, the one you could almost trust) to bring him a couple of flagons of port. Implicit invitation for them all to return, despite Ruby's rudeness.

A drink would get him on top of things, give him a vantage point to see a way out beyond the mud and tangled bracken of his thoughts. Too much time for thinking and none of it useful.

No news from the world, not even a letter from his sister Helen. Who would be waiting for news of the baby. Not hanging out to know, but interested. He ought to write, if only to explain why her loan repayments had, in the meantime, ceased.

No TV set — if he'd managed to buy one would Lisa have stuck around to watch the soaps? — and the battery radio unable to pick up even the nearest station. Nothing to read but the school books Ruby brought home to stare at after tea. Dogging the corners of the pages, her tongue rasping her bottom lip in concentration. Consulting Frank now and again, maybe out of kindness.

His schooling had been at best sporadic but his memory was fine. He remembered the certainties his own school books, and those who taught from them, had imparted about the universe. And now found it startling to learn from Ruby that a large

39

number of those facts had turned into discredited fallacies. As if learning was some kind of household appliance to be traded in and updated every few years.

When the baby was fretful in the night Frank would recite to him riding-alone poems that he could no longer remember learning. *Wide were the Kroombit paddocks and wild the Kroombit steers.* Hearing his own voice, rough as the bark on an old pine. *And fearless were the horsemen whose fame has crossed the years.*

He could ride alone around Titahi Station and not one poem would rise to mind. If they had, Frank wouldn't have given them voice — the words would have hovered, displaced, above those alien hunched hills and shrinking gullies.

THE PORT CAME, just as ordered. Not with Ian, though — but in his car, lent to Jason, Carol and an overweight boy called Wyatt. Leila, they said, was intending to join them, would sneak out her window, through the trees and across the paddock. A journey she hadn't thought to mention when Frank relieved her of her baby-care duties late that afternoon.

'They're not bad kids,' he placated Ruby smouldering in her bedroom. 'Not a patch on you, but not bad kids all the same.'

Ruby pretended to be deaf. He tried harder.

'They even brought beer. Bad kids would've turned up empty handed and drunk my port.'

'Sometimes,' Ruby said, 'you're pathetic.'

He read it as absolution.

The soothing motion of cup to lips. He sat among them. Saw, for the first time, how wary they were of each other. Words and gestures like a licked finger on hot iron. Until the beer (in Carol's case, his port) lullabyed them into rowdy confidence.

Leila didn't come. Caught in the act of climbing out her window? At any moment an enraged Jack Samuels might come hammering on Frank's door. The more they discussed this possibility, the more entertaining it seemed. Reminded Frank of the time his mate Kanga Kristofferson took up with the wife of a professional wrestler. But he'd only got to the part where the wrestler — a great big bastard, arms as big as Frank's two thighs pressed together — was dangling Kanga from the balcony of their third-floor hotel room in Athens, when the baby woke up famished.

Cries stopped the minute Frank stepped into view. Warm stench of shit. Lambs and babies, their shit even smelt yellow. Why was that?

Frank laid the baby, nappyless, cleaned up and pink, on the kitchen table while he heated the bottle. The youngsters wandered in. Jason wanted to know what happened to Kanga. Frank said he'd come into money, bought himself a nice bit of land. Jason said he meant about the wrestler.

While Frank finished the story — an anticlimatic kind of ending, despite the postscript about Frank seeing the wrestler years later on TV — the three of them gazed at his baby. Each of them reached out and rather tentatively laid a finger on the plumply naked flesh, as if the infant was a ouija board.

Frank lay on his bedroom mattress beside the baby because that way they could both drink in comfort. And fall asleep.

At a point beyond waking Frank became aware of an obstruction beneath his ribs and chilly fingers scuffling at his beltline. The two seemed somehow connected. He felt his shirt riding up, belly hair tweaked by a zip, warned himself against breaking the surface of the sleep that so kindly engulfed him. He turned slightly, a weightless movement, to offer greater accessibility, and felt the thinness of the girl's limbs, her grasping fingers. The baby's bottle jammed beneath him, oozing milk.

Finally was obliged to open his eyes. She laughed into them.

'Don't worry. I'm on the pill.' Folding her thin bones down beside him. Snuggling.

'For God's sake!' Removing the baby's bottle. Dampness everywhere. 'You can't sleep here.'

She laughed her odd little laugh that reminded him of Lisa. The baby was still asleep, thumb jammed in his mouth. Even this seemed unconvincing, done for effect.

Carol slid from the mattress, a sullen movement, and stood looking down.

'Who said I wanted to?' She slammed his door behind her. The baby started, sucked at his thumb noisily.

In the morning they had gone, all three of them.

'Your friends were here last night,' he told Leila, as if she didn't know.

'They like you, Frank.' Her smile told him he was no match for her.

41

'They were expecting you.'

'I know.' She did a ballet movement, a kind of swooping curtsey as if she was graceful and good to look at, instead of big and clumsy and plain. She smiled again. 'I changed my mind. I'm sick of Jason. He's boring.' Another little swoop, then some shuffling steps on the toes of her sneakers. 'School starts again in five days. What ya gonna do then?'

'I'm working on it,' he lied. He'd done nothing, didn't know where to start. The minding of his son was an insoluble dilemma.

'Carol would. She told me. Had enough of school. If you asked her.'

Carol in his kitchen, in his bed, minding his baby. 'No,' he said, then carefully. 'Don't reckon she'd manage. She's not a capable type like you.'

'Thank you.' A curtsey. 'You'll be happy to know you're knocking off early today. So that I have time to get ready. My brother's birthday. We's all of us going to town for takeaways and the movies.'

FRANK HAD TO remind Jack Samuels about these plans. Not sure if that was the prudent thing to do, but sure enough Samuels had forgotten. Did not, however, appreciate being reminded.

When Frank rode up to unsaddle Maguilla, Leila was waiting at the open door with her jacket on. She'd spent all day filling Ruby's head with stories of the film they were going to see, for Leila and her brothers had seen it once already. *Eaty*, it was called. About some alien come down to earth.

'Reckon I saw that years ago,' said Frank. 'Not one alien but half a dozen. Real ugly bastards as I remember. And they were in some kinda —'

Ruby gave him a mean little punch. 'No,' she wailed. 'This one's famous. Not old either. And everyone in the world but you has heard about it.' Her voice dropped and she turned away so he didn't have to keep listening. 'And every kid in the world but me is gonna get to see it.'

Frank pretended he hadn't heard. What was there to say?

Fetched the second flagon of wine he'd hidden in the wash-house. Reused the cup stained pink from the night before. Gulped it down, his mind on the Samuels family. Had they no eyes? No feelings? One skinny child among all those brawny ones — would that have ruined their evening?

A second cupful, sickly though it was. Ruby crouched on a kitchen chair, hugging her knees, head full of *Eaty*. He hated to look at her, went into the bathroom and stared at his own face in the rusting little mirror. Her sadness inhabited him. Their life was desolate and she was right — he was pathetic.

'Do something,' he told his mirrored self.

'We're going out too,' he told the folded-up girl. 'Visiting. We'll pack up some gear for his nibs and we're on our way.'

Her head towards him. 'Someone's coming to get us?'

'We're going on Maguilla.' Reaching for the bridle.

She'd never taken to riding, despite his initial coaxing. Had never got beyond the fear of being far from the ground and at the mercy of a beast with a skull as hard as steel.

'I'll hang onto you, Rube. Hang onto you with my life.'

'But — baby?'

'Reckon we can sling him in a sack,' he said. 'Good enough for little lambs.'

She was too easy to tease, eyes wide with concern.

'S'okay,' he retracted. 'Got it all worked out.'

They filled a bag with dry nappies, spare clothes, a full baby bottle wedged upright, then Frank put on his oilskin coat and went out to catch and saddle the stallion. Coming back in, he slid his leather belt from his jeans and fastened it tight around his coat, making a marsupial pouch. But the buttons of the old coat lent no confidence. He tried again, this time adding a big old sweater of Lisa's with a large neck and buttoning the coat around it.

The baby woke as they eased him between Frank's shirt and the voluminous jersey, but made no protest. A top baby, this, after all. Ruby tied a shop-knitted hat over the soft dark fur on his bobbing head. She was wearing heavy clothes beneath her school raincoat. It was cold outside, would be even colder coming home.

It was nearly dark as Frank untethered Maguilla. Not much cloud but the moon was still hidden behind the ranges. But then, darkness could be an advantage — Ruby might feel less fearful not seeing how far away the ground was.

He strapped the bag onto the saddle, and they led Maguilla up the track to the gate and out onto the main driveway. Light flickered through the trees that surrounded the homestead. Frank hoped it was an outside light, that the family had left already for town. He didn't want to meet up with them and face questions he'd rather not deal with, comparisons he'd sooner didn't get made. Reminding himself that he was a better stockman, a better horseman, a better human being than Jack Samuels would ever be.

Outside the main gate he lifted the girl up. 'Get on your high horse,' he said.

He guided Ruby's hands down to grip the pommel, then edged her forward until her thighs were almost on top of her rigidly clutching hands. He swung up behind her, adjusting his balance to accommodate the baby, who was dribbling into the hollows of his collarbone. He encircled the girl with one arm and slid the other arm, holding the reins, past her armpit. Maguilla was standing to attention.

Frank had bred this horse, matching a thoroughbred mare whose wind had broken with a magnificent quarterhorse temporarily in the possession of Kanga Kristofferson. Had raised the foal, broken him, worked him, got together the money to bring him — forsaking all others — across the Tasman. Better to have lost Lisa than to lose Maguilla.

'Okay.' Touched his heels against the horse's ribs. Ruby was rigid with fear. The stallion moving easily, confident. Frank thinking of the tobacco in his pocket, the lack of a free hand to extract and roll it.

Ruby's tense legs beginning to relax. Why hadn't he thought of this before?

Maguilla's brisk hooves treading the verge of silent roads. Ruby whispering. Frank whispering back. Because of the baby, because of the weight of darkness. Two vehicles passed, one from each direction. The first slowed almost to a stop, a glimpse of faces peering. The second barely altered speed. Past Ruby's school and the teacher's house beside it. Not too far now, he told the girl, and hoped it was true.

As they turned up Bradford's Road the baby struggled and whimpered. Frank talked to him, same way he'd talk to a horse. Calmed him into silence.

Frank knew he had the right place when Maguilla picked up speed. Soon after came the whinnying and a small stampede to the fenceline up ahead. A latched gate and the smell of wood-smoke drifting from the house. Frank halted Maguilla and told the girl to climb off onto the gate post. Balanced her with his free hand while she found her footing, a distrustful eye on Maguilla's head. That mouthful of teeth. Frank waited while she climbed to the ground, then swung out of the saddle, a cushioning arm around the baby.

Up the driveway, light streamed from uncoordinated geometric windows. Frank considered the child's-play house and the sapling native trees lit by its windows and had qualms. The home of someone intent on saving the planet. Not in itself a bad thing but, in Frank's experience, concern for the planet could make a person strangely indifferent to the everyday problems of human beings.

Not Judy Gordon. She opened the door, made noises of pleasure and concern, reached into Lisa's jersey to help remove the baby while Ruby leapt past them into the warmth and light of the house.

Judy fed them soup and bread and cheese, setting it before them without even asking. Took Ruby upstairs to the television set. Sat a half-full cardboard wine cask on the table midway between herself and Frank. The baby by then dry-bottomed, full-bellied on the rag rug, cooing and gurgling.

Frank explained the last few months of his life — apart, that is, from the previous night — and drank the wine as slowly as he could manage. One mouthful per thousand words or thereabouts, but worried still that Judy might get the lion's share.

Depressing himself with his own story. A conspiracy of circumstances that could defy belief. Frank thought he could sense a vein of scepticism — possibly his own — but saying it through did seem to untangle the knots in his head.

'On my own —' he concluded. 'No problem. Take my dogs and my rifle and ride away.'

He thought of the journey that night. The three of them swaddled and sedate, Three Wise Men on a horse. 'I'm trapped, y' see. Never was a settling kind of bloke but this time I'm on my knees with a gin trap round my neck.' Glanced at the wide-eyed baby, ashamed. But there it was, the truth.

'No need to stay there,' said Judy.

For a dissolving moment Frank thought this was an

invitation, even a proposition. Saw that he'd be just the man for a set-up like this. Would make some changes, get the place on its feet.

'Leave,' said Judy. 'Why not?'

'Where would we go? How can I work? With *him*.' Holding his breath.

'Welfare,' she said. 'If she's not coming back, you're a deserted husband.'

'We weren't married exactly.'

'So what? You're a solo father. Get on a benefit. Rent a house.'

Brisk as a yard broom sweeping away his dilemmas. Relief and a kind of helplessness. 'Where?'

'Anywhere. If it was me, I'd get as far away from Titahi Station as I could.'

Frank felt a gust of freedom, gates swinging open. Thought of the house they'd ridden away from, squatting ugly and barren on the side of the hill. Imagined Mac and Sal's kennels empty, Frank and his family driving straight through town and out the other side.

In what?

One horse, two dogs, one adult, one child, one baby, no car. They'd managed it getting here. But that was two adults (loosely defined) and one child.

Shaking his head and seeing, from the corner of his eye, Ruby sliding off one wooden stair and onto the next. Furtive. Eavesdropping.

'You want to stay?' Judy crashed her glass down on the table. Incredulous.

'Jesus no,' he said. 'But . . .' No way he could spell it out and not have it sound like a plea for help.

Ruby stood up. He pretended surprise at her appearing like that out of nowhere. She sidled up next to him. In this house she became a kind of Ruby he'd not yet met, girlish and wheedling.

'We can't leave,' she whispered. 'Please don't. 'Cause then how's she gonna find us when she comes back?'

46

JESS HAD A claim on them — on the girl, the baby, the man, but most of all on his horse — from the day she went with Judy to help move them to the rabbiter's cottage. Their possessions waiting in an unprepossessing pile. Jess wanting to stare, wanting not to stare, keeping her eyes averted as she ferried tired goods across the mud to the horse float hitched behind Judy's ute. Knew then that she was on their side, no matter what, abetting this escape from Jack Samuels, the overlord in the big house.

'Miserable arsehole bastard.' Frank muttering to himself. Jess could taste his words, unfamiliar and rich as chocolate in her own mouth.

Frank set off on his perfect horse with the two dogs at heel, and when he was gone Judy, Jess and Ruby wiped down windowsills, shelves and cupboards with rags and Ajax, though Frank had said not to. Leave it grubby as they'd found it. Leave it grubbier. Serve the bastard right.

'Least,' said Ruby, squeezing her rag beneath the tap, 'least he can't say we didn't leave it clean.'

It made Jess crumble inside, hearing the girl say that. She began to rub harder, battle the circled glass stains into obliteration. Wanting the place to be left not just clean but pristine, spotless, sparkling. For Ruby's sake.

When they'd done they crammed themselves into the cab of the ute. Ruby taking the baby on her lap. Jess on the outside to open and shut the gates. A first scary few minutes as Judy negotiated the rutted greasy track. Ruby braced herself against the dashboard and clenched her eyes shut.

They caught up with Frank just past the bridge. A dead rabbit slung over the front of his saddle. Mac had bailed it up against the bridge's concrete foundations. Frank, grinning and boasting on

Mac's behalf, passed the limp body in to Jess through the window. The fur was still warm.

'A rabbit to christen the rabbiter's cottage,' said Judy.

Before they unloaded the horse float, Jess and Ruby ran from room to room, Jess remembering wallpaper, faded now and curling where it joined, but inside her like childhood. A windowsill still raw wood where Jess had pared it with a kitchen knife. Marion's wrath. Owen placating.

Ruby was awed by the house. Everything from the smoky palm trees in the cracked glass door to the linen cupboard stacked with tattered magazines. *People*, *Pix* and *National Geographic*. Perfect for school projects.

This was the moment for Jess to say, 'Mr Bennington — he's my father.' She didn't. Ruby maybe knew already but didn't feel inclined to mention it. It was an odd feeling, having other kids know your father maybe as well as you did, only in a different way.

They unpacked the baby equipment, Ruby taking charge. She was no older than Corin, yet he took charge of nothing. Wanted, still, to be everyone's baby.

Jess helped Judy wipe out the fridge and cupboards. It wasn't fair, Jess thought, to have to clean both houses. 'That's life,' Judy said. 'Life's unfair.' She said it as if that was the way of things and nothing could be done. Owen thought unfairness was the fault of groups of people — the rich, the greedy, the Western world — and could be changed. Marion believed misfortune was something you brought on yourself by not trying hard enough. So Judy's version of unfairness — that it just existed and you had to put up with it — was new to Jess.

Ruby didn't care about cleaning this end of the shift — nothing to prove. She carried things to her bedroom and closed the door. Jess opened the kitchen cupboards — spilt stuff, dark and sticky. She felt obscurely pleased at knowing that the wife of Leila's hairy second cousin had left the house uncleaned.

Last week when school started Jess had said to Leila on the bus, because it was in her head, 'He never would give you his horse. Not that one. Never.'

'I wouldn't take it,' said Leila. 'It's a useless horse, just like the owner.'

When they'd unpacked the kitchen stuff (old dungy stuff that

Marion wouldn't have even allowed on a picnic) Judy made a pot of tea and they sat on the concrete steps in the sun waiting for Frank and Maguilla and the dogs. Jess was happy, aware of being that way — an easy riding-alone feeling she didn't expect to get when there were people around.

Each year, it seemed to Jess, winter took longer. The Benningtons trapped through long nights in the house that wasn't theirs, surrounded by land they didn't own and had no right to walk on. None of them wanting to be there — at least that's how it felt to Jess. Unseen angles in the air above and between each one of them. Why?

It used to be different. Weekend picnics and a week each summer in a crowded camping ground. Movies on TV that they watched together. Jess and Sheenagh dribbling pikelet mixture onto the skillet in Js and Ss and Cs and never a cross word between them. Marion baking butterfly cakes in corrugated pastel patty pans.

'Used to be tadpoles in the trough,' Jess remembered out loud. 'I liked living here.'

'Me too,' said Ruby with feeling.

If Corin had said that Jess would have poured scorn. 'Y'only just moved in!'

'Here he comes,' said Judy. A glimpse of Frank and the horse where the road turned.

A bit closer and he must have seen them, moved the horse into a canter. Up the road towards the open gate, then swinging out before he reached it, setting the stallion at the fence, sailing over it cleanly, easily. The two dogs tipping torsos between the wires, racing behind the man and the horse. Then Frank swung his horse towards the Chaneys' boundary fence. Leapt it without hesitation, a sheep skedaddling in terror. A tight turn and they jumped back over the fence.

'Skite,' said Judy. But they were grinning wide, all three of them, as they watched, raised up by this unscheduled entertainment. Maguilla's hooves pounding, then, towards the patio steps, so close that Ruby leapt up and took refuge way back behind the palm-tree door. The black hooves skidded to a halt. Frank set his hat back smugly, all but bowed.

'AND WHAT ADVENTURES did you have today, Jess?' Her father at the

49

dinner table, reaching between the voices of Marion and Sheenagh to hand Jess the opportunity to exist among them.

'Nothing much,' she muttered, wishing he wouldn't do that concerned stuff. She'd been thinking about the stallion, the gloss of his haunches, the haughty curve of his neck; it made her heart pound, her throat run dry.

HE WALKED ON his back legs, rubbery black dong wavering like a massive antenna.

'Jeezus,' breathed Jason, stepping back. 'Jeezus, look at that!'

Pride warmed Frank, throbbed in his hammer-mashed thumb.

'Like owning a Harley,' said Wyatt.

Jason brayed. 'Harley hard-on!'

'If I was a biker,' affirmed Frank to Wyatt, who was in need of kindness, 'he'd be a Harley-Davidson right enough.'

Wyatt gave Frank a grateful look.

'Should've called him Harley,' said Jason. ''Stead of that whatever. What did you call him that for?'

'Just came to me. Out of nowhere. An odd thing that — I looked at him and I saw the word, like it was written out. Can't explain it.'

Frank had the boys out working off the night before. In the junk pile under the trees he'd found enough old timber, enough reclaimable staples and wire, to raise the fence of the small paddock behind the house. Make it high enough to discourage the stallion from jumping into his neighbours' larger, lusher paddocks.

His change of address hadn't shaken the youngsters off. They'd arrived on his doorstep the afternoon before with one crate of beer, one well-defaced acoustic guitar and a pram Jason had rescued from the Windsor tip. Jason, Carol, Wyatt and Lynette.

'Don't let them in,' Ruby had hissed.

But they were smiling at him and bearing gifts, and there'd been no one but Ruby to talk to since Judy and her off-sider helped them move.

They'd played poker using matches, the four of them and Frank and Ruby. Carol watching Frank with her streaky smile, so he knew he was set up for the night and didn't mind at all. Jason and Lynette entwining legs in promise. Poor Wyatt the odd one out, but lucky at least in his cards.

Ruby went to bed. They finished off the crate. Wyatt's lucky hands stopped coming. Frank held the baby's bottle in one hand and his cards in the other. There were teeth piercing the baby's front gums. Lynette fell asleep, her hair spread on Jason's thigh.

Frank issued no invitation but Carol was in his bed when he reached it. She gave her weird taunting laugh as he slid in beside her. Frank told himself he hadn't heard it. That laugh was full of complications he didn't wish to know about.

Needy people — the buggers could sniff out misery and loneliness. When your own life was a mess you attracted all the hopeless, luckless sods in your neighbourhood. Water finds its own level. His Mother's Voice. Frank's little old joke — his mother, the cracked record.

Lisa had taken up the same song. 'You're like a sick dog. Y' attract vermin.'

'That's right,' he'd sneered. 'And you're the proof of it.'

She'd moved in front of the mirror, to look at her own reflection. She was bruised, that morning. Mouth like a nibbled doughnut, split and swollen.

'Yeah,' she said. 'Look at me.'

But he'd turned away.

'You have to live with yourself,' he'd said, not talking about her broken lips but about the hangers-on. 'In the end, that's what it comes down to — you have to live with yourself.'

'Listen to you,' she'd said into the mirror. 'You're fuckin' unbelievable!'

Before Frank fell asleep Carol began pestering him about work, coaxing. Frank could find a job and Carol would replace Leila. He wouldn't need to pay her even, just her food and a packet of cigarettes now and then. Frank thought of the way she laughed, and how many hours until daylight. Said, just to be on the safe side and not have her roaming round the house in the dark feeling vengeful, that he'd think it over.

Working on the fence with Wyatt and Jason and he still hadn't told her no. Last seen she was still wrapped up asleep on the lounge floor where he'd half carried her because he didn't need Ruby finding them together in the morning. Didn't need that at all.

JACK SAMUELS HADN'T been too happy when Frank handed in his notice.

'Quit!' He'd roared. 'Quit to bludge off the state. Our state. My taxes.'

'Yup,' said Frank. 'I guess so. Thank you.'

Samuels' big arms flexed but didn't swing. 'The cottage went with the job.'

Cottage. That's what it'd been called in the advertisement. Such a pretty word. It had tipped the balance for Lisa, the thought of that country cottage.

'We've got a place.' Frank, telling Samuels this, couldn't keep down his grin. 'I understand it belongs to your cousin.'

Judy Gordon had found them the house, ferried them all into town on Frank's day off to sign a rent agreement with a lawyer and visit the Welfare office.

That day Frank had all three of them scrubbed and spruced, a mattress crease in his best strides. Knew appearance was what counted with the people who made decisions about other people's lives. Ruby was a dilemma. She'd filled out a bit, shot up. He had her try on her only dress, then her skirt but neither would do, so they settled for tracksuit pants, and a jersey of Lisa's, shovelling through the box for one that would suit.

'All this gear going to waste. Reckon we could do some alterations and you'd have heaps of clothes.'

'No,' she whispered. Hanging onto hope. Making Frank feel sad and clumsy.

Polishing his boots with mutton fat to a fancy shine. The glow of nourished leather. Glow of virtue. Frank's mother smiling from above as he buffed the heels, with an approval she'd rarely shown him in life.

He'd asked Judy to stop off at her place so he could iron his shirt. Was uncertain about his hat.

'Leave it on,' said Judy. 'Why not? It's you.'

She was a good woman, Judy, but in some ways she hadn't a clue.

As it turned out, either way the hat wouldn't have mattered. All it took was the baby gurgling and sparkling on Frank's lap. The woman behind the Welfare desk set her eyes on this motherless tot and was hooked. Ready to help Frank and his baby, but not so keen about Ruby. Legal problems, lack of ownership papers. She thought it might be advisable for the girl to be returned to Australia, back to the home in Dubbo.

Ruby had turned to Frank with a bleat of anguish that took him by surprise. Made him speak up firmly. Ruby was his daughter, good as, and old enough anyway to decide on her own account who she'd live with.

'You,' said Ruby, quickly. 'Him. Frank.' And finally, desperately, 'Dad.'

The Welfare woman was swayed to indecision. She'd leave it, pending the social worker's recommendation. This person would visit them within the next few days. Was there any time that wouldn't be convenient?

'I'll be there,' Frank said. 'We don't have a vehicle so I'm bound to be there. But for Rube it'd need to be after the school bus gets in.'

She scribbled a note. 'I imagine there are things you need?'

Frank was still examining that sentence for trickery when Ruby stepped in. 'We need a cot for the baby. And we need a TV.'

Frank cringed. He'd been starting to think along the lines of essentials — a garden spade, hoe. A flagon or two of something to sustain him.

'You don't have a TV?' She was astounded, impressed. Here was self-denial of major proportions.

Ruby, thought Frank, you little beaut!

There was, of course, a catch. The money was just a loan, repayments to be deducted. Ruby and the welfare woman had trapped Frank into buying something they didn't need with money they didn't own. But 'Dad,' she'd said. How could he protest?

Judy had taken them to Windsor's only second-hand shop where they'd found one cot, livid with stickers. Frank took a closer look. Cartoon figures, comic-strip animals, words he'd never before met up with.

'Brand names,' Judy explained. 'That one there's a type of pushbike.'

Enlightened, Frank saw words he recognised. Pepsi. Tip-Top — children weaned to words on brand names? How long had this been going on?

He scratched one with his thumbnail. 'Soak'em off, we can.'

'They'll learn him to read,' said Ruby.

'Teach,' he said. 'Teach him. But never, not that brainwash rubbish — no son of mine.'

He was shouting, a sudden choking rage. They were all staring at him, even the shop woman, glued to TV, who had showed no interest in them until now. They thought he was making a fuss about nothing. Didn't see what this defaced yellow cot was telling them about mankind and where it was heading.

They looked at TV sets. A choice of those, including, perhaps, the one the shop woman was again watching. Hunched on a stool beside a one-bar heater, knitting by heart.

Frank liked one with cabinet doors to conceal the screen, and little cupboards on the side that could be made use of.

'It's ancient,' said Judy, unimpressed. 'And probably dead.'

No electrical plug in sight so Frank had to ask. The woman sighed and set down her knitting, a cruel shade of orange and all curled in on itself in a secretive way. She kept her eyes on the screen until the canned laughter rang out like rain on a tin roof.

Ruby had hopped in to watch by then. Frank craning forward. Two men shouting at each other. The woman dragged herself off to find an extension cord, glared at the cabinet TV in passing. 'It goes good.' Irritated about having to prove it.

It did go good. The same two men. A sweep over the ecstatic faces of their audience. The sound rolled in behind, like thunder. Judy leapt to turn it down. Ruby knelt in front of the TV, her raised, enraptured face smiling at a screen full of raised, enraptured faces. Frank felt his grip on life diminishing.

The price seemed fair but as Frank unfolded the notes Judy jumped in with an offer so mean Frank had to look away. While he studied a formica chest of drawers Judy and the woman haggled, settled on a price that left him in pocket. Ashamed but pleased at the same time.

From the motley collection of tools he picked a spade and a sad hoe and took them to the counter. He paid the prices inked on the handles. He wasn't opposed to bartering, but places like this you looked at the poor sods in charge and knew you were all in the same boat together.

'Maybe they just want you to think that,' said Judy, when he put this theory as they roped the cot upside down over the TV set. 'For all we know that one goes home and drinks out of Waterford crystal.'

'She'd still be poorer than me,' said Frank. 'Anyone who watches crap like that all day is worse off than me, no matter what they drink out of.'

Realised with those words that he was thirsty and still a pocket of loose change. So when Judy nipped into the bank he off-loaded the baby onto Ruby's lap — the girl was still glassy-eyed with happiness — and shot off to the bottle store. The same bottle store he'd stood in four months before — seemed more like four years — when they were on their way to Titahi Station. He remembered himself stepping in, looking around at the shelves, and he wished he was back at that moment and could try it over again.

They'd arrived at Windsor in hired transport — a stock truck whose driver was prepared to let three people and two dogs ride with him for not too much more than the fare for the horse. An uncomfortable trip with the three of them squashed together and Lisa like an over-ripe peach ready to split. Sally and Mac had it even worse, sharing the back with a short-tempered Hereford bull and a travel-worn stallion.

They were to be met at Windsor. Frank had supposed that a sheep and cattle station would run to horse transport of some description, or at least could borrow one. But Jack Samuels came in a Landrover and drew a rough direction map for Frank on a leaflet advertising calf food. Titahi Station was twenty-three miles from Windsor. Frank didn't mind the prospect of riding out but he hadn't figured on Lisa and the girl arriving without him at the 'cottage' they had such high hopes of. Lisa could not be relied on to take disappointments in her stride.

The job was a pig in a poke but Frank had told himself that any man willing to hire him unseen would be the easy-going kind. On meeting Samuels he saw more likely that this was a boss who had trouble finding and keeping workers, and Frank should have guessed as much.

He'd saddled Maguilla and watched his family and dogs drive off before he went looking for a drink. A fast beer with a whisky chaser in the Windsor Royal, and then he'd stepped into the bottle store. Rum, a good drink for a man on a horse with distance to cover.

NOW FRANK LOOKED wistfully at the spirit bottles, then sighed and

55

moved on towards the unmarked flagons. He couldn't feel good about climbing into Judy Gordon's wagon clutching a jar in a brown paper bag.

When he got back Judy was there jiggling a small white bear with a tartan collar in front of the baby.

'Oughtn't go wasting your money,' Frank told her. He passed the bottle over Ruby's head. 'Inadequate token of our gratitude.'

Judy protested. 'You can't afford . . .' She looked at the label. Glenevis Sweet Muscatel Wine.

'To have with your dinner,' said Frank.

'That's nice,' said Judy. 'Well, thank you.' She smiled. Frank looked out the window in case his chagrin showed.

As Judy turned the key and eased into first gear, Frank slid the baby off Ruby's lap and onto his own. The hoe rolled in the back as Judy turned into the main street of Windsor. Frank felt something cold pressing against his closed fist and looked down; Ruby's fingers were trying to creep between his. He opened his hand to let them in. Well, he thought, holding her cold hand, well, fancy that.

JUDY HAD UNLOADED them and left. Frank was connecting the aerial wires to the back of the TV set when Ruby produced the bottle of wine. 'Judy said your need is greater than hers.'

Ruby was onto him, he saw that. Her look was half amused, half contemptuous. For a nine-year-old she was too smart by a half.

Lisa would have liked this new home of theirs. A fridge that didn't leak and a washing machine that was just a matter of pushing buttons. A green formica table with the chrome flaking from its legs. Three square bedrooms — Ruby had the best one, with the extra window. And fair enough, life owed Ruby.

Yet a dishonest kind of house, Frank thought. Walls substituted by breakfast bars and fold-back screens in pretend leather. Well suited, though, to raising babies. Frank could stand at the sink scrubbing potatoes and, just by turning his head, have a view right through to the baby, pillow-propped on the colourless carpet in the pale afternoon sun.

WHEN FRANK AND his fence-raising assistants, Jason and Wyatt, went back to Frank's house for a pot of tea, Ruby, Lynette, Carol

56

and Frank's baby were lined up on that same carpet staring at TV. In hell that's how it would be, people in rows doing nothing. Staring ahead. Outside, the sun shining, trees growing.

It made it easy to tell Carol. In front of them all so she couldn't pretend to have misunderstood. 'Carol, that offer you made. Been thinking about it. Seems to me since I'm in a position to look after my own baby, that's what I wanna do.'

'I could keep house,' she renegotiated. Her look mining him for concessions, invitations.

'No,' he said.'Thanks, but no.'

She kept on looking at him for too long. Her eyes still drilling but now just for the hell of it. So he started talking. Always his first line of defence. Telling them, as he brewed up tea, about him and Rumbo after Gina had died and Rumbo couldn't bear to stay in the house because it was like Gina was there but not there. So Rumbo and his son Kenny, who would have been, then, four or maybe five, hitched up to join Frank who was just about to go on the road with a mob, a big mob, of cattle. Taking them from Normanton to Chilagoe. The northern stock route, which runs . . .

Constructing his homeland on the green formica out of spoons and forks, to show them.

AND FRANK WAS glad he'd been firm with Carol, because it wasn't a bad life being an all-day father. Plenty to do and time to do it. A vegetable garden, chooks, maybe a tree-house for Ruby. Might cure her fear of heights.

He had in fact started digging his garden, between the house and the macrocarpas, when the chestnut-headed girl rode in. The dogs escorted her from the gate while Maguilla churned and whinnied behind his raised stockade. Frank dredged for her name, ashamed that it had deserted him. Barely a week before this girl had helped them move house.

'Hi.' She shrugged schoolbag straps from her shoulders. 'Brought you some things.' Slid from the saddle clutching the bag. Patted the gelding's neck.

'You've got a pram!'

'Youngsters gave it to us.'

'Leila's lot?' The shadow of a grimace. 'Well, this is nothing much. Not like a pram.' Tipping the contents onto the ground:

notebooks, ballpoint pens, colouring pencils, cutlery, a small saucepan. 'Thought Ruby could use the paper and that.'

'Bet she can,' said Frank. 'But isn't someone gonna miss it?'

'It's just sitting round. We've got heaps of stuff just sitting round at our place. Electrical stuff and all that too. Like, if you could fix it?'

'Probably not,' said Frank, picking up the saucepan. 'But this — just the thing for brewing up cocoa. And all this other — young Ruby can use all that, she'll be over the moon. Cuppa tea, eh?'

Pushing the pram across the rough ground. The gelding at the girl's heels, green slobber catching in her hair. She remarked on the newly raised fence. Was Frank sure it was high enough? The stallion certainly can jump.

Maguilla was strutting at the fenceline for the benefit of the gelding. Eat-your-heart-out bravado which her horse had the nous to ignore. It was the girl who stopped to stare, bringing them all to a halt.

She turned to Frank. 'I could work him for you.' A small, breathless voice. 'I mean . . . I guess with the baby you don't get much chance. After school or in the weekends?'

Frank felt fatherhood curdling. Chains clanking, keys turning, air thinning. Claustrophobia. Trapped. Coffined. Buried. And this bit of a girl shyly offering to dance on his grave.

C H A P T E R 7

JESS CAN TASTE fear like honey between her clamped teeth.

This is the fourth time she's borrowed the stallion and still there's nothing about him to take for granted. He's obedient — so far he has been obedient. And so far she has been vigilant in keeping him on a tight rein. But he's biding his time. They both know it's a charade, this master/servant stuff.

She watches his ears — perfect ears, thin, dark teardrops framing the route ahead. Straining impatiently forward or swivelling politely to catch her words in a forest of hairs. Then, abruptly, those ears slam back to flatten, tips pointing at Jess. Accusation or threat?

Those flattened ears, their contradiction of his demure façade, excite Jess.

They travelled, this time, up the main road almost as far as Titahi Station. Then they turned back and onto the old road. Maguilla high-stepped over the first river crossing and cantered with restraint across the early spring grass where the shadow road curved beside the river. She set him at a clump of manuka bushes and he took them in a condescending hop.

Now they ford the river once more, and he steps down the slope of ancient concrete with more confidence than the slippery green slimeweed should allow. A front hoof slides and he flounders sideways into the deeper water beyond the ramp. Jess yanks her feet from the stirrups as the cold river rushes towards her, but the horse has found a foothold among the slippery boulders and steadies himself. The water is now up past his belly and lunging at Jess's boots.

Maguilla is inclined, at this point, to turn back but Jess urges him on. He moves with caution, positioning each hoof before resting his weight, until he hits the weed-smothered concrete. Then he scrambles from the water, and Jess is unprepared, slack-reined and stirrupless. She struggles for control and has an advantage, for here the river bank rises steeply, and Maguilla heads straight up, spurning the snaking sheep track.

The climb curbs his speed, gives Jess time to regain her stirrups, reclench the reins. She's grateful for Frank's saddle, ostentatiously rolled and padded for maximum grip and comfort.

They reach the top of the bank and Maguilla has the bit between his steely teeth. Jess hauls on the reins, without effect. She is tiny, weightless and ineffectual, he is huge and powerful. She pulls on the left rein with all her strength and manages to drag his head around just far enough to see the white of his eye.

Maguilla continues to gallop, but the moment has gone. His pace slows, his teeth relinquish the bit, his flattened ears rise to flutter indeterminately.

'You bugger,' Jess says, realigning the reins, stroking the hair beneath his mane. 'You rotten, sneaky, wonderful bugger.'

She knows it was a warning about where they stand, him and her. Beneath her hand his wet hair is glassy in the sunlight.

'WHO'S THAT WOMAN?' It had been bothering Frank for at least twenty minutes, the taunt of familiarity.

Wyatt's eyes didn't move from the screen. 'She's the one with all the money and that old geezer's who she used to be married to.'

'I got that. I meant who is she in real life?'

'Dead,' said Wyatt. 'By now. Whoever she is.'

'They would've said at the beginning,' said Frank. 'In the whatchamacallits.'

'They wouldn've known when she was gonna die. Not when they made the movie.'

Frank let it go. What did it matter? Things came on the screen and hovered about a bit then went away. Still he watched, even in the daylight. Not at first, swore he never would, but then the TV looked out one day and saw him shackled and softening with disuse and dragged him in. He'd had to force himself to finish the vegetable garden, lost interest in a hen coop. If he had a newspaper or one of those programme guides he could have made choices and eliminations. Should he order one of those on the rural delivery? Would picking and choosing solidify his softening brain?

Judy had taken Frank to the Windsor Four Square to organise an account. This meant he could leave a list for the rural delivery van and the stuff would be left at his gate next day. He could have done the same at Titahi Station but nobody had bothered to tell him. In case they'd be held responsible for his unpaid bills? Picking him, right off, for a wastrel and satisfied, now, that their judgement had been confirmed. He hated to give them that satisfaction, could feel it grating his bones.

'I hope she's dead any rate,' said Wyatt. 'She deserves to die.'

Wyatt seemed to have moved in. Or perhaps the others had just forgotten him when they last left. Frank had supposed they would come and collect the lad in due course, but it was already several days. Through which Wyatt slept and watched TV on the mattress in the living room. On the second day Frank had raised the matter of education. Windsor High School, Wyatt assured him, was always grateful for his absence.

That name — what had possessed the boy's parents? Frank could have worn it with some degree of insouciance, but this boy was pinkly plump with a face that could be boiled down for brawn. Those bristly pale lashes — and eyes like a glassy sea in which, now and then, Frank seemed to see a desperate signal like a drowning arm, but too distant to be sure.

Genetics. Hitler had made a lot of decent people squeamish about the word, but Frank set store by genes. It stood to reason. Mate two brainless dogs and you'd get a useless mutt. So what could you expect from a couple of human beings who had by-passed all the perfectly adequate boys' names and grasped, instead, at Wyatt?

'He's eating all our food,' Ruby had complained. 'And using up all the toilet paper. Make him go.'

'Rube,' he reasoned, 'if he was some mangy half-grown dog who'd come scraping and whining at our door, what would we do? Take him in, feed him up.'

'Mac'd chase him off,' said Ruby, reasonably. 'And if he was eating all their tucker so would Sal. They'd bite him and chase him away.'

'So bite him,' said Frank. 'If you feel inclined that's okay by me.'

She made a face.

'If he was a dog,' he persisted, 'we'd take him in. Feed him up. See how he went.'

But if he didn't shape up. If eight days on he was just eating and crapping and lying on the carpet gazing mournfully at a flickering screen, well then he'd take the mongrel outside and put a bullet in its head. Out of its misery. Kindest thing. Frank could see this was where the problem lay and was expecting Ruby to point it out.

Instead she said, 'He's not mangy even. He's fat.'

'You can be fat and mangy.'

Frank was idly picturing the rifle propped in the corner of his bedroom and thinking that wasn't such a bad idea. Good animals getting killed off all the time and hopeless people being kept alive to breed more of their kind.

But Wyatt was still a youngster, and youngsters and Frank were on the same side. With some care and attention Wyatt might turn into tolerable company, might curb his appetite and be persuaded to pull at least a proportion of his weight . . . In the meantime he was there and he was only fifteen, so what could you do?

'You have to live with yourself,' Frank told himself and Ruby, and gathered from her face that she'd heard it before. He didn't let this throw him off stride. 'That's the thing to remember. Whatever you do, afterwards it's yourself you've gotta live with.'

The woman from Welfare had visited, fortunately, before Wyatt had joined them and before Frank had been zapped into submission by cathode rays. A cold snap, late afternoon. Frank had rabbit stew simmering sluggishly and the house was full of it. The fire was burning. Ruby was spread on the carpet with her exercise book and rubber, unscrambling words. RCAOHCKCO — an insect.

'Cockroach,' Frank told.

'I know that.' Ruby hiding the list beneath her hands. 'You're not s'posed to tell me.'

The baby lay between them, slashing the air with a yellow plastic funnel. The dogs had given Frank plenty of warning and the sherry bottle, almost empty, was back in the cupboard.

The woman, young enough to be Frank's daughter, tickled the baby's cheeks, enquired about his diet, drank a cup of tea and took Ruby off to her bedroom for a chat. While he waited Frank stood stirring flour paste into the stew and grinning, certain already that Ruby would stay.

JESS THINKS SHE will sense it, that moment when the stallion tires of pretending. She believes that, crouched on his back, she will know. Or will she be certain only when she tries to rein him in, like a toddler tugging at the brake of a steam train?

'Just keep him under control,' Frank had said the first time, 'and you should be right as rain.' But he'd watched from the steps, squint-eyed, until they were out of sight.

Jess doesn't want Maguilla to be a horse she can control. Doesn't even want to be the rider. Wants to be the horse himself. Bolting.

Sometimes with Lucky or Pedro she'd remove the bridle on the way home, or jump on bareback in the paddock with nothing but the mane to clutch, and kick them into action. Always it was disappointing. Lucky was cunning rather than reckless and Pedro was simply too nice to bolt.

But Maguilla . . . he is flying, now, along the flat; the old house site with its crumbling chimney ahead . . . beside . . . behind. His ears tipped back but not severely, so perhaps it is just the wind tilting them before it slides, cold, down the neck of Jess's shirt and cold, too, among the roots of her hair. She closes her eyes to feel it all: windsmell of river, mint, cattle, sweat . . . coarse mane lashing her face . . . hooves drumming above the yodelling of magpies and new lambs bleating . . . motion of muscle, sinew, leather beneath her fingers . . . the sweet, dry taste in her mouth.

Beyond the flat there's another river crossing and no reason to suppose that Maguilla knows or cares. Jess opens her eyes, braces her knees against the saddle and hauls at the reins. One hand, then both hands. The stallion's dark ears flatten in resistance, he raises his head a little higher. Jess tries again. Chooses the right rein — to the left is the river bank hidden by manuka, to the right is the boundary fence to the Turnbull property — drags on it. Maguilla veers to the right with no perceptible change of pace. The fence is ahead of him. Jess gives in and they clear the fence. Sheep scatter and flee, stiff-legged.

'WHEN MY MOTHER died,' Frank told Wyatt, talking over Elizabeth Montgomery, whom he'd got to like, and her twerp of a husband. 'After she died well then we were orphans near enough, only my sister had these people who took her in. Well one stage, after m' mother died, they put me in this orphanage, but I didn't take to it at all. Just kept clearing off. A couple of times or so they nabbed me and I was taken back, but the next time, well I guess they just couldn't be bothered. I must'a been thirteen or so by then. I reckon they thought I was old enough and ugly enough to look after myself.

'Well, I hitched north — I had this idea I'd get work on a station, or seasonal work. That's how I met Jack Hobson and he took me under his wing and he taught me everything. Everything I needed to know to keep myself alive.

'He was a cattle thief, Jack, a convicted cattle thief and a very impressive bloke.'

Way back when he knew no better, Frank had pondered over the apparent contradiction.

'Every word Jack Hobson told me I've remembered. Like the wrong and the right things to do in the bush; things like how to catch a scrub turkey without a rifle — without anything. He'd have to have been the best bushman in New South Wales.'

'Tell us about the dog,' said Wyatt. 'The dog you used for rustling them calves.'

Frank was coming to love Wyatt, the lad listened so well.

The others had again come visiting — Jason, Ian, Lynette. Plus a dozen of beer and a bottle of port. Frank insisted on chipping in; they'd never have asked and he gave them credit there. Lynette had managed to corner Frank in the kitchen and ask how did he feel about Carol, because Carol was wanting to know. 'She really, really likes you, Frank.' And for a moment there he saw himself as the teenage boy he never was — that open freckle-faced kid in *Happy Days*, someone like that, making dates, confessions, lovable social boo-boos. And for a moment he liked the flattered and goofy feeling that came with the vision. Then it was gone.

'Jeezus, Lynette,' he said. 'Look at me, will you, I've got enough troubles as it is.'

'Oh. So what d' you want me to tell her?'

'Nicely,' he said. 'Put it nicely. You know —'

Lynette with her white patterned sweatshirt, her hair fluffy about her motherly face. A couple of years on and she'd be shacked up with Jason or Ian, nursing a baby of her own. All she thought she wanted from life, so it was all she'd get — Frank feeling regretful on Lynette's behalf for her life yet to come. His own life was no great shakes but at least it had an edge to it. No one could say — could ever have said with confidence — this is how Frank Ward's life will be ten years from now. That was something to hang onto.

Before the youngsters left Frank took Jason aside and said it would be appreciated if they took Wyatt back to town with them.

And they did. But, like any befriended mongrel, Wyatt was back three days later. He'd walked out of town with a few clothes in a plastic bag and flagon of sherry to oil his welcome. He'd made modest inroads into the sherry while waiting on the roadside for a lift.

When Wyatt arrived back at Frank's place Frank was bathing the baby, which he did to no particular schedule in case his boy should grow up to be a prisoner of routine. Frank saw the flagon but he also saw the way Wyatt's jeans hung low beneath his rolling flesh and there was a moment, a narrow aperture of time, where he steeled himself to say — no, you eat too much and this isn't the YM. But they were words that didn't sit comfortably on Frank's lips and, came the point, he couldn't assemble them.

The girl Jess came after school now that the evenings were lengthening. Bringing, each time, small gifts which she insisted her family had no use for. A kettle, a packet of metal clouts, notepads and ballpoints monogrammed Barker Hanley Realtors, a small yellow teddy bear with fraying ears, condensed three-in-one *Reader's Digest* books, a tea tray with a castle rusting in circles . . . In return she rode Maguilla, with a growing and irksome confidence.

So that now and again, when Ruby was home and Wyatt was awake (between his years and her sense they could surely handle a crisis with the baby), Frank saddled up his horse and called the dogs to heel. A short, sharp ride to remind himself he was Frank the stockman, horseman Frank with his handmade saddle and shit-hot horse. Though the girl would for sure have been seen about, devaluing Maguilla as an object of awe.

In the saddle Frank rode through memories like clouds: horses he'd owned, horses he'd wanted, horses he'd buried. Cars he'd owned — bloody disasters, all of them, but some worse than others. Journeys, accidents, lucky escapes. Women. The fill-in ones whose faces he couldn't remember. Lisa, pushing resentment aside long enough to reveal her heavily pregnant, pendulous breasts resting on her extended belly, and happy with it. Happier than he'd ever seen her, so he'd told himself motherhood was what she needed and things would come right. Though Ruby had been there to put the lie to that little dream, if only he'd had the sense to see.

Before Lisa, going back a bit, there was his wife Jean and the babies — two or was it three? — who never made it through to full term. Frank had ambitions then, and a good job, a very good job. Nineteen, and managing a property near Brewarrina. Setting money aside for his own place, a long haul, but possible he'd never doubted. Seeing him and Jean and a family and his mother looking down, incredulous that her intemperate son had come so far so fast.

When Jean died, the whole lot went with her; the dream of his own place and the sense of himself as a person of solid prospects. Jean died and his mother was proved right. Except it seemed to Frank that he was a better person now than he had been back then. The old Frank wouldn't have let himself be trapped at home with a couple of kids and a voracious adolescent. Yet in Curvey's Creek the old Frank would've been respected, even envied. Strange, that. Approval was a worrying word. Right now, under the circumstances, he wasn't doing too badly. A fire in the grate, clean clothes on their backs, food on the table.

The food bit was getting harder. Ruby was right — Wyatt's appetite was more than they could afford. So, under cover of night, Frank the provider and Mac hopped through the fence and quietly cornered a cross-bred wether which Frank upended, clamping its furious legs, and dragging it to the fence. Beneath the macrocarpa trees he slit the sheep's throat, draining the blood into a bucket because he was partial to a drop of black pudding. Then he strung the carcass up and skinned it. Already he was planning a meal — forequarter, pumpkins, potatoes. The taste of gravy watered his mouth.

While Frank was rehanging the carcass in the wash-house Wyatt came in. He studied the skinned sheep from various angles like a tourist taking in a famous statue. Eventually he turned away and picked up Frank's knife where it lay in the washtub with the blood smeared along the blade. Tested the blade cautiously with his thumb.

'I could go a cuppa.' Little by little Frank was training Wyatt in useful tasks.

'Bloody sharp,' said Wyatt.

'Oath,' said Frank. 'Have your balls off before you could blink.'


JACK SAMUELS TOOK a couple of steps inside the door of the schoolroom. Kids scuttling past him through to the lockers in the porch. Silenced to whispers, back glances, nudges. Something up. Wayne's father. Wayne already out there in the Landrover, waiting. Maybe in trouble, maybe in *big* trouble.

Owen felt the change in his kids and looked around. The poster buckling, half secure. Life cycle of the hydatids worm, updated version.

'Hi.' Jack, he should say Jack. Easily: Jack, howgoesit? 'What can I do for you?'

'A word,' said Jack.

Owen's stomach tightened. 'Wayne?' He tried to remember every recent exchange he'd had with the boy.

'No.'

Suzanne Chaney dawdling out, earwigging. 'Off you go,' Owen told her. 'On the bus. I'll be out in a minute.'

She went, the last child, dragging her feet over the wooden floor.

Owen waited for Samuels to explain, felt the poster brushing his arm. 'Excuse me, I'll just —' Turning his back to fasten the paper with two more pins. A sheep, a dog, a child of non-specific gender. A moment to remind himself that Jack Samuels was merely an overgrown farm boy. Owen remembered his kind, plank-headed schoolyard bullies, contemptible. Yet thirty years on and Owen's instinct was for deference.

'Yes?' He turned back.

'Frank Ward,' said Samuels.

'Ruby's father?'

'So he'd claim. You know him?'

'I met the mother.'

'Missus thought you'd be the one to talk to. Be better coming from you.'

The kids would be in the bus by now. Waiting.

'What would be better coming from me?'

'Ward. Was working for me and now he's in the rabbiter's cottage. Well, you know that. Thing is, seems he's been rooting some kid from the high school.'

Rooting. Owen imagined pigs, Samuels leaning on the fence above them staring down, hat crushed in his hands.

Leila, thought Owen without surprise, but vaguely flattered. The Samuels had come to him, oblique and embarrassed, for advice.

'Name of Carol Green. In Leila's class.' Jack Samuels reading Owen's mind. 'Under age and all.'

'Then it's a police matter.'

But Jack wanted more, stood waiting.

'Surely?' Owen prompted.

'It's not just that one girl. All these young kids from town hang around at his place. And that's what's going on.'

'Leila?'

'I put a stop to it fast where she's concerned, but there's these others.'

'Their parents . . .'

'Riff-raff. Townies. Point is, first it's that lot, then it'll be kids from Curvey's Creek. If we don't do something.'

'So what,' said Owen carefully, 'do you have in mind?'

'We thought you'd know for the best.' Meekly. Almost with deference. For fifteen years Owen had waited for this moment, wondered if it would ever come. For fifteen years he and Marion had sat in the district like potted plants in a cottage garden. Among but not with. Awaiting removal.

Back at the start he'd joked to his wife about the local

anthropology. Males out wielding clubs, swaggering and gossiping; females back in the caves sweeping, breeding, rearing. Owen the eunuch who minded their children and might one day be elevated to the role of Wise Man.

His parents had thought it a fine thing to have a teacher in the family. Owen had trained with enthusiasm and served his trainee years in a suburban primary, believed himself a person of worth. The sole position at Curvey's Creek had seemed a definite advancement — independence, a salary increase, a healthy start for their expected child and a way of keeping Marion away from the shops.

He'd anticipated respect, even a measure of gratitude. It was 1967 and rural teaching positions weren't much sought after, especially at schools where the roll was liable to fall below what was officially considered a viable number.

But embarrassing, that's how they found him. Nothing said, but he knew. A nanny, a ninny. Men drove tractors, whistled dogs, mustered, leant on saleyard rails. In private Owen scoffed, but when he talked to a father he heard himself being respectful. He bought himself checked brushed cotton shirts to wear in the weekends, and tried never to listen to himself or look at himself, because that was surely the secret of their inner confidence.

Owen would imagine neighbouring males calling on Marion while he was stuck in front of the blackboard. Bedazzling her with their weathered forearms, their nonchalant black armpits. He should have looked then at the vacancies in the *Gazette* but Sheenagh was already on the way and he dreaded upheaval. Next thing, he was teaching his own daughters and seeing them easy among their peers, belonging as he and Marion never had and never would. His children had put down roots. That seemed reason enough to stay.

When Corin, their third and last child, started school, Marion found herself a desk job in the county council office. She commuted each day to Windsor and cheered up — once again there was money for spending. Marion would open the *Windsor Mail*, even the *Herald*, and look at the ads before anything else. He hated to see it. Knew she was shallow like that, had always known, but at the start had set that knowledge aside because she was lively and lithe and lovely beyond all his youthful expectations.

Marion having a job lowered Owen's status further. He read the subtext in every sentence the Curvey's Creek mothers offered up. Wives here might help out on the farm but they didn't demean their husbands by earning a living. Wouldn't think of having a male preparing dinner, mopping floors, folding the washing. Poor Owen, poor sap.

Problems within the community came and went but Owen learnt of them second hand. From absence notes, from the children, from the *Mail*. Accidents, death, erosion, drought, the removal of government subsidy on stock prices . . . dramas that brought the locals together but left Owen and Marion on the outskirts.

Marion didn't mind. She'd made friends in town, went off with them on shopping sprees to Hamilton, even Auckland, where shops were bigger and better. At night she did her real estate course, called it a career. But Owen minded, couldn't help it. He replaced his blazer with a speckled jacket the colour of Lou Wilson's hills in autumn and bought a hat the slimy shade of green that Pedro's slobber left on Jess's shirts. Wore it to Windsor over his receding hair.

Now, at last, Owen was being asked for advice on a matter beyond spelling lists or the logic of new maths. Asked by Jack Samuels, whom Owen once regarded as the epitome of rural brawn and ignorance, and what Owen was feeling was gratitude and an eagerness to please.

'I could have a word,' he offered. 'With . . .Ward.'

'A word!' Samuels rolled his eyes. 'Fella's a devious. One of them. Smartarse with it. Oughtn't you be thinking about that little girl of his? She's not really his, y'know.'

'Perhaps . . .' The children were waiting in the bus. Owen was driver, teacher, housewife and — at last — sage. But Jack Samuels was a busy man, had taken the time . . . Farmers worked day and night.

'The girl,' said Owen. 'Leila's friend —' thank God Jess had grown out of Leila — 'if she was persuaded to make a complaint . . . That would be the appropriate way . . .'

Samuels scratched his thigh, fast like a dog scratches. 'I'll find the name and address,' he said. 'Get you on the blower tonight.'

THE DOGS WOKE Frank. Ten past two by the fluorescent hands of his alarm clock. They kept up the racket, Sal's bark choking as she leapt to swing on her collar. Frank pulled on his trousers and sneaked barefoot up the passage. Heard the back door open as he reached the kitchen door, waited clenched and ready though it was pitch black out there.

But the bulk and the walk were unmistakable. Frank reached for the light and Wyatt stood blinking and wobbling, thighs pressed together like a woman, feet splayed. Put Frank in mind of a top about to reach the end of its spin. Wyatt was breathing hard. There was a smear of blood on his arm.

'Where the hell ya been?'

'Nowhere.' But keeping his eyes away from Frank's.

'Bullshit.'

'Thought *I'd* get one.' Wyatt's voice had gone up an octave. 'For a . . . you know. Contribution. Only, ha ha, you must be able to run bloody fast, Frank. Bloody fast.'

'You fall or what?'

Wyatt followed Frank's eyes to his own arm. 'Musta cut him a bit. I had him, only he got away.'

'Cut him with what? Pocket knife, I bet. You were gonna kill some poor bloody sheep with your pocket knife!'

'No,' said Wyatt, his eyes wayward again. 'Had a proper knife.'

'Let's see it.'

But Wyatt's eyes stayed on the warming drawer at the bottom of the stove. Frank marched back to his bedroom and checked the leather sheath on his belt. Empty. Back to have it out with Wyatt.

'Where is it? Where the fuck is it?'

He'd had that knife for ten years, more, the blade now whetted to a state of lethal elegance. Lofty Carson had carved Frank's initials, F.C.W., at the top of the handle one night in a pub in Wagga. Lofty was dead and buried with his head, they said, under his arm. Severed in the crash, clean, they said, as a knife through a mushroom stalk. A knife that sat easy in the hand, as Frank's knife did.

'You'll find that knife.' His pointed finger shaking in rage. 'With the first glimmer of daylight you'll get out there and find my bloody knife.'

'Wasn't my fault, honest, Frank.'

'You'll find it. That's all.'

Frank kept himself awake, waiting for daylight. He read five and a half chapters of *The Pastures of Heaven*, which Jess had borrowed for him from her father's bookshelf. He'd written down the authors' names — Jack London, John Steinbeck, Charles Dickens, Zane Grey — so she wouldn't turn up with some rubbish he couldn't be bothered with. The *Reader's Digest* book had been better than nothing but he'd sooner stick with what he knew.

Maria Lopez was harnessing up old Lindo when dawn light reached the rabbiter's cottage in Curvey's Creek. Frank put down the book and went with Wyatt, who couldn't be relied upon to find his own arse in a hailstorm. They climbed the fence and trekked up the hill, Wyatt sighing and sniffing as his eyes skipped over the ground with an air of certain failure. Seeing this, Frank demanded details.

Unable to hold the sheep, Wyatt had stabbed it. The knife had gone in a short way then hit bone. This wasn't what the woolly surface had led him to expect — apart from its brutal feet, the sheep in his arms had felt like a solid teddy bear. As his stomach heaved, Wyatt had let go and the sheep had fled.

'Idiot,' said Frank. 'You stupid bastard.' But there was no mileage to be had. One look at Wyatt and you knew the poor bugger had been sworn at all his life.

Frank found drops of blood blackening the grass and followed them to the top of the hill, but there was no glint of metal to be seen. Beyond the hill they would be visible from the neighbouring house, a well-established affair with tidy gardens and freshly painted sheds. C.B. Webster, according to the rural delivery box on the roadside, but C.B. had not felt inclined to make himself known to his new neighbours. Nor had he any children attending Curvey's Creek school. Ruby and the youngest of the Chaney kids, their neighbours on the other side, were the only two kids to catch the bus from Turnbull Road.

Frank and Wyatt came back down and made a search of the gully just in case. Found only a fly-blown ewe bogged behind some bulrushes. They pulled her out and stood her on dry ground. Twice her mud-encased legs gave way, but on the third attempt, splayed and rigid, they held and she was off. Wyatt spewed up behind a clump of manuka. He'd seen the maggots writhing. Frank could raise no pity for him.

'Well, that's that then.'

'I was only tryin' to be useful.' A splatter of vomit had caught on Wyatt's belly-stretched jersey.


THE NEXT AFTERNOON, as Frank was hammering a shoe on Judy Gordon's latest save from the knacker's yard — a roan skeleton who didn't yet answer to the name of Cobra — the green Landcruiser pulled up at the gate. Mac and Sal tore over and set up a chorus but Frank barely looked up. He'd half been expecting . . .

C.B. Webster unlatched the gate, showed Frank's dogs the sole of his boot, got back behind the wheel and drove on through, leaving the gate open. Arrogant prick.

'A neighbourly visit?' Judy clasped the reins tight under Cobra's chin. The horse was vehicle shy, bird shy, cow shy, plane shy . . . just plain paranoid.

'Doubt it.' Frank mumbling through the two nails clenched between his teeth. He knew the vehicle, and who owned it. Had watched it from his vegie patch, raised his hand the first time or two but nothing in response.

Cobra wrenched back his upturned hoof and reared clumsily as the cruiser pulled up only a few yards away. As Frank cursed and cradled a torn finger, he watched Webster jump out. The hunting knife dangled between the man's finger and thumb.

Cobra and Judy reached a truce a few steps back from where they started.

'Mr Webster,' said Judy. Polite as a child giving cheek.

'Miss Gordon.' He looked like a polo player, that kind of weathered and well-heeled confidence. Sixty, maybe, but fit. A man who still looked in his mirror with satisfaction.

Webster held up the knife, his eyes on Frank. 'Lost something?'

Frank shook his head. 'Useful-looking knife, though.' Past Webster's head he saw Wyatt's face sink beneath the window ledge.

Webster let the knife drop, then caught it, gripped the handle, turned it slowly until the blade pointed to the sky. 'Very useful. If you're into slaughtering your neighbour's sheep. I'm Charles Webster, by the way.' He aimed the thumb of the knife-clenching hand towards the boundary fence. His left hand stayed in the pocket of his jacket.

73

'Frank Ward.' Frank pushed his hat back just a fraction, in neighbourly gesture.

'I know your name,' said Webster. 'What about the C? What's the C stand for?'

'Sorry . . . not with you?'

'Your second name?'

'My second name?' Frank scratched the back of his head below the hatline. 'Odd kinda question. Etheridge, as a matter of fact.' The word had just come to him out of nowhere. Such a smooth and improbable invention. 'Family name. Francis Etheridge.'

'FEW,' said Judy.

They looked at her.

'F.E.W.'

'Right,' said Frank. 'Some have worse, though. Phew.'

'Phewwww!' Judy began to giggle, turning away. Frank pretended not to notice.

'So what's the story with the knife?' Looking straight into Webster's eyes.

Webster looked straight back. Flinty, squinting grey eyes. 'Stuck fair through the ribs of one of my wethers. Paddock just through the fence. Handy when you're running low on tucker.'

'Hang on,' said Frank. 'Hang on. If I was gonna knock off your sheep, mate, I'd make a decent job of it. The culprit here, from what you're telling me, is some townie who wouldn't know a sheep's arse from its nostril. Come out this way Sunday driving, you know the story — looking out for mushrooms . . . blackberries . . .'

'This time of year?' Nostrils fluting, eyebrows raised.

'What do they know! And they see a fat lamb . . .'

'I get them.' Judy weighing in with Frank. 'Strolling through the paddocks, pulling up native seedlings, chasing the Shetlands, pelting them with stones. Not often but I get them. You must've too.

'On a dead-end road?'

'What's the difference?' said Judy. 'That kind think the country's public property, they go wherever they please.'

'I'll keep an eye out, though,' said Frank quickly. 'From now on I'll have an eye out, that's for sure.'

Nothing Webster could do. The flint eyes said he didn't

believe Frank, not for a minute. He shrugged and climbed back into the Cruiser. Frank was sorry to see his knife departing.

Judy dragged Cobra back beside Frank. 'Your knife?'

'Not me,' he told her. 'Was young Wyatt.'

'Killed Charlie Webster's sheep?'

'No,' said Frank, picking his way selectively through the truth. 'Had a go at it, though.'

Judy looked sick. 'Get rid of that boy, Frank, is my advice. Send him packing.'

'YOU'S A RELIGIOUS or somethink?' Three teeth missing right in front, a teapot belly, hair in its death throes. Yet Owen suspected she wasn't much older than him.

He wanted only ever to see people like this on film in other people's countries. He told his pupils about it year after year — plague, famine, need. Slanting his message towards inevitability and the virtues of giving. Save the Children and Corso cast as heroes, but never a villain in Owen's teaching scenario. No political overview or whisper of man's inhumanity to man to challenge their young brains, enrage their parents, jeopardise Owen's future.

Just last year the whole country in a kind of civil war because of a rugby tour and Owen walking a non-committal tightrope. Racism, intolerance, brutality — words that did not cross his lips in public. *Apartheid* was safe, a reversible jacket of a word, that could be defined as the listener chose.

There were no brown-skinned children at Curvey's Creek School, in Owen's time there never had been. No poor kids either. Ruby Ward was as close as it came, but even she had shoes to wear and lunches to eat. And Ruby was why Owen was here. He needed to remind himself of that, think of Ruby's sharp little face, her knowing eyes and what might have made them that way.

'No,' he told the woman, 'not religious. Nothing like that. I was hoping to have a word with Carol. If she's home?'

'Word? What about?'

Should have foreseen this. He looked at his shoes. Khaki canvas, selected by Marion. A rusted section of downpipe lying beside them.

'Her future,' he said.

'You's from the school then?'

'Yes.' Smiling at her. 'From the school.'

'She's quit.'

'I know. May I see her?'

She turned her head. 'Care . . . ool. Someone to see ya.'

Carol came to stare at Owen. Thin, pretty face, mouth hitched sideways in a kind of a smile.

'Hi Carol,' he said. 'I'm Owen Bennington. I was hoping to have a word with you.'

Carol shook a cigarette loose from a packet of Benson & Hedges, lit it with a pink lighter.

'Perhaps we could go for a stroll?' said Owen. The mother, if that's who she was, still stood there.

Carol shrugged. 'If you want.' Pushed past the woman to join him.

They stopped a few yards up the street. 'I wanted to get you in private.'

'Oh yeah?' She laughed inanely, her eyes clutching at his whenever he let them.

'How old are you, Carol?'

'Sixteen.'

'I could check it out.'

'So what are you asking for anyway?'

'You know a man called Frank Ward.'

'What's it to you?'

'You've been sleeping with him. Is that right?'

'So?'

'If you're under age it's against the law.'

'Gonna arrest me? Go on then.' The laugh starting again.

'He's the one breaking the law, not you.'

She laughed again. Owen looked down the street at his car. Wished he was in it and moving. 'I'm concerned for his daughter . . . step-daughter, Ruby. What sort of man he is . . .'

Her laughter died away. She dropped the stub of her smoke on the footpath. 'You're gross,' she said. 'You're disgusting, that's what y'are.' Turned and ran back towards her awful home, running with her shoulders round her ears and her knees coming up too high.

Owen waited, gave her time to get inside the house. Told himself no one need ever know about this futile mission. He saw that his life was insulated and easy, felt a surge of gratitude for his own family and the lives they led.

Their Jess, almost the same age as Carol Green and much prettier in a decent kind of way. Little disappointments he had nurtured, perhaps because she was the oldest; not as clever as he'd hoped, nor as outgoing. Marion's genes and Curvey's Creek had claimed Jess from the start, shaped her in their own image. An outdoor child, uncommunicative, oblivious to the pleasure of books and learning. Stubborn too. The horse thing, which at first he'd encouraged because it was such a *natural* kind of interest, had grown into a sulky obsession. Hormones, said Marion. Nothing to worry about. And now he saw that she was right.

If Owen allowed himself a favourite child, it would be Jess.

# CHAPTER 9

CARS PASSED WYATT, spitting out mean little stones. To avoid them he had to walk in the long grass, stumbling over hidden rocks and rabbit holes. His right arm ached from holding out his thumb. One old Austin truck and a new Honda Civic had passed him by already and he was only seven telegraph posts past the turn-off to Frank's place.

The cows in this place were friendlier than the people. To the cows Wyatt was a big attraction. They came pounding to the fence, a whole stampede, and lined up dribbling and staring. Fans. Wyatt stopped and bowed. He raised his hand and waved to shy ones in the back row. In those big stupid eyes he was Meatloaf, or maybe Robert Plant. He gave them a few bars. *There's a da dada da, and da da dada da, and we're BUIL-DING A STAIRWAY TO HEAV-EN.* His voice was a small squeak in a vast universe.

The cows liked it, he could tell. He reached out a hand towards a wet black nose and it revved back out of reach. Emboldened, he leant on the fence. The beasts shouldered and shuffled themselves into an attentive half-circle before him.

'You'n' me,' he told them. 'You'n' me, eh.' A couple of them nodded, saw the connection.

He pushed on along the fenceline as far as the gate. The cows followed.

'Join me,' he invited them. Leaned over to unfasten the metal hook and push the gate back. Only a few inches, for he suddenly lost confidence in their affability.

'You'n' me need to talk,' Frank had said and Wyatt almost knew what was coming.

'Buy you a new knife. I will, Frank. Promise.'

'Not m' knife, mate. It's not even you in particular. Just right now I've got problems enough and a chronic lack of funds, if you see what I mean.'

Wyatt had heaved himself up into sitting position. 'Not really.'

'Want you to go, mate.'

The ground hundreds of feet below and Wyatt teetering at the door of the plane, clutching Frank's arm.

'I hope you're not gonna regret this, Frank.'

'I hope so, too.' Frank pushing him out the door into the nothingness.

Wyatt had lain down again. 'Be gone first thing in the morning, Frank. Wouldn't wanna stay where I'm not wanted.'

'Okeydoke,' Frank had said.

The *Coronation Street* music came on at that moment. Wyatt listened to it for a while then promised, 'I am gonna get you that knife, Frank, like I said. A class knife.'

'Don't worry,' Frank told him. 'Was only a knife.'

It wasn't quite first thing in the morning. About eleven o'clock. But almost first thing for Wyatt by the time he'd got up and had a bit of breakfast. He'd half thought Frank would've changed his mind but the only thing changed was his temper. He'd snarled at Ruby, booted Mac out the door and didn't look Wyatt right in the face. Not once.

OWEN UNLOCKED THE schoolroom as Charlie Webster had asked him to, and waited. A confidential matter, Charlie had said. For the eight years Charlie Webster had been chairman of the school committee Owen had avoided calling him by name, but on the phone the day before it had been 'Charlie' and 'Owen' without hesitation. Owen, no longer on the periphery, was embarrassed by the satisfaction this gave him.

They arrived in three vehicles. Rick Chaney — father of Peter, Calvin and Suzanne — came with his bachelor brother, Phil, while Charlie Webster and Jack Samuels came alone. As Rick said, this wasn't a matter for women to worry about, best leave them out of it. They took off their boots at the door, though the school floor was uncarpeted, and sat rather stiffly on top of desks to discuss what to do about Frank Ward.

'All of us here,' said Charlie Webster, 'have good reason to want to get rid of the sod. I've got two sheep gone, Rick and Phil had their gates opened. Dan Bradford too. I couldn't get hold of

Dan but he lost a beast. It got bowled by Dr Chase on his way to attending to old Mary Menzies when she came down with pneumonia. And Jack here wanting to keep his girl out of Ward's clutches now we know what the sod's like. And Owen, well, Owen's got his own reasons.'

He had to mean Ruby. And Owen could almost believe now that Ruby was in need of saving. Thinking of small gestures, expressions, silences . . . signs Owen might have recognised as pleas for help. But the connection between paedophilia and wandering stock seemed obscure.

'Why would he go round opening gates?'

Revenge, Charlie told him. Charlie had had a run-in with Ward over a hunting knife Ward denied was his. Ward must have opened the gates to pay Charlie back.

'But then,' Owen wondered, 'why didn't he open Charlie's gates?'

'Too cunning for that,' said Phil Chaney, with a degree of admiration.

Owen looked around at their faces and saw not a trace of uncertainty to match his own flicker of doubt. And surely these men would have a better grasp than Owen of a stockman's logic.

'The question is,' said Charlie, 'what do we do?'

Jack Samuels scratched his leg in a sudden frenzied movement. 'If only I could track down Kevin,' he said, 'I'd get him to evict the bastard.'

'That wouldn't help Ruby,' said Owen. The girl Carol came into his head with her sliding eyes and silly skittering laugh.

When, years ago, the rabbiter's cottage had served as the schoolteacher's house, Charlie and May Webster and Rick and Edith Chaney were Owen and Marion's neighbours. They'd lifted hands to each other in greeting when their cars passed on the no-exit metal road.

'Y'ought to drive by, Owen, see what he's done out back of your old place,' said Rick, as if he'd been reading Owen's mind. The Chaney children all had reading difficulties. 'Raised the fence, bloody fortress. Keep in that crazy stallion of his.' Turning to Jack. 'Got no okay from Kevin, I bet?'

Jack shrugged he doubted. 'What gets my goat is the likes of him getting paid to do nothing out of my taxes. That's what gets to me.'

'Bad enough the way they dish money out to women these days,' moaned Rick. 'Breaking up marriages, that's all it does.'

Phil Chaney whacked his brother's arm. Haw hawed. 'Scared Edith's gonna take off, are you? Have to get your own bloody dinner.'

Owen wondered, not for the first time, if these men were aware that he cooked and cleaned? Laughed about it over saleyard fences?

'That's the key!' Charlie slapped his tweeded thigh. 'If his kids are taken off him, he'll have no income. He'll have to leave.'

Owen said, 'I think we'd need rather more evidence than we've got.'

'Get his little girl examined,' said Phil. His face looked wolfish and excited and, seeing this, Owen felt unease.

'Not just like that,' he said. Ruby, with her bony arms and wispy hair, the way she sidled up to him at playtimes and chatted as if she was Owen's peer, her sly diplomacy in playground wrangles . . . 'I'll look into it — have a word with her.' It sounded lame, and Owen felt cornered and uncomfortable, as if he'd reneged on a promise of adventure.

'Maybe,' said Rick, 'it's your girl y' should have a word with.'

'What?'

'I see her often enough,' Rick was uncomfortable now, looking away, 'careering round on that crazy stallion of his.'

''Fraid I have too.' Charlie Webster gave Owen an apologetic grimace. 'I took it you knew. Couldn't figure out why you hadn't put a stop to it.'

'WHAT DO YOU do there?'

Jess looked at her father in disbelief. 'Why?'

'Just answer me!'

'I ride his horse.'

*And . . .* his face was saying. *And . . . go on.*

'Sometimes I have a cup of tea.'

'You don't drink tea.'

'Just to be polite.'

*And . . . and . . .*

'And talk to Ruby . . . Why?'

'You're not to go there. Never again.'

'What?'

'You heard me.'

'Why?'

His face screwed up as if he was trying to remember the reason.

'Dangerous. That horse. Stallions can't be trusted.'

Jess laughed, patted his arm. 'You know nothing about horses. That's just stupid.'

'I'm not arguing, Jess, I'm telling you. Stay away from the place.'

'Not even visit?'

'No, not even visit.'

'Why?'

'Because . . . it's time you knuckled down, miss, and did some schoolwork. What about your exams? What about them, eh? Or don't you care?'

Jess bowing her head in the hangdog way that talk of her schoolwork required, but also to hide her face from Owen. Who *always* and with infinite patience would give reasons for rules he laid down, but this time had lied, and clumsily because of chronic lack of practice. Which was kind of endearing, but also pathetic. So something secret and interesting was going on and it was to do with Frank Ward.

'You understand me?'

Jess raised her head. 'Yes,' she said.

'Good,' said Owen. He got as far as the door before turning round. 'Not to Judy Gordon's either. No riding off anywhere.'

This was beyond belief. 'But Pedro has to be ridden.'

'You can ride him round the paddock.'

Ride him around the paddock! It was hard to believe that someone could live, for years, surrounded by farmland yet remain so pathetic. *Ride him around the paddock.*

'What did I do?'

'Perhaps you should tell me.' The barest hesitation, then he walked away.

Unfair. Marion was no great respecter of fairness but Jess had to dump her outrage somewhere. So she waited until her mother came home, and then waited for a moment to get her alone. But the only time Marion was alone she would be glued to the telephone. They went with the job, those never-ending calls. Marion would take them on her bedroom phone where she could hear herself think.

So this night Jess would get to the bedroom door and hear her mother's real estate voice, which was deeper and happier than her normal voice, and would retreat. Until finally she gave up waiting and quietly pushed the door open and heard her mother using a voice that belonged to neither work nor home, a softly playful and intimate voice, as shocking as a flash of inner thigh, flabby with disuse.

Jess had to look, then, and saw that her mother's expression was as silly and shimmering as the voice. Until Marion saw Jess standing there, and the voice and the face rearranged themselves, covering up with indecent haste.

'Sorry,' Jess mumbled. 'Nothing. Never mind.' Retreating.

To be found a bit later by her father — her poor, kindly, deceived father — who couldn't bear to let the sun go down on an argument.

'I think I owe you some kind of an explanation,' he said. 'All I can tell you is Frank Ward is someone you should keep well away from. There've been complaints.'

'What sort of complaints?'

'Girls.' He said it reluctantly. 'Unpleasant stuff. He shouldn't have access to children.'

'He's got kids of his own.'

'That may well change.' Owen touched Jess's arm. 'Are we friends?'

'I can only ride in the paddock?'

'Well, if I can trust you to keep well away from Ward?'

She looked at him, felt pity. 'Okay — friends.' She smiled at him. She was no better than her mother, but he was so easy to deceive.

JESS COULDN'T SLEEP, fleshing out Owen's uneasy words. An awful sort of excitement mingled with disbelief. She had told Frank she'd be back on Thursday, after school, and that was tomorrow. She couldn't just not turn up without a reason. Whatever he was supposed to have done it had nothing to do with her, or with Maguilla. They were picking sides, her father ordering her into his team, but she should have a right to choose.

Quietly Jess slid from her bed, tugged off her yellow winceyette pyjamas and dragged on clothes. Sheenagh's breathing rasped steadily on. Jess opened the window wide, her hand like a rapist's over the swinging latch to muffle its sound. She was scared of the dark. Not the close-by dark but the further-off stuff, the solid blackness of it. Wished she dared risk a torch, but the blackness would still be out there all around her.

Should she take a bridle? Pedro or redundant old Lucky for the comfort of their company? But alone she could shortcut over fences, across McElvey's paddocks. And, alone, when crossing the road, if a car came she could crouch in the ditch or duck behind the clumpy flax.

The moon was muffled in cloud, almost useless. And Jess was running, stumbling on grass she knew by heart and even so something was behind her, its warm breath blowing aside her hair, exposing her neck, reaching out to grasp . . .

Over the road, through the fence wires, into McElvey's paddock. Walking, making herself walk now, trying to sort out shapes before she was upon them, sheep struggling to their feet and leaving camp on her account, blundering blindly off single file. Jess's eyes getting smarter all the time, until there were minutes on end when she felt free and fearless. But then the stalking blackness would be back again, breathing on her neck.

Not even sure why she was doing this. To catch him out or to warn him? But thinking already of his kitchen as a refuge.

Close now, she jumped Webster's creek by guesswork, gauging the water's edge and laughing in relief when she landed on grass. Up the bank and as she reached the fence there, at last, was Frank's kitchen light, second hand through the laundry window. Jess slid between the wires, then began to sprint. Only a few steps and she stumbled. Something stabbed her knee, but the pain eased as she scrambled to her feet, limping now, and feeling suddenly uncertain, even ridiculous. What was she doing here? She reached down to her left knee and felt a rip. His dogs were barking. When Jess called their names softly they whimpered recognition.

The kitchen door opened and Frank stood there. A slash of light between his horse-bowed thighs, a stick in his hand. No, a rifle. Jess's stomach lurched with fear. She stepped into the window light, raised her hands like a captured outlaw.

HE DABBED AT her knee with the corner of a folded nappy. Cloudy water soaking the torn denim of her jeans.

'Sting?'

'Not much.'

She'd told him as much as Owen had told her. As soon as he'd seen it was her and hurried her inside, she knew she would tell him.

'Can't believe I was holding a gun at you. Stupid. Only these last few days I've had a feeling, y'know. So I've been keeping m' rifle handy. Scared they'd try and get at Maguilla.'

'Who would?'

'Some stupid bastards are saying I opened all the gates up along the road. Judy Gordon told me. Your knee — how'd you do that? I ask you, why would I want to go opening gates?'

So Jess had told him. 'That's not all they think you're doing.'

Now Frank sloshed disinfectant in a bowl of water and ripped the torn flap into a larger hole. 'Yer Mum'll patch it up no problem.' He didn't know Marion.

'Could've been Ruby's mother. She's not what you'd call an emotionally well-adjusted person.' He poked a corner of the nappy into the bowl and grew more certain. 'Yeah, either she's rung 'em and spun some bullshit or she's put someone else up to it.'

'But,' said Jess, 'then how did my father know?'

'Maybe she rang him too. Wouldn't put it past her. Maybe I should have a word with your dad.'

'Then he'd know I came here.'

'Right. Bad idea.' He handed Jess a packet of plasters. 'I'll make us a cuppa.'

While she was spooning in sugar to cover the taste he said, 'I'll tell you this. Any bastard reckons on taking my kids he'll have to wrestle them off me.' His eyes rested on Jess for a time. 'That's a fair walk,' he told her. 'From the school to here. In the dark, on your own — that's one helluva walk. Just to warn me. Only a top person would've done that.'

Jess glowed.

Then Frank talked about fear. 'When I was about your age I used to ride around a lot in the bush on my own. Like if I'd left a job and was going on to another I might ride forty miles through the scrub at night leading a packhorse. And in the middle of the night there's this horrible feeling. There's just bush, just the trees, the scrub, the tree fern — which you call pongas here. Y'd be riding down through the trees in the middle of the night and you couldn't see the horse's ears in front of you. And there were sounds — koala bears, they make a sound like a newborn baby, awful noise, but you knew what they were. And the screaming woman owl — it petrifies you the first time, but once you know . . . After a while you know every noise in the bush. And yet you're scared . . .'

He knew, thought Jess, had sensed fear on her when she arrived, the way a horse would, or a dog. She still had to go back, and soon. She straightened her grazed knee, which barely hurt.

The baby, Frank was telling her now, was a little bottler. Sleeping right through the night. And Ruby he could leave a note for, just in case. He'd walk with Jess, not all the way home maybe, but some.

WITH FRANK BESIDE her the night is as tame as knitting wool. Jess improvises lies to tell in case she's been missed at home, and Frank turns into a parent and says if it was Ruby had taken off at night he'd tan her hide. They cross the road and no cars pass them. They follow the sheep track over Turnbull's ridge and Jess is waiting for Frank to abandon her and turn back, but he doesn't.

On McElvey's hill Jess trips on a coil of rusted wire and staggers a bit. Frank takes her hand.

'That's better,' she says, and he leaves his hand there holding hers.

Jess's hand, in Frank's, pricks up its ears and quickens its pace. She lets it stay there, the ground is uneven — she could stumble again and fall.

Jess's hand, in Frank's, has bolted. It shoots heat, then chill, through her body and makes her feel loose-jointed and slightly dizzy. This is unexpected yet somehow not surprising; she'll hang on tight and go with it.

But suddenly, sharply, Frank pulls his hand free. 'You're on the home straight,' he tells her. 'Reckon you'll be okay from here?'

'Of course,' she says.

Jess looks back to wave but he's already part of the dark. She sinks down to sit for a moment, her wayward hand pressed against her cheek.

# CHAPTER 10

THE WELFARE PEOPLE came two days later — the woman who'd come before, and a man with a ponytail, which Frank took to be a good sign. The kitchen floor was washed and he was as ready as he ever could be.

At first the woman made it seem as though they'd just dropped by to say hello. Frank went along with this. He showed them his vegetable garden, which he'd got back into since Wyatt had left and the TV was no longer always on demanding attention, and he brewed up tea. The woman took the baby on her lap and volunteered to change his nappies. Frank fetched her a clean, ready-folded replacement from the pile in the airing cupboard, and hung around, feeling smug, for the unveiling of Ben's plump arse — chlorine-smelling but unblemished except for the faintest and inevitable chafe marks on the inner thighs.

The woman walked out to meet Ruby off the school bus and for a time they sat together in the car. The man played rattle games with the baby and talked with Frank about the amount of toxic spray used by orchardists. The man had spent two summers picking apples and now ate only apples from his own tree; packed them in tissue for keeping, though cool storage worked better.

When Ruby came in the man joined the woman on the concrete apron. Then they asked Frank whether he was aware of anyone who might have a grudge against him. He mentioned Lisa, and the rumours that he'd opened gates. There were other names he might have mentioned, depending on how far back you wanted to go, but naturally didn't.

They asked Frank if there was someone who might vouch for his character. He sent them to Judy Gordon, hoping he hadn't yet worn out her patience.

All the next day he was half-waiting for the woman and man

to come back and try to take away his kids. Ready to wedge the doors and bar the windows. His rifle as a final resort. A picture in his head of failure; of Ruby's skimpy face peering out the back window of the white monogrammed car as it turned onto the road. The boy swaddled up and clutched on her lap. The distance between the children and Frank stretching and stretching until it snapped.

'IF THEY'D TAKEN you and the boy,' he told Ruby, 'it'd be like they'd sliced my innards out and dragged them behind the car all the way back to town.'

'Would it?' Ruby was picturing this. Awed.

He didn't let on to the girl that her mother could be behind all this. Yet if Lisa wanted to get at Frank, why involve Ruby's school?

What had the schoolteacher been told?

Now that the Welfare people had been, Frank had grounds for a word with the teacher without involving Jess.

So he waited, the next day, by the gate, with his dogs, and his boy in the pram. Stood there bare-headed in a raging southerly that bunted the pram and whipped the cigarette paper out of his hand when he went to roll up.

And at last the rattling snub-nosed bus came round the bend unleashing dust. The schoolteacher at the wheel seeing Frank there but showing no sign of it. Slowing as if to stop right beside Frank, but turning in at the driveway instead and pausing there with the motor running, just long enough for Ruby to jump out.

She leapt down the steps, her schoolbag clutched to her chest, a drawing flapping from her clenched fingers. She shouted at Frank, some question that he lost in the wind, and the bus backed up to turn around. Frank was still trying to catch the teacher's eye, and did for a moment. Cool grey eyes in a freckled, boyish face. Frank remembered that the daughter had been forbidden to visit. The schoolteacher could not know that Frank had been given Welfare approval, still believed that he was a monster. Perhaps he should send a note tomorrow with Ruby?

Yet, having met Frank's eye, the schoolteacher gave a cursory nod as he accelerated away. Ruby waved to the two last kids watching and grinning from the back window.

'What happened?' She furled her drawing and slid it beneath the wicker hood of the pram.

'Nothing. Just thought you might blow away. Up over the hills.'

'Like dandelion fluff?'

'Yeah. Bony ones.'

When he'd latched the gate she took his hand. 'Now I won't.'

The car appeared in a sweeping sail of dust as Frank was pulling the pram up their fat front steps. A sixties style of car in mint condition, winking chrome and honking as it slowed at their gate. Frank sat down on the step. Whistled the dogs back to heel.

'Shall I run over?'

'Nah,' he told her. 'Let them do it, whoever.'

Something huge and dark rose from the passenger door and teetered to the gate. From where Frank sat it looked like a buffalo learning to walk on hind legs. The car rolled through the gateway, the buffalo swung the gate closed, pussyfooted back to the car and edged itself in.

'Mum,' squeaked Ruby. 'My Mum, Lisa, it's her.'

Dark glasses shaped like colliding teardrops, blue-black innersprung hair. *Elizabeth Taylor alights from her limousine.* Frank reached blindly for the pram and pulled it closer. He wanted to be sneering but his lips had gone soggy. The way her buttons slipped from their buttonholes and her shorts rode up to nestle in her crotch — did she work at that, or was she just born tasty? He'd seen this same quality in other women, but only a few and none of them what you'd call normal. A certain kind of crazy woman made men's mouths water.

She walked towards them. Ruby was standing stiff as a soldier, hands clasped together. Lisa stopped in front of Frank. The black teardrops slid a finger's width down her nose. She smiled.

'Hiya, cowboy.'

*You bitch. You rotten lowdown heap of shit.* 'Gidday Lisa,' he said.

'SHE HAD HAMMOCKY eyelids,' Frank remembered from the movies.

'Hammocky? *Hammocky!*'

'Or maybe it was that bit above the eyelids?' Frank pinched out flesh in demonstration.

'He's right,' Debbie Reynolds told Lisa. 'You're much too young to remember.' Turned back to Frank. 'She's still around, you know. Runs a casino in Vegas. Someday I'll go there. As a fan, of course, ardent. And you're right, her eye sockets droop. But of course, darling heart' — lunging around the table leg to squeeze Frank's thigh with her huge clawed hands — 'that's not a word you'd be familiar with!'

Lisa raised her eyebrows and drained her glass. Didn't like her friend (her 'best friend' so she'd claimed on introduction) making a fuss of Frank. They were drinking the rum and Coke she had produced as a present for Frank. Ruby had got a doll, a skinny little thing in her own image, except it had a decent crop of hair. For the baby there was a smiling sheep, its eyes stitched in dazed crosses as if it had had a whack on the head. Frank had done best — the Coruba, before they got into it, had the same voluptuous coffee-bean sheen as Debbie Reynolds' massive arms.

His woman was back and Frank could forgive her for leaving. He wasn't the easiest bastard to live with. Nothing of this had been said but sometimes that was the best way. And he'd been wrong about her dobbing him in to the Welfare. She swore she hadn't, was shocked that he could have suspected her of such a thing, and, oddly enough, he believed her.

So someone else was out to get him. Most likely Jack Samuels. But not to worry, life had resumed. Frank would now find a way of getting them all out of this Godforsaken valley.

The girl was asleep with a smile on her face, the scrappy slip of a doll beside her. And they'd hours ago soothed the baby out of his trauma at seeing Debbie Reynolds' vast shaved chops and snaking hair loom down towards him. Lisa had been playing the prodigal mother for all she was worth and, even with Lisa, it surely couldn't be all for show.

Yep, they'd be okay now! Frank poured himself another drink, concentrating. Manoeuvred the bottle towards Lisa's glass, but she pulled it away shaking her head.

'Bed for me.' She lifted the corner of her mouth at Frank in an ambiguous smile.

'Sleep tight,' mumbled Debbie.

Frank raised his glass, his hand wasn't quite steady. Lisa was retrieving her shoes from beneath the table. Frank smiled at their guest and began to roll a smoke.

When he realised the big transvestite (no, transsexual, she'd stressed that point, he must try to remember) had fallen asleep, Frank drained his glass and, with difficulty, spread garments that might constitute bedding on the living-room mattress. He tapped

Debbie on the arm until she swatted at him blindly, a lioness's swipe. So he left her sprawled at the table and got himself to bed.

Lisa was there. A peachy curve of back beneath his bedding. He collapsed on the mattress beside her while in the act of unzipping his boots.

DEBBIE REYNOLDS WAS shaking him awake. The sun hitting Frank's face, so it was around midday. A moment of panic before he had things in place. No more sole charge. No more alone.

'Tea,' said Debbie, holding a mug by its upper rim. 'I'm sorry it's not something stronger. I hate to be the bearer of bad tidings.'

Frank elbowed himself up to take the mug. With both hands free Debbie clutched her chest.

'She's gone, darling heart. Not even a note. They've all gone. Your kids, my car. Even the cash from my handbag. The hussy.'

Debbie could not tell him when. She'd woken during the night and found the mattress. Collapsed thereupon and slept like a baby.

Frank examined the bedrooms — the baby had recently graduated from Frank's room to a bedroom of his own. Both the boy's room and Ruby's were virtually cleaned out. An oblong of entrenched dust showed where Lisa's suitcase had sat since they moved into this house. Frank felt hollow, aware of anger skulking in the wings.

Debbie had followed him through to the bedroom with the abandoned mug of tea. 'You can cry, darling heart, don't mind me. Get this down you and if you feel like weeping I'll join you. That car was precious.'

Frank sat down at the table, stared at the Coruba bottle, all but empty. Saw how well she knew him, how easy he'd made it.

'What'd she tell you?'

'She wanted to see her babies. And her brown-eyed handsome man.'

Frank leant forward and drummed his forehead on the table.

'Don't be hard on yourself, darling heart. You were thirsty. We both were.'

'We'd better report your car.'

Debbie sweeping her hair back, twisting elastic. 'I keep away from the boys in blue. They do their thing, I do mine. I might ring home. Maybe she'll drop it off when she no longer needs it.'

'Where was she living — before your place?'

Debbie didn't know. 'Here and there. Where d'you keep your phone, darling heart?'

'Not on the phone.'

'Of course you're not. Which is your closest neighbour?'

'Forget it. Like as not they'd shoot on sight.' Frank raised the rum bottle, gulping down an inch or two. 'Either we take a *very* long walk or I'll go on my horse.' He could now — anytime, anywhere. The freedom he'd sometimes missed so badly, this was it.

JUDY HAD HOUSE guests. A couple who had grown up in nice homes with nice parents, you knew just by looking. Frank accepted a cup of coffee — the proper kind — and spooned in sugar. He was the centre of attention and thinking how he must seem to these people — a carless careless man who couldn't even manage to hang onto his own children. Judy's gaze felt stern.

'Did the Welfare people come here, then?'

'They did.'

'Thanks,' he said.

'You don't know what I told them.'

'You're honest,' he told her. 'That's all I wanted.'

She sighed. 'You don't think maybe . . . this time . . . from the kids' point of view . . .'

Even Judy!

'No,' he said. 'I don't. Their mother is not a well-adjusted person.'

Aware of the three of them weighing up his unreliable judgement

'I'll fix you up,' he told Judy as he waited for Debbie Reynolds' flatmate to answer the phone. 'Let me know the amount when they bill you.'

She nodded, unconvinced. Judy had grown weary of Frank with his everlasting problems, and who could blame her. But who else could he turn to?

The phone was answered. The flatmate — a husky voice of non-specific gender. Frank introduced himself, explained. The flatmate demanded to talk with Debbie. Frank explained again.

'I warned bloody Reynolds,' squawked the flatmate. 'You only had to look at the eyes to know that little whore was off her trolley.'

Frank read out Debbie's bank account number. 'Forty dollars should get her on the bus. And if you need to get hold of us leave a message with my friend at this number.'

Debbie's bank account number was written on the back of the school newsletter. *Friday 17th Sports Day Please Come Along and Join Us. Sack races . . . egg and spoon races . . .*

Frank imagined Ruby creeping away as if they'd never been mates. Perhaps looking in at him sleeping, in all his clothes on top of the bed, goobing and snoring. That's it, Rube — remember me drunk the way your mother would want it.

'Why not notify the cops?' said Judy. 'And Social Welfare? They'll have to know.'

'Not yet. Not just yet.'

'What'll you do?' The husband blinking concern through rimless glasses.

Frank had thought on that while riding over. He could ride to Auckland. That's where she'd been, so he figured that's where she'd head for. For Frank three days on the road, maybe four. A couple of weeks to find her. Or, option two, accept it. Stay on in Curvey's Creek, find work and get the money to get him home.

Wherever that might be.

'I'll find them,' he said. 'One way or another. Only . . . in the meantime the . . . ah, friend Lisa came with needs a ride to Windsor to catch a bus . . .' As good as asking.

'We could do that, couldn't we, Jude? No problem.'

But Judy followed Frank outside and stood there while he untethered Maguilla. 'There's talk going round, Frank. About you and schoolgirls.'

'Christ! You didn't tell the Welfare that?'

'I almost did. Maybe I should've?'

'So you believe it?'

'I'm asking. I'm the one who got you shoeing young girls' horses. I need to know.'

He swung into the saddle. 'What do you think?'

'I don't know what to think. That's the trouble, Frank. First there's Webster and his sheep . . .'

'You figure I'm knocking off their sheep so I must be knocking off their daughters?'

'And stuff you, too,' she hissed, walking away.

But she arrived, all the same, with her friends the next

morning to take Debbie Reynolds to the bus depot. Frank went along for the ride; there was no one to stay home for.

Debbie rewarded her benefactors with foul jokes and indiscriminate endearments all the way into Windsor.

'We mix in such limited circles,' regretted the visiting wife. But Judy drove in silence, her smiles fleeting and hedged with irritation.

JESS NOW UNDERSTANDS her mother. The way Marion can be there yet elsewhere, that naked white voice she used on the telephone — Jess sees now that these things are not of Marion's volition, but have befallen her in the manner of a landslide or freak hailstorm. How Marion's daughters and son, or even her husband, may feel about them is not relevant. One minute you're living your life and the next minute a situation exists and there's nothing you can do about it.

Jess would like very much to talk to Marion about this matter, and Jess's newfound appreciation of it. But of course this isn't possible; Marion would ask questions and Jess has a dangerous need to tell someone. Almost anyone, except her friend Janine, who suddenly seems too childish to be entrusted with such an astonishing secret.

Jess knows now how Linda Quigley felt after she went to the revival meeting and took God into her heart and couldn't talk about anything else for months. Without warning, God had *inhabited* Linda. Just as Frank Ward has inhabited Jess. Perhaps without even knowing. He held her hand and suddenly she's some kind of vampire, unable to sleep at night or swallow food. Needing, not blood, but mention of his name or things concerning him in order to survive.

Jess watches for signs, she manoeuvres conversations — seeing herself, hearing herself and feeling appalled. I am *pathetic*! She can't help it.

*Frankly*, bullies the science teacher, *I see no hope for any of you*. Jess hears only his first word and is nurtured. She prints Frank's name on the top corner of her maths exercise book punctuated by two pricked and perfect ears, lays an arm to protect it from Janine, and stares at it for minutes on end. On the school bus she strains fruitlessly to hear gossip that may concern him. At home she offers to put Sheenagh's golden hair into skinny plaits for the crimpy look that Sheenagh envies, and tells her bored but captive sister about Maguilla's beauty and waywardness. Wayward. Ohhh.

Scraping carrots for Marion, who for once is home early enough to take charge of dinner, Jess remembers out loud how the frogs used to breed and croak in the water trough at the rabbiter's cottage. And, later, as she and Corin butter bread for the school lunches Jess hears her mouth casually mentioning Ruby's name. Did Corin like her?

'She's okay, I s'pose.'

'Just okay?'

'Okay is okay.'

'Like . . . you talk to her and that? She talk to you today?'

'Hardly!'

'What?'

'Well, how could she? She wasn't there.'

'Why not?'

'Dunno, do I? Not yesterday or the day before either.'

'She hasn't left?'

'I dunno. Maybe she's sick. Ask Dad. Why? What's it to you?'

'You ask him. Go on.'

'Nah.'


JESS CONFRONTED OWEN, an exercise book in front of him, writing one of his carefully encouraging remarks beneath the mess of untidy printing.

'Ruby, has she left school?'

He didn't look up. 'If she has I haven't been notified.'

'But you're hoping she has! Aren't you?'

He looked at her then, resting his chin on his hand. 'You know nothing about this. I believe you don't. I sincerely hope you don't. So let's just keep it that way.'

Jess looked down at her father. He was losing his hair; from above he was all naked scalp. Whereas Jess had lashings of hair, and just the same shade as his. It was as if she was taking his hair away from him year by year.

She was her father's favourite child. He didn't show it but Jess had always known it was so. Now suddenly they were on opposite sides. Enemies, and there was nothing could be done about it. Jess turned and walked away. And it was like walking away from a railway station after someone you love has left on the train. This had never happened to Jess but she knew how it felt when she saw it in movies — unpreventable and final and enormously sad.

She glanced back over her shoulder. He should have been sitting with his elbows propped on the desk watching her go, but he was back with the exercise book.

# C H A **11** T E R

OWEN WOKE ALONE in the bed. Eighteen minutes past three. Marion had said she would be late, but not this late. Some kind of dinner with colleagues or clients? She'd said last night. Why didn't he listen? Had registered only that, once again, she wouldn't be home to eat, to help, to talk to their children.

Too much wine so she'd decided not to drive? But never before without ringing. Had left it too late, didn't want to wake him? The obvious reason was usually the right one. Get back to sleep.

Couldn't. Listened to the rain bucketing down outside. Turned on the bedside lamp — the one on her side — and watched the shadows it wove around the walls. A cottage garden eternally circling on her bedside table. The price of it could have fed a family in Uganda for a month. He should draw the line, but if it makes her happy . . .

Around his walls the colours churned and blurred. Never before had Owen lain this long and watched them. Neither, he'd swear, had Marion. The thing she liked best about buying was opening the boxes and plugging things in. After that she lost interest, neglected to adhere to instructions or post off the guarantees. When an appliance broke down Owen would mess about ineffectually with soldering iron and screwdriver before packing the thing up in the box it had come in and storing it in the garage. Several months later Marion would notice its absence and a more advanced gadget would be unpacked in replacement.

Three o'clock in the morning and Owen, a man of regular habits, had entered a secret dimension. Who else was out there sharing it? Insomniacs tuned to talkback radio, people with empty lives. Or with crowded, impromptu lives that spilled right through the night, unfettered by obligation.

Owen was missing out. Had been born to miss out. Couldn't

even hang onto the old image of himself as a person of principle. Where had he been last year when the friends he ought to have were putting their convictions, their personal safety, on the line? Great-grandmothers even, children . . . massing outside rugby grounds. Safety helmets, placards. Owen, living in rugby country, had kept his mouth shut in public. Had written letters to the city newspapers signing himself *Incredulous* and *Ordinary Kiwi*.

Couldn't even manage to make his own wife see what was at stake. 'Interfering,' she called it. Minding your own business — was that tolerance or the death of conscience?

Owen had 'interfered' with another man's life, but out of social concern. So why hadn't he given his name when he rang Social Welfare instead of acting like some furtive heavy breather who worried, afterwards, that they might trace the call.

Was it his discomfort at being on the same side as men he'd once despised as rednecks? Or guilt for not having known that one of his pupils was in need of saving (and the squeamishness of imagination that made him, even now, not wish to know)?

He'd been hoping Ward would be investigated and absolved, Owen knew that now. His own conscience would be clear, his worries about Jess dispersed, and his status in the local community still a little higher than it had been. When Ruby wasn't there, three mornings ago, to catch the bus, he'd wished on her the strep throat that had been doing the rounds. But noted, on the second and third mornings, the absence of nappies on the clothesline and a sense of inactivity about the house.

Jack Samuels rang Owen that third day, at lunchtime, to report that Rick Chaney had been up his back paddock with binoculars, morning and night, and had seen no sign at all of Ward's children. 'We were right!' The note of triumph in Jack's voice rang on in Owen's head all afternoon and when he bent over the children's desks he could smell sweat from his armpits as if he'd been mustering sheep like their fathers.

'We'll give the creep . . . what? . . . five days? . . . to bugger off,' Jack had said. *And if he doesn't?* But Owen had preferred not to ask.

On Ruby's last day at school Owen had finally set eyes on Ward. A lean, weathered-looking fellow, eyes from a Drysdale painting, jaw from a Marlboro ad. Not, you'd think, the face of perversion, but the least obvious are the most likely — isn't that what they said? Jess. Did she really know nothing about it? Marion had made light of it — Jess was quite able to look after herself. But then Marion would be happy to see Jess wearing skirts half up to her ears and going on dates, pretty and empty-headed just like her mother.

Once Owen had found Marion's ignorance appealing. Had called it honesty, a lack of artifice. Besides, she was eager to learn. And must have, since now she earned more than he did. Her colleagues told Owen he must be proud of her. They thought he was shy and intellectual, so Marion reported. He cited that shyness as a reason for excusing himself from the Barker Hanley staff social functions. It seemed kinder than saying he'd sooner stay home and read a book.

Outside the rain had stopped. The revolving colours were making Owen nauseous. Like the octopus rides at the A & P show when the children were too young to go unaccompanied.

Owen switched off the lamp and in the relief of darkness saw with clarity: Marion was having an affair!

The certainty of it drove him out of bed and up the unlit passage to the kitchen. It wasn't a brand-new thought. The possibility had come to him now and again like a shape pressing against a window he preferred not to open. Now that he'd let it in, Owen wanted to find it ludicrous, grotesque — Marion spreadeagled on newly laid carpet beneath a trouserless client, whispering interest rates and terms of mortgage. But instead he saw damp hair glued to her cheek, heard her whimpering like a puppy.

Beneath the kitchen light, the room seemed foreign and unconvincing. Owen filled the safety-switching, non-breakable, untoppleable electric jug and switched it on. It took a long time to heat. At this hour of night, time clearly extended. Talkback hosts dealt with more callers per hour, wandering minds clocked up improbable mileage on uncharted roads.

Slow down, he told himself. Rethink.

An accident. Returning home, Marion had failed to take a bend. The road greasy from the heavy rain. The car had slid and rolled, pressing down fence wires, crushing gorse and manuka. Owen's wife was at this moment trapped between seat and steering wheel, semi-conscious, hidden from passing vehicles. He considered where, exactly. The approach to Thompson's Saddle?

*99*

Hurley's corner? The hairpin bend before the bridge just past Phil Chaney's? Or perhaps some other road entirely. What had Marion planned to go to, and where?

Back in his bedroom Owen pulled on clothes. How long would the search take him? Wake Jess or leave a note in case one of the children woke before he returned? Emergency rooms in hospital, terrible places, you could be waiting hours and hours.

He tapped on his daughters' door softly before he entered.

'Jess. Jessica.' Whispering in the dark until his eyes told him her rumpled bed was empty.

The bottom window unlatched. No point in asking Sheenagh; his daughters had never been close the way sisters ought to be. Owen made a cursory search of the house, seeing Jess as she'd been this past week or so, toad-puffed with reproach.

He left Sheenagh sleeping, penned a note just in case. Made it cheerful. *Don't panic. We haven't been captured by aliens. Back soon. Dad.* Left it on the table secured beneath the salt pig. Outside there were puddles on the lawn.

On the road he remembered Marion and kept an eye on the right-hand verge in case. But there were only five miles of road between the school house and the Turnbull Road turn-off. Two more to the rabbiter's cottage — seven in all. As the crow flies . . . as the snake crawls . . . considerably less.

He stopped, first, beside her horse paddock, swept it with his car lights. Both the horses were there.

The rabbiter's cottage was in darkness. Dogs barked as Owen switched off the motor and then the lights. He sat for a while, his certainty gone. Considering and rejecting various alternatives. Imagined himself going home, crawling back into bed, handing the problem over to Marion.

Who, at this very moment, was clutching at bracken, dragging herself through the Toyota's shattered windscreen, demanding he *do something.*

Owen pressed the car door closed and kept to the grass but still Ward's dogs heard him coming. Amid the barking was a reassuring rattle of chains so he kept on walking. Skirting wide past the dogs then up the curving concrete steps. A light came on. Owen walked softly. The barking took on a desperate note but through it he thought he heard voices.

The light was from the passage. It slid through the open inner door and lit the frosted palm trees. Marion had saved for that shameful door, out of the housekeeping, in their days of a meagre single income. Since Owen's old friends had never made it to Curvey's Creek to visit, the embarrassment of the door hadn't really mattered, and the girls had liked it. Now one panel was taped up with brown paper.

Owen tried the door handle. Not locked. While he stood there undecided, the door swung inward. Ward was standing just inside, his free hand still fastening his belt. Naked feet, naked chest, tight grey-peppered curls. On his head as well. That head pushing forward. 'Okay, shut up now.'

The dogs fell silent. Ward looked at Owen, then down at his own scrawny bare feet.

'I'm looking for my daughter.'

Ward nodded thoughtfully. 'Right,' he said. 'I figured. You wanna cuppa tea?'

'For Christ's sake!' Owen pushed past the man, through to the lit hallway. He strode right into the bedroom he and Marion had shared, his hand straight on the lightswitch. The room was empty but for a cardboard box and some horse gear.

'Jess . . .' Owen heard Ward calling, and a muttered response.

That door was half open. It'd been Jess's room, her baby room, then Jess and Sheenagh's. Owen walked in.

She was sitting among Ward's filthy tangled sheets. A fetid male smell. Her boots lay discarded on a heap of leather and iron. She wore a shirt, a man's shirt, and her thighs were palely naked. Ward had entered the room. Now he turned to Owen and Owen's fist shot out of its own accord. Missed the elongated jaw but struck on cheek bone. Ward's head flew back, hit the edge of the door. Owen readied his startled fists to defend, but Ward just stood there. His shoulders squared off, his Adam's apple rose and fell in his ropey neck, but he didn't raise a hand.

Owen hit him again. This time the mouth, knuckles grating on teeth. The Australian's eyes watered. He lowered his head. Continued to stand there, hands behind his back.

Jess screamed then, and threw herself between them. She hammered at Owen's chest and upper arms until he managed to trap one flailing wrist and twist it behind her. Hadn't done that since his own schooldays, forbade it in the Curvey's Creek playground. Was startled by the easy way it came back to him now.

'Home,' he said.

'No.'

'Yes. Get dressed.' Freeing her arm, he saw that her lips were puffy and dark, her face pale. She backed to a corner, rubbing where his fingers had clamped. Looking down, shaking her head.

Ward slipped past and out the door. Owen, helpless now, let him go, unable to sustain an adequate rage. Felt only a mumbling anger such as might have come from letting the washtub overflow. A disaster of his own making. Too soft, too liberal, too trusting. Marion had said so often enough.

'Jess —' He didn't know this girl. Didn't want to look away at the mess of bedding, the saucer spilling matches and pinched fag ends.

Ward returned with a bundle of clothes and held them out to Jess.

'Drying them out,' he said, for Owen.

Jess took the clothes limply, her eyes on Ward.

Ward turned to Owen, cleared his throat. 'If you . . . ah . . .' nudging his head towards the doorway, 'and Jess and I could have a word?'

His look said they were on the same side, he and Owen. Cheek of the sod! But Owen turned and walked back to the living room. Switched on the light, saw the leaking mattress that served as a sofa, studied his aching knuckles, then stared at the palm trees until tears stung his eyes. *What have I done to deserve this?*

'YOU BLOODY HAVE to. There's no alternative.'

He watched her eyes filming with tears.

'Please?' he said because she was a decent caring sort of girl. 'Y'know how it looks to him.'

She pushed one foot into the jeans that weren't yet dry. 'You let him hit you. You just stood there.'

'You think I ought to have hit him back? He's your dad, girl! He was entitled to thump the shit out of me.'

'I'll tell him,' she said, dragging the denim over her hips with sudden haste. 'Tell him he got it wrong.'

'He won't believe you.' He reached to unbutton his shirt that she wore, to hurry her up. His fingers were shaking, though he hadn't had a drink since Lisa's rum ran out. 'Why should he?' he croaked. 'It's near enough true.'

Her face lit up. It shone at him. He held her then, tightly but briefly, in case the father should walk back in.

'Y' won't take off without us seeing each other? Promise, Frank?'

'I promise. So long as you go now with your dad.'

Christ almighty! How had he got himself into this? Life came falling on him, uninvited, like chunks of sky; saw Frank Ward down below, just trying to get along by minding his own business, and became excited — *get this dozy bastard again!* And down it would fall right on top of him, some new disaster or complication.

If he'd seen it coming he might have dodged aside. This time at least. On the other hand, he might not.

He'd been sitting around trying to figure what was his next step. Same thing he'd been trying to figure out all day and most of the night before. Trying to look at it first one way and then the other and most of all from Ruby and Ben's view. Which could only be guessed at. Lisa wasn't going to be the best kind of mother a kid could hope for, but she was their mother and, to be fair, she wasn't as partial to a drink as Frank.

Maybe she'd taken her kids because she wanted them, and maybe she'd taken them just to get at Frank. But how was she to know he wouldn't be glad to be free of the kids? Enough times he'd thought he would be, but instead of unshackled he's feeling like a piece of old seaweed left behind when the tide went out.

Some time after the TV had turned to static the girl had arrived at his door, looking like a sheep that had just been dipped, hair plastered, clothes stuck to her skin.

'They've been taken, haven't they?'

'They sure have.'

'The bastards,' she said. 'I'm sorry. How could they?'

He found a towel and some dry clothes and sent her off to Ruby's room. She returned in a shirt that nearly reached her knees, wet clothes bundled. He arranged them in the hot-water cupboard. Had run out of the firewood he'd kept under the house, not bothered because there was only him to keep warm.

By then he'd put her straight about who had taken the kids. Not that it made much difference, gone was gone.

She'd come out of kindness. 'I knew you'd be really upset.' Trudged all that way in seeping rain, scared of the dark.

He knew then that he was right in the path of another great chunk of sky. And okay, maybe he'd still had time to dodge but his reflexes were blinded by that look in her eyes, telling him he was more than an everyday sort of cove. Soaking him up inside her.

A decent kind of person, not half-crazy, out-for-herself, like Lisa. He'd made them toast and tea and they'd talked about the kids and what he should do for the best. It took a long time but even so her clothes weren't dry. He thought she should take a nap or they'd want to know how come she was so tuckered out next day. Dragged out his own blankets to tuck her beneath on the living-room mattress.

Set his alarm clock for 4.30 and covered himself with a few stray garments, though he suspected that, with one thing and another, sleep was out of the question. Then, maybe half an hour later, she'd shuffled through in the dark draped like an Arab. Complained this was stupid, she couldn't sleep and he must be cold. Crawled in beside him, rearranged the bedding, slid beneath his arm.

Her mouth was warm. They kissed and whispered, they giggled, kissed some more. She told him she didn't want him to leave but knew he would. Asked him to take her with him. He said he'd come back for her. Saw himself in that moment as a man who made plans and had them work out.

OWEN AND JESS travelled in silence. *How could you?* he wanted to shout. *You promised you wouldn't. I trusted you.* But they felt like words from a movie script. Besides he didn't want to hear the answer. Imagination was bad enough.

Until he needed to ask. 'Did he force you?'

She gave a hard little laugh. 'Don't be stupid.'

Owen's jaw had clenched, forced him to hiss.

'For God's sake Jess, he'd be older than me.'

'We didn't *do* anything!' Her voice full of scorn.

She could even lie to him, barefaced. Owen felt despair, then. Loss flowing into his veins. He remembered Marion.

'Your mother wasn't home either.' Harsh and childish, wanting to injure. 'Probably for the same reason.'

No response. Owen was ashamed. 'Maybe an accident,' he muttered. 'I was going to drive up the road a bit . . . Get you home first . . .'

'So she doesn't know? About me?'

Looking at him the way she'd done all her life. Small accidents or misdemeanours that Marion would carry on about. Pleading for intervention; Mum needn't know need she? Owen clenched his teeth.

'Not yet,' he hissed.

MARION'S CAR SAT beneath the carport. She had run a bath and was about to step into it.

'We went out looking for you,' Owen told her. 'Thought you'd gone over a bank.'

'I drive very carefully,' said Marion.

Owen signalled Jess to go to bed, and stepped into the bathroom.

'I was worried,' he said to his naked wife. 'Did it never occur to you that I might be worried?'

'Ohhh, sorry,' she said in the sort of snuggling, soothing voice she used for the cat.

*Where were you?* But he didn't ask. He was exhausted, wanted only to sleep.

'You woke Jess? To go looking?'

'She was already awake.'

Marion's breasts lay against her ribs, her belly was a small round island in the water. Her body had rearranged itself when Owen wasn't watching.

'We were worried about you,' he said.

# CHAPTER 12

THEY WATCH EACH other, father and daughter, sneakily and without affection. Owen thinks of it as watching an empty stable door, though the horse analogy is one he could do without. He tells himself that Jess is just a child and children are something he knows how to handle. Patience and encouragement, it works in the classroom. But when he catches her glance in the act of escaping his, he sees such contempt it leaves him breathless. *Pathetic*, her eyes sneer and he's reduced to wondering if she's right. 'Pathetic' just another perspective on what Owen would prefer to call *liberal* and *reasonable*.

As a result of which his daughter has gone off the rails? Possibly, though in his heart Owen blames Marion. Adolescent girls need a mother with time to pay them attention.

Marion hasn't yet been told. There's no way of telling how she will react. Police, medical examination, charges laid? Or shrug it off as hormonal misadventure? And either way she would talk about it in the office, even maybe to clients. Turn it into some kind of rueful adventure in which her family is embroiled.

Word would get around. Jess would be called a slut, Sheenagh and Corin would be questioned by their peers, Owen might even be forced to resign.

So Owen has delayed telling Marion, but at times is sorely tempted, for despite her unpredictability and her inability to be discreet, Marion would surely have some practical ideas about what should be done. Whereas Owen is simply — *pathetically?* — watching and waiting. Watching his daughter and waiting for Ward to leave.

Over the weekend he takes all three children, plus Sheenagh's friend Kay McElvey, for a picnic on the coast. Only Corin is eager to go. Sheenagh and Kay don't mind, so long as they're together. Jess says, looking not at Owen but at the new coffee-maker, 'I s'pose I have to?' He tells her yes. So she comes, but only in body and even that has a lifeless air about it.

Under Owen's surveillance Jess nibbles at sandwiches and dangles a fishing line until an icy west wind blows up and drives them back to the car. All the way home Corin examines the only fish that was of legal size — a snapper caught, alas, by Kay — while Sheenagh and Kay whisper and giggle in the back seat and Jess sits silently beside them, looking out the window.

On the Tuesday afternoon Owen drives the school bus up past Chaneys' gate, the kids all chorusing a reminder that he doesn't need to — Ruby's left, *remember*? Silly Mr Bennington! He turns at the driveway. Can see no sign of a horse, can hear no dogs. Relief floods through him.

THAT NIGHT HE called Rick Chaney from the schoolroom phone. 'I reckon Ward's left us.'

'No such luck,' said Rick. 'Tinny bastard's got himself work with the bloody Gordon woman. Dan Bradford said. An' I seen him m'self this morning, heading up with his dogs at the cracka dawn.'

Owen clenched his teeth. He looked at his knuckles, the bruise now yellowed. 'You reckon he plans to stay on?'

'Looks like it,' said Rick. 'Jack won't be happy. Nor Charlie either.'

'Perhaps we should get together,' said Owen.

They met at Charlie's place over Scotch on the rocks from a cut crystal decanter. Charlie's wife, May, delivered fruit cake and cheese busters and returned to the kitchen to iron Charlie's shirts. Owen hadn't tasted cheese busters like those since he left home to go to training college. Marion didn't bake, not even the occasional afghan.

Dan Bradford, who'd not only had his steer bowled but had had to pay the doctor's insurance excess, came along this time. Jack arrived late and while they waited Rick told the others, in strictest confidence, what Rick's wife Edith had been told in strictest confidence by Win Samuels. Their Leila had got herself in the family way and Win had to take her to the clinic in Hamilton to get rid of it. Leila wasn't saying who the father was but they'd worked out dates and it had happened in the holidays when she was looking after Ward's kids.

Owen felt ill; the man was unstoppable. Could Jess be pregnant? A child *with child*. It happened all the time, yet it was a possibility Owen hadn't allowed himself to think about. He was tempted to tell these men — to *share it* with them. Looked down at his knuckles around cut crystal and imagined himself saying, *I punched the bastard over*.

Truth was, they wouldn't believe him.

'One of us should have a word with the Gordon woman,' said Charlie, as he poured Jack's drink.

'Waste of time,' said Jack. 'We should call on Ward.'

'All of us?' Rick stubbed his cigarette in an oval china ornament that only vaguely resembled an ashtray.

Charlie was doubtful. 'We can't just go taking the law —'

'Just to put him in the picture,' said Phil.

'Let him know we mean business,' said Dan.

Charlie looked at Owen. 'What d'you think?'

All of them looking at Owen, waiting, respecting his judgement. Owen tossed back the contents of his glass, felt it go down, grimaced.

'I think,' he said, 'the sooner we get rid of him the easier we'll all sleep.'

'Right.' Jack slapped him on the back, and now they were, all of them, exchanging grins.

'A top-up, Owen?' Charlie lifted the decanter.


DEBBIE REYNOLDS' CHRYSLER Valiant had been found in the parking lot at Auckland airport. Debbie had rung Judy to pass on that message. But, as Frank explained to Judy, the location of the car meant nothing. Lisa was too cunning for that.

Unless, of course, it was a double bluff.

If she had the fare Lisa would surely return to Australia. But where would she find the money? One fare for her and a half for Ruby, and the baby travelling free. But then, she could be resourceful when it suited her. To Lisa the world was fair game.

She would expect Frank to be searching already, crazy with anger. The thought would give her pleasure. But Frank was using his head, had his priorities sorted. First get some money together, then find the children. Judy — top woman that she was — was back on side, giving him work until he found a proper job. It could break a man's heart, working for Judy. The hopes she'd hold for pigeon-chested old mares and broken-winded ponies. Hard to see how she ever hoped to turn a profit.

And now putting herself out on a limb for Frank. Though in return he was working like a dog. And happy to do it. Riding off at dawn, the dogs at Maguilla's heels, a smell of summer already in the air. A sense, in the mornings, of life and hope.

But the nights. Empty bedrooms. The loss, then, being as he'd imagined it. Worse, because he didn't trust Lisa to put the kids' welfare ahead of her own. How long till she wearied of the inconvenience and dumped them somewhere?

Frank, frying himself up supper — eggs, left-over potato, pumpkin — heard Sal barking out front by the trees, maybe an opossum. He'd been leaving the dogs loose since the night of Jess's father. Poor irate bugger, hopping about like a butterfly with a broken wing, and who could blame him? Not Frank — certainly not Frank.

He hoped the girl had managed a satisfactory explanation. It was more than Frank could do. Her father would know what he saw and technical innocence would be scant consolation. With luck the memory of his schoolteacher fist hitting Frank's mouth might serve him better.

Now there's a tale, Frank told himself. Grinning a bit as he turned his supper to brown on the top side.

Mac's grumbling bark had joined Sal's. Frank stepped outside and whistled. The moon was behind the hill, and his eyes were useless in the sudden dark. Mac slunk up, a growl still rumbling in his throat. Maguilla's hooves thudded up to the fortified fence.

Frank stepped away from the house. Behind him the kitchen glowed, he'd been standing there like a spotlit roo. Sal yelped. Mac cowered, growled afresh. Frank thought he heard voices. Waited. The demanding bleat of a teenage lamb, water trickling in C. B. Webster's creek . . .

Frank called the dogs inside. Sal was favouring her left hind leg, but Frank could find no cause. She whimpered at the closed door, her eyes begging, but he left it closed. A hunk of doctored meat, a bullet — who knew what craziness could be out there.

He left the kitchen light on and sat in the darkness of his bedroom with his rifle beside him. The dogs lay at the door. Like Frank, they were high from a whiff of danger, possibly of their own invention.

A morepork calling from the macrocarpas; the same morepork Frank had heard for the last three nights, only now its hoot seemed ominous. Frank rolled himself a smoke. Had to light a match just to see which side of the paper was glued. The Aussie papers had one corner clipped off so in the dark you knew which way up it needed to be. Little things like that made you homesick.

Sal raised her head and gave a growl, the faintest purring in the back of her throat. Then nothing. She sighed, subsided. But Frank now heard something — a breaking twig, a footfall? He fumbled for Mac, muzzling him with his hand. Sal was smarter. *Shhhh*, he told her, his voice no louder than a socked foot on bare boards. Then, almost outside his window, someone stumbled, involuntarily hissed, 'Shit!'

Frank crept up the short passage and through the back way into the wash-house. Rifle readied, his dogs pressing behind. Opened the back door, softly, slowly. Now he heard voices, two at least, somewhere round the front. He heard the clomping of boots, his french doors being thrown open — they didn't lock, the key was lost. 'No one needs keys out Curvey's Creek,' had boomed Kevin Samuels' cheerful Windsor solicitor.

Frank and the dogs went beneath the clothesline, across the silver beet and cabbage plants and reached the macrocarpas. The morepork hooted no more. Frank pushed himself in among the low branches that gave at least a partial view of the house. He laid the rifle beside his feet and placed restraining hands on his dogs. Watched lights come on to bathe the grass outside the windows. Glimpsed figures passing inside. Heard voices, then, and laughter.

The laughter was a relief — Frank had got himself round to thinking about Lisa's Asian connections. No longer did anything seem beyond possibility. But what kind of Asian hit men, on finding their prey had escaped, would let loose a barrage of locker-room guffawing?

THEY'D MET AT Phil Chaney's because Phil had no wife to go interfering. They rinsed out cups and poured themselves a couple of tots of Phil's Johnnie Walker while Charlie, who'd done his military service back even before Vietnam, ran through the *modus operandi*.

Owen propped himself in a corner, sipping out of a chipped

mug, and wondered why he'd always been privately contemptuous of team sports and the people who played them. Seeing himself as he had been till now — pale and peculiar, cocooned in a belief of his own superior sensibilities. A man ignorant of the ways and pleasures of men.

Rick and Phil had produced, on their own initiative, a variety of hats and scarves and balaclavas. Everyone tried them on, kids at a dress-up party. Dan had brought his son's cricket bat. The sight of this caused a moment's silence. Dan practised batting strokes on Phil's encrusted lino, got defensive. 'Bugger might set his dogs on us.'

'Boot on the head'll soon fix them.' Rick raised a boot so chapped, so ageless and colourless that Owen thought of tuataras on sun-baked mud. He glanced at his own brown canvas slip-ons.

'Besides,' said Dan, 'I thought the idea was to scare him shitless?'

They waited for Charlie to decide.

'It is,' said Charlie.

Owen found a hand-sized piece of metal out by Phil's chopping block. It fitted in his pocket.

They piled into Charlie's Landcruiser and drove past the rabbiter's cottage. At his own first paddock gate Charlie switched the motor off. The others climbed out and they pushed the vehicle down the track as far as the creek, keeping their voices and laughter down. Phil was recalling opossum shoots that were this much fun.

A light was on in the kitchen of Ward's house, and his dogs were loose. They came as far as the fence, kicking up a racket that had Charlie's dogs joining in from their kennels over the hill. Nothing could be done about that.

As Charlie had instructed, the men advanced separately, making full use of the trees. Ward had conveniently called his dogs inside by then. Owen's relief at this was tempered by a sudden queasiness. Up until that point he'd eliminated Ward from the adventure, but, as he eased himself slowly between fence wires, he imagined the Australian at a darkened window taking telescopic aim.

They assembled, as Charlie had instructed, at the north-east corner of the house. All except for Phil who had got it wrong and was found pressed against the wall on the north-west corner.

No sign of the dogs now, and the light was streaming from Ward's kitchen window in open invitation. Confidence grew. They walked onto the concrete patio. Dan opened the glass door and they all trooped in. Owen pushed aside the vinyl divider; the kitchen was lit but deserted.

'Ward?' Rick called. His voice was muffled by wool. He rolled up his balaclava and called again. No response.

They divided up and searched the house. Owen followed Dan into Ward's bedroom. Same smell, same state as last time. A reminder to Owen as to why he was there.

Owen, Dan, Phil, Rick and Charlie met up in the kitchen.

'Take off that damn fool thing, Phil,' said Charlie.

Phil ruefully tugged off his balaclava. 'Felt like a real commando.'

'He's scarpered.' Rick kicked at the wall divider. 'Yellow rat's scarpered.'

Dan had picked up a paperback from the table. Flicked over the cover. 'This is yours,' he told Owen. 'Got your name in.'

All four of them looking at Owen as he took the book Dan held out to him. *The Pastures of Heaven.* Owen turned the cover, read his own name there, his own teenaged handwriting.

'Never thought of that,' Phil was saying softly. 'What's in it for you, Owen?'

'Yeah.' Rick. 'All the rest of us got a reason for being here.'

'You were agin it, I seem to remember,' said Dan. 'And the bugger's not here, is he? Funny that!'

'My daughter,' said Owen, trying a smile. 'Used to go riding. As you know. Must've left it here.'

'Ah,' said Charlie.

Owen was aware of the strip of iron in his pocket. Of Dan's cricket bat, Rick's knobbled branch. Aware of them watching him.

'You're wrong!' he said. 'Jess . . . he raped my girl.'

'Jeezus . . . why didn't y' say? . . . we'll do him, Owen . . . we'll make the bastard pay . . .'

They clapped their hands on him, on his arms, his back, his shoulders. Rick gave him something that resembled a hug. Owen felt removed from it all, watching it happening.

Suddenly Rick was sniffing fiercely. 'Hey, can ya smell . . .?'

'We'll turn his horse loose,' Dan was promising Owen.

'Shit!' bellowed Rick, who had followed his nose. 'Come 'ere, look!'

In the bedroom that once was Corin's, flames were leaping up the curtains and skiing across the wallpaper.

'Holy hell,' said Dan and they ran for buckets and pots, holding them beneath taps that did little more than trickle.

Jack came in from outside. 'Fuuuck.' He looked in at Phil, whacking at fire with a horse blanket. 'You turkey, you're makin' it worse.' Hauled Phil out as Owen came in to toss a saucepanful of water. The flames hissed derisively and shot higher.

'Shut the door,' ordered Charlie.

Owen got out and slammed the door. Inside glass shattered with a sound like gunfire.

'Let's get the hell out of here,' said Dan.

'Everyone out,' barked Charlie. 'Leave everything as it was.'

Owen returned the saucepan to the cupboard. The Steinbeck with his name in it lay on the table. He snatched it up.

Running behind Rick, drops of water or mud splashing Owen's face.

At Charlie's boundary fence they stopped to watch flames writhe from the windows.

'I hope your cousin's insured, Jack,' Rick said.

'I'd reckon so. I'd say most likely he is.' Jack's voice sounded tight, as if on the edge of tears or laughter.

Owen's socks were damp. He crouched to touch the ground. Dry grass. It hadn't rained, not since the night . . . Almost a week ago. He touched his face. Wet mud on his cheeks.

FRANK SAW THEIR faces when the flames shot up. Charlie Webster and the schoolteacher. And the big coot behind them would have to be Samuels. Five, he counted. A posse.

He watched them climb through the fence and disappear into the darkness. Then couldn't afford to delay any longer; he ran to the house.

The front room was filling with smoke and when Frank opened the door flames nibbled the passage. He slammed that door shut and took the kitchen entrance to the wash-house. Snatched up his saddle, his bridle, his oilskin coat. Dumped them outside, well back from the house. Heard the stallion's shrill trumpeting above the spit and cackle of the fire.

Back inside again he reconsidered the passage access to his bedroom. Decided against it. His bedroom window was open so Frank scrambled over the sill, closed the door against the passage of flames and groped in the dark. His farrier apron and tools, his clothes, hairbrush, bedding. Hurling it all out the window, over the head of faithful Sal, who waited and whimpered.

Smoke billowed in from beneath the door, wood splintered and crashed. The synthetic curtains were beginning to melt. Frank jumped out and dragged his salvaged belongings to the edge of the firelight. By this time even the kitchen was full of smoke. Frank groped blindly and backed out clutching a sack of dog biscuits and a plastic bag containing two sprouting potatoes.

Outside he talked to his wild-eyed horse, gruff, empty words of reassurance, as he pulled on the bridle. Those things he didn't need or couldn't carry with him Frank hid beneath the trees. He threw the potatoes into the sack with the dog biscuits, took the cup, the saucepan, a jersey and a pair of socks and bundled them in his coat. Strapped the bundle to his saddle.

As he rode off, the south-facing wall of the house detached itself and toppled to the ground.

# C H A P T E R  13

EDITH CHANEY, WIFE of Rick, had seen the night sky scorching yellow and run up to the paddock behind their house. Then back to the house to ring the Windsor Fire Brigade and drag the kids from in front of the Friday horror movie and up the paddock to watch the real thing.

By midday Saturday half the residents of Curvey's Creek had driven down Turnbull Road to gaze at the blackened remains of the rabbiter's cottage. When Marion and her children got there it looked like the Windsor A & P Show: kids kicking through the debris, parents clustering, rows of vehicles parked in the rabbiter's paddock.

Having reassured herself that Maguilla was gone and there were no blackened dog skeletons, Jess returned to her mother. She felt impatient to leave; why was everyone standing around?

'I was twenty-two when we moved here,' said Marion, looking not at Jess but at the mess, the vast dead campfire. 'I thought I knew it all.' She gave a sharp little laugh.

Jess wondered if this was directed at her. She still didn't know whether Marion had been told about her and Frank Ward. She lived in a household where nobody talked about stuff that mattered, so you didn't know where you were or what was going on.

'Let's go home,' she said, then saw Judy Gordon's yellow ute pulling in. 'Hang on, it's Judy, I'll just have a word.'

Judy switched off the motor. 'Jess,' she said.

'Is he at your place?'

Judy shook her head. 'Yesterday, he was. Doing some work for me. But last night . . . today . . .? I guess you've heard? About the fire brigade?'

The Windsor Voluntary Fire Brigade had screamed out to Curvey's Creek like a squeaky hinge. In time, possibly, to save something, but someone had left on the outside tap of the water tank. The firemen were squishing about in puddles, no water in the hoses, and Webster's creek too far away.

'So they're saying it was arson,' said Judy. 'Except it makes no sense. Why would he? And where the hell's he gone?'

He wouldn't leave without telling Jess. He wouldn't. He couldn't.

Corin had found a tortured piece of metal and a blackened ten-cent piece.

'They're not yours,' said Jess, but Marion was letting her drive home so she had no free hands to grab them off him.

'He was drunk,' said Sheenagh. 'Frank Ward — he was pissed as a fart and he dropped his cigarette on his mattress.'

'Language,' said Marion. 'Who told you that?'

'I heard.'

'You know nothing.' Jess looked for Sheenagh in the rear vision mirror. 'You're full of shit.'

'Jess!' hissed Marion. 'Watch the road.'


JESS TOOK FOOD — left-over sausages, cheese, tomatoes, slices of buttered bread — when no one was in the kitchen. *In case she found him.* Except she blackened those words out of her mind, replaced them with *He'll be hungry.* She covered the food with plastic wrap, pushed it into a paper bag and stowed it in her pack beneath her parka.

Owen and Corin were cleaning Owen's car. Jess walked past them on her way to the horse paddock with the saddle over her shoulder, the pack on her back, the bridle in her hand. Owen seemed about to say something but didn't.

Pedro was glad to be out of the paddock, eager to please, almost spirited. They splashed over the fords and cantered along the flat. Jess had her mind on a very tight rein to stop it leaping ahead beyond *after this where else would she look*? Even now the phone might be ringing . . . but he wouldn't risk ringing her at home. Perhaps a campfire? Smoke snaking and beckoning from the hills, just for Jess. But likely he'd had enough of fires.

The other possibility — that he'd ridden off into the night regardless of Jess, his promise perhaps forgotten as soon as it left his lips — stood at the edge of her mind like a large, cold, empty room, not to be entered.

As she approached the old house site a neigh rang out and was cut short. A grin started on Jess's face. There was no sign of life among the tumbled bricks, the tangled rose and gooseberry bushes, but Jess felt confident now, slid from the saddle. And saw him walking out of the bush. He was wearing a cautious kind of grin. She was grinning back.

'I brought you some food.' She shook off her pack.

'You're a bottler,' he said. 'You dunno how glad I am to see you.'

Jess's grin wouldn't stop. 'The outlaw of Curvey's Creek!'

'That's me. Bit exposed here.' He jabbed a thumb back the way he'd come. Jess handed him the pack, took Pedro's reins and followed Frank into the bush.

She watched him eating.

'Sure you don't want some?'

'I'm not hungry.' Haven't been ever since . . .'

'A feast. This is a feast.'

He told her about his intruders, the fire. He didn't sound angry as much as amazed. Never before in forty-five years had Frank had a posse on his tail. 'That's a first,' he marvelled. 'A first in my lifetime.'

'Did you see who they were?' Owen had gone out last night, which he didn't often do. A teachers' union meeting in Windsor, he'd said, explaining to Corin why the boy couldn't go with him.

'Webster,' said Frank. 'And I reckon Jack Samuels. The others . . . couldn't see well enough.' He wasn't meeting her eye.

Jess looked around at the two horses tethered apart in awkward spaces, Frank's pathetic bundle of possessions. 'You reckon they're still after you?'

'Them? Nah. I'm not afraid of a bunch of rednecks. They've done their worst. It's the coppers I'm worried about. On account of the fire. It had to be lit and they'll figure that out. Some bastard emptied the tank, so it had to be arson.'

'So you tell them what happened.'

'Coppers?' He thought that was funny. 'Think about it. My word against the words of five upstanding law-abiding locals. Who's gonna be believed? Who would you believe?'

'You,' she told him and put her hand, the one without the warts, close to his in case he might wish to hold it, if only for comfort.

He seemed not to notice, grew suddenly uneasy, as if the police might even now be surrounding them. Jess would save him, would give evidence at his trial, persuade the jury that Frank was innocent.

'You knew I'd come here,' she told him. Wanting to hear him say it — that he'd remembered her telling him it was the place she liked best, and so figured it was the first place she'd come looking.

He said, 'Truth is I couldn't think where the fuck to go, so I left it to Maguilla.'

It was almost the same thing.

'I'll look after you,' she told him. 'I can come every day. Bring you food. Tobacco. Tea . . .'

He was shaking his head. 'I'm gone, girl. Soon as it gets dark we'll be out of here.'

'We?' Hope stole her breath away, her voice just a whisper.

His face was all over the place — sorry, startled, pleased, then sorry again.

'Me and Maguilla and the dogs.'

''Course,' grinning away her own stupidity. *Of course* he'd meant them. A little laugh, getting herself back on track. Frank would leave and Jess would finish school and get a job in the Windsor Four Square or Woolworths, like any other girl who had no plans. She would marry and have children. She would grow old yet still be scrabbling and gnawing at this particular afternoon, trying to refashion it into something that demanded a future.

'Won't I ever see you again?'

'Don't,' he said. 'Don't look like that. Please.' His voice was Corin's age, plaintive. 'A few days and you'll hardly remember me.'

Tears trickling down her cheeks. She sniffed. Wiped them away with the back of her hand. More came. He wiped them away with his hand. He put his arms around her. She pressed her wet face against his neck.

'God almighty,' he said. 'This is not a good idea.'

She raised her head and pressed her salty mouth against his.

OWEN WAITED ALL weekend for a police car, rehearsing in his mind the story they'd agreed to tell if anyone asked. A card game at Phil Chaney's, a poker night that wives hadn't needed to know about.

No one would ask. They had no reason to.

But, if there *were* questions, Owen would be the weak link. No one had said this, but Owen knew and the others surely suspected. Omissions of information and small deceptions he could manage. But an outright lie? To police, trained in detection? If nothing else, they would smell the sweat breaking out.

What if they asked how you played poker? Owen hadn't played poker since he was a student. How many cards? How did you bid? He'd wanted to ask those questions that night before they all went their separate ways, but couldn't. Poker was like rugby or backing a trailer — no man should need to ask how it was done.

Who would their lies be protecting? No one had mentioned the cause of the fire. Was that because the others all knew? Or did they, like Owen, just have suspicions they didn't care to voice?

The more he thought back, the less Owen was sure about. Could the fire have been part of the plan? All of them in on it except Owen? Yet the decision to act had been his own. Hadn't it? Or had they been setting him up?

See, he was sweating already. Shirt sticking to his armpits.

Why was he prepared to collude in a lie when he had witnessed nothing that couldn't be acknowledged and, technically, was no worse than trespass? Yet he was guilty because, at the time, it had felt so good. Not the teeth-gritting satisfaction he'd imagined revenge might provide, but a kind of surging, crazy glee.

For three days Owen had been waiting, but no police car had yet arrived.

SUCH A NIGGARDLY heaven, distant and squashed between the hills. Looking up made Frank homesick.

*The love of fields and coppice*
*Of green and shaded lanes . . .*

His feet marching out the rhythm of the verse, a nagging pressure below the toes of his left foot where the hide he'd glued last week to patch the gaping sole was curling loose.

*Of ordered woods and gardens*
*Is running in your veins . . . '*

The words rolling out so nicely, the way they always did. Public bars, campfires, huts . . . with or without public demand.

For solace or celebration. 'Shit Frankie, all that poetry. Off by heart!'

He liked that. *By heart.* Not something you've had to learn but something that's seeped quietly into your inner being.

*. . . grey-blue distance,*
*brown streams and soft dim skies —*
*I know, but cannot share it*
*My love is otherwise.*

She'd been thinking, Dorothea Mackellar, of England. But the *otherness* applied as much to New Zealand — or what he'd seen of it. Frank was battered by a great wave of homesickness.

*I love a sunburnt country,*
*A land of sweeping plains . . .*

Lisa back over there. Whereabouts? Little Ben and Ruby. You can't hang onto anything, Frank scolded himself. Vaseline fingers.

Even Jess?

Thinking of the way her hair fell across her face, how it had felt against his skin, her voice in his ear. Best to put her out of his head, the very last thing his life needed right now was another complication.

He'd left Maguilla in Curvey's Creek, and Mac and Sal, so he'd have to go back there. Sooner or later.

He'd sent Jess home a couple of hours after. Watched her ride off until she was out of sight. Had felt . . . not regretful, as he probably should have, but stunned and slow, with bruising around the heart.

Once she was gone he waited until the ranges were eating into the evening sun. Then he packed up, untied the horse and saddled him, strapped on the bags. Called the dogs to heel and rode out onto the main road. Telling himself that any copper with an ounce of sense would now be home sipping an ale and watching the mid-evening news. But, all the same, riding fast and with his head tucked low and his ears straining.

Only one vehicle passed. It was a small truck with a gaping muffler, which meant Frank misjudged and stood hiding, with Maguilla and the dogs, for a good ten minutes behind the flax and thistles, wishing his tobacco had managed to last just a little longer.

Judy was home, which proved luck was sometimes on Frank's side. He didn't hold with flogging a willing horse, but there was no one else to turn to, so he drank Judy's coffee and filled her in about the fire.

A couple of coppers had called on Judy that afternoon, asking Frank's whereabouts. Now Judy wanted to drive him into the Windsor Police Station to tell his side of the story. Frank felt depressed; the only two people on his side in this sorry business were naïve to the point of stupidity. He tried to recall Australians he knew who had this problem of wide-eyed innocence. Could think of none. Told Judy, no way; he'd go and see the coppers in Auckland where maybe he had a decent chance of being believed.

Frank needed a temporary place for Maguilla and the dogs. It was a lot to ask, but he had to. He and Judy went out with a torch and moved a pregnant mare and the twitchy Cobra so that Maguilla could have the high-fenced paddock.

'If he's still here in four months he's mine,' said Judy.

'Fair enough.' Frank cleared his throat, felt himself reddening like a schoolboy. 'Young Jess might like to come up and ride him for me.' He was glad of the darkness.

His dogs knew he was leaving them. Sal held her nose in the air and pretended indifference, Mac nudged at Frank's legs and blinked in slow motion. Had Frank close to giving in, but he couldn't take one dog and leave the other.

Judy made salami sandwiches, despite his protests, and drove Frank out past Windsor. She paid him what he'd earned plus a little more and waited in the car while he bought Park Drive and papers.

'You're a top person,' he told her through the window just before she U-turned off to leave him under the stars. Her reply was lost beneath the roar of the ute's motor. Frank pictured her driving back to Curvey's Creek, growing more cheerful by the mile in her relief at having got rid of him.

Hitch-hiking in the dark was pushing his luck. But daylight would come, and leaving Curvey's Creek behind at walking pace was better than not leaving it at all.

Frank didn't mind hitching, wasn't one of those who held a grudge against the luckier bastards behind their wheels. A hitch-hiked journey was like a condensed version of life. You started out with some kind of general hope about where you might end up, and sometimes you got lucky and were carried the whole way. Other times it was all stones and wind and rain, though a flame of hope would keep flickering, pushing you on. And maybe at last a car would pull over and a door would open. Then you'd find it was only going half a mile up the road. Sometimes your luck was so bad you might as well just give up on where you were hoping to go and settle for staying wherever you'd got to.

And sometimes, if you were Frank, you might stop in at a roadside pub and get sidetracked off into someone else's life for a week or a year or two. Public bars were another kind of condensed life. You'd walk in the door and never know who you might get talking to or how that meeting might change your life for good or bad. The important thing was to be open to possibility.

This particular little life — from the northern side of Windsor to the heart of Auckland — turned out to be an easy one, despite the disadvantage of setting out in darkness. Frank's first ride was with a tanker driver who took him just past Te Awamutu, the second ride (a couple from Taihape heading north for her sister's wedding) took Frank and the boy right to the waterfront of central Auckland.

Frank had met up with the boy about twenty minutes after the tanker dropped him off. It was just before dawn and he was trudging up a steady incline that could well go on for miles. Reciting.

*The stark white ring-barked forests,*
*All tragic to the moon . . .*

And the moon was tragic all right — the size and shape of a fingernail clipping, so he couldn't see where the tarseal ended and the verge, with all its pitfalls, began. He was gaining on the boy, who knew he was there. He would hear the rasping of Frank's patched-up soles, as Frank could hear the occasional skitter of dislodged stones and — as the distance between them lessened — the harsh little gasps of exhaustion or fear. Frank called out, then, made himself known.

The kid was maybe twelve or thirteen. Jeans and a jacket, the whites of his eyes like pale birds' eggs. His name was Jacob and he was going to Auckland to stay with his Aunty Anne. Frank went uh-huh as if hundreds of kids walked through the night from city to city to visit their aunties.

They walked together. Jacob came up with a story in case some nosy parker should ask about them. 'You're m' dad, see, 'n' we got a car — a V8 Holden — only it ran out of gas.'

122

'That's no good. They'll drop us off at the first service station.'

Jacob kicked a stone. It dribbled off into the dark. 'Okay. Someone stole our car. At this gas station, see. We went in to buy pies and you left the keys —'

'Jesus, I did too.' Frank slapped at his pockets. 'How could I have been so bloody stupid!'

'You's thinking 'bout the pies. We was that hungry!'

'Right. I remember. Steak 'n' mushroom.' And pastry that showered flakes as you bit. Frank's mouth watering. 'Did we get the pies anyway?'

'Nup. Your wallet was in the car.'

Frank clutched the crown of his hat. 'Oh lord, I'm such a wally. Such a goddamn stupid bastard.'

The boy laughed.

'Still,' said Frank, 'they were top people that ran the garage. Hadn't the heart to send us away hungry.' He swung the bag from his shoulder and crouched on the road to loosen the cord. Judy's sandwiches, neatly wrapped, sat at the top. Frank divided them up.

'All *right*,' said Jacob. 'Good one, Dad!'

Some three hours later they stood side by side in downtown Auckland.

Jacob studied the skyline. 'Do people go out on them roofs, and walk about and that, you reckon?'

Frank remembered, a long time ago, that same feeling. That those wide open yet secret parts of a city were the interesting bits. But he knew now that there was seldom anything up there to make them different from the cramped and junky back yards you got to glimpse from the windows of suburban trains.

Jacob didn't know where Aunty Anne lived and they couldn't find her in the directory. It was too early to ring Debbie Reynolds so Frank bought them breakfast, then came across a pub that was open and left the boy outside while he went in and downed a handle or two. Got talking to a young bloke in riding boots who'd just thrown in a station-hand job on the east coast. None of the workers stuck it long, he whined — the manager was a mongrel. Frank got him to write the name of the place on his Zig-Zag packet all the same.

When he got out of the pub, Jacob had disappeared. Frank waited a while, then searched, but not too hard. He got the feeling the boy was watching. That the kid had seen how Frank was a soft touch, incapable of shaking him off, and had, considerately, removed himself. He could have searched longer but he'd come across a phone box where everything seemed in working order, so he dialled Debbie Reynolds' number. The flatmate gave him the address. Frank bought a mini-map from a service station and found he was almost there.

'Darling heart,' said Debbie Reynolds at the open door, 'you look quite, quite dreadful. Has that baggage come back to you? Crystal,' she yelled over her shoulder, 'remember that two-faced thieving Aussie bitch . . .'

Crystal was wearing a pink and orange bathrobe and the faintest five o'clock shadow.

Debbie and Crystal set breakfast in front of Frank before asking why he'd come running to Aunty Debbie. He'd asked himself the same thing as the husband from Taihape drove clenched and anxious along the motorway. Now, looking at Debbie, he found the answer.

'Because, apart from Judy Gordon and a slip of a girl, you're the only straight person I know in the whole goddamn country.'

They liked that, Debbie and Crystal. Tickled their fancy.

Frank told them about the Curvey's Creek posse burning his house down. Each time he told this story it seemed less believable. Debbie and Crystal were aghast at the idea of Frank making a statement to the city police. Only a country boy could be so gormless.

But Frank had thought it through. 'Gotta go back home and find m' kids. Soon as I get some money together. And so long as they've got this arson business on me here they won't even let me out of the country.'

Debbie clapped her big sausage fingers over her face and peeked between them at Frank's future. 'Don't do it,' she intoned. 'There must be some other way. Don't do it, darling heart. Listen, please do, to your Aunty.'

WARD WAS GONE, no policeman had come to Owen's door to ask how you dealt a poker hand. Marion had, in response to a clumsily contrived enquiry, assured him both his daughters understood about contraception ('Sheenagh,' he bleated, 'is barely thirteen') and were sensible girls.

It was over and Owen must put it behind him. But flames and Phil Chaney's derelict kitchen kept creeping into his dreams. He needed someone to tell. Even an acknowledgement, a phone call from Charlie, or Rick or Dan on any pretext at all; just the sense of them all being in it together. He wondered if they spoke about it to one another, but not to him. He tried to despise them, the way he once had, but it was different now. Owen had gone with the big boys behind the bikesheds and taken part in a thrilling and shameful ritual. A blood brother.

He couldn't tell Marion, not this far down the track. Besides, she had contempt enough for him already. Did other blood brothers tell their wives?

Jess was avoiding him, but in a quiet way not obvious to the rest of the family. The defiance had gone from her eyes, been replaced by a Mona Lisa glow. Owen attributed this to relief that her childhood had been restored. That much he had given her. But the satisfaction he gained from this thought immediately led him back into the maze of suspicions.

THEN, ONE WEEKDAY evening, the police drove in and parked in full view of anyone driving past.

There was a policeman and a policewoman. Their identical blue shirts, his navy trousers, her navy skirt and sockless lace-up shoes, overshadowed their faces. They were two uniforms with voices that said to Jess,

'Frank Ward. Is he your friend?'

'He raped you, didn't he?'

'Don't try and protect him, Jessica. He doesn't deserve protecting.'

'Where is he, Jessica?'

The words spattering on her shirt and falling away. Jess heard them but from somewhere deep inside herself. From that distance she watched her mother's face moving, as if some unseen hand was pressing it this way and that. Saw her astonishment turned on the police and then on Owen. What was all this? Why hadn't she known?

Saw her father, white-faced, trying to calm things down. The policewoman joining in, apologising. 'We assumed you knew, Mrs Bennington. It seems to be widely known.'

Marion then staring at Jess as if into a fish tank full of

stingrays. 'Is this true? Answer me?' Shaking Jess by the shoulders to make her surface. *'Is this true?'*

'No,' said Jess in a loud voice. 'No, it's lies.'

They expected more. All of them waiting. Jess hung her head so her hair would shut them out. One of the warts had dropped off her left hand, leaving behind a small pale blemish. Frank had tickled his tongue across all three, said he had cane toad saliva — intoxicating and lethal, especially to warts. Told her of toads jostling for space on front lawns, so Jess saw hundreds of toads stumbling over snakes, and housewives trapped in their houses unable even to fetch in the mail.

'You're fifteen, is that right?'

Her father answered softy. 'Yes.'

The policewoman persisting, beyond Jess's curtaining hair. 'You're not in trouble, Jessica. You've done nothing wrong.'

*Then leave me alone.* But the words jammed in her throat.

'We could arrange for a doctor to . . .'

'You're not pregnant, are you?' Marion wrenching aside hair, pushing her face through. 'Are you?'

Jess glared back. 'Maybe I am.'

Marion pulled away.

'You're not the only one.' The policeman's voice. 'There have been others, Jessica. Girls like you. Maybe younger.

She pushed back her hair then. 'Who? When?'

Her father said, gently enough, 'It's true.'

'He doesn't deserve your loyalty. You see that now.'

'He's run off, Jess. What does that tell you?'

'Which girls? Who?'

'I suppose he told you he loved you,' the policewoman said, and sighed.

Jess was crumbling away. Tears like needles and pins in the eyes, her jaw locked yet trembling. Her hands shook. She pushed them between her knees, saw that another wart was hanging loose. Coincidence. He was all lies and bullshit. Jess was nothing, not to him, no one.

DEBBIE AND CRYSTAL took Frank on a circuit of clubs and pubs and living rooms, showing him off. They encouraged him to tell the stories of his past adventures, drew attention to his bowed thighs and the half-cured leather patch on the sole of his boot. Crystal took flashlight photos, posing him against baroque satin drapes and surrounded by drag queens; she liked the incongruity. They shouted him garish cocktails with swizzle sticks and umbrellas, he shouted them depth-charges with whisky chasers. They propositioned him frequently and inventively and he couldn't be certain they were joking. But around dawn he would crash out on their sofa, fully dressed, to sleep unmolested.

One day — he tried to count back how many he'd been there, only four, or was it five? — he woke up early, at least before midday, and knew he had to get on with his own life. He felt like a man who had eaten nothing but waffles with maple sauce and whipped cream for a month.

No one else was up so Frank had a shower and a shave, consulted *Wises' Street Directory* and let himself out. Debbie and Crystal's flat was expensive, decaying and central. The Chrysler crouched like a gleaming blue ladybird beneath the carport. Frank thought of Ruby and the baby in the back seat as their mother drove them north.

At the Central Police Station Frank told his story to a bald and increasingly impatient copper. It took a while. Frank had to fill in the background — Wyatt's misguided attempt on the sheep, the allegations of gates being opened, the odd digression into some matter of general interest — but when he finally got to the fire, the copper cheered up. Dusted off a saucer for Frank to use as an ashtray while he went to check the computer files.

When he returned the bald copper brought another cop with him. One look at their faces and Frank knew Debbie was right — this had not been a good idea. They obviously had his past on file. Nothing terrible — drunken driving, the cattle rustling, assault — but on paper, plucked clean of detail and circumstances, these things would not impress. Especially not coppers who were a judgemental breed.

'Francis Copeland Ward,' said the bald one. 'I'm arresting you on a charge of the carnal knowledge of Jessica Marion Bennington.'

# C H A **14** T E R

AT FIRST JESS had thought of funerals. Her own body, reproachfully young and virtually wart-free, being wept over by Owen and Marion. Sheenagh smirking and already wearing Jess's shockproof, water-resistant fifteenth birthday watch. Frank's deceitful body, rotting undiscovered and deservedly maggot-ridden beside a country road. But his horse, his dogs, remained at his side, selfless and distraught. Jess couldn't bear their suffering; brought Frank back to life.

He'd be taking back roads, looking out for work. A poem and a dead cigarette on his lips. Two dogs and a swag. Maguilla's coat finely powdered with the dust of unsealed roads. The police would arrive in two cars, box Frank in. *A warrant for your arrest, cowboy. Your girlfriend dobbed you in.*

Would he say, *Which girlfriend?* Bemused by profusion? Which young girl among the many? Jess reran this part of the story over and over in her head. As the blinding pain eased she knew she didn't believe it.

If he asked, *Which girlfriend?* it would only be because he couldn't credit it, not of Jess.

She remembered his stubbled jaw so close to her eyes that the whiskers resembled slashed manuka trunks, his tobacco breath, his fingers on her skin. The policewoman's claims became unreal. Larger than life yet insubstantial in the manner of a road hoarding. And Jess had believed it.

She has done a terrible thing. *I'm sorry*, she cries out to on-the-road Frank, *I didn't mean to.*

HIS WIFE THUMPS down on the bed beside him and tugs at the duvet. Her nightdress spills on his thigh like a cool dry breath. A slippery garment, dark blue, with a midnight cobweb of lace. She has a drawer full of nightclothes and underwear that has slithered

128

from the bodies of lithe young models in glossy double-page spreads. Owen likes cotton. White, simple, old-fashioned.

She is still furious with him. *It's going to get worse*, he tells her in his head. If they catch Ward — and they will sooner or later — and charge him, he's bound to say about the fire. Anyone would. How much does he know, or guess? Where did he get to that night and how much did he see?

Which one of them had told the police about Jess? By coincidence or design? If only Owen had kept his mouth shut that night. He now has a motive on record. Vengeful Father Resorts to Arson. They've set him up to take the rap, just as it's done in third-rate movies.

Marion is now filing her nails beneath the small swivel light. Owen switches on the dreadful bed lamp with its moving summer garden of colours.

'What did you put that on for?'

'I felt like it.'

He wants to attack. An unfamiliar feeling.

'Actually,' he says, taking up from where they discontinued hours ago, 'I did want to tell you but I figured you had enough on your plate already.'

'Like what?'

'Your extra-marital sex life.'

The nail file freezes in the air and trembles slightly.

'What's that supposed to mean?'

'What it usually means. You're having an affair. Aren't you?'

The filing resumes. 'And therefore I didn't deserve to know about my daughter?'

'Something like that.'

He's better at this than he thought he would be. Marion has gone quiet.

'Are you?' He directs the question loftily at the suitcase on top of the wardrobe. 'Having an affair?'

Silence again. Is she trying to remember?

'I have been,' she says quite calmly. 'For some time now. It's more or less over.'

'Oh,' says Owen. 'I see.'

Suddenly there's no fun in this any more. Owen feels panic, a two-year-old-lost-in-a-supermarket feeling of terror.

'Are you planning to leave us?'

'No.' Marion turns to glance at him, not unkindly. 'In fact it's not like that at all.' She arranges her pillows, stacked high the way she likes them. 'I've got an early start in the morning. Can you turn off that light?'

Owen reaches to turn off the lamp, feeling relief. As if someone has reached down, taken his hand and said: it's all right, we're going home now.

'I hit the bastard,' he says in the dark. 'When I found him with her. I punched him fair in the face.'

'You?' Her voice astonished but not disbelieving. 'Good God.'

A moment or two later her hand gropes for his arm. 'Did you really?'

Owen's smile scrapes the flesh of his cheek against the sheet.


IN HER LUNCH break Jess hung around with Leila and Lynette just long enough to find out what she wanted to know. Carol Green had got to sleep with Frank, Leila probably hadn't, Lynette certainly hadn't. Carol broke her heart over Frank, just like she'd done over Aaron Smythe and Michael Jackson and Kenny Whatsisname and Michael Keaton. Apart from their crowd and Judy and the prim little girls who got their ponies shod, no one seemed to have visited Frank.

Carol Green. Jess could barely put a face to the name that had Leila and Lynette giggling and rolling their eyes. Carol Green didn't seem to count.

From the phone box outside the tuck shop Jess rang Judy Gordon.

'Jess,' said Judy. 'I was meaning to ring you. Frank thought you might . . .'

'He's there?'

'No. But between you and me, the stallion is, and his dogs . . .'

He was going to come back! All along he'd been planning to come back. *Forgive me, my darling.*

'He thought you'd want to come over and ride Maguilla.'

*I'm sorry.* Jess whispered, 'You've heard from him?'

'Not yet.'

'I need to get hold of him. Some things he lent me, I should return. You don't have . . .?'

'If he gets in touch I'll let you know.'

'You don't have any kind of address?'

'Well, there's a number somewhere — friend of the ex-wife. Hang on . . .'

Gavin Cawley tapped on the glass door. Jess was writing the phone number on her inner arm. Gavin was waving something at her, pointing and grinning. His driver's licence. He'd passed. Could borrow his parents' car.

'TAKE INCEST,' SAID Desmond Snail in a treacle voice. 'What is it? An expression of love, just an expression of love. And you want your children to know love. Of course you do. Everyone does. You have children?'

Frank manufactured a small snuffling snore and kept his eyes tightly closed. Was Desmond, with his tidy moustache, his mobile, fleshy face and alabaster fingers, part of Frank's punishment? Or was it intended as a kindness, like with like?

Jess had made a complaint, had pushed her hair back out of her eyes and held a pen just below the second wart on her index finger and signed a statement. Under what duress? Or did Frank fool himself, redefining violation as an act of affection? Was he in fact no better, no less deluded, than his cellmate?

An answer to that on the faces of the balding copper and his associate. And again on the face of the judge, the prison screws. Fastidious distaste, a fear of contagion.

He'd told Desmond — an initial instinct of self-protection — that he was up for drunk-in-charge.

'No need to pretend with me.' Desmond's flesh-eating smile was a harbinger of confessions to follow.

From the moment of Frank's arrest the police had lost all interest in hearing about the house burning down. 'Ladybird, ladybird,' the bald copper chirped and the others cracked up laughing.

'Listen, mate — that was my possessions. Near enough everything I had. I don't normally hold with ratting to coppers but I can give you names.'

'Sure, y' can. Wanna call your lawyer, Francis? I'd want to if I was in your shoes.'

Frank fumbled at the numbers on the dial, hoping he'd remembered right.

'When do I go up?' While the phone rang, and rang again.

'In the morning. We'll be giving you bed and breakfast.'

The bald copper picked up an extension phone just as Crystal answered in her lady muck voice. 'Queen's Chain B & D Department.'

The copper looked over at Frank, eyebrows soaring.

'Listen,' said Frank, watching the copper listening in. 'I'm ringing from the cop shop in town. I came to tell them about the arson and they've arrested me. Now the bastards are listening in on this call.'

'Is that right? Get off the phone, you brute.'

The cop's snort was loud in Frank's ear.

'Was that him? Is he still there?'

'Never mind.' Frank turned his back. 'I'm in custody. I go to court in the morning.'

'Oh cowboy. There's no joy in saying I told you so. We'll be down in a tick to bail you.'

Frank glanced round at the copper, who shook his head.

'Not today,' Frank told Crystal.


LATE NEXT MORNING from the dock he searched the half-filled public benches for his friends. No sign of them. Self-pity trickled. It was always the same in his limelit moments, no one there who belonged to him. Frank at school prizegivings (most improved pupil, even, once, top of the class) and nobody watching. His mother working shifts at the clothing factory, then too ill to come, then dead.

He could tell a psychologist all that stuff. Now he was on the books as some bent kind of weirdo they'd be wanting to fish up his past and shovel about in it looking for reasons. Well, with Frank they'd be like pigs in shit — he could give them the works. Father a boozer, soldier, deserter — not of the army but of his two children and his tight-lipped, teetotal wife. Who saw in the son too much of the father and battled against it with a razor strop and a God who, in return, raised not one hallowed finger to guide her through the misery of poverty or tuberculosis.

Frank's sister Helen, as virtuous as Frank was wayward, had leeched herself quietly into the family of a primary school friend. So when their mother died Helen was formally adopted and Frank, at twelve, was passed to the orphanage.

Helen finished her schooling, became a secretary and married her boss. By thirty-five she was a widow. Not rich, but certainly not poor. Her adoptive sister sent her a news clipping about riders on a rodeo circuit; Frank photographed parting company with a long-horned steer. Helen tracked him down, said she felt guilty for having abandoned him. Frank had been startled — he was, after all, a couple of years older than Helen — but not displeased. They had nothing in common, as far as Frank could see, beyond their parents' genes, but since then they'd kept in touch. Frank still owed Helen $210 of the money she'd lent them to come to New Zealand.

Oh, Frank could make a case for the psychologists, no trouble at all. Could give them the blocks from which they'd construct a tower of logic so impressive, so intricate yet plausible, that it would be impossible to tell where reason ended and exoneration began. They'd weave in words of social apology — *deprivation, disadvantage* — absolving Frank of responsibility even as they endorsed his guilt.

To hell with that. Frank was on to them. Stick him in with one of that lot and he'd present them with a childhood so rosy and glowing they could sell the rights to Disneyland.

THE JUDGE HAD a cauliflower ear. On seeing it Frank's heart sank. A former rugby player! Luck couldn't get much worse. The same kind of thoughts in the judge's mind, you could tell. Having read the charge, he wanted to flick Frank onto the floor and squash him beneath his heel.

Fair enough, too; in the judge's shoes Frank would have felt the same. He threw the judge a look to convey as much, but His Honour just looked away.

'Is this . . . man represented?'

'No,' said Frank. 'No sir. I'll be speaking on my own behalf.'

This raised some interest among the spectators, but the judge wasn't impressed. He flicked his hand impatiently and turned to the lawyers in the front seating. 'Will somebody kindly see to this?'

The lawyers glanced up at the dock then busied themselves shuffling papers. No one wanted Frank on their side. The judge cleared his throat ominously and a teenager in a three-piece suit raised his hand and murmured, 'Your Honour.'

'Thank you,' said His Honour sourly and scribbled on his pad. 'Remanded in custody until December the fifteenth?'

'Yes sir, thank you, sir,' said the teenage lawyer inexplicably.

'Step down,' the judge ordered Frank.

'Hang on,' said Frank. 'I want bail.'

'I think not,' said the judge. 'Bail denied. Step down.'

Back at the prison Frank was placed in Desmond Snail's cell. 'Have a nice day,' the officer said as he closed the door.

CRYSTAL CAME TO visit on the Sunday. She passed in tobacco and papers and thirty dollars in cash for Frank to receive the next day, and she slipped him emergency tailormades. Debbie sent her love, was unable to come; ex-inmates were not allowed to visit and she could hardly hope for *incognito*.

Debbie and Crystal *had* turned up at the courthouse to give Frank their support, but were directed to the wrong courtroom. They'd sat there for three and a half hours, through traffic violations, unpaid fines, possession of cannabis, vandalism and a protracted debate on — Crystal smirked — what constituted a concealed weapon.

'Just now I read the rules on the wall out there,' Crystal told Frank, loud and unstoppable. 'Been there since nineteen fifty-two. Things we're not allowed to do with each other. Conversation is one of them. I kid you not. So I guess that just leaves boring old oral sex.'

Frank winced.

'Oh dear. Am I embarrassing you, cowboy? I dressed down and everything.'

'I haven't told you why I'm here yet.'

He started from when Lisa left him; context was important. Before he'd got to the present, a squawk of laughter escaped from Crystal's tragic orange mouth.

'I'm sorry. It's just — you need to come across like Charles Bronson, and the only friends you have in the whole of Auckland are a couple of raving queens.' She clamped her lips against another gust of laughter, blue glass beads quivering on her scrawny chest. 'Sorry dear, but there is a funny side. Best I stay away?'

'No.' Frank heard the desperation in his own voice and was embarrassed. 'Truth is,' he confessed, 'what scares me most is thinking that by the time I get to court they'll have me convinced I'm the bent kind of bastard they think I am.'

Crystal consoled. 'We'll find a good lawyer.'

'Nup,' said Frank. 'Far as this case is concerned I've already had one lawyer too many. Gonna do my own defence.'

Crystal threw up her hands. 'That's just asking for trouble. No, listen to me. It's like this — go into a licensed restaurant with your own bottle, and they'll act magnanimous, let you sit there and drink it. But you can bet they're gonna get even when it comes to the corkage fee.' She saw Frank's face. 'Well, perhaps in cowhide country that's not a great analogy. Let me put it this way: The main function of law is to keep lawyers, cops, prison officers and various other uniformed types gainfully employed. This means that lots of people must be arrested and quite a few of them sent to gaol. Whether they're guilty or innocent isn't really the point.'

'Hang on,' said Frank. 'What's that got to do with the licensed restaurant?'

He watched as Crystal strained to recall the thought, the link of logic. Laying odds that she wouldn't be able to. Even a seasoned expounder like Frank had trouble retracing his steps.

'I meant,' said Crystal, 'there's always a price. If you don't pay in the approved way, you'll have to pay in some insidious fashion.'

'Insidious,' said Frank. 'Now that's not a word you hear very often. I like it. I could maybe use it in my plea.'

'Jesus wept,' moaned Crystal. 'Listen to me, cowboy. The law is not a level playing field. As *the accused* you start with a disadvantage. It might be different in Ockerland, but *we* don't have a heritage of lovable convicts. You need a lawyer.'

Frank was adamant. 'The turkey they gave me wanted to throw it back on Jess. Say it was my understanding she was at least sixteen.'

'And what do *you* plan to tell them, dare I ask?'

'Guilty. Well, I am, strictly speaking. But I'll put it in a wider kind of philosophical context.'

'The mind,' said Crystal, 'boggles.'

'Well, I'll say, "What you should be measuring, Your Honour, is the emotional situation. The crime is when you don't care — the hasty poke with nothing on your mind except maybe last night's dinner. And, if we're honest, we've all been guilty of that. And we've probably all been on the receiving end, one time or another. But that's not how it was with me and this girl. Neither one of us was taking advantage. And, that being so, where's the crime?"

Crystal looked at the ceiling. 'Beam me up,' she begged. She looked back at Frank. 'It's hayseed. Say that and you'll be looking at at least five years. Keep this in mind — laws are just people in power making sure they keep it that way.'

'I know that,' said Frank. 'That's why they want you to have a lawyer. Lawyers make damn sure nobody gets to ask or to answer the simple questions, like what's right and what's wrong. But — and this is the cunning bit — show me a judge who doesn't like to think of himself as, at heart, the kind of straightforward man who can relate to a straightforward man like me? Y'see? *Y'see?*'

'I'm bedazzled,' said Crystal limply. 'Not since Perry Mason has such a fine legal mind leapt into motion.'

JESS PEERED IN the window of the car and ran the order through in her mind. From the right — accelerator, brake, clutch. A B C — as simple. With practice it would be as easy and thoughtless as walking, Marion said so. But Marion's car was automatic and smaller than this one. Owen disapproved of Japanese cars, said they were lightweight and full of gadgetry. Worst of all they were shamelessly modern. Marion and her daughters cracked jokes together about how Owen was so hopelessly behind the times.

Jess had driven Owen's car only once. Down the drive and up the road for a mile or two. She'd turned into the Chaneys' uncle's driveway, on Owen's instructions — though by then she was getting the hang of the gears — and Owen drove home.

'I'd sooner drive Mum's car,' she'd muttered.

'I'd sooner you did too,' he'd said.

Yet in all other matters Owen was the patient parent.

So Jess peered into Owen's car thoughtfully, yet without intent. And she saw, spilling from the dashboard pocket, among envelopes and paper clips and crumpled sales dockets, the cover of the book she'd borrowed for Frank.

She opened the car door and edged the paperback out. There on the cover was a sultry dark-haired woman, in a peasant skirt and off-the-shoulder top, standing in front of a rough little shack, and a man in a wide-brimmed hat walking up the side of the house in a purposeful way. Looking at it, you got the feeling he didn't know the woman was there, and would not be pleased to find she was. Jess had been intrigued by the cover, though not sufficiently to want to read the book. Now she turned to check inside. *Owen Bennington*, in handwriting not unlike her own.

The same book.

Which should now be ashes. Which could not have been back in her father's possession unless someone had returned it to him, or he himself had been, quite recently, in Frank's house.

Jess marched into the house where Sheenagh was talking on the phone and Corin was watching TV and her father was hunched at his desk writing report cards. In the bedroom she wrote on a piece of paper *Dear Corin, please can you see that Lucky and Pedro are looked after. Judy G will tell you what to do. Your loving sister Jess.* She left it under his pillow beside a piece of chewed bubble gum.

Back in her own bedroom she took the remains of her pocket money, her Post Office savings book with the phone number of Frank's ex-wife's friend tucked beneath the plastic cover, and a change of clothes. The key to the Ford was on the hook in the kitchen. Marion's dark glasses were on the windowsill. The closed-in porch her father used as an office was at the back of the house; there was a chance he might not even hear. The important thing was not to stall.

And she didn't. Reversed out fast and not straight but she missed the gate posts and swung onto the road. Then into first, left foot on C, right foot on A, and she was off, thinking she heard them yelling but not at all sure and she couldn't risk taking her eyes off the road to look in the mirror. And when she felt able to do so, then to reach up and adjust the mirror for a view beyond the back seats, by then the school house was long out of sight — a hill and several bends behind her.

By the time she reached Thompson's Saddle, Jess knew she could drive this car anywhere. She was dizzy with capability. The gas tank was one-third full, and she had fifty-three dollars in the bank and two dollars thirty in her pocket.

She took the stock truck turn-off just before the high school and by-passed the town centre. Cunning. North of the town she cruised past state houses that looked like the rabbiter's cottage, then was back on the main road.

She'd passed the saleyards and was just changing down to third gear for the hill climb when the police car overtook her. A policewoman — *the* policewoman — was in the passenger seat shouting out the open window. 'Pull over, Jess. Pull over, there's a good girl.'

Jess put her foot down. The police car dropped behind her, but as the road straightened it again drew abreast.

'Jessica —'

Again Jess's foot went down, but it was unsteady, struck B instead of A. The car skidded, screeched, spluttered, stopped. Jess ground it into neutral, turned the key. She was rolling backwards. A B C . . .? C B A . . .? *Which?* To her left, beneath its disguise of bush, the hill fell sharply away. Jess wrenched at the wheel. The car was rolling faster.

# C H A 15 T E R

DESMOND WENT OFF to his trial and Frank was on edge all day, waiting for news, afraid the case would be remanded. The odds weren't good; remanding cases was the legal system's main activity. Remands, false starts, delays, confusion — the thing about courts was that nobody ever seemed to know what they were supposed to be doing or when they were supposed to be doing it. This might be deliberate, remands being the worst kind of punishment. Better to be serving a sentence, getting on with it, than trapped in the timeless, useless limbo that was remand. In remand cells men tried to kill themselves, sometimes succeeded. If Desmond returned and the next day Frank found him dangling from the window bars, purple-lipped, what would Frank do?

But Desmond didn't return. He got seven years and a transfer south. 'Seven years. You should think about that, Frank,' said the woman officer who gave Frank the news. 'The law's getting tougher on you lot. Not looking good, matey.'

Frank kept his mouth shut. This got easier. There was enough complaining, explaining, protesting going on without Frank adding his bit. And with Desmond gone, Frank's life improved. He could read without interruption the eclectic armful of paperbacks Crystal had brought in for him on request. She'd chosen them randomly from a mission shop, not being one for reading herself. Under the circumstances Frank wasn't fussy. They all filled in time and dulled the aching images of his children: of the baby's plump limbs and wide crumpling smile, of Ruby's hand sliding into his, of the two children waiting in some bitter room for Lisa to come home, for Frank to rescue them.

Sometimes, of course, the ache inside him was not for his children but for a drink — the warmth and promise of the liquid sliding down his throat.

With Desmond gone Frank was able to talk to the decent screws, get to know them and benefit from the small concessions that came with being assessed, despite his charged offence, as a reasonable sort of bloke. Alf, who did night shifts, would leave Frank's light on so he could read late. With Desmond sharing his cell the nights had been a long stretch of scuttling roaches and impotent regrets. *If only*, he would think. If only he'd sold his saddle, begged, borrowed, whatever it took to get on a plane. He might have found his kids by now. If only he hadn't let Debbie and Crystal distract him. If only Jess had been a sour lump like Leila Samuels. If only he'd never left Australia . . .

Among the gang insignias, the drawings of devils, motorbikes, snakes, flames and sexual parts, and the inked propositions and obscenities in Frank's cell, someone had written in a neat, slanting hand, *At least I've still got my health.* Frank liked that. No matter how often he read it or how bad he was feeling it could still raise a small internal grin and a feeling of kinship with the joker who'd written it.

Until one day Frank read it and thought that maybe it wasn't a joke. Maybe it had been put there by some sanctimonious prick who really meant it?

THE POLICEWOMAN, JENNY Tripp, helped Jess out of Owen's car and instructed her to move her head and shoulders and arms to make sure they were all in working order, while the policeman looked at the back of the car, which seemed to have imbedded itself in rock, and pronounced it undrivable. He called up on the RT for a tow truck while Jenny Tripp put Jess and her plastic bag of belongings into the back seat of the police car.

They questioned her as they drove back to Windsor.

'I'm Jenny, remember? Call me Jenny. Where were you going, Jess?'

'Anywhere.'

'Why?'

'Dunno.'

'Of course you do. You'll have to do better than that Jess. Who were you running away from? Your Mum and Dad?'

'No.'

'Who then? Frank Ward?'

Jess gritted her teeth.

'He can't hurt you now. We've picked him up. He's in gaol, waiting trial.'

'In gaol? Where in gaol?'

'Miles away.'

Auckland?'

'You've heard from him?'

'No.'

'It's your dad's car?'

''Course.'

'How's he gonna feel? About you smashing it up?'

'Guess he'll be laughing and dancing.'

'Dancing maybe.'

'Anyway, it was you guys' fault.'

'Our fault?'

'Running me off the road.'

'What's he gonna say?'

'How would I know!'

'Car conversion. It's a crime you know. Kids get sent away for that.'

'So send me away.'

'Somehow I don't think your dad'll want to lay charges. We'll take you home and see what he says.'

'I'm not going home.'

'You don't have a choice, love.'

'I'll just run away again.'

'You're still in shock. You'll feel different after a good night's sleep.'

At the station they gave her hot tea thick with sugar, then Jenny Tripp told her, 'We need you to give evidence, Jess.'

'You're gonna take me to court?'

'No, Jess. I'm talking about Ward.'

'No, I can't. What I said — I made it up.'

'I know it's hard, but he has to be stopped, Jess.'

Jess put the cup down and ran. Out the door, past the counter and out onto the street. Jenny Tripp was behind her and might never have caught her except that Jess saw the Barker Hanley office ahead of her and hesitated, afraid to run past it.

Jenny walked her back to the station.

'You're making things worse for yourself.'

Joke. What could be worse than the way things were? She was a traitor, a car thief and a rotten driver.

At least she knew where Frank was. But how could she get to

Auckland now? They would be watching her. She tugged the policewoman's sleeve.

'Will they bring him back here for the court?'

'I doubt it.'

Jess threw herself into a chair, sat there scowling and plaiting small strands of hair. After a time she blurted, grudgingly, 'Okay, I'll go to court.'

'Good on you, mate,' said Jenny Tripp.

'But only,' said Jess, 'if I don't have to go home.'

MARION IS MAGNIFICENT in a crisis. Owen is filled with admiration for his wife. *Nothing daunts her.* He senses that inside himself he's shuffling closer to her, as if her dauntlessness is an umbrella that will shelter them both.

He exhumed his guilt, his parental culpability — too soft, too permissive — and Marion, who has always reminded him of these failings, laughed and cast it aside. Owen then dug further, came up with their shared failure; a flawed marriage, short on mutual affection — Jess instinctively reacting to a void her parents had chosen not to acknowledge. Marion poured scorn and this theory, too, shrivelled.

Marion lays blame in only two quarters — Frank Ward's lack of scruples and Jess's adolescent hormones. Now that Marion has recovered from the outrage of not having been told, she's taking things in her stride. Even the shameful fact that their daughter was now a resident of the Wharekoha home for wayward girls.

'She might learn to appreciate what she has,' said Marion. Though he heard her on the phone to one of her colleagues, skirting the truth by saying that Jess was staying with friends. The rest she told with a kind of martyred glee; an abridged and daggish version. Jess, doing her teenage rebellion thing, had taken off in Owen's car, rammed it into a bank and emerged wiser and miraculously unscathed.

Owen and Marion saw Jess in the privacy of an office at the Windsor Police Station before she was taken to Wharekoha Girls' Home. *At her own request.* Officer Tripp had asked that they bring in clothes for her. It was a distressing meeting; Owen wanted Jess to come home with them, wanted to forgive and forget, but Jess appeared more dogged than distraught. Marion believed punishment was in order and an institution would best know

142

how to deal out discipline. So Owen gave up, listened to Marion delivering messages about how Jess could have killed herself, the effects of delayed shock, the clothes they'd brought in, the care of Jess's horses and the irresponsibility of trying to palm that off on her little brother. Jess made minimal response.

'She's probably still in shock,' Marion said as they pulled in at the panel-beaters.

'So am I,' said Owen on seeing his car. The rear right end was stoved in and the back axle buckled. In fact he'd been expecting worse. He hadn't yet checked on the insurance, but with Jess driving it was unlikely to have been covered.

Hearing this, distress caught up with Marion. 'Oh no. Oh God, it'll cost a fortune. Can't we say you were driving?'

'Witnesses,' he reminded her wearily. 'Who are also police officers.'

Officer Tripp, having been called away that day before Owen and Marion arrived at the station, came to see them the following evening. She was breezy and reassuring. Everything would be fine, Jess was a good kid going through a bad patch. She, Jenny Tripp, was on their side, and also on Jess's side, and these were one and the same. Listening to her cheerful confidence Owen felt better than he had in a long time.

Then Jenny Tripp had told them — smiling, the bearer of glad tidings — that Jess had agreed to give evidence at Ward's trial. It was a brave decision and she would need their support. Marion was saying, of course, they would be there for Jess. Owen could hardly object, especially to the nice Ms Tripp, but was stricken by a vision of Ward in the dock pointing at Owen. *That man is an arsonist.* A muted gasp, heads turning to stare.

AT WHAREKOHA JESS realised that, as an outlaw, she had much to learn. Taking your father's car was for beginners, though pranging it showed some promise. Friendships at the home were of the hothouse variety, blooming brightly, bruising easily, dying fast. Jess promised Elpie, without too much prompting, that they would be friends forever. But Wharekoha was the best place Elpie had ever lived and she was ready to stay as long as they'd have her, while Jess knew it was only a pause in her life, a kind of preparation.

Marion came to visit, confirming this. A date had been set for the court hearing and Marion was on the verge of a good sale, anticipating the money. They would go shopping in Auckland, just Marion and Jess, with Owen to drive them round. Sheenagh and Corin could stay with their schoolfriends and Owen had arranged for Mrs Cawley to relieve at the school.

'You don't need to come,' Jess said. 'You guys don't have to bother. They'll take me there.' She gave her mother a trembling smile.

'But we want to, dear. To support you. And then we'll all go home and everything'll be back to normal.'

*Back to normal.* Jess tried to remember, like visualising wallpaper that you'd seen for too long and hadn't chosen in the first place. Never, she thought. Never, for me.

FROM THE MOTEL in Herne Bay they could see flashes of the harbour, even a small section of the bridge. If not from their unit, at least from the balcony that circled the upper floor. Jess glanced at the water briefly, then turned to squint at the jumbled, roaring city or rather the buildings that blocked it from view. Even now Frank could be looking out at those very same buildings, a view distorted by bars, but the same ugly, glittering concrete towers. Did he have a sense of this — of their proximity, his and Jess's? Did he know she'd agreed to come? Did he hate her?

They had driven north, Jess, Marion and Owen, in shining weather. One of those days before summer's been around long enough to be taken for granted, when the land sparkles and the air is thick with honeysuckle and jasmine. Their bags were in the boot — Jess's big bag with the clothes she had at Wharekoha, beside Marion and Owen's overnight bag. Jess had waved to Elpie until she was no longer in sight.

Marion had chatted most of the way, about the sale she'd pulled off, the things she would buy, the possibility of drought, the strain of Christmas, the deteriorating quality of fifteen denier pantyhose. To Jess her mother's voice was like rain on a roof, impersonal yet comforting. Owen drove in almost total silence. Jess would sometimes turn her eyes from the window and study her father's scalp beneath long strands of pale hair, his freckled arms. She tried to think about nothing.

Only once in the three and a half hours of their journey was Frank or his court case referred to. Attracted by the festive air of people clustered at the picnic tables of a roadside tea-rooms, the Benningtons had stopped for Devonshire teas. As they returned to Owen's freshly panel-beaten Ford, Marion suddenly said to Jess, 'So — tomorrow I'll finally set eyes on your fancy man!'

Owen made a small incredulous sound. Glared at Marion, glanced unhappily at Jess. Who was dribbling the words around her mouth, sweet and sharp as honey. *Her fancy man.* Jess and Frank. Bonnie and Clyde. Some couples just made to be larger than life.

Having examined their motel unit — bathroom, double bedroom, and a space that served as kitchen, living room and single bedroom, recurring brown and gold and slightly shabby — and laid claim by way of scattering a few possessions, Marion and Jess hit the shops.

Not appliances this time, but clothes. Marion manoeuvred them adroitly in and out of cavernous showrooms, flipping through racks, clutching coathangers to her chin as she gazed in mirrors, stroking, poking, peering, dodging. Jess trailed in her mother's wake, passing opinion when requested.

'Will I regret this, d'you think? Too bunchy here? Too tight across the shoulders? No? Yellow or green? I've suddenly got a taste for yellow. With my hair this colour yellow seems to . . . Is it me? No, tell me the truth. Why don't *you* try it? The blue one. Just pull it on over . . . There! Don't scowl. Have a look. What do you think?'

Marion bought herself yellow slingback shoes with lacy fronts and plain white courts with medium heels. White was *in* — shoes, trousers, jackets, tops: racks and shelves of whiteness. 'It grows on you,' said Marion. 'It definitely does.' She bought a white jacket and skirt and trousers. An ensemble. Marion and the saleswoman tossed the word between them as if they were about to shoot a goal. To go with this she bought a yellow blouse that wouldn't crease, and a grey and yellow sweatshirt.

Clutching the bags with their assorted labels they found a coffee bar. While Jess ate caramel éclairs Marion peeked into the bags and lamented on Jess's inability to make a decision on her own behalf. So they returned, then, to a previous shop and Jess chose a grey sweatshirt and a pair of fat white sneakers but rejected the dresses Marion and the salesgirl paraded before her.

Hours later, back at the motel, Marion showed Owen the

ensemble that she planned to wear to court in the morning. She complained about Jess's refusal to have a nice new dress for the event. 'It's not a wedding,' said Owen, then glanced quickly at Jess to see if the remark was somehow offensive to her. Marion unpacked Jess's only dress — high collar and flared skirt, green and blue daisies on a white background — and sent her to the motel laundry to iron it ready for the morning.

Jess hung the ironed dress on a coathanger she'd found in the laundry. Then she put on her new sneakers and new sweatshirt and brushed her hair and tied it back, and cleaned her teeth. She walked between her parents to a Chinese restaurant that Owen had sorted out while they were shopping. They walked past other restaurants, where city people sat on display right next to the windows fiddling with forks and wine glasses, and on to the Chinese restaurant that was much like the Chinese restaurant in Windsor, and where you ate in private in the diffused red glow of ornate lampshades and you could be anywhere at all — Bangkok, Sydney, Windsor.

'Tomorrow,' Owen said to Jess after the waiter had taken their orders, 'it's only a matter of answering their questions. You'll be fine.' He looked ill.

'I know.' Jess didn't meet his eye.

'You're doing the right thing,' said Marion mechanically. She was looking around her disappointedly at the other diners, only a handful of them and casually dressed. 'Tomorrow,' she told Owen, 'we'll find a menswear shop and get you a decent jacket.'

When they'd eaten they walked around the block, looked in at cafés where other people were eating and at the big old shambling houses, counting the letter boxes, imagining all those people living cheek by jowl and maybe not even knowing their neighbours. Then back to the motel and to bed, a big day ahead.

Jess was discomforted by her parents' proximity. They closed their door, but not entirely. She heard them exchange a few brisk words then fall into silence.

She lay awake, wide awake. Listening to the roar and whine of the city, watching the yellow numbers on the bedside clock taking their time. Forcing herself to wait just a little longer.

Even so, when she finally crept out of the motel, leaving the daisy dress on its hanger and taking only a few clothes crammed into the crackly plastic bag from the department store, she knew at once that it was too early; that, at four o'clock in the morning, she was absurdly conspicuous on these lit but deserted streets.

So she headed, at first, downhill to the snatches of bush that could be glimpsed between the old mansions with multiple letter boxes, the motel hoardings and the new concrete mansions like high-rise water tanks with balconies. All of them jostling for space, and Jess scuttling past and between them, taking note of shrubs or fences she could duck behind if a car turned into this street, or the next one. Zigzagging so her path led not just down but further away from the motel where her parents were sleeping.

At the bottom of a street she came to wooden steps that took her beneath the pohutukawas and down to a tiny stretch of sand banked by tide-worn clay. Through the branches she could see snatches of the harbour bridge, the arcing car lights. She sat with her knees pulled in beneath her chin and waited for daylight and its trickle of early workers.

From a phone box outside a service station she rang the number of Frank's ex-wife's friend. Was about to hang up when it was finally answered. A dark and crumpled voice. 'I'm Frank Ward's friend,' Jess whispered. 'I need to see you.'

At the service station counter she bought two Crunchie bars and a minimap of the city. Sussex Street was only five blocks away. She took a roundabout route, choosing small streets and a leisurely pace.

She climbed the stairs and knocked on the door. Then knocked again a little louder. Heavy footsteps, then the door opened fractionally. A big brown woman staring at Jess through a mean slit of space.

'I'm Jess. I rang. A while ago.'

The eyes in their shadowy circles considered Jess for a moment longer, then the door was pulled back.

'I'm sorry,' said Jess, stepping in, 'but I didn't know where else to go.'

Behind Jess the door was slammed and bolted. The woman pointed Jess through to the kitchen and disappeared. Jess heard her voice, urgent and angry but indistinct.

The woman returned accompanied by something in a bath robe. A man of sinister ugliness. *Big Bird*, thought Jess. He was tall, pale, beaked and bald. Skinny, veined legs and scrawny feet. They stared at Jess; she felt their contempt.

'I'm Debbie Reynolds and this is Crystal.' She looked at the man beside her and winced. 'I think she'd like you better with your hair on.'

The man clutched at his scalp. 'Oh dear.'

Debbie said to Jess. 'Now perhaps you could tell us what's going on?'

OFFICER JENNY TRIPP, who had travelled to Auckland independently, rang the Benningtons' motel unit at eight thirty.

'Good morning, Owen. Jenny Tripp here. Everything okay?'

'I think so, Jenny. Jess isn't here at the moment — but I imagine she's gone for a stroll. Marion says her good clothes are still here.'

'When did she go out, Owen?'

'We only woke . . . maybe an hour ago. She was gone then. You think . . .?'

'She may have got cold feet. That'd be quite understandable. I'll get them to put out a call, just in case. And I'm on my way round.'

Owen replaced the receiver. Marion, in a lacy white slip and stockinged feet, waiting.

'She's coming round.'

'Oh great. So what do I wear? I mean, are we going or aren't we?'

'There's still plenty of time,' Owen soothed. 'She'll turn up.'

He had an urge to laugh. The whole thing was surreal. With luck, Jess might change her mind and they could all go home and forget the whole sordid business.'

Marion was sliding her new white skirt from the hanger. 'I'm going,' she said. 'I'm going anyway. I want to set eyes on this monster my husband punched over.'

Was she mocking him?

'Then go,' he said. 'No one's stopping you. But I'm only here because of Jess. I've no desire to see the sod. None at all.'

Jess, he thought, please change your mind. Be a coward, disappoint the nice Jenny Tripp, get us all out of this ridiculous nightmare.

HE STOOD AGAINST the wall of the courtroom corridor — not quite against it because it had that sense of grime removed but remaining, in the way the tossed-down cigarettes stayed forever as small black bullets in the lino, and the scratched obscenities were etched beneath the paint. The people flowed past him, dreadlocks, scars, tattoos, black stretch pants with the double white stripes bulging like raw sausage skins. Lawyers in rapid conversation, court officials, the lost and the bored.

Marion was inside the courtroom, decked out like a wedding guest. If he stepped to the door with its peep-hole window he could see her there, conspicuously — suspiciously — overdressed. The young man with the disfigured face, skin tucked into his collar like a draw-string bag pulled closed, was still in the dock. What had he done? Owen was stirred to curiosity but not enough to enter the room. He would ask Marion later. As long as Jess was still on the loose there was no reason for Owen to be in there.

Jenny Tripp's face in the corridor traffic, bobbing and twisting towards him like a leaf on the water. Jaunty. Seeing Owen she shook her head.

'Don't worry. I'm sure she'll be all right.' She'd reached Owen, touched his arm. 'I feel responsible. It was a lot to ask. Too much, I guess.'

'You're not to blame.' Owen's voice boomed in his head, he turned it down. 'If it's anyone's fault, it has to be mine.' He hoped she wouldn't ask him to explain that. He didn't even believe it.

She was smiling at him.

'What?'

'I see a lot in this job. The parents I would hold to blame are almost always the ones who insist they're not.' The smile again. Such approval. Again Owen imagined Ward in the dock, pointing and accusing. Jenny Tripp's smile gone forever.

'So what happens now?' he asked her.

'They won't give us much longer.' She looked at her watch, grimaced. 'Shall I let you know when he's called?'

'Don't bother,' Owen told her. 'I'd be happy never to set eyes on the blighter again.'

'Blighter! I haven't heard that word since my dad died.'

She moved off with a little wave of her hand. Owen watched her bobbing away upstream, probing unhappily at her parting remark. Her father? Was it the baldness?

WHEN FRANK WAS, eventually, called into the courtroom it was past lunch time. His eyes fell at once on Debbie Reynolds and Crystal and he felt a trickle of dismay. They were, after all, his only support; he'd rather hoped they would make an effort to blend in. Then he felt ashamed of himself. Were they not top people?

From the dock he half turned and caught their eyes, threw them something a little less blatant than a smile. They immediately responded with bizarre eye signals and semi-surreptitious fisted salutes that Frank could do without and pretended not to notice.

He would remember, later, the woman in the white suit and blood-red lipstick. Would remember her clearly, but only because he'd thought at the time that there was a stylistic resemblance between her and Debbie Reynolds and had looked closer, though unsuccessfully, for signs of emerging stubble on the jaw.

He'd had plenty of time to gaze about him. The judge was in conversation with a court official. The murmuring of the public grew as people waited. The judge was glancing across at Frank. A different judge, lean-faced and possibly younger than Frank. After a time the official moved back to his seat. The judge slapped down his gavel and, in the swift silence, announced that this case had already been held off for two hours at the prosecution's request and he felt that was enough time to have been wasted.

'The prosecution's crucial witness has' — the judge smirked, perhaps at his own grasp of the vernacular, perhaps to punish the police for inefficiency — 'done a bunk.' He looked across at Frank. 'The case against you, Mr Ward, is dismissed.'

C H A **16** E R

JESS STARED OUT the window, looked at her watch, thumbed through a magazine, looked at her watch, opened the fridge though she wasn't hungry. They'd offered her breakfast, watched her trying to swallow toast and honey. Had softened towards her after she'd told them her story, but still she'd felt they didn't like her.

They'd dressed for court. Big Bird in a wig rigid with hairspray, and a screaming green dress. Jess wanting to laugh, though partly just from satisfaction at all this being so *remarkable*, befitting the story she'd now stepped into.

The two of them parading, primping and adjusting jewellery, no better than Marion. Then leaving Jess with the television and four issues of the *Woman's Weekly*, stuck in a vacuum, waiting for the story to unfold.

Then, as the hours went past, the waiting became something in itself. It caused her body to tremble and her teeth to chatter. It made her lonely and scared. If they sent him back to prison . . . if he couldn't forgive her . . . what kind of a story would that be?

WHEN THEY ARRIVED the afternoon was halfway gone. She heard voices but couldn't even look out the window in case it was only Debbie and Crystal.

Then Frank stepped inside and stood there looking at Jess, and her shaking got worse, until he came forward and put his arms around her and she inhaled the lovely musty booze smell of his breath.

'This,' he told Debbie and Crystal over her head, 'is a top person.' And Jess was no longer trembling, was no longer waiting.

Yet, within the hour, Frank was wanting to take her back to the motel and her parents. Making it sound like a reasonable thing to do, though his voice was a bit blurry due to the bottles Debbie Reynolds had carried in.

Jess, on only her second glass, was feeling a turbulence in her stomach. She sat there, struggling with disbelief, while Frank explained how easy it would be — Jess would tell her parents she was sorry but she just hadn't felt able to go through with the court thing. They would understand, they would be so happy to see her. She would go home with them, get on with her schooling and wait the ten months until she was sixteen.

And then?

Then, in all probability, Frank would come and get her. Depending on how he was placed.

Jess's jaw jammed. Words of dismay and rejection buzzed in her head like caught flies. She could read in his face that she was another problem he didn't need.

'Don't worry,' the words rasping her throat, 'if you don't want me I won't hang around. I can look after m'self.'

He rubbed his hands down over his face, pushing the skin into new folds. That's how he'd look when he got old. Older.

'Don't be bloody daft,' he said. 'We'll sort something out.'


IN VERY SMALL printing Frank could fit all his problems on the flap of a Zig-Zag packet. Kids taken. Broke. No job. No house. Jess under age. In terms of magnitude he couldn't decide what order they should come in, but some were clearly easier to tackle than others.

They took Jess to stay with Crystal's sister, Cheryl, in Point Chevalier, for the police were bound to track Frank down to Sussex Street and come searching. Which they did.

Frank went each day to visit Jess, eyes on the run like a spy in case he was watched, though logic told him one more missing teenager was scarcely a matter on which the police would waste immense resources. He rather liked it — this cloak and dagger stuff of taking different routes, getting off at different bus stops. Always she was waiting for him, her face lighting up, shining as though they hadn't, either of them, a care in the world. Except they both knew better.

'I been thinking,' she'd told him the second day. 'I been thinking that really you're right — best I give m'self up. This way I'm just causing you heaps of trouble.' Inside him it was like a fuse shorting: not relief but profound dismay.

'If that's the only reason — on account of me — it's not reason enough.' He watched her face coming back onto full beam.

'Crikey,' he said, 'we're good to each other. I never felt this noble in me whole life.'

Her laugh was like rapids in sunlight. He wished he could find her more things to laugh about.

It wasn't a great arrangement. Cheryl wandered her own home and the city streets in an amphetamine daze, her moods swinging on a fine string in a breeze of suspicion. Her two small boys had learnt to dodge, deflect, dissemble. Jess became their baby-sitter, from choice as much as obligation. She slept on the sunporch sofa and ate as little of Cheryl's food as possible, though Crystal had made it clear Jess shouldn't feel indebted, not to Cheryl, who owed her sister more favours than she had puncture marks on her inner arms.

It wouldn't be for long Frank had promised, believing it. Jess made him feel like a man with solutions at his fingertips. He'd already jacked himself up some casual work in the kitchen of Excelsior Hotel where Crystal worked, disgruntledly, as second cook. The money was less than he needed to pay his own way, let alone Jess's. She had almost fifty dollars in her savings book but he'd told her best not to draw it out, they'd be waiting for that, would get the local coppers to keep an eye out. Besides, he wasn't so low as to have a schoolgirl plunder her life savings on his account. Not yet, at any rate. What he needed was a proper job and place for them to lie low in.

Within a week he'd sorted something out. Recalling the conversation he'd had with the disillusioned stockman when he'd first arrived in Auckland — the phone number lost — Frank had stood in the library, methodically searching out East Coast stock and station agents. Had rung them with a yarn near enough to the truth and tracked down a few numbers of possible employers. More calls that evening and he'd come up with two possibilities. One of them had a couple of vacancies but wouldn't take anyone sight unseen. 'I'll be there Friday.'

He was ready to hitch. On foot wasn't the smartest way to turn up for a job interview but at least it would show he was keen. If they took him on, and he figured they would, he'd find some local trucker who was willing to fetch Maguilla and the dogs on time payment, and as soon as he could Frank would send Jess the bus fare. So he was ready to hitch, but Debbie Reynolds offered to take him. She had relations in Masterton who might or might not be pleased to see her, she was happy to take a long route there, she was bored with Auckland.

Frank could see the disadvantages. Fronting up for a job interview in the company of Debbie Reynolds could be less auspicious than arriving on foot. But what could he say? 'You're a bottler, Debbie.'

Then Jess wanted to come too, her bottom lip quivering like a toddler's so he nearly gave in, but, 'Believe me,' he told her, 'the less the employer sees the better. Least at this stage.'

'You could drop me off,' she said.' Me 'n' Debbie could wait in Wairau.'

'Best not,' he told her. 'I reckon not.'

His bones informed him that Debbie Reynolds' offer had been to Frank alone. The problem with being beholden was this need to second-guess the conditions applying.

THE VALIANT WAS burning oil so they stopped regularly at gas stations. Frank, too, needed topping up, but Debbie would throw a quick glance at the pubs and press her foot down. This was dangerous country.

'I'll bring you one out to the car,' coaxed Frank.

Debbie made a sharp nasal sound, not quite a laugh. 'When I want to revisit my childhood I'll let you know, darling heart.'

At Rotorua they compromised. Frank bought cans at a bottle store and they drank them on the way. It wasn't the way he liked to do it; pubs were part of travelling. Another town, another bar-room.

They drove up into the ranges in silence. Frank felt his heart quickening as he looked out at rugged hills, at bush. He touched the skin above his wrist, the inside of his arm. The sight of hills, the smell of them, the old opossum trapper he'd got talking to as they waited to be called into court had told Frank that the sight of natural country tightened the skin. Frank thought he could feel it — his limp city skin retracting to fit his flesh.

He'd have discussed this phenomenon with Debbie, but Debbie was driving like someone watching a friend die of terminal illness. She had turned off the radio the better to hear the intermittent muffled shriek that came from somewhere beneath them. They'd already stopped and searched the chassis but seen no clues. Frank's knowledge of motor mechanics was sparse and

Debbie's was nil. They should ask at a garage, but Debbie wouldn't have it. Burning up oil was enough to worry about.

So Debbie drove and listened and regretted (Frank figured) the rashness of her offer. If she'd stayed at home the noise might never have happened. He decided he couldn't ask Debbie to let him drive alone up to the station. Even if having her with him meant losing the job, the whole journey for nothing.

At Wairau they had steak and eggs and chips and a trickle of grated cabbage. Debbie had edged herself into the space between stool and table and, like a sliding door on its tracks, could go nowhere but sideways. If she ate too much, possibly not even there. In Debbie's enormous hand the greasy cut-glass bottle of Worcestershire sauce disappeared from view.

'How far is this farm place then?'

Frank had the map set between them, was studying it. 'I think it's this road here. Hang on.'

He asked the pale young woman selling grocery items in the other half of the room.

'Ah, yeah. Follow that maybe twenty minutes then left at the fork then maybe another ten minutes and you'll see it on your left.'

'Twenty minutes then left and ten minutes and left again. Thanks.'

'Depending on how fast you drive.'

'I drive slow,' he told her, in case Debbie was taking it in.

'Twenty minutes then. You looking for work?'

'Sure am.'

She looked him up and down, looked past him at his large friend and said nothing. Frank went back to Debbie.

'Ask about motels,' said Debbie, then swallowed. 'I wanna find me a bed and a TV set. Cheapest.'

So Frank got to leave Debbie at a camping-ground cabin and drive back up into the foothills alone, listening to the metallic screech beneath him and reciting Banjo Patterson.

He got the job. A month's trial. The manager was the jumpy type — pinched-in nostrils and busy eyes — but the wife seemed a decent sort. Three kids still at primary school. Frank had his story about Jess, which had been waiting in his head unassembled till he saw how the land lay. But even now he couldn't be sure who he was pitching to. Decided on caution, said she was his niece; could ride like nobody's business but didn't have a horse of her own; had worked on her old man's farm up until he died and the second wife — her stepmother — grabbed the lot.

'To look at her,' he told them, warming to it, 'you'd think she was still a kid, but in fact she's going on nineteen.'

The manager walked Frank down a metal road to show him the quarters where they would live. The manager hadn't bargained on taking a young woman; it would mean two of the men sharing. Frank said that was okay by him but he pitied his room-mate, he'd been told he snored something chronic.

Frank met his two fellow workers, Wipo and Hans, and the manager walked him back to the main house. 'About your niece,' he said. 'I'll give it some thought.'

''Preciate that.' Frank removed his hat to scratch his head. 'How soon were you looking at me starting?'

'Soon as you can. Is there a problem?'

'No, no. Just I have to ride my horse over from Te Kuiti way. Figure it'll take a few days.' Frank slapped his hat back on. 'Tell you what, if you could write me out a few lines just to say I got a job here, I'll be okay for credit. That way I could get a carrier.'

'Hire a float,' said the manager. 'Stick it behind that flashy old auto of yours.'

Frank had the job, was safe now. 'Only problem with that is she ain't mine.'

They had stepped into the kitchen. Frank could see the manager's face, watched it closely, but could read no reaction.

When he got back to the camping ground Debbie was pretending to be asleep. Waking up ostentatiously, all that stretching and blinking. That's how it seemed to Frank. Like a woman when you came home late, pretending she hadn't been waiting, her fury on hold.

Debbie acting that way made him nervous, had him talking fast and hearty, hoping he had it wrong. He owed Debbie Reynolds, no denying. Owed her everything. Almost everything.

'So what now, darling heart?' Her voice like a big cat purring.

'What now?' Frank heard this feeble echo, pulled himself together. 'I gotta work out how to get Maguilla and the dogs out here.'

'You tired?' Debbie propped herself up on her elbow, lemon

nightdress like a stage curtain rippling from shoulder to shoulder, a hint of cleavage. Like looking from high above into calm deep water, the impulse to jump was there. Frank wrenched his eyes away.

'Depends,' he said.

Debbie began to shake quietly. Her hormone-assisted breasts wobbled against the yellow curtain. She pursed her lips and blew Frank a kiss then lumbered out of bed. Moving slowly, deliberately like some big animal. 'I've had a nap,' she said. 'If we leave now we'll be in Windsor by daylight. You can sleep on my shoulder.' She widened her eyes at Frank and giggled again.

He gave her a sick sort of grin, the good-sport kind, but he was angry. She'd looked inside his head and laughed. One of those big tough mean girls from the school playground, pointing and shrieking at your pissed pants.

MAC AND SALLY came hurtling up the road towards the Valiant.

'Christ,' said Debbie. 'Look at that. I don't believe it. They knew.'

''Course they bloody knew,' said Frank.

Debbie had woken him an hour ago to take the wheel. He'd slid across while Debbie got out and went round the back. Above the idling motor he'd heard her piss hitting the road.

He'd driven for maybe ten minutes before he noticed.

'Hey, Debbie, you know something? That noise's gone.'

She yawned. 'It stopped way back. So either it was something caught up that shouldn't've been there, or something's dropped off that ought to be there.'

'That's a point,' said Frank and eased his foot from the accelerator.

Now he pulled over and got out to meet the dogs. Sal leaping up, a grin on her face. Mac on his belly writhing like a stranded fish. 'Didn't I tell you I'd be back!'

He let them in on the back seat, saw Debbie wince a little.

'They're not too dirty, ' he said, 'and it's been a while.'

Debbie heaved herself round to stare at the dogs as they drove to Judy's gateway.

'That love? Or just that you've got a smell that carries a long way?'

But Frank was thinking how he hadn't been in touch with

Judy all this time and how much did she know, and how much did she need to know?

'Now Judy Gordon,' he said to Debbie, 'she's a top woman and all, straight as a die. That's the trouble. So maybe I ought to do the talking?'

'You do anyway,' said Debbie.

Judy was still in her dressing gown. Frank apologised — for the hour of the day, for burdening her with his animals, for his failure to keep in touch.

'But I guess you heard what happened?'

'You were acquitted — that's what I heard. Insufficient evidence.'

'Yeah,' said Frank. 'That's about it.' Trying to read her face, the strange little smile it wore.

'I should bloody hope so,' she said. 'The place was insured, you know. Well insured. And now Charlie Webster's buying the property. What does that tell you?'

She thought he'd been facing a charge of arson. Frank caught Debbie's eye for half a second. 'I dunno,' he told Judy. 'I don't wanna think about it. Just want to get on with my life now.' What did she know about Jess? Safer, maybe, not to ask.

While Judy made them coffee Frank took the bridle and went up to get Maguilla. The stallion ran towards him but dodged away when Frank reached out. On the skinny side and his hooves in need of attention but still his good looks had Frank standing there with his jaw dangling.

Again the horse stepped towards Frank then leapt aside. 'I know,' Frank told him, 'but it couldn't be helped. And you did okay.' He looked around at Judy's land, the grass cropped like a threadbare carpet (and he hadn't even asked her if she'd made any sales, how she was managing) and the stallion moved up again and, this time, pressed his nose against Frank's face. 'Yeah,' said Frank, his hand had been missing touching this hairy skin. 'Yeah, yeah, boy.' Frank's nose had missed this smell of horse, the best smell in the world. 'Yeah, mate, Maguilla old boy.'

When he got back to the house Debbie told him, 'The girl's missing.'

'What girl?'

'Jess,' said Judy.

'The police came,' Debbie reporting, enjoying this, 'and wanted to know if Judy had heard from her.'

'She could be back home by now. She hasn't been in touch. I didn't like to ring her family and ask, and no one's mentioned. But then I keep pretty much to myself.' She was looking at Frank. Seeing what? 'You could ring,' she said. 'And see.'

'Why?'

Judy looked bewildered. 'I thought you and her were friends.'

He almost told her — some people made even the necessary lies clog up your mouth — but then thought better of it. Told her, instead, about the job.

'How will you get Maguilla there?'

'I'll ride,' he said. 'I'll give him new shoes this afternoon and I'll ride him over.' He didn't look at Debbie. She'd got him this far and he was grateful. All the same he was hoping for her to offer, the way a hitch-hiker who keeps walking is banking on the psychology that people are more inclined to help the man who seems willing to help himself.

'I'll take you,' said Judy.

'No,' said Frank. 'No. You've done too much already.' A chink of uncertainty in his voice to show he'd be open to persuasion, though he was still hoping Debbie would put in an offer. Better if no one from Curvey's Creek — not even Judy — knew where to find him.

'Hey,' said Debbie, 'she's got a horse float. Don't be a fool, darling heart.'

'I'd like to take you,' said Judy and gave Frank a steady look into which he read that she was lonely and really would be glad of an excuse to get away from this sour little valley. (Though driving in on a fine day such as this, when it sparkled with willows and toi-toi, the physical beauty of the place had felt almost edible.)

Beside the dusty Valiant, Debbie enveloped Frank in her arms and whispered, 'You owe me, darling heart.'

'I owe you,' he agreed.

Her tongue crawled into his ear — a large pink slug. His head jerked sideways. Debbie laughed. 'But I can wait,' she told him. 'I can wait until you're old and derelict and unwanted. I'll pick you up from some cockroach-infested pavement stinking of meths. And I'll take you home, cowboy, and have my way with you.'

Then she wedged herself in behind the wheel and drove away.

Judy and Frank set off the next morning with Mac and Sal in

the back of the ute and Maguilla behind. Frank had a feeling of completeness, of optimism, that he hadn't felt in a long time. He watched the roadside pubs roll past with only a small yearning and now and again he thought of the girl who would be expecting him back maybe about now, although his plans had always been open-ended. He'd write to her from the station, send her the bus fare out of his first pay. He should feel pleased that they were prepared to give her a go, but it was all too fast, too easy. He could hear things falling into place and the sound was ominously similar to that of a cage door snapping shut.

Judy talked occasionally about her horses, seeking Frank's advice or reassurance on this one or that. Lately, she told him, she'd been regretting her move to Curvey's Creek. She'd imagined that the land, her animals, would be enough, that the people didn't matter — and in any case would in time come to accept her in a neighbourly fashion, which was the most she would ever require of them. But since the fire, since Frank left, she had not felt at ease in the valley. There was a sourness in the air, it gave her headaches. With no one in sight she often felt under observation.

Frank said, 'I stuffed it up for you. You'd've been fine if I hadn't come along.'

'Maybe. Maybe not.' Suddenly they'd caught up with the rainclouds that all morning had been peeling back as fast as they drove towards them. The windscreen became a creek in the seconds before Judy got the wipers into action, and there was a jolt from behind as Maguilla rearranged himself. Frank looked round at the dogs. Sal was pressed against the cab for an ounce of shelter but Mac, stupid Mac, stood braced against the downpour, eyes screwed shut, a drowning rat.

The rain stopped as fast as it had begun. 'At the time,' said Judy, now that her voice could be heard again, 'I thought I was glad to see the last of you. But, if you want to know the truth, I missed you, Frank.'

He heard the way her voice changed, saw her head tilt aside. Thought, oh shit — he didn't need this, neither did she.

'I didn't hear that, Judy. Sometimes I get this partial deafness, y' see. Didn't hear it.'

She gave him a look he couldn't read. Perhaps it was loathing. If she had any sense it would've been gratitude. Some other man might have taken advantage.

The rest of the journey they made small talk like a couple of social misfits at a party. Frank wanted to find something to say to put them back where they'd been, make it all okay again, but let himself down by not being able to. It seemed such a waste of a friendship, with no one having done anything wrong.

But at least this way, if she found out he hadn't quite told her the truth about things, it wasn't going to matter.

IT WAS TEN days before his first letter reached her. A black time with her trust seeping away. Even Curvey's Creek seemed okay compared with the boredom, the tarseal, the grinding ugliness of Cheryl's life. Jess began to suspect she *should have known better*.

The city felt and smelt muggy and metallic. Day after day moisture hung in the air, an oppressive greyness, nicotine-stained where the sun was attempting to get through. Jess was a listless ant stranded inside a tin can. If she went more than a few steps up the street she might not hear the phone ringing.

Then his letter came. Seven pages of words that sang shingle-voiced in her head. He was waiting for her, so was a seventeen-hand station hack and a job — a real job. Her new name was Gillian — Gillian? — Ward and she was Frank's niece. Next week he would send her the Road Services ticket. And maybe she should put some dye through her hair. Brown was a good service-able kind of colour. A twenty-dollar note.

She wrote back to him in the printing kind of writing her teachers had despaired of. Then copied it out, but still it looked no better. She hoped he wouldn't hold her letter against her. She signed it *Gillian*. She wore a wispy fringe and her dark brown hair ended unevenly just below her shoulders. She was still grieving for her dead father, and shocked by the depths of her step-mother's greed. Within a week the bus ticket came.

A DESERTED STREET and an empty bus stop. The driver wasn't happy about leaving her there in the dark, alone.

'He'll be here,' Jess told him. 'Any moment now.'

She smiled at the driver, backing across the footpath as his door slid closed. And she kept on smiling at the bus until it disappeared around the corner, in case the driver was glancing back. Then she took the drawstring bag from her shoulder and sat down on it, to wait.

The day before she'd drawn her savings out of the Post Office and bought some work clothes from St Vincent de Paul. There wasn't much choice but they'd have to do. She'd also bought the bag.

When the bus stopped at Rotorua Jess had found a post box and dropped in a letter to her parents, the way Frank had told her she should. Just a few words saying she was alive and well and not to worry. Otherwise, Frank wrote, they'd be in the same state of not knowing as he was in over Ruby and Ben.

Jess was happy to wait. Happy to be out of the bus, to be breathing fresh air, to be at last in the vicinity of Frank. Was happy for the first ten minutes and only a little anxious for the next ten. Then had just begun to look around for a phone box when Wipo came running up.

'You Gillian?'

'Um . . . yeah.'

'I'm Wipo.' He giggled and held out his hand. Jess shook it vigorously. He didn't look a whole lot older than her. Wipo picked up her bag and slung it over his shoulder, jerked his head to show her which way they were going.

'Been waiting long then?'

'No,' said Jess.

'Must've brought the good weather with you.'

She couldn't find anything to say to that. Where was Frank?

'Been heaving down, last couple of days. Shearers had to pack up and leave. Don't s'pose you done any shearing?'

'No,' said Jess, but trying to sound interested. This was what she was meant to be here for.

'A bit under the weather.' Muttered, as if to himself.

'What?' Politely.

'Your uncle,' he told her.

'Sorry?'

Wipo sighed patiently.

'Your uncle. Pissed as, y'know. I'm teetotal, me.'

The frosted pub windows, voices like the low buzzing of bees. Wipo followed Jess between the parked cars, reached over her shoulder to open the heavy door into the bar. Jess looked past the empty tables, saw Frank's hat, Frank beneath it, his head turned up to the tall bearded man leaning on the bar beside him.

Jess floated towards Frank. The bearded man had seen her,

gave Frank a nudge. Jess's smile broke through as Frank turned his head. She took the last few steps towards him.

'Hi,' she whispered.

Frank stared at her.

*He doesn't know me.* Jess grinned at him, but uncertainly. He was looking at her yet she felt as if that person he was looking at was someone Jess didn't know.

'What is it?' Still whispering.

'Look at you!' So loud he could have been heard from the deserted bus shelter. 'Take a look! Who d'you reckon you are? Eh?'

The bearded man held his face very still. His eyes swung from Frank to Jess and back again. Out of the corner of her eye Jess could see Wipo lowering her bag to the floor.

'What the fuck took you so long?' Frank near enough screaming, hurling the words into the frozen face of Jess. Or Gillian. Or whoever it was his reddened eyes were seeing.

PART *T* WO

C H A P T E R **17**

'SO ON THE bus she gets, her hair dyed and hacked off like you'd swear someone took shears to her. This Gillian. I tell you, I was so nervous about the whole set-up, how we were gonna carry it off with none of them putting two and two together, and the day she arrived and the shearing had been rained off so we went in early. And I was bloody apprehensive so I'd downed a few drinks.'

'You were rotten drunk,' Jess says and glances at their friend Del, who rolls her eyes.

'Moderately pissed,' Frank amends, 'and with good reason. There's Jess, a straightforward kind of girl and I've got her set up to pretend she's someone else, that there's nothing between us. And of course if someone cottoned on that there was, and me being her uncle and all, well it would've looked like . . . well they'd've thought, this guy is as bent as a barnacle.'

Monty guffaws appreciation, slaps his thigh. Del is grinning as she edges a menthol tailormade out of the pack. Frank refills his glass and Monty's.

'But they never did catch you?' prompts Monty.

'There was some close shaves. Her tippy-toeing into my room and Hans, a Dutchman, big hunk of a fella he was, sees her, so she says, quick thinking, there's this mouse in her room, she was gonna get me to come and grab it. So there's the three of us pulling her room apart in search of a bloody mouse which two of us knew never existed.

'Another night there was this helluva storm, so we knew it was risky and sure enough the manager comes to get us to move the stock in the river paddock — it was right up, way over its bank — and I had to scramble out Jess's window. Grabbed a shirt on the way — and it was hers too, only one of those plaid jobs so it wasn't too obvious — then had to come in wearing nothing at all bar this bloody shirt and pretending I'd just nipped out for a leak.'

'I reckon Wipo knew,' says Jess.

'Only if you told him,' says Frank and his voice has a steel edge.

Jess sighs into the silence that follows. All four of them avoid each other's eyes.

Del comes to the rescue. 'How many workers were on this place?'

'Us and two others,' says Frank. His usual voice.

Del looks at Jess. 'And you were doing the same job they were?'

'Sort of.' Jess looks at her glass, half full of Coke, and thinks that if she learned to like beer she wouldn't feel like the odd one out.

'Only she worked harder.' Frank was back in stride. 'Put us all to shame.'

'Rubbish,' says Jess, embarrassed but pleased.

'Well you did a darned sight more than the Dutchman,' says Frank. 'Hans was a laid-back sort of coot, wouldn't lift a finger if he didn't absolutely have to. Whereas Jess — well they set her up with this mean-minded gelding —'

'Dougal.'

'Manager and his wife had Scottish connections. Dougal! A bad-tempered lump of horse-flesh like you don't expect in a gelding, but maybe they'd cut him late so he knew what he was missing out on and was sore about that.'

'He wasn't *that* mean,' Jess defends.

'Not with you, he wasn't. With Jess he was like a goddamn lamb. Wouldn't know him. With Gillian, I mean. First day out and I'm fair shitting myself on her behalf on account of what I've got her into and there she is cool as could be, so you'd almost've sworn she was this young woman who'd been running her dad's farm single-handed while he was croaking on his death-bed. Sometimes I bloody near believed it m'self. Wouldn't've taken her for a schoolteacher's daughter.'

'But there were farms all around us,' Jess points out. 'Besides, I just did stuff the way you told me to do it.'

'Well, Frank'd know,' says Monty. 'Never met anyone knows animals the way Frank does.'

Frank grins and scratches his head.

'Worst part,' says Jess, who is locked into the memory now

and doesn't want to let it go, 'was keeping up all that bullshit. Specially with the boss and his wife who were good people. I hated us lying to her.'

'But then, if we'd told them the truth it would've put them on the spot as much as us. I reckon, anyway, she'd figured it out, sometimes the way she'd look at us. But she would've thought the less she knew soonest mended.'

'They didn't want us to leave,' says Jess. A hint of reproach.

'They knew we would. Hell, we were working our arses off and scrimping and saving every penny. I had to get back here and look for Ben.'

'That wasn't the only reason.' Jess says this softly and again she glances at Del.

'That and having to sneak about like we were trapped in a monastery.'

Jess smiles faintly and lets it go, but later, when the men have gone out to look at the perished hose on the Torana's radiator and Del is helping Jess sort and fold yesterday's washing, she tells Del. 'Y'know the real reason he was so keen to leave? He was jealous. And there was no cause. But it got so I couldn't even talk to Wipo or Hans without him getting into a state. And he'd take it out on me when he got drinking.'

'Typical,' says Del. Jess knows she's talking about men in general and Monty and Frank in particular.

Perhaps she shouldn't have told Del, who is bound to tell Monty, who will report it back to Frank, who won't be impressed. Jess isn't sure why she needed to tell, especially that last bit. Which Frank, of course, will absolutely deny if it gets back to him. She remembers how, at the time, his jealousy had made her feel good. Proof of his love. Even now it pleases her, to tell the truth.

BUT FRANK WAS right in saying they had left the Lands and Survey block because of Ben. Left even earlier than they'd planned to because a letter had come from Frank's sister, Helen, in Australia saying that, out of the blue, Lisa had rung her. Not for any apparent reason, but she had mentioned that she was now living in Maitland, and Helen thought Frank would want to know.

'Just mentioned it, my arse,' said Frank. 'What Lisa says she says for a reason and the reason must be she wants me to know.

And why would she do that? What I think is she's wanting to off-load the kids but won't come asking. Won't lower herself, and anyway doesn't know what kind of reception she'd get after what she did. That's what I figure.'

'Maybe she wants you back,' said Jess. This woman she'd never met but already feared.

'Fat chance,' said Frank. 'I'd sooner put my head in a gas oven on the first day of spring.'

So after that they were in a hurry to get the fare together before Lisa changed her mind. But it wasn't just the two of them, there was also Maguilla and Mac and Sally. Frank began shopping around for the cheapest way they could do it, but even so it was going to take them another few weeks. Then, on an afternoon off when Wipo had driven them all into town, Jess bought a raffle ticket in Frank's name, and two weeks later they found Frank had won a Triumph 650. So they each had a ride on it, up and down the street, then they took it to the motorbike shop and sold it for just over half what it was worth. Enough, with their savings, to get them all on a rancid tub of a boat that was leaving from Napier in ten days.

The day before they won the motorbike Jess had turned sixteen without anybody but Frank knowing. Also, for the third month running, her period hadn't come and her breasts felt tender.

Being pregnant had made things simpler. It meant Jess didn't have to think about her family and whether they were missing her and whether the intermittent gusts of sadness that came upon her meant that she was missing them. Being pregnant made staying with Frank the right thing to do.

Jess vomited her way across the Tasman: seasickness, morning sickness — both at once, then taking turns. Frank held her, wiped her, told her tales from his past and of their future; she felt weak and grateful and in love.

TWO DAYS BEFORE they docked Frank made a decision without even knowing he had been giving it thought. He would sell Maguilla. That way he could pay Helen the remainder of the loan — money she'd have written off as a lost cause — and get him and Jess into a place in Maitland.

He should have made this decision before; everything would

have been easier. But leaving the horse in New Zealand would have felt too much like desertion. Frank still wasn't sure when or how it had happened that the girl had come to matter more than the horse.

She didn't want Maguilla to go. 'We'll manage. We have so far.'

But his mind was made up. From the wharf, while Jess was still considering what lay beneath her feet, Frank rang Kanga Kristofferson. Sliced through the catch-up talk. 'You still want that stallion of mine?'

A silence. 'What's wrong with him, Franko?'

Frank was pained. 'Ya old bastard. Fact is, I need the money.' Looked at Jess, who was still practising walking on a steady surface. 'Reckon I'm in love.'

THEY STAYED AT Helen's the first few days. Frank's letters had been selectively penned, so seeing Jess was a shock for his sister. She pulled him into the bathroom. 'She's a child.'

The tilting motion of the boat revisited Frank. He steadied himself on the handbasin. 'Calm down,' he told her. 'It's not as bad as it looks.'

Helen made Frank a bed on the sofa and gave Jess the spare room. She acted as though Jess was incapable of conversation, and Jess made no effort to prove her wrong. Frank would see them circling each other cautiously, like dogs on a footpath.

A deal was made with Kanga. The act of selling Maguilla had the same feeling as standing near a cliff at very high altitude. Frank felt inclined to clench his eyes shut and pretend he was elsewhere.

'I gotta foal you ought to have a look at some time,' Kanga told him. 'Five and a half months. A little bottler.'

'I'll do that. Yeah. Soon as we've got our shit together I'll come up and take a look.'

'You'll both come. And stay a while.' Kanga had taken a fancy to Jess right off.

Frank didn't say goodbye to Maguilla or even help load him. He went alone to the nearest pub and got drunk. Helen didn't allow alcohol in her house; even as Frank slept it off she'd opened the windows and turned on the fan to remove the fumes of his outgoing breath.

Frank bought a 1972 Falcon stationwagon with a radio and

sloppy steering and he and Jess loaded it up with Sal and Mac and some household stuff that Frank had stored in Helen's garage when his life was a little more straightforward. They headed north, full of the pleasure of being on their own and having a future.

In Maitland they found a flat where dogs were allowed and Frank picked up a job laying cement. After work and in the weekends they went looking for Lisa. Frank never doubted they'd find her. He guessed she'd be back to her old ways, and in any city it was easy enough to pinpoint the areas favoured by the druggies, the jobless and the marginally psychotic.

As it turned out, she was almost their neighbour. Three streets away. Jess spotted them in the supermarket — a child who looked, as far as she could remember, like Ben, and a woman in jeans and a purple shirt. Dark hair, down just past her shoulders. And not fat but . . . there was quite a lot of her. And pretty, sort of.

'That's her,' said Frank. 'Could be her. Next time follow them. Take the dogs. No don't, hell no, she'll know them, and they'll know her. Just follow her — see where she goes.'

Jess hung round the supermarket for the next two days, she had nothing else to do. But when she saw the child and the woman again it was in the chemist's and they were with a man. The man, Jess observed, wasn't a patch on Frank; straggling hair and face like an unshaved dinner plate.

She followed them to a flat little different from the one she and Frank lived in, except instead of Sal and Mac there was a doberman.

That night Jess and Frank went back there together. There was no sign of the dog. If they had the wrong place, Frank planned to say they were looking for their own dog, which had run away.

As soon as Frank knocked, the dog inside went crazy. Lisa opened the door, grabbing the doberman by the collar as it lunged. She was wearing a Chinese robe that she'd bought way back when she and Frank were together. She'd put it on to show him and danced with surprising grace until the fabric belt fell undone.

'Well,' she said. Her eyes moved from Frank to Jess, who was behind him, and back again to Frank. She shook her head, a tut-tut movement. The dog was barking in a strangulated fashion. Lisa turned aside and shouted, 'For Christ's sake,' and the man appeared behind her. He pointed the fork that was in his hand towards the inner recesses of the flat and shouted at the dog, who cowered and slunk away. With the dog silenced, canned laughter rattled from the TV.

Lisa stepped back and Frank walked in past her. The man was shutting the inner door against the dog. Ben sat on a dark brown rug, its pile like the coat of an English setter. He was pressing an orange plastic truck pitted with tooth marks against the strands of the rug and didn't look up. Frank wasn't sure he'd have known his son; his head seemed to have grown faster than his body. He could hear Lisa introducing herself to Jess.

'Where's Ruby?' he asked, and saw a look pass between the man and Lisa. Who shrugged, for Frank's benefit.

'Took off — after causing us a heap of shit one way and another.'

'Took off to where?'

The Chinese robe rose up in another shrug.

'How long ago?'

Their eyes consulted. 'Two . . . three months?'

'I'm taking the boy.' Then wished he'd chosen a softer way of saying it; Lisa would be loath to pass up a confrontation.

'He doesn't even remember you.'

Frank slid his hands beneath the child and lifted him; he was too light. He struggled and bleated, holding his arms out to his mother.

'I'll have to think about it,' Lisa said. She made no move to take the whining child. 'Me and Les'll have to talk.'

Frank turned to the lanky young man and held out his hand. 'Frank.'

'Yeah. I figured.' He passed the fork into his other hand and reached for Frank's.

'Malnutrition,' Frank told Jess as they walked home. 'She likes all that bullshit food they plug on TV.'

So did Jess. Seemed like real food was out of fashion.

'We should've just taken him,' Jess said. 'They could do a flit.'

'They won't.' He was certain Lisa was just making him sweat a little, that she had, once again, grown tired of motherhood. Why else would she have made an apparently purposeless call to Helen? If he hadn't turned up would she have dumped the boy the same way she'd now twice dumped Ruby?

FRANK AND JESS returned, as agreed, in the weekend. Lisa had the boy's things crammed into a battered case. 'If you want the cot, twenty-five dollars is what it cost me,' she said. 'And the stroller was thirty.'

'What about the stroller you stole from me?'

'It was junk, it fell apart.'

'I'll give you thirty for the both.'

'Forty.'

He counted the notes out. Jess's eyes were large with dismay as she watched their grocery money depart.

'You saw me coming,' Frank told Lisa. 'Right back at the very start, you saw me coming.'

A lesson there. Except, when he thought back he couldn't for the life of him see what he could have done differently and not ended up feeling like some kind of arsehole.

Now they had Ben, Jess would have something to do while Frank was at work. Now they could look to getting on with their own life.

'What about Ruby?' said Jess in the passenger seat of the Falcon, rocking the whimpering Ben against her.

'What can we do? Besides, I'd have no legal leg to stand on there.'

It bowled him over, the way this girl had moved into his life and never once balked at carrying a share of all the past crap and baggage that came with him.


FRANK DECIDED THEY should stay in Maitland at least until after the baby was born. A big move in those last months could befuddle a mother's proper instincts. He'd learnt that the hard way and even though Jess and Lisa were chalk and cheese there was no point in taking risks.

So Lachlan Francis Ward was born in Maitland on a chilly spring morning, and that afternoon Jess asked Frank to bring her in a writing pad and a pen. 'My mother should know she has a grandchild.'

'And your dad.'

'She'll tell him,' said Jess. (Radiant, she was. Warm and milky and glowing, so that the memory of Lisa's post-natal rage seemed all the more aberrant.) She took Frank's hand. 'I can't just forget what he did to you as if it didn't happen. I'll never forgive him.'

Frank looked at his second son, pinkly sleeping. 'I'd probably have done the same,' he said. 'It's water under the bridge.'

JESS'S LETTER ARRIVED four days after the funeral. Marion read it aloud, although he wished she wouldn't. When he read it for himself her voice would overlay Jess's voice. But the letter was not to him; Marion was entitled to claim the contents.

'She sounds happy enough.' Marion refolded the letter. Her fingernails were the colour of flame and long enough to be disabling. She tipped her fingers back and used the cushioned pads, like a sheep with footrot.

'At least we know where she is now.'

'Yes,' said Owen. His voice came out as a whisper, but was the best he could do, for there was nothing inside him, not even spare breath.

'A son!' said Marion. 'Good God.'

She clasped her hands together. *Wringing her hands*, Owen thought dully. *Is that how it's done? Is that a* clutch *or a* wring? Last night he had looked at her nails and asked, what colour was that. Apricot, she'd told him. Afterwards he'd lain there thinking. That's the calibre of our conversations! Holding her responsible. Then had felt ashamed. All she'd done was answer his question.

'It's almost,' said Marion softly, 'as if this one's a replacement . . . '

Owen looked away, inwardly wincing. The same thought had crossed his mind but was too mawkish to be voiced. Besides, Corin didn't deserve to be so readily replaced.

'She'll have to be told,' he murmured. Thinking of Jess. He was losing his children one by one.

With Corin his first thought had been, *Thank God it's not somebody else's child.* Meaning one of his own pupils. Imagining, even as his son was carried from the field, how it would have felt to tell the parents. Even if he was not to blame — and he wasn't, a freak accident, Jimmy McElvey's kneebone and Corin's skull colliding — *how would you tell a parent?*

That thought ahead of his own anguish. What sort of a man was he? Eleven years old. The very least a boy could expect from his father was unadulterated grief.

An inter-school sports day at the Windsor Domain. Normally an occasion to be dreaded, but Jenny Tripp would be there, off duty. Her own idea. They might not even get a chance to speak to each other but in a sense they would be together. Within sight. Those who knew her would imagine she was there in the course of duty; those who didn't know her would think she was just another parent. Jenny liked sport, knew the finer points of difference between league and rugby and the names of the regional netball team. Since knowing Jenny, Owen had started watching the occasional match on TV. He liked the thought that they were both watching the same thighs at the same time.

About mid-morning he saw her behind the long-jump pit. She was wearing blue and green tartan trousers, a navy jacket and a green scarf that flapped in the wind. Owen imagined her standing in front of the mirror and choosing clothes that she hoped he would like to see her wearing. He wanted to tell her she'd chosen exactly right.

Corin had been picked as a half-back for the combined rugby team. He seemed unsurprised by this. Owen, with his recently developed interest in the sport, was gratified by his selection and hoped that the boy would play well enough to gain Jenny's approval.

While Corin had no reason to recognise or remember Jenny from her visits in connection with Jess, Jenny would surely pick out Corin. Perhaps with some anguish. Owen and Jenny had agreed that guilt was not a relevant emotion in a relationship such as theirs, driven, as it was, by inevitability. By unspoken consent, and with the exception of Jess, they never discussed Owen's children. Nor did they allow themselves to talk of the future. 'One day at a time,' Jenny would say. And, sure, it was hoary old cliché, but on her lips it turned into the wisdom of ages.

Ten minutes into the first half, and Owen was organising the junior relay, had barely glanced across at the rugby where the ball was up the wrong end. Just a couple of minutes before. A freak accident, they said. If Jimmy's knee had been better padded, or even an inch or two to either side.

If Jenny hadn't been there it would still have happened. Owen keeps having to remind himself of that.

It seemed like the whole population of Curvey's Creek turned out for the funeral. Such immense kindness. For the first time Owen felt himself to be a truly accepted part of this community. Corin now in the Windsor cemetery, just behind the domain. Owen had resisted that plan at first — his child's bones lying alone in a town he had no affection for, in a region he'd always seen himself leaving. But after the funeral he saw it was the right thing — this place was Corin's home, possibly also Owen's.

Jenny had no complaint with Windsor, no desire to transfer to some stressful city police unit. She came to the service. She took Marion's hand and whispered damply, 'I'm so sorry,' and tears ran down the furrow of her nose. She did not take Owen's hand. Mascara smudged across her cheek, surprising him. He'd thought she wore no make-up. His son was being buried and he was thinking about his mistress's cosmetics.

Phil Chaney, dredging his teeth for remnants of cold chicken with one hand, offered the other to Owen. 'Still,' he said, 'couldn't be a better way to go. On the field, eh?'

Owen had felt his mouth quiver into something that could be construed as a smile. Life had culled out Corin and left Phil Chaney; there was no logic, only grounds for contempt.

A house was now being built on the burnt-out site in Turnbull Road. The frame already up, at least twice the size of the rabbiter's cottage. When it's finished Charlie and May Webster will move in and their son and daughter-in-law and their three children will fly out from England, where the son has been made redundant from his managerial job. The son and his family will live in Charlie and May's old house.

The subject of Ward and his house has never been mentioned to Owen. Not by Charlie, Jack, Rick, Phil, or even Dan, whom he sees regularly because of the school committee. Owen wonders if they ever think about it. With shame or pride? Or, like Owen, a see-saw ride between the two.

He would like to tell Jenny. Deception like the first spot of rust on the shining chassis of their love, demanding swift removal. But there is her job to think of; telling her could be a disservice, a cowardly off-loading of guilt.

LEANING AGAINST THE garage to catch the last patch of sunlight before the hills stole it away, Owen unfolded Jess's motherhood letter and read it for himself. It was a child's letter — clumsy with clichés and mis-spellings and he winced over it. He'd expected his children to be clever, especially his first-born, but written communication from Jess semaphored his inadequacies. As a teacher and as a dispenser of genes.

177

Still, it got her message across, and without a single reference to Owen. Jess was a mother, she was euphoric, she was with Ward, she was in Australia, she was fine.

She was a child, not even a smart one, who had been entrapped, bedazzled, taken advantage of. But even that was not quite as dreadful as some of the fates he had conjured up in the seventeen months since the brief, cruel little note with the Rotorua postmark. (Jenny Tripp had followed this up, had them out looking. Consulting with Owen, perhaps more often than was necessary.)

Owen and Ward were now related, this baby a product of their combined genes. You almost had to laugh. And, if it wasn't for Ward, Owen might never have met Jenny Tripp. The thought of how close he had come to not meeting her, or meeting her but not getting to know her, filled Owen with a kind of cosmic terror, compared with which Ward was nothing.

Well, maybe a blowfly.

*One day at a time*, Owen told himself, refolding Jess's letter.

# CHAPTER 18

'ONLY CLAPPED EYES on her once before,' Frank says, easing a sausage off the long fork onto Del's plate. 'And that was from the dock in the courtroom. At the time I didn't know who the hell she was, but I noticed her all right. Couldn't help but, the way she was got up. Looked like she'd come for a wedding. Or maybe a funeral.'

'Doesn't she look like you then?' Del asks Jess.

Jess is pinning the toddler's napkins to her singlet to stop them falling down. She shrugs. 'You must've seen her in the photos. She looks like my sister. Used to. Or the other way round.'

The toddler jabs her sausage at Jess's face, squealing with pleasure. Jess takes a bite. Her face contorts, she blows chewed sausage onto the ground beside her knee. The toddler laughs.

'Ta to Mummy.' Jess yanks the sausage from her daughter's fingers. 'Dirty. Yuck. You put it down on the ground, didn't you? Yes, you did.'

Jess tosses the sausage to Sal, who pushes herself forward on arthritic old shanks to grab it.

Frank takes a just-warm sausage from the very edge of the hot plate and holds it out to the toddler. 'Come on, bub. Come and get it.'

The toddler moves forward on chubby, bandy legs. Her chin raised, her eyes fixed on Frank and the sausage. The adults all watch her. In a few more days she'll have got the hang of upright balance and her spectators will lose interest, but right now it's the girl against gravity, and the odds are in gravity's favour so she needs their united support.

A yard away from the sausage her chest outspeeds her feet and she topples. Monty groans as though he's backed a loser. Del and Jess go *ooops* in unison. Frank flaps the food. The toddler reassembles her face, then looks around her and chuckles. On hands and knees she races towards the extended sausage.

Del remembers and turns to Frank. 'Yeah. Go on — yer mother-in-law.'

HE RECOGNISED HER straight off — or maybe just responded to her own fierce glance of recognition. She stood still for a moment in that stream of incoming travellers, and then changed direction. A fleeting glimmer of forced brightness, like a faulty lightbulb, as she stepped towards them. A glimmer that wasn't revived as her eyes slid down to take in the boys.

He held that against her, even now; for anyone could see these were top kids. He'd spruced them up, searching out the clothes Jess had specified, not allowed them to eat or drink anything on the journey in case of spillage.

Marion had reached them, sleek in high heels and the kind of hairdo that took a lot of upkeep. Her shoulders jutted square and military, as if she'd pulled on her green jacket with a padded clotheshanger still in place.

'I wasn't sure if I'd recognise you.' Damned if he'd call her Mrs Bennington, but 'Marion' might be stretching his luck. He had his hand ready in case shaking was in order, but hers stayed clasped on her overcoat and the black travelling bag.

'You,' she told him, 'look exactly the same.'

He liked that; the acid in her voice telling him right out he was yet to be forgiven. She looked down at the toddler.

'This is Lachlan,' he said, though it was hardly necessary. He expected her to pick the boy up, at least to touch him, but she just stood staring down.

'You look like your mother,' she told the child, then looked back accusingly at Frank. 'I didn't need grandchildren,' she said. 'Not yet.'

'I didn't need a mother-in-law,' Frank said, 'but I'm prepared to give it a go.'

She very nearly smiled.

He put a hand on Ben's shoulder. 'This is Ben.'

'Hello,' said Marion, her eyes sweeping past the boy. 'Where do we pick up the the baggage?'

JESS HAD REHEARSED this scene in her mind — over and over with

*180*

dread and longing. Had been rehearsing it, it seemed to her now, ever since the day she fled from the Herne Bay motel. At first, of course, she'd imagined all of them: parents, sister, brother. In that scenario they'd come intent on dragging her home, and she would refuse.

So much had changed since then. Especially on their side. Developments hurtling airmail across the Tasman like bullets from a war zone. Corin's death, Owen and Marion's separation. Her father's girlfriend — the woman cop who'd have had Jess put Frank away. A marriage-wrecking bitch.

'Don't judge,' said Frank. 'What does anyone know except them? Never can judge from the outside.'

But Marion's letters had crackled with pain and rage and Jess, disarmed by the discovery that her mother had real emotions, and pleased to have confirmation that her father was contemptible, had quickly lined up on Marion's side.

Thrown out of her own home, Marion had rented a flat in Windsor. Sheenagh had elected to stay with her father, which Marion saw as another act of betrayal. Worse, she'd continued to stay there when Owen moved his new woman in.

No chance of a reconciliation, Owen was panting for a divorce. Off with the old, on with the new. 'Bastard,' muttered Jess, reading that letter as she blindly undid Ben's skew-whiff buttons.

Marion quit Barker Hanley and fled to Wanganui, where she got a job as national administrator of Welcare Health Aids. Home sales, she wrote, were the bright future of retailing. Party plan and mail-outs. Welcare also operated in Australia — could be the way for Jess to make some extra money. The letter had been forwarded on to Jess by their ex-neighbour in Maitland.

'Maybe I could.' Jess had felt a surge of possibility.

'Jesus wept. Who do you think you'd sell the stuff to? The cows? Or the roos? And even they'd have enough sense to turn their noses up.'

'You know nothing about it,' Jess told him, but lightly, as if it was of no consequence. He'd had a few drinks so she might've known better than to even raise the idea.

Marion's new job kept her very busy. The letters became fewer and shorter until they were postcards with a hasty note on one side and, on the other, photos of civic rose gardens, war monuments and farmers herding sheep. Frank had bought Jess a camera, so in return Jess sent photos of Lachie laughing, Lachie standing, Lachie pulling Sal's hair, Ben cuddling Lachie, Lachie and Ben paddling, Jess, Lachie and Ben standing beside the Falcon.

Marion sent a photo of the unit she'd bought after the divorce settlement. No-maintenance brick and aluminium with eight polyanthus plants standing to attention beside the path. Frank and Jess examined the photo for some time in wonder, then Frank said he'd seen public toilets that were cosier. Jess had to agree. 'It's not a grandmotherly kind of house,' she said.

As Marion's communications dwindled, Sheenagh began to write to Jess. Complaints about living with the policewoman. Not that Jenny was unkind, but that she was nice to the point of sickening, and she and Owen were so disgustingly lovey-dovey that Sheenagh felt embarrassed and in the way. Jess would imagine the letters she sent in return — the envelopes with her shameful printed handwriting — being pulled from the school-house letter box by the policewoman and left on the kitchen table where Owen would see them, see they were never addressed to him.

Serving him right.

The prospect of seeing her mother had dried up Jess's milk supply. The nurses were stuffing her with vitamins and food supplements but she knew these would do no good. Marion was doing the motherly thing, flying over for the birth of her daughter's second baby (robbed, thank heaven, of attendance at the actual event by the baby's earlier-than-scheduled arrival), and in response Jess's body had seized up with an anxiety that bordered on terror.

'What's the worst that can happen?' Frank had asked her. Then gave her the answer. 'The worst that can happen is you and her don't manage to get along too well. Be a shame, but even so, you'd be no worse off than you were before.'

Except he was wrong, that wasn't the worst that could happen.

Even thinking that, she'd had to look away. From *this* Frank who sat on the bed beside her stroking their new baby's silky ginger hair.

FRANK HAD PROPOSED dropping Marion off at the hospital and

leaving the two of them together, but Jess wouldn't have it. They must all come in to see her and then Frank could take the children to the playground for a couple of hours. She needed Frank there at the start; it was his insurance and hers — though she didn't tell him this, didn't even, at the time, know it herself.

If Jess did not see Frank that morning Marion's presence might obliterate him. Her half-a-mind to leave him might crowd out the half that hated them being apart.

Now Jess hears the children's running feet on the glossy lino of the passage. She looks at the baby who is sleeping and perfect and entirely beyond dispute, and is suddenly no longer certain of being, twice over, a mother. Is just a teenage girl sitting on a hospital bed with the sun almost reaching the window. She's got herself in trouble but her mother is coming to get her.

Ben and Lachie come in first, slowing their footsteps, grinning and walking as if they're on glass because of the strangeness, still, of the room and because of the baby. Lachie can't see over the edge of the crib so he comes straight to Jess, scrambling into her arms, pressing his nose hard against her cheek.

In the doorway Jess sees Frank standing back to let Marion go first and this unnerves her. It's as if he's handing her over — handing her back.

Jess looks hard at her mother, tries to find familiarity within the creation of clothes and hair and careful cosmetics. As Marion approaches, Lachie slides from Jess's arms and escapes to Frank.

Marion hugs Jess. She holds her daughter against the green lapels of her jacket and murmurs, 'Lovely to see you.'

Jess starts to cry. Tears spill down and mark the green fabric with splotches the shade of card-table felt.

'We'll see you in a while,' says Frank from the door. But Jess protests that she hasn't had a hug from Ben, and frees herself from Marion's arms. She gets out of bed, hoping the back of her nightgown is as yet unmarked with blood, and half-runs to the door. She bends to hug the older boy, then another quick hug for Lachie. And a kiss for Frank. She tries for a real one but, embarrassed, he holds his lips closed. For a moment she wishes that Marion was already gone, or had never come; wants it to be just Jess and Frank and their kids.

Other people are always the cause of their troubles.

LACHIE WAS FOUR months old when they left Maitland. Not enough people wanting paths laid and Frank's work was fast running out. So he jacked up a job further north on a mixed farm. The owner was an ex-brother-in-law of Frank's old mate Rumbo McFee; his health had packed up and he needed a man to keep the place going until he recovered. There were married quarters, semi-furnished.

'Hate to profit from another man's misfortune but,' Frank grinning at Jess.

They'd done a flit from the Maitland flat because that was the only way their money would possibly stretch the distance. Sneaked away at one o'clock in the morning, the Falcon crammed with bedding, clothes, nappies, the cot and mattresses tied to the roof.

Comical, it looked, when the daylight came and the heat with it. To Frank and Jess, if not to the passing traffic. Jess thought aloud, 'I bet to them we look pitiful. No better than all those boat people.' They were on TV, the boat people, night after night, homeless and landless. 'Jeezus,' Frank would say. 'Makes me feel bad enough looking at that lot. How'd you feel if you were some rich bastard, fancy house, posh car, and looking at that? How could you sleep at night?'

'Are we homeless?' Ben worried, sardine packed in the back seat.

'No,' said Jess. 'It's just a long way away.'

Frank launched into verse.

*. . . where beneath the clustered stars*
*The dreamy plains expand*
*My home lies wide a thousand miles*
*In the Never-Never Land . . .*

These were the best times of all. Just the four of them and Sal (Mac, at fourteen, had died in his sleep), disposable nappies, eye-spy games and one eye out for takeaway places. Ice-blocks and the smell of melting tar. Landscape she had yet to get used to. The road spinning towards them like a future rich with possibilities.

Of course there were small disasters — a hole in the radiator, Ben tossing up his breakfast into the baby's carry-cot, smoke from the ignition wiring . . . Nothing, though, that couldn't be cleaned up, patched up, cobbled together.

And, admittedly, they hung about — Jess, Sal and the children — too long and too often in the car parks of roadside pubs where Frank had nipped in for a quick one. But at least they knew where he was and he knew there were plenty more bars waiting for him on the road ahead. Often as not, there'd be other women waiting in cars, other kids for Ben to play with.

The drawbacks of the job with Rumbo's ex-brother-in-law quite quickly became apparent. The 'quarters' in which they were to live was in fact an extended lean-to that had been built onto the eastern wall of the farmer's house. Frank and Jess saw right away that this was not auspicious. John and Wendy de Vere were in their fifties and, even in the best of health, wouldn't need a baby crying in the night or a small boy loose in their careful garden.

John de Vere had a debilitating illness. One of the symptoms was insomnia, another was an over-sensitivity to sound. Furthermore, the de Veres were religious. To their ears, run-of-the-mill curses would screech into the realm of obscenity and blasphemy.

'If you get pissed here,' Jess whispered, 'we're done for.'

'For someone so pretty you talk some terrible nonsense.'

On the good side, the place was slightly bigger than the grim little flat they'd left, and it was country. Windows looked out on plains scattered with rocks, and trees with pale writhing trunks that reminded Jess of comic-strip ghosts. Gazing at their new surroundings, she felt her heart ungripping. True, this was alien country — bleached-out shades of flame where there should be a thousand variations of green, tenuous shrubs and rocks strewn like misshapen marbles and slithering, surely, with snakes — but still it was country.

The de Veres had no appreciation of horses. Another cause for concern. The husband had a morose, knock-kneed chestnut mare called Goldy that Frank was expected to ride.

'Apparently it's a quarter horse,' said Wendy de Vere, waving her arm vaguely in the creature's direction.

'Right,' said Frank, 'it's the other three-quarters that worry me.'

Mrs de Vere just looked perplexed. Jess had to bend down sharply and attend to her shoelaces.

Stuck with Goldy, Frank became bitter about the loss of Maguilla, talked about buying him back, or maybe the colt that

Kanga was holding onto. Just as soon as he could raise the money. A good horse was an investment. He would look at Jess, then, as if he was weighing her up, measuring her value against Maguilla's and regretting a decision made in haste and not even on dry land.

John de Vere's illness kept him, for the most part, indoors. Doctors had failed to find a cause for his condition. A virus, they said, attacking his immune system. They could treat only the effects — the aches, the dizziness, the insomnia, the blurred vision, the aural sensitivity, the lack of energy. He had pills for all these things.

Her husband's illness had taken over Wendy de Vere. The randomness of the disease suggested divine purpose. Prayer meetings were held at the house every Thursday. She wasn't sure, she told Frank, whether they should be praying for a cure or just for an explanation. Then she gave a small laugh and said that of course it didn't really matter; *He* would decide which request was in order.

Frank was appalled. He related the conversation to Jess.

'She'll let the poor bastard die while the Almighty is kicking his heels and looking out the window.' He couldn't understand how any rational human being could just hand themselves over like that.

Jess thought about this. 'I have,' Jess told him. 'I've handed myself over to you.'

'That's totally different.'

'No it's not.'

'Bloody hell it is. At least you know that I exist.'

Jess took another small sweatshirt from the clothes basket, folded it up. 'Yeah,' she agreed. 'But God, if he does exist, is good. Everyone knows that. And I'm not sure that you're good. So who's the dumb one out of her and me?'

He wasn't listening, just grinned at her silly logic as he stirred white sauce.

The anger that suddenly rose inside her was directed not at him but at herself.

MARION EXTRACTS PHOTOS from her handbag and shows them to Jess one by one. Sheenagh in jeans and a white crocheted top, with a perm still crimping the ends of her hair, posing for the camera; Marion in white high heels, straight red skirt, white jacket in front of the Welcare office; the immaculate living room of Marion's 'townhouse'; the bedroom of Marion's 'townhouse'; Sheenagh, in an off-the-shoulder dress, snuggled beneath the shoulder of Gavin Cawley. Jess looks at the back of the photo in case something is written there.

'The Cawley boy.'

'He was in my class. Where was it taken?'

'I think some school dance.'

'And Sheenagh goes round with him?'

'He was her beau at the time. I'm not sure about now.' *Beau! Townhouse!*

'He can't be still at school?'

'That would've been a couple of years ago. He's at medical school.' Some people's children, Marion's tone says, were a cause of pride.

She peers, again, at the baby, who is still sleeping. She stands with her hands clasped and her neck bent forward like someone examining a display case in a museum.

'You can wake her,' offers Jess.

'Wouldn't dream of it.'

Marion returns to her seat beside the bed and recalls her own babies. Jess was solemn but undemanding; Sheenagh was the handful — not sleeping, turning herself purple with rage, hurling things. It was supposed to be the other way round; the first baby the hard one.

Jess says Lachie was easy. A good child. But then maybe he was a second baby, because of Ben. She sees the way Marion's mouth straightens at the mention of Ben; sees it but tries not to notice because it is unfair. She wonders if her mother will talk about Corin.

THEY WERE DECENT people, John and Wendy de Vere, and, even living on each other's doorsteps the way they all were, things didn't go too badly until Debbie Reynolds and Jock came to visit.

Jock was a small, stocky man with ragged ears and a flattened nose. He'd left his wife and kids for Debbie. The top of Jock's balding head reached just above Debbie's shoulder, but they were in love. They'd spent four days in Sydney, then come looking for Frank. It wasn't difficult, he'd kept in touch and c/- J. de Vere was as much as you needed in the country.

Frank gave them the double bed and he and Jess camped on the squabs from the sofa. That first night the four of them drank the two casks of wine the visitors had brought with them and Frank helped Jess put together a stew. They sat around the table until late, drinking, yarning, laughing and smoking. Reviewing their shared chunk of the past and presenting it to Jock. When Lachie woke Jess took him to the sofa in the corner. His teeth were coming through, he was weaning himself from the breast but still seemed to need this last feed. She listened to Frank turning her into a gutsy person, weaving the worn and tangled threads of their time together into a story as good as any. Sad and happy and funny. Making it seem that their lives made sense.

Jess tucked Lachie back in his cot, hovered for a time in the grip of dazed and incredulous pride that she had produced this perfect creature, then rejoined the others. The force of Frank's voice, the concentration he put into placing tobacco along the length of the rice paper, told her he was drunk. So was Jock — the nozzle of the flaccid bladder in his hand groped and nudged at the rim of his glass then trickled its contents onto the table. Jess didn't mind. They were with friends, they were at home, they were happy. She took the wine bladder from Jock and squished out the last half-glass. Debbie had fashioned, out of the foil from her Benson & Hedges packet, a silver buttercup on a two-leaf stem. She held it up in front of Jess.

'That's lovely.' Jess plucked it from the huge fingers — yet capable of such finesse — to examine it more closely.

'What the fuck d'you think y' doing?'

At the top of his voice. In the house through the wall it would crack like gun shot, but Frank was directing the question at Jess, who was not even an arm's length away. His voice a cleaver hitting the table. They froze. Ben's half-awake voice from the bedroom, 'Mum? Mu . . . aa.' Jess opened her mouth to reply then closed it again. Smoke, drifting from Jock's cigarette, was harsh in her throat.

'What kind of mother are you?' His voice lower now. An unsteady finger pointed to the glass beneath Jess's hand.

Jess looked from the glass to Frank. She told herself she was learning to handle these thin-iced moments. Must keep her face and her voice calm, empty her eyes of fear and contempt. 'It's only my second glass.'

'Your second! But you're bloody drinking it out of a bloody tumbler. It's not cordial, you know. That'll go straight into my son, curdle his guts, addle his brain . . .'

'Hey.' Debbie lurched towards him across the table. 'Hey darling heart, hey, come on . . .'

Frank squinted at Debbie, suddenly uncertain. But moral support made Jess careless. 'Then that'd make two of you,' she hissed at Frank. 'The addled brains. You'd know for sure he's yours!'

It was that last sentence that did it. She'd meant nothing, the words had just rolled off her tongue to round out her scorn, but they went into Frank like boxthorn and stuck there for days, festering.

That's what he told her later. That he thought she was saying that Lachie's father might have been Wipo or Hans. She'd almost forgotten the jealousy. That and the drink together — she should have known better and buttoned her mouth.

But one thing that puzzled her from that time was — how come Frank could remember her saying that? He never could remember anything he'd done or said when he was that drunk. 'Did I?' he'd whisper next day when she told him. 'Oh Christ almighty! That's bloody terrible. I did that? And the kids — did they see? Did they hear? Look, I wasn't *really* that bad an arsehole, couldn't've been.'

And, shaking but safe now, like someone saved from a shipwreck, she'd see that it hadn't been him but the insane stranger that swam into Frank with the alcohol and stared out through his eyes.

On this particular night the stranger simply cast his shadow. Jess gave in about the wine. Silently, pointedly, she emptied her glass into his, which, of course, was nearly empty. Then she rinsed her glass under the tap and sullenly refilled it with milk. Well, he was right, wasn't he? It wasn't fair, men getting off so easy when it came to babies, but that was scarcely Frank's fault.

The following day when Frank finished work, Jess stayed home and peeled the vegetables while Frank and their visitors drove to the pub to get supplies. She boiled up swede and potato while she got Ben bathed, then she mashed the vegetables and laid a soft poached egg on top.

'Baby's food,' said Ben happily. He spooned it down while Jess shovelled mushed vegetable at Lachie's mobile mouth and worried about how to cook a meal for four adults without Frank there to help her. Saw now why Marion had never invited people round to dinner. How could you have things cooking in different pots and arrange it so they were all ready for eating at the same time? How could you know how much would be enough? And whether to fry or roast or boil?

She could not keep relying on Frank to handle the difficult things, must learn for herself. Staying home and cooking dinner was what mothers did, apart from a few like Marion. Lots of clever, rich women on television saying it shouldn't be like that, but stick them out in the backblocks with a man out working all day, and the money his, and what would they do?

All over the world men went drinking and women stayed home and put kids to bed and dinners on top of pots to stay hot. It was how things worked, so why should Jess expect anything different? And it wouldn't go on forever because children grow up, and then . . . Well, then you could both go drinking. If you wanted to. Though possibly staying at home on your own with the TV would seem more interesting than listening to drunk people saying the same thing over and over.

It's not the kind of future she'd envisaged for Frank and Jess.

The longer Frank and their visitors stayed at the pub, the more they drank, the less they would want to eat. How many potatoes was enough?

When, finally, the three of them staggered out of Jock and Debbie's rental car with much guffawing and clinking of bottles, Wendy de Vere's prayer group were leaving the house. The sight of Debbie Reynolds, overdressed in royal blue Thai silk, turned the prayer group into witless sightseers. They pointed and made small excited noises, shuffled forward for a closer look while Wendy de Vere stood on her front step, waving to no one.

Frank nodded around at them, balancing the crate against his chest while he raised his hat.

But Jock took offence. 'What's the matter? Eh?'

Debbie yanked him away, closed her arm around Jock's neck and flashed their audience a smile. 'Lovely evening.'

The prayer group got a grip on themselves, were suddenly waving to Wendy de Vere, smiling, murmuring, nodding politely.

Jess watched all this from their unlit bedroom window, where she'd been sitting for some considerable time, looking out at the night. She continued to watch as Wendy de Vere stood on the path gazing unhappily from Debbie's rental car to the rusting Falcon and back again.

'What you doing?' Frank stood in the doorway.

'Nothing,' she said. 'Dinner's not ready. I didn't know when to put it on.'

'I'll give you a hand,' he said. 'Come on. We bought you Coca-Cola.'

Funny, she'd thought, sipping the Coke — you'd think after those months at Curvey's Creek with the two kids, stuck there, waiting for Lisa to come back, he'd know how it felt.

Later, Jess felt compelled to ask Jock, 'You didn't love your wife?'

'I thought I did,' he said. 'But it was, you know, a phantom love.'

'What's that?'

'Like a phantom pregnancy. You can convince yourself it's the real thing, but only so long as you don't know any better. And now I know better.'

He reached over and pinched Debbie on the thigh. She gurgled happily, grabbing his hand and raising it to her lips. Nibbled at it. Jess thought of her father and the policewoman.

'I BROUGHT YOU a present,' says Marion, 'and for the baby, and . . . Lachlan, but they're down in his . . . in the car.' She looks set to run down and fetch them.

'They can wait,' says Jess. 'Anyway, we don't need presents. It's just nice that you came.'

'I should've come sooner,' says Marion. A *but* hangs in the air between them. 'So much has happened,' Marion murmurs. 'One thing after another.'

'Sorry,' says Jess, because she doesn't know what else to say. She sees now that no submerged maternal intuition is going to alert Marion to the possibility that her daughter may be in need of rescue. If Jess needs Marion's help she will have to ask.

THEY STAYED SIX days, Debbie and Jock. 'We're gonna miss you guys,' said Frank. And it was true, even for Jess, though she was glad to have their own bed back. They had been top visitors; entertaining, generous and nice to the kids.

They left, heading for Brisbane, and it was as if, in driving off, they had snatched life from Frank and Jess. Their days, which had been full of colour, were now spent in bleached-out penitence. They'd overspent — not just in money but in conviviality.

In Debbie and Jock's company they'd lived carelessly; Frank would wake in the morning exhaling fumes, still drunk and exceedingly cheerful. He'd whistle off to work and Jess would tidy the house and feed the children and wait for Debbie and Jock to emerge, which they'd do about midday. In the afternoon the three of them and Ben and the baby would go for a walk or a drive in the rental. Jess or Ben got to choose.

Through last week's eyes Jess and Frank looked at themselves and saw that they were poor and shackled.

Frank drove to the pub to console himself and returned four hours later with a bottle of Coruba on already over-extended credit.

'You stupid bastard.'

She never thought, that was her problem. His fist got her face before she even saw it coming. While she raised herself from the floor slowly, slowly, he turned the keys in the outside door, their only exit, and dropped them into his pocket.

She edged towards their bedroom, taking small steps and keeping her eyes on him, thinking horse sense — watch for the hooves, watch for the teeth, move slow and calm. Inside the room she pushed the door not quite closed — that final click could be provocation — and went to the window, listening, listening, as she silently raised it.

If only he would crash, fall asleep, die if need be.

'If you saw yourself,' she'd told him after last time. 'If, just once, you could get to watching yourself in that state, then you'd grab your gun and put a bullet through your head. You wouldn't think twice.'

'Not with a bullet in my brain. I wouldn't even think once.' He was kissing her neck. Morning after a night like that and he'd be fond of everything. She'd pulled away.

He circled her wrist with his finger and thumb. 'You're not gonna go all righteous and bitter on me? Don't be, love. Promise me you're not gonna turn into some sour dried-up little woman who turns her back on life.'

'If I do,' she told him, 'it'll be you who made me like that.'
'Me?'

He had no idea. He was never there to see himself.

So this night, the worst so far, she was out the window and possibly safe. There was no moon and the light was on in the de Veres' living room. Sal rattled her chain, saw it was Jess and didn't bark; she knew the score.

Frank was at the front door, Jess could hear the scrape of the key searching for the lock. She let herself in through the de Veres' fancy little gate and crouched behind the hedge. Hide-and-go-seek. You never knew what childhood games would stand you in good stead. *Good stead* — what on earth did that mean?

She heard him mutter something to Sal, heard him stumble and curse. 'Hey,' he called, loud in that thick voice. 'Hey, where are you? Hey, bitch.'

The de Veres' useless dog had started barking. Their outside light came on, lighting Jess up. Mrs de Vere parted the curtains and looked out.

'Evening,' said Frank, 'you gotta whore in your garden.'

MARION IS HERE for two more days.

'About Dad . . .' tries Jess. If they talked about Marion and Owen maybe Jess could say about Frank.

Marion's eyes make a rush for the window. 'I'd rather not discuss it.'

After all those bitter letters. Has she forgotten she wrote them?

*Corin, then,* Jess wants to shout. *Shall we talk about my brother?* It's beginning to seem that Marion is the one in need of rescue, and that's not fair!

The baby wakes, lies silently staring. Everything those wide blue eyes see is out of focus. Blurred mother picking her up, handing her to blurred grandmother.

Frank is a lovely father. Talks to them, plays with them, reads to them. Jess doesn't want to leave Frank. Never ever. She just wants him to stop drinking.

'She looks just like you did.' Marion looks down at the baby in her arms and her mouth is soft and smiling. Jess has a memory flash of Marion's face looking down at her, a smile like this one.

MRS DE VERE gave them a month's notice. Beyond that she made no mention of that disastrous night. She'd remained at her open window for a few uncertain seconds while Frank stumbled and blasphemed and collapsed into the hedge. She'd told Jess, then, to come inside.

In the kitchen with the door locked twice-over Wendy de Vere had silently dabbed water on Jess's face, then made her a cup of tea.

'What do you intend to do?' she finally asked.

Jess just wanted to escape — from this kitchen, from her life. She went to the window and pulled the curtain aside; the light shone on the sparse hedge — there was no sign of Frank.

'He'll have flaked,' she said. 'I'll be okay now.'

'We don't need this kind of thing, you know.' As if it had been Jess's idea of fun. Jess's fault.

So the Ward family moved once again.

This time the journey was not quite so buoyant. But it would be a relief (they told each other) not to have anyone breathing down their necks.

This time they headed back east to the coast. Frank was hoping for casual work on the fishing boats, had done a bit of that in his time. And it was only for the meantime, until the baby was born. After that they'd do some serious thinking about the future.

MARION REACHES FOR a magazine and turns the pages while the baby attaches herself to Jess's insufficient breast. The suction this baby achieves is unnerving in something so small; her lips smack greedily against Jess's flesh.

'Oh, nice,' says Marion. 'I like these.' She holds the book so Jess can see. The page is filled with towels, draped and folded. They have sculptured pile in a paisley sort of pattern and rich shades.

'Yes,' says Jess. 'Mm.'

Marion repossesses the page and stares at it for a few more moments. Jess looks down at her daughter's hand encircling her finger, the way the thumb is out on its own. The baby's mouth and the crackling of the pages in Marion's hand are competing for attention. Jess wishes she could think of something real yet not upsetting to say to her mother, who has come all this way to see her.

Frank comes back with the boys. He keeps them there by the

door while he looks at Jess. His eyebrows reach for the brim of his hat. Her smile urges him in, and for a time the boys take over, touching the baby, babbling, laughing. Lachie carefully unclutches the baby's fingers and lays claim to his mother's freed arm.

Eventually the boys can no longer be relied on to fill the space. Frank leaps into the silence.

'Terrible blow about the boy,' he says, as if he'd known Corin. 'Jess was heartbroken — not being there and all.'

Jess lets go of Lachie and concentrates on moving the baby to the other side.

'Yes,' says Marion. 'Terrible.' She blinks and furls the magazine into a funnel.

'So how's life on your own?'

Jess is aware that she's holding her breath.

'Fine,' says Marion. A sharp smile. 'Once I got over the shock of being thrown aside for a younger woman.'

Jess thinks of her father. Remembers that once they were on the same side, an unspoken alliance against Marion — or at least against some strangeness they sensed within her. She says to Marion, 'But you had someone. I know you did. You used to talk to him on the phone.'

Marion is for a moment disconcerted. Then her face softens in a smile.

'That!' she says. 'He was just . . . well.' The smile fades. 'It was foolishness,' she says briskly. 'I put an end to it. It had nothing to do with real life.'

Jess catches Frank's eye and reaches for his hand, as if Marion is a chilly wave that could wash them all away.

A TESTING COUNTRY, was how she saw it. A blazing, taunting land where she was constantly on trial. A place where you gritted your teeth and breathed deeply; she liked that.

They had, at last, their own place. Near enough theirs. They'd seen such advertisements often enough. For sale or lease — abandoned farm. You'd think the owners would lie a little in their own interests.

'No point,' said Frank. 'Soon as you looked you'd know the story.' Bleached bones, dried-up waterholes, dismembered vehicles.

But this one was south of the Queensland border and Frank could work that country, was sure he could. He'd gone on his own to look. Met the owners and talked them out of the advance lease payment they had in mind.

So once again they were on the road. This time Kanga Kristofferson came with his stock truck to give them a hand. He'd sold them Maguilla's foal, a leggy colt they'd named Genghis, and Bridey, a nine-year-old stockhorse. Frank had a terrible urge to buy Maguilla back but the stallion wasn't for sale. Besides, he was getting on a bit, and Frank couldn't offer him the kind of fancy conditions he enjoyed at Kanga's.

'Wish I'd hung onto him.' Frank, at Kanga's place, sliding from Maguilla's saddle and taking baby Kathryn so that Jess could have her turn. But then, Australia was full of horses Frank should have hung on to.

As well as the two horses they had new dogs: a goofy bitch called Kelly that a neighbour had been eager to get rid of, and a puppy, Jed, with rather more potential. And they still had Sal.

This time the journey was overshadowed by their impatience to arrive. The house was rough, he'd told her that. There were burrs around the door, mothers-of-thorns, that could tear your feet to ribbons. But there was water — he'd discovered a frog among the green slime in the toilet bowl, left it there so the boys could find it. In the end water was all that mattered. It was the cost of the bore that had put the owners out of business.

Same old story, said Frank. Any old suit with a yen for the open spaces thought he could be a stockman, thought all there was to know you could learn out of books.

A roof over their heads, land to work and no boss. What more could you ask for? Jess had no doubt about Frank's ability to deal with burrs and plumbing and snakes and drought. Set Frank down any place in the world and he'd find his family shelter and food. Plague, floods, nuclear fallout . . . Frank could survive them all. Him and the cockroaches.

They'd had two homes since the de Vere place. Both in town: — Werris Creek, then Tamworth. In Tamworth they lived in a semi-detached flat and the boys played with the kids from the other half of the building. Their mother was Jody, much older than Jess, a reformed alcoholic. When Jess first met her she told Jody about the places they'd lived in so far. 'Ah-ha,' said Jody. 'Doing a geographic!' Then saw Jess's confusion and explained. A geographic was the drinker's trail from place to place, home to home. Mess up and move on. Jody and her children's father had done it for years. Australia — maybe the whole world — was full of families criss-crossing the land in constant migration. A culture of its own; fast friendships based on the bottle, easily made, easily severed. After a while, said Jody, you'd meet up again in another town. If you survived long enough you'd get to know every second alcoholic in the country.

Jess told Jody it wasn't like that, not for Frank and Jess. Was just that, one reason or another, things hadn't worked out up till now. And Jess didn't drink, hardly at all. Didn't like the taste and anyway Frank didn't much like to see her drinking. 'We're gonna settle down,' Jess told Jody. 'We definitely are, now with Ben at school and Lachie starting soon. We're gonna settle. Except not here.'

But Jody's words had got jammed in Jess's brain, stuck there and bothersome like corn-cob husk lodged between the teeth.

THEIR FIRST NIGHT on the abandoned farm Jess stood in brand-new gumboots among the burrs and felt the earth's slow turning beneath that vast and astonishing sky. She considered the miracle of gravity that kept her rubber feet fixed to the dry earth when her every inclination was to step off in the direction of the largest, brightest star.

She saw how it would not be possible to live here, in such proximity to the universe, and remain unchanged. She imagined people, generation after generation, sleeping beneath this sky, and understood that this would have to involve some kind of intimacy with the cosmos.

Frank had a story about working as a mustering cook in the Northern Territory. Much condensed, it went like this. One day the station manager arrived at dinner time and was outraged to find Frank serving the Aboriginal workers on plates; meat and vegetables, same as the other men. Accepted practice was to feed the Aboriginals as you did the dogs, tossing the meat in their general direction. When Frank not only disregarded the manager's objection but went on to serve up rice pudding for all, the man was beside himself. He ordered Frank to saddle up and leave, and he swore the workers to secrecy. Never again would he be able to hold his head high if word should get round that, on his property, Abos had got to eat pudding.

Sometimes Jess thought that everything Frank was, the good and the bad, could be explained simply by saying he was Australian.

In the first three weeks they slashed down the burrs and the nettles, scrubbed out the house, repaired fences, dug over a vegetable garden and surrounded it with high chicken netting. Frank caught a snake on the verandah and took it across the paddock and let it go again. He poked around beside the house looking for others but found none. Their nearest neighbour, Pally Simmons, called in to introduce himself. He and Frank discovered someone they knew in common. An old friend of Pally's.

When Pally left, Frank told Jess that Pally's old friend was almost as big an arsehole as Jack Samuels.

'That doesn't mean anything,' said Jess. 'I used to be best friends with Leila.' Whenever she thought back to Curvey's Creek it seemed not quite real, like something she'd seen in a long and boring movie.

To bring in some ready cash Frank took a droving job: ten days on the road, moving a mob down to Narrabri.

They had no choice, Jess understood that. The money would get them started — a few head of cattle — and fill their stomachs. Yet she wanted to clutch and beg. *I'm only nineteen. I'm scared of the dark, the snakes, the size of the stars, accidents and dingoes.* How could she look after a baby and two young children with not another human being in sight?

She would have the car. (No longer the Falcon but a Holden Torana.)

Frank was watching her closely. 'I can change my mind.'

'Leave me Sal,' she said.

And she got through it.

Frank had made her a list of things to be done each day, and extra jobs if there was time, and she crammed the hours so full of doing things that the fears were pushed to the periphery. At night she shared her bed with Ben and Lachie and their breathing kept the stars at bay. The baby slept alongside in her cot, the rifle was on top of the wardrobe, and Sal was on the bedroom floor listening out for snakes. Jess would think of Frank sleeping beneath the sky.

A letter came from Sheenagh, who had left school and Curvey's Creek, and was now a polytech student flatting in Hamilton. She wrote about parties and boyfriends with Cortinas, and had drawn a sketch of her new hairstyle. Jess looked at herself in their only mirror and wondered whether people ever really chose the lives they led, and if, knowing it all, Jess would have chosen differently.

Frank rode right through the last night to get home at daybreak, thumping on the locked door a day before he was expected. Fumbling to get the door open Jess felt as if she was stepping out of cold storage; her blood suddenly moving again, her lungs filling right to the bottom.

'Just one more,' he told her that night. 'One more job and we'll be on our feet.'

But by then they'd got to know Monty and Del, so when Frank was away Del drove out with the kids and stayed for the weekend. And Jess knew if something went wrong she had friends who would help her.

Frank had chummed up with Monty in the pub and Monty had taken him home to meet Del and the boys. The next weekend the family drove out to visit Frank and Jess and ended up staying the night. Monty and Del were in their thirties. They lived in town. Monty had no regular job but took casual work and was good with cars; Del worked at the supermarket checkout. They had two boys — one a bit older than Ben, the other a bit younger than Lachie. Del and Jess got along. Del wanted a daughter, and made a great fuss of Kathryn, who was now no longer a baby.

Which was just as well, because Jess was pregnant again.

ONE DAY THAT first summer Frank and Monty Cray had driven east, to the hill country where there were wild pigs for the taking. Monty had his little mutt who looked like a lapdog but was a demon with pigs. Frank had Kelly, who'd turned out smarter than anyone ever would have credited. They went in Monty's big old Bedford truck, so the minute Frank saw the bull he got excited.

'I could use that bastard,' he told Monty. 'I surely could.'

'Yeah, he'd fill a few freezers.' But Monty sounded doubtful.

'No way,' said Frank, 'we're taking him out alive.'

On horseback they might have roped the brute where he stood, but on foot they had to chase him, along with the couple of scrawny cows that tagged behind, for maybe an hour until they reached a fenceline. Then up and down, wearing a track beside the fence, until, with dogs and ropes, they got the crazed beast down and roped his legs.

After that a boar would've seemed an anti-climax. Besides, they didn't trust the bull not to struggle free. Monty went back for the Bedford while Frank sat around admiring their trophy and figuring out how they would get him onto the truck. He was still a young bull — unmarked, untagged. Weighed maybe a ton.

In the end they slung a rope over a branch and hoisted the beast up bit by bit. Drove home carefully, stopping off to buy a dozen but foregoing even a quick celebration glass in the pub.

'The girls aren't gonna believe this.' Monty scarcely believed it himself.

Del and the kids were out at the farm with Jess. There was no question of disbelieving. The kids lined up at a distance to watch as Frank untied the ropes and prodded the bull into the yard.

'Couple of inoculation shots,' said Frank, 'and he'll be good as gold.'

'We can go back tomorrow and try for a pig,' hoped Monty, who now had nothing to show for the day.

'You're a beggar for punishment,' said Frank. It would mean another four o'clock start. 'Fair enough, mate.'

A live bull in the yard and half a pig in the freezer. Living high.

A couple of weeks later Jimmy Pacino, one of the local coppers, turned up, accusing Frank of cattle rustling. Turned out he meant the bull. Frank was incredulous. That was a feral bull; it had no owner.

Jimmy Pacino explained with patience. There was no such thing as a feral bull. Every stray cattle beast, if only through its antecedents, had an owner somewhere.

'I see,' said Frank carefully. 'So what you're telling me is that all those pigs up in the ranges, they belong to Captain Cook. So every bastard who's ever shot himself a pig has been ripping off the captain's descendants.'

'Ah,' said Jimmy Pacino. He rubbed his chin. 'Well in actual fact . . . probably.'

'I've got a hunk of cured pork hanging up in the kitchen. You gonna charge me with that too? Take it in as evidence?'

Jimmy Pacino took a very deep breath.

'You charge me on account of that bull and there's gonna have to be a lot of pig hunters cloggin' up the courts.'

'I'll let you off, this time, with a warning.'

Frank liked that bit best of all. The dignity of it. Not even a trace of a grin as Pacino climbed into his car.

'But it is a warning,' Frank told Jess. 'Someone put him up to that. Some vindictive bastard who's got it in for us.'

'Pally?' wondered Jess. 'Coulda seen the bull from his boundary fence and figured we don't have the money to buy a beast that good.'

'But the copper knew where we got him.'

'Then you must've been skiting around.'

'Who've I seen to skite to? Been living like a bloody monk just lately.'

'Monty,' said Jess. 'Monty would've been on about it, you can bet. Could've told anybody.'

'And *they* could've told anybody. Bloody hell,' he said, 'we just start getting it together and some arsehole's out to drive us away.'

Made him so fed up he had to drive to town for a drink. Jess had a short memory, waved him off thinking, why not? He hadn't had a drink since the night he and Monty brought home the pig. As he'd always told her, if it wasn't there he could do without it. Proof that he had no drinking problem. 'Your alcoholic, now he's addicted, can't stay away from the stuff. Which goes to show y' don't know what y' talking 'bout, do ya.'

Maybe she didn't. And now things were starting to mess up already but it wasn't Frank's fault. Proving Jody was wrong with her 'geographic'; they'd moved a lot, only not any more.

IT WAS SPRING when Jimmy Pacino again pulled up at Frank Ward's house. Frank was handstitching a stretch of cured rabbit hide onto worn-out saddle lining. Beside him baby Eve dangled in a canvas bouncer while her sister sailed a hub-cap ark full of plastic animals in the paddling pool.

Pacino closed the car door behind him. 'I came to see you some time ago.'

Frank glanced at his younger daughter and calculated. 'Eight months ago,' he said.

'Guess it was. About an allegedly wild bull.'

'Christ almighty,' said Frank. 'What is it now?'

'You still got the animal?'

'I have.' Frank snipped off thread, pulled it through the small groove in the candle wax.

'You don't mind if we take a look at it? Seems we've got someone who lost a bull in those parts.'

Frank laid a hand over his eyes. Pushed it up his forehead, nudging his hat back. 'It wasn't tagged,' he said. 'No markings at all. I tell you, the thing was wild.'

'Can't hurt to take a look then.'

Frank gathered up the saddle, the candle, the needle and thread and put them on the shelf on the porch, out of child reach. 'Grab your shirt,' he said to Kathryn, 'and bring me your shoes.' He looked at Pacino. 'It's a fair stretch away and my wagon's not mobile at the moment.'

This wasn't true, but there was no point in inviting an officer of the law to sit behind an unlicensed windscreen. He expected the copper to ask how they managed, therefore, for transport, but Pacino just glanced at the Torana. 'We'll take mine.'

'I'll have to bring these fellas.'

Pacino drummed cheerfully on the car bonnet while he waited for Frank to manoeuvre Kathryn's feet into their pink sneakers and tie the laces. Frank took his time. He extracted the baby from her suspended seat and readjusted her hat. The brown-limbed sweetness of his daughters could still startle him.

In the second paddock they overtook Jess on the mare she had only just broken in (all on her own, and a bloody good job she'd done too).

'Mummy,' squeaked Kathryn, winding down her window.

'I'll just explain,' said Frank.

The copper slowed to something less than a crawl and Frank caught the look on his face as Jess turned towards them. Remembered that, last time, she'd stayed out of sight.

'Your wife?' Pacino sounded stunned.

Frank wasn't offended. Knew how the copper felt. Like her daughters, Jess could cause him these flashes of total amazement when it seemed he must have blundered into someone else's life. Every year, it seemed, she grew more lovely. The sun had bleached her hair to the colour of powdered ginger and tanned her skin the shade of her darkest freckle. She would grow large with child and then return, without concern or effort, to an impeccable shape.

Frank hadn't bargained on beauty. He didn't require it and, while he appreciated it in the way he'd appreciate a great sunset or a well-turned fetlock, looking at Jess — really seeing her, the way Jimmy Pacino was now — always gave him a jolt. Made him nervous as much as anything else. Some day she would look in the mirror and see that, without even trying, she could find someone better than Frank.

But at this particular moment the look on the copper's face — a look that should have made Frank jealous (her family had a weakness for coppers) — was making him happy. He saw that, come a legal crisis of any kind, Frank had, in Jess, a trump card.

Viewing the bull proved inconclusive as Frank knew it would. Pacino got close enough to see there was no ragged tear on the ears, but already seemed less than interested. He was craning around staring past the fence into the south paddock which belonged, at that moment, to the cows with calves. As Frank had been suspecting, the bull was not, had never been, the object of the exercise.

Finally Pacino's glance fell on two calves bunting each other for sole possession of the udder of their Hereford mother. Pacino's eyebrows leapt.

'I'd've said one of those was a Murray Grey.'

'Mmm,' said Frank, 'there's a resemblance.'

'That's its birth mother?'

'Yup.' Frank kept his own eyes safely locked on the two stocky calves. 'Twins, she had. Reckon that one could be a throwback.'

'Right.'

A bubble of laughter dribbled around like indigestion in Frank's stomach. If he caught the copper's eye now Frank would laugh, would be unable to stop himself. Perhaps the copper would laugh too.

'And that other one over there, the Friesian — another throwback.' Pacino's voice was deadpan, and Frank didn't dare take a look at his face.

Someone had laid a complaint. Maybe a number of people had. But what could they prove? A newborn calf, spirited away in the night. One from here, one from there and not from those that couldn't afford it.

'You got a high percentage of twins out there,' Pally Simmons had said.

'I have,' said Frank. 'Indeed I have.' Looking Pally in the eye.

'If I didn't feel right about it I couldn't've done that,' he told Jess later. 'He seems a decent enough kind of bloke. If I had a bad conscience I never could've told him bullshit while looking him straight in the eye.'

Frank should have known how it would be out here. Not a whole lot different from Curvey's Creek. Country people no kinder or smarter than their own poultry when it came to accepting newcomers. Landowners knew their own kind at a glance, and even if Frank had owned this land he'd never be the landowner kind. Wouldn't want to be, no thanks. Arrogant bastards. Thought that someone like Frank was too stupid to recognise rudeness, too pathetic to resent it. Or maybe just figured he was fair game, having no way of getting back at them.

Big mistake.

Since Jimmy Pacino's first visit Frank had been keeping tally of snubbings, insults, even innuendos. Those he perceived as being directed at him and the ones encountered by his family.

Two weeks at his new school and Ben came home to ask, 'What's a cradle snatcher?'

'Why d'you want to know, son?'

'Peter Cain said you're a cradle snatcher.'

Kids didn't come up with stuff like that of their own accord. 'Cain' went into Frank's mental ledger and, came the spring, Gerry and Susan Cain had a young Friesian calf just disappear into thin air.

Pally Simmons, already suspect, drove right past Frank as he stood poking in the bonnet of the conked-out Torana, near enough twelve miles from home. Went past with a sneer on his face. It was Pally who ran the Murray Greys.

The Cavendish woman from up by the crossroads waved Jess down when she was out riding. No reason but nosiness, though Jess took it at first for friendly. Until the old crow couldn't restrain herself, hissed at Jess, 'What are you doing with that old man? He won't even have a penny to leave you.' The Cavendish property went on Frank's list . . .

'One thing I've learnt,' he advised Jess. 'Unless you're one of those rich bastards the only way you're gonna get justice in this life is to do it yourself.'

Jess didn't care about the justice. She objected to lying awake wondering if Frank would be shot at or arrested those nights he went out to extract it. And she fretted on behalf of the cows left lowing into the night for their missing babies.

'They soon get over it.' They might, all of them, be bovine Lisas, and Frank doing them a favour.

'You don't know that. I'd never get over it.' Even the thought of it making her sad and sleepless in the night. Frank, alongside, thought about his first wife, Jean, the one he'd married, and how maybe she hadn't got over her lost babies. Maybe it was the grief that killed her. Frank thinking how strange it was to have had a life going on when this woman who lay beside him was not even born.

Jimmy Pacino dropped Frank and the girls back at the house and drove off. Nothing he could prove. Who would identify a newly dropped calf that had disappeared before he'd even set eyes on it?

YOU WON SOME, you lost some. When Jimmy Pacino returned it

was late summer and he had a warrant for Frank's arrest. As they drove towards town they both looked out at the distant flush of green spreading across the blackened paddock. Frank had been burning off. Well of course he had, and any farmer with half a brain was doing the same. Only by burning that carpet of yellow straw would you see the grass regenerate. A blanket fire ban was an absurdity dreamt up by city morons in air-conditioned offices. They did not have to watch their stock starving, their debts mounting. Not to burn off would have been much the bigger crime.

He could argue this in court but all they would hear was an admission of guilt. An unprincipled law demanded unprincipled tactics. 'You prove it,' he told Pacino, ''cause I'm not admitting to lighting any fire.'

Pacino smiled at him. 'We've got witnesses.'

The fire had swept through the back section of Frank's property and licked the edge of the Simmons' station. Frank and Jess and Monty and the boys had been out there with wet sacks, keeping it under control.

'Let me guess,' said Frank.

'You were also seen moving stock from the area the day before the fire started.'

'Yeah. I was a bit lucky there.'

Pacino's eyes whipped up to look at the ceiling of the car, then back at the road. 'If I was you I'd be getting myself a good lawyer.'

It wasn't a threat, more like friendly advice.

'Right,' said Frank. 'Who would you reckon?'


'NO ONE,' FRANK told the lawyer, 'can stand up in that court and swear he saw me light that grass. If he does the bastard's lying. All any of them could've seen was me and the others out there getting it under control. And even then I could've been any bugger about my height and wearing a hat — they'd've been too far away to know for sure.'

The lawyer made an I'm-less-than-confident face. Their witness, or witnesses, might feel justified in elaborating a little on the detail of what was, in fact, seen. Frank pictured Pally Simmons seeking vengeance for his missing calves, and knew the lawyer was right. Pally would put his hand on the Bible and swear that he watched Frank extract the match, smelt the phosphorus as it burnt. Standing in court with his hat clutched obsequiously in his hands, seventeen strands of hair coyly straddling his scalp.

Whereas Frank would have Jess. 'No worries,' Frank smiled. 'My wife will give evidence.'

The lawyer didn't cheer up. 'You haven't seen her,' said Frank. 'She's coming in to get me. Soon as the kids get home from school. I'll bring her in — what time d'you shut up shop?'

But the Torana packed up on Jess halfway in. A fuel blockage, it turned out, when a stranger finally stopped to lend a hand almost two hours later. Jess and Ben with engine grease up to their armpits from trying to fix it and all the kids fractious and hungry. Frank had been waiting, as he'd arranged, at the bottom pub, drinking on credit when the money ran out. He vaguely remembers Jess turning up, but the lawyer would have been long gone by then. Beyond that he doesn't remember. Only that she got him home.

They had two weeks before his court case. Two weeks for her to rehearse. *We saw the smoke. Frank said, 'Oh gosh I do believe it's our place and ran towards the car.* Jess would carry baby Eve onto the stand. Or perhaps, at the last moment, pass her to Frank? It was those little details that, in the end, counted.

Frank wanted the boys to take the day off school. He could see his whole family seated in a row — healthy, handsome and well-scrubbed. 'Wholesome!' he said. 'That's what we'll give them.'

Jess objected. 'How d'you think they're gonna get an education if we drag them out of school every time you break the law.'

She arranged for both boys to go to Lachie's teacher's house after school. 'We have a legal appointment,' she said on the phone to the teacher, 'and could be delayed.' The modification of truth slipping off her tongue so smoothly. Frank took credit. His confidence zoomed. And it was more than just acting, he told himself with pride; each day Jess grew just a little more like him.

She was right about the boys. Turned out they weren't needed, might in fact have been an overstatement. Sufficient for the lawyer to record their existence and whereabouts, leaving Jess and the girls to convey the right amount of innocence, poverty and self-respect.

As Frank predicted, there was no competition between Pally

Simmond's self-righteous fabrications and Jess's shy but unshakeable lies. The case was dismissed, just as Eve registered her empty stomach and began to bellow.

Frank was triumphant. He took a twenty-dollar note from his wallet and waved it at Jess.

'Buy yourselves something. I'm just gonna nip in for a jug.'

She got that look on her face.

'Christ almighty,' he said. 'I *deserve* a drink. We could've got fined to buggery. I might've even been sent away.'

She softened a little. 'Which pub then?'

'Royal Arms. Just round the corner.'

'We'll see you half past four. At the car.'

'Right, Serg.' He saluted, a click of his boots. His daughter laughed.

SO HE WENT to the pub, and there was Ruby.

He wouldn't have known her. Could have stared at that face for an hour with the niggling thought that it was somehow familiar, but would never have figured it was Ruby's face.

She saved him the bother. Plodded over and stood in front of him.

'Frank? It is Frank, eh?' No smile or anything. 'I'm Ruby.'

Poking her chest so he'd be sure. Knew she was beyond recognition. Frank stood there with his tobacco pinched out on the oblong of paper, his fingers suddenly boneless things incapable of a simple action they'd done unsupervised maybe a million times.

Ruby had blown up. Not puppy fat, not even a matter of piling on the beef. Skinny little Ruby had filled out in the manner of an air cushion or a waterbed bladder. At her joints the flesh indented as if some rubber band, idly rolled onto her arms and legs and neck during childhood, remained there buried and forgotten. Frank felt that if he took out his pocket knife and punctured Ruby's skin a rancid suppuration of grief and loneliness would well out.

How old would she be? Ben was six so she would be . . . fourteen, but he must have it wrong. Dark indented circles around her button eyes.

'Shit. Ruby. Jeezus. Sit down.' Pushing a barstool towards her, a tiny round circle of wood that surely wouldn't hold her.

She reached out a hand and pushed the stool behind her. Possibly beneath her. Anyway, out of sight. 'How's Ben?'

An edge to her voice. Frank had the feeling of being caught in the act of doing something shameful. He couldn't meet her eyes.

'Good,' he said. 'He's fine.' Asking after Ben meant Ruby had been in contact with her mother. Knew how long Frank had been back in Australia.

'We looked for you,' he blurted, wishing it was true. 'I wanted the both of you, Rube.'

He felt her disbelief. Pushed the focus back on her. 'What made you take off? From . . .'

Her face said it was an overly large and stupid question. Frank looked around the bar to see if there was hope of rescue; someone he knew or someone she'd come in with. No one was looking in their direction.

She read his intent. 'I don't know anyone here.'

The thought hit him. 'You were looking for me?'

Her face wobbled out a laugh. 'No. I'm waiting for my man. Only maybe he said the pub on the corner. I can't remember.'

'You're living here?'

'Passing through.'

'Aren't you a bit young . . . for . . . ah, y'know?'

'Tell me about it!' She pushes her face towards him. 'I was turning tricks at twelve. Girl's gotta eat.'

The implicit accusation.

'Jeezus Rube, I'm sorry.'

'No big deal.' Her head toppled back and she drained her glass. He refilled it from his jug.

'I don't eat that much,' she said. 'Not the way it looks. I got this disorder.' She dragged out a cigarette packet. Empty. She screwed it up. Frank nudged his tobacco towards her.

'I kept thinking you'd come and get us. That first few months.'

Frank watched the puffy fingers trying to roll a smoke. 'I couldn't,' he said. 'Honestly, Rube, I was stony broke. Then all this other rubbish was happening to me. You wouldn't believe. I was really in the shit.'

He glanced up at her then and saw the old Ruby in her look of ironical, weary amusement.

'Anyway, legally,' he said, 'with you I wouldn't've had a leg to stand on. They'd've laughed me out of court.' And he remembered that he'd come to the pub to celebrate.

'I heard you's married.'

'Same as,' he said. 'Jess. Remember? Used to come and ride Maguilla.'

Ruby's mouth slipped open. 'Her! They told me she was just a kid.'

'You see Lisa then?'

'I was passing through.'

Frank didn't want to know more of that, changed the subject. 'Jess is doing some shopping. With our girls. She'll want to see you. You could come home with us and see Ben. Just one more jug, eh, and we'll go.'

He slid the empty jug towards the barwoman.

'You haven't changed,' said Ruby. She looked at the clock. 'I think I am at the wrong pub. What other ones are there?'

'One a couple of blocks up the road. Another over the railway lines.'

'You could show me,' she said. 'Could come and meet him.'

'Yeah,' he said. 'Reckon I better. See if he's good enough for you.'

It was clumsy, he knew, but somewhere in there was the old Ruby and she'd give credit for good intent.


AFTER A GREAT deal of walking, comparing and unfolding, Jess bought tracksuit pants, on special, for all four children, and an ice cream in a tub for her and Kathryn to share. Then they walked back towards the car at toddler pace. The straps of the baby carrier bit into Jess's shoulders and Kathryn's hand was sticky in hers.

Frank was not in the car, but she hadn't expected him to be. Jess laid the baby on the back seat to change her nappies and put the dirty one, rolled up, into the plastic bag already rank with ammonia.

She tucked the baby into her carry cot and sat Kathryn alongside.

'I'll be back in a minute.'

She walked through both bars of the Royal Arms in case he was tucked around a corner or hidden behind some bulky drinking companion. No sign of him. This didn't surprise her;

nor did the bar-room whistles, the wobbling, leery invitations. If she waited in the car with the children, eventually he would join them. They would argue briefly and, with luck, she would drive home with her teeth clenched while Frank snored beside her.

But, this time, as she approached the car she looked at her daughter watching out the window, her mouth drooping at Jess in commiseration, and she looked at the clock above the war memorial, which said four forty-nine. And she thought, very calmly, 'I'll give him exactly half an hour.'

At five twenty-five she started the car and drove out of town.

It took seventy minutes, more or less, to the teacher's house, and another twenty to get home. She waited for regret, compassion or fear to take hold of her, but instead, with every mile, she felt herself growing calmer and cooler.

When the boys were settled in the car, nursing their schoolbags and a small fleet of improvised battleships, and the car doors had been slammed and locked, only then did she reply to their questions about Frank's whereabouts.

'As far as I know,' she said, 'your father's still in the pub.'

It shut them up. Perhaps the ice in her voice reached out and froze their tongues.

There was much to be done when they reached home. They emptied the car boot of the groceries Frank and Jess had bought while waiting for the court to open, then Jess sent Lachie to feed the motherless calf and the half-grown pig and Ben to fill the water troughs.

'Up to the brim,' she told him, though at that point she was still not admitting to herself any definite intent.

She fed the dogs and checked the horses — six of them now, and one of the mares in foal. Another two sold last month, show ponies, one with ribbons for jumping. As long as the feed could be found, Frank and Jess could make money from horses.

With Kathryn's help, Jess gathered the eggs from the known nests, and fed the cat and heated baked beans from a family-sized can (canned food was disapproved of by Frank, and therefore a treat). And all the time she was waiting for the phone to ring.

Then, when it did, she stopped Ben in his tracks. 'Don't. Don't answer it.'

The two boys stared at her. This was something different; this was life about to turn upside-down. They stared at her, then stared around, like strangers, at the walls, at the ripped and colourless lino beneath their feet, but they said nothing.

'After tea,' Jess heard herself telling them . . . 'After tea we're gonna pack up your clothes and toys and go away for a while.'

None of them asked why. After a silence they began to clamour about what they would take, but none of them — ever — asked her why they were going away.

*They knew.* That was the thought she kept in her mind. *They knew — they didn't need to ask.*

If she told Frank that he'd never believe it.

# C H A **20** T E R

NOW AND AGAIN the Torana coughed, like a sheep in the night, and lost power. The headlights would dim, then revive. Their future would be decided by an aging motor; if it stopped they would push it to the side of the road and wait to be rescued. They could sleep, bundled together, and when help came in the form of some kindly motorist Jess would invent some story and drive, or be taken, back home.

The children were silent, only the steady snuffling breath of Kathryn in the front seat. Hayfever. Songs of leaving and pain bobbing, half-submerged, in Jess's head. The motor running smoothly now. 'Anyone awake?' Softly. Hopefully.

'Me.'

'Lachie?' The boys' voices are hard to tell apart.

'Mmm.'

'You okay?'

'Where we going, Mum?'

She makes a decision. 'Grafton.'

'Grafton. Graafton.' Rolling it in his mouth like a lollipop.

She'd never been to Grafton, knew no one there. He'd have no reason to look for her in Grafton.

He would think, first, of Del's place — though they'd gone away till the weekend. Then maybe Jody's. Beyond that who might he think she would turn to? His sister Helen? All those places he would have found her and she doesn't want to be found.

Not yet, anyway.

One time Del had noticed a yellowing bruise beneath Jess's eye. 'Run into a door?'

'Yeah.' Jess touched her cheek. Seemed like it had happened a long time ago.

'Men!' Del slammed in the drawer. 'All the bloody same.'

213

So Monty too!

'Only when he's drunk,' Jess half-defended.

Del rolled her eyes. 'I drink, and I don't beat anyone up.'

'I know, but . . .' trying to get it clear in her head, 'some people it affects different ways.'

Del wasn't listening. 'I've left Monty twice. But living with Mum drove me up the wall and boys need a father. And there's a lot worse than Monty and Frank, that's for sure. Monty's sister stayed in one of those women's refuge places, and some of the stories you wouldn't believe. Except she's pretty fucked in the head, Monty's sister. Always has been.'

Monty walked in right then, and Del gave Jess a look and said, 'Runs in the family.'

Monty looked at the grins on their faces and said, 'What does?'

'Brains,' said Del, 'and sex appeal.'

Monty smirked, put an arm around Del and nipped at her neck until she was shrieking and struggling.

'I COULD SEE the irony,' he would have told Jess. 'There I was, feeling like her father and wanting to take a whack at the prick. All het up about what she was doing with a loser like him and what sort of arsehole was he to be taking advantage, and her no more than a kid.'

He'd tried to like the coot. Cord, his name was — he'd spelt it out with a beer-wet finger on the bar, as if it was a word Frank might not have come across. A skinny weasel of a bloke, with eyes set close and a brown moustache dribbling beer. Frank had sat there and listened to bullshit about inhabited planets and alternative soundwaves, an eye on Ruby, who used to have so much sense but now sat there like she was lapping up the wisdom of Solomon.

Frank thinking it still wasn't too late, they'd find room for Ruby, a family was all she needed. But not including idiot Cord. And how could he make that kind of offer? She really seemed to admire the guy, and even if it was just pretence, she would no doubt put great store on loyalty, the way people do when they've received bugger-all of that commodity themselves.

He was waiting for Jess to come and drag him out. Anticipating how the crabby-wife set of her face would melt when he introduced Ruby. (Better if she recognised Ruby without introduction, but what was there to know?) And picturing Cord's face when he realised Jess belonged to Frank.

Eventually he got to wondering why it was taking Jess so long, and by then he knew there was trouble ahead. Could see her green eyes slicing through him, the contemptuous twitch of her upper lip. It was the wrong thing to do, looking at him like that. Left a taste in his mouth that needed washing down.

He remembered that he'd told her he'd be in the other pub. But she knew by now if it wasn't one it'd be another. Ought to get moving all the same. He persuaded Ruby and Cord to come with him back to the car. Meet Jess and his little girls. 'One more jug,' said Ruby and Frank wasn't up to arguing.

As they paraded along the footpath Cord got playful, whacking at Ruby's improbable arse with the back of his hand. Ruby would cuff him away and giggle. Their routine depressed Frank. Even Ruby didn't twig that Frank had asked them to come mainly in order to defuse Jess's certain anger. They were appalling but innocent.

On discovering the Torana was not where it had been, Frank led the way to the Royal Arms, where he and Ruby had met, so that when Jess returned from wherever she'd gone he would be easily found. He was angry, now, at her irresponsibility; the boys would be waiting to be collected. Had she forgotten that?

It was almost dark before he began to think that something might have gone seriously wrong. He rang Monty's place but no one answered. He rang home, collect, from the public phone in the bar-room but got no answer there either. He decided they must be still on the road; he'd try in another twenty minutes. He couldn't believe Jess would go home without him, but it started to look like that's what had happened. The thought of it brought a terrible taste to his mouth.

It was almost an hour later when Ruby reminded him to ring again. And still there was no answer.

He scraped up enough change to put through a call to the schoolteacher's house. He told the teacher he was still in the big smoke, he needed to leave a message for his wife.

'But Mr Ward,' said the teacher, 'your wife collected the boys a couple of hours ago.'

'Then she'll be home,' he said. 'It's our damned phone on the blink again.'

215

He repeated the conversation for Ruby and Cord. 'Always could think on my feet,' he told them. It was no great comfort. He drained his glass and fumbled around in his pockets. A five-cent piece, which he tossed on the table.

'Here I am, not a penny in my pocket and my family's buggered off home and left me.'

Though right now, most likely, they'd be on their way back to pick him up. Jess, having made her point, would not be so heartless as to leave him penniless a hundred and ten miles from home. Frank decided he could forgive her.

'We'll take you, man,' said Cord. 'Can't just fuck off and leave a good bloke in the lurch.'

'He's my dad.' Ruby was drunk. 'The only one I ever had.'

She laid her swollen fingers over Frank's and, just looking at the gnawed and grubby nails that were still recognisably Ruby's, he could easily have cried. He, too, was a little drunk.

'Gotta full tank almost.' Cord raised reverential eyes towards the grimy ceiling. 'Fate,' he said.

Frank acted as if the possibility of Cord's offer had never crossed his mind.

It was a silly little Toyota, a city car ragged with rust. Frank drove; his companions had been falling about once they got out on the pavement, and Frank knew the way. When he moved, Cord spread a smell like footrot, and it was stronger in the confines of the car. Frank wound down his window. All the way home he was expecting to see the Torana's lights coming towards them.

Even when they walked into the house and no one was there he wasn't seriously worried. When he rang Monty's again, there was still no answer but he saw now that this meant nothing; Jess and Del could be there with the kids just letting the phone ring. Failing that Jess must have taken off to some camping ground. Just for the night. Giving him time to sober up. She had sense, Jess, common sense and guts. He was proud of her.

She had been home. The dogs had fresh water and the cat wasn't whining, the groceries had been unpacked.

Frank and Ruby propelled Cord to Ben's bed. Frank could air the bedding and Ben would never know. He sliced cold mutton from the bone and opened a packet of supermarket bread. While they ate he explained to Ruby how Jess and Del were letting the phone ring unanswered. Aiming to serve him right, scare the shit out of him. 'So I won't be ringing any more.' He grinned across at Ruby. 'Two can play that game. The phone doesn't ring she's gonna start getting worried.'

When Ruby fell onto Lachie's bed — not much more than a camp stretcher, but it juddered and held — Frank lay down on the double bed, thinking he could've offered it to Ruby. His own lean bones were better suited to a single bed. But then Jess might still come home before the night was over.

Finally he went to the phone and rang Del's number again. Monty answered, half asleep. They'd got home an hour before from Del's mother's place, knew nothing of Jess.

'She's probably on the way home right now,' Frank said. 'Reckon we just got our wires crossed about time and place. Get back to bed, mate.'

The next day he waited. And the day after that, which was the day that Cord and Ruby left. Frank had managed a private word with Ruby, told her they'd be happy to have her stay there awhile, only he was almost certain Jess wouldn't agree to having both of them — Cord being a man and pretty much a stranger.

Ruby looked at him the way she used to, a long counting-to-ten look, and told him, 'She's not coming back, Frank. This is how it goes, remember? Your women leave you, and they take the kids. Is that why you suddenly want me to stick around? So you won't be on your own?'

She was entitled to that — having a go at him. He wanted to tell her she was way off the mark, that Jess and Lisa were chalk and cheese, that Jess was straight as a die and never just out for herself the way Ruby's crazy mother was. But he just said, 'That's not fair, Rube. We were mates, you'n' me. You know we were.'

Ruby looked out the window at Cord, who was sitting on the chopping block examining the sun through a fragment of yellow cellophane. 'I stick by my mates,' she said.

'Well,' he said sourly, 'good on you Rube. So I guess you two gonna be leaving me soon?' He had wanted to feel charitable towards Cord but sober had been no improvement on drunk. Cord encased in an armour of suspect universal facts, like a tough little beetle. A borer, quietly digging his way in, causing weakness and finally collapse.

'Right now if you want.' Her eyes spitting out little stones.

'Don't be like that,' he said. Then added, a little plaintively, 'It's up to you.' But already he hardly cared one way or another; the last two days had drained him of emotion. He couldn't remember ever experiencing such a sucked-dry absence of feeling. It must be to do with growing older — the heart hardening, the capacity to care about others shrinking. The world being run, on the whole, by a bunch of old codgers. And it showed.

Ruby and Cord left the next day. Frank poured his spare can of gas into their sad little car, would have given them money but he had none on him.

'I wish you'd got to see Ben,' he told Ruby. 'He's a top kid. Doing well at school.'

'Maybe next time.' She gave him a sudden hug, and he stretched his own arms around her.

The night before they'd talked of Curvey's Creek, dragged their memories out and stood them back to back and found that hardly any measured up the same. And once or twice Rube had got him laughing.


Owen had moved Jenny Tripp in with indecent haste. Hadn't intended to — six months was the time span he'd allotted, six months between Marion's bitter departure and Jenny's arrival. Time to see if their affection waned, time to blur the unpleasant portrait of a man casting aside his wife for a newer model, time for Sheenagh to come to terms with the prospect of having a stepmother. Time to reassure the Curvey's Creek parents that he was still the right man for the job.

But, as Jenny had protested, they'd already waited. One of them might die, to leave the other with everlasting regret. The margins of scandal had rolled back, even in Curvey's Creek. Police officers knew these things — incidents, skeletons in cupboards.

So they packed up Jenny's possessions, hired a trailer and moved her in. Sheenagh and her friend Kay watched from Sheenagh's bedroom window, made no offer to help, and that was the way it would be with Sheenagh from that time until she left school and home. Passive resistance but never confrontation. Civility without warmth. Owen should have been wounded, at least concerned. Was surprised by the lack of sympathy he felt for his daughter, how unambivalent he was about taking sides in this cold war. Discussing the girl behind her back, two against one — though Sheenagh had Kay, and they were thick as thieves, always had been.

Sheenagh would learn to accept, and if she couldn't that wasn't Owen's problem. Same with the Curvey's Creek parents. Once Jenny was there with him Owen had stopped caring what others might say or think. It no longer mattered. If they wanted to remove him from the school, let them. He'd find another job, and Jenny would come too.

Sheenagh enrolled at Hamilton Polytech. They drove up and got her settled in at the YWCA until she found a flat. Kay McElvey had moved to Auckland.

Owen and Jenny were alone and unrepentant. He took up jogging when Jenny was working evenings. She deserved a body in good condition. He'd run along the barely visible track on the road verge, once used by Jess on her ponies. Both of them gone now — the horses. They gave the old one to Judy Gordon when she came to collect Pedro.

Judy had since left the district, sold her farm to a Japanese consortium; the land sat empty. Judy took the horses she couldn't sell off and moved north. The spectre of wealthy Japanese reaching in and buying land in their midst had united Curvey's Creek in fear and outrage. They saw it as the beginning of the end, were disenchanted with a government that had allowed such things.

Owen didn't wish to align himself with rural xenophobia, but Jenny shared the local outrage. 'It's our land and our children's land,' she lectured Owen. She was speaking in broad terms but it still made Owen a little anxious. Jenny envisaged having babies. Owen saw babies as stepping back into the cycle he'd just staggered out of. Babies grew into children, they died, ran away, resented you. It was a subject they'd pushed aside in the meantime. Jenny was only twenty-nine, they had time in hand.

Owen still hadn't told Jenny about the burning of the rabbiter's cottage. The longer he left it unsaid, the more deceptive he would seem to have been. If he didn't tell her she might never find out, but that had begun to seem unlikely. The New Zealand for New Zealanders Association held meetings at the school and when she wasn't working Jenny went along. Rick Chaney was the chairperson and Win Samuels the secretary. The cars that arrived were testimony to the popularity of the cause, and Jenny reported that the meetings were convivial. Owen took some satisfaction from the thought that, a few years back, he would have felt obliged to pretend allegiance. Now he was his own man.

Yet, as long as Jenny remained ignorant about that night, Owen would be vulnerable. In his more anxious moments he imagined himself being blackmailed. These were not totally scrupulous men. If Phil Chaney, for instance, demanded money as the price for not enlightening Jenny, what would Owen do?

And if Jenny found out for herself through gossip, idle or malicious, how would she react? Shrug it off as justifiable outrage that went awry? Or see only the crime and deception?

In bed one night, long after the New Zealand for New Zealanders cars had dispersed, when Jenny and Owen fell back on their pillows damp and happily depleted, Owen took a few moments to gather his strength and broached the subject, though obliquely. Started with mention of their first meeting, then asked her how she and her colleague knew about Ward and Jess. Who had told?

Jenny was shocked. 'I can't tell you that. You know I can't. It would be most unethical.'

'Of course,' muttered Owen. 'I'm sorry.' Told himself that at least he'd learnt something. Jenny Tripp was not the kind of officer to shrug off her lover's criminal transgressions.

'We may have misjudged Ward,' he said, either to annoy Jenny or by way of private atonement.

'No way,' said Jenny. 'I know his type. I don't want to upset you, Bennie' (her private name for Owen, since the first time they made love) 'but no one deserves a man like that.'

And then, bizarrely, the phone rang. As if somehow they had summoned Jess up. 'Just a minute,' said Jenny and passed the receiver across. Mouthed, 'It's *her*.'

Jess's voice was ragged and tearful. 'I've left him,' she said. 'Me and the kids. Dad, will you help us?'


SHE'S REALLY LEFT *me*. A whole week had gone past but Frank was still shoving that thought out of his head. Lisa, but never Jess. It wasn't possible. Frank and Jess had seeped into each other. Severance would leave both of them maimed.

Frank on his own. Nothing new for him in that. And this time better set up than he ever had been: a home, horses, dogs, a pig, cattle, Rhode Island reds and guinea fowl, the half-tame roo they'd found on the road.

Sure, the house was on the rough side, but they had everything they really needed. Why would she take off now when things were the best they ever had been?

A man, a young man, had come prowling round and turned her head. If Frank knew that was true he might believe she had gone. Concentrate on how to get her back, 'cause it wouldn't last — not with four kids at heel. If necessary he'd kill the bastard.

Thought he'd had bad times — who didn't think that? — but they were nothing compared with this. In his head Frank goes over and over that day she went, as if that way eventually he'll get it right and when he and Ruby and Cord reach the house it'll be lit up with Jess and the kids there waiting. She's shitty at him, of course, but only until she gets the picture. *You'll never guess who I ran into.* She's heard that one before, but this time he's brought the evidence with him. 'Ruby!' she says. 'This is *really* Ruby?'

But Frank can't make it happen that way, so here he is, all set up with everything he really needs, and it's a ball and chain around his feet. The animals' need to be watered and fed, while it lends a hazy purpose to each day, also shackles him. The stretch of black soil which had become the single significant spot on the globe — *You are here* — is now just another patch of semi-desert. Less than that; it's limbo. The air is insufficient to fill the lungs, and time fails to pass.

Kelly, Jed and the cat rub and curl about his legs in tender concern — or do they simply sense emotion going begging? He prefers to believe concern, but it's scant comfort.

Even unshackled, Frank couldn't leave. With Ruby and Cord gone there is no transport bar horseback. Anyway, where would he go? And what if, in his absence, she rang and her call went unanswered and she never rang again.

JENNY, AT LEAST, had felt vindicated. She'd known Ward's type, had seen too many perpetrators of domestic violence, even her own father. Common as dirt under the fridge, and just as easily remedied. Rearrange and scour.

That was what had attracted her to Owen, his lack of rage.

Owen was seeing a bunched fist collide with his daughter's

soft mouth. He winced and shied away. Jess had given no reason. It could be anything that had caused her to flee. Another woman . . .

'Look at Marion and me,' he told Jenny. 'There are all kinds of reasons why people . . .'

'Not to a refuge. With four little kids.'

She was right. Of course she was.

'After everything that's . . . I won't know what to say . . . how to talk to her.'

'You will, Bennie.' Jenny kissed Owen's neck.

ON THE TRAIN a foreign woman entices Kathryn to sit beside her. *Entice* is the word that comes into Jess's head and keeps her turning to check that her daughter is still there, exclaiming out the window and being taught, Jess supposes, selected words in the woman's language.

At first the woman catches Jess's eye with smiles and gestures intended, clearly, to reassure. And Jess smiles back, her fears for the moment allayed. Feels, even, grateful that she has one less child to worry about now the novelty of the train has worn off.

But then unease floods back, as if anxiety is now her natural state, and she jerks her head round, expecting to see two empty seats where the foreign woman and Kathryn sit.

Already Jess has been forced to separate the boys, who had begun to elbow, pinch and punch each other. That is Jess's fault. It must be. Her children have learnt about punching and pecking-order from kids at the refuge, have discovered the bleak benefits of recycling their pain. At home Jess's children were almost always nice to each other. Doesn't that mean they used to be happy children but now they're not?

The baby is not unhappy. She is cheerful and stroppy and eager to entertain. Already she's forgotten her father, and the cat with his irresistible tail, and the dogs Kelly and Jed. Her eyes don't get the unoccupied glaze Jess has come, already, to recognise in the older children as a yearning for home.

When they talk about the chickens, or Bridey — the gentle mare that even Kathy could ride — the half-tame roo, or the cat they never have agreed on a name for, Jess sees her children's faces light up. But she has to spy on them for those moments, for in

222

her presence they censor themselves. They are protecting her, she understands that, but she's not sure from what.

Do they think, like everyone else, that she isn't old enough to be a proper mother? With or without Frank, Jess is used to being mistaken for her children's older sister. (Some day, Frank used to say, she'd get a thrill out of it. Whereas he was never going to get a great deal of joy out of being taken for Jess's father and his own children's grandfather.)

Alongside Jess, Lachie is kicking the seat in front of him, which is Ben's. A steady thump, thump, that may or may not be intentional. Ben's head peers around at arm-rest level.

'What about that sea?' Jess's voice in her own ears sounds both childish and phoney. 'Who's gonna be first to see the sea?'

Only Eve shows enthusiasm. Ben's face now appears above the seat. 'What's it worth?'

'Don't be stupid,' Jess tells him, but she feels chilled. Frank would be appalled to hear a child of his speak like that. Ben would never have said that if his dad was there. In the absence of Frank are her children going to turn into grasping, petulant creatures?

'Don't keep wading through the bog,' Gloria had said, meaning stuff like this, sloshing and swirling in Jess's head. 'You can't see anything while the mud's flying. Let it settle, let it dry. Take your time. One thing's for certain, you did the right thing. You know that, don't you?'

'Yes,' said Jess. 'I know that. But —'

'Just keep that ticking round in your head. You did the right thing. Say it.'

'I did the right thing.'

*I did the right thing, I didtheright thing ididtherighthing ididtherighthing* . . . until Jess sees that the baby is copying the silent movement of her lips. Jess smiles at Eve then glances quickly back at Kathryn, who is sucking at something unseen and possibly narcotic. The foreign woman is also sucking. Or pretending to? Jess can't tell if the woman's face is placid and kindly or scheming and malevolent. She wishes she was a good judge of character, but in fact — except when it comes to heavy drinkers — she has more faith in Frank's assessments than in her own.

The train is moving, the windows are open barely a fraction, there are several other passengers in this carriage. Even if the woman is a demented kidnapper, not foreign at all but merely incoherent, there is nothing at this moment to be gained by snatching the child away. Too many witnesses, nowhere to push or drag her.

Jess wishes they'd stayed on at the refuge, despite the overcrowding and a sense that the needs of the other families were more urgent and dramatic. She wishes *at least* that she'd chosen to stay in the area and keep in touch with Gloria and Vicki. Especially Gloria, who despite her awful braying laugh and faintly mouldering odour, is the person Jess would most like to have been her mother.

This thought causes Jess to remember her childhood fantasy that Judy Gordon was her natural mother. Which in turn reminds her about the policewoman stepmother who now sleeps in Marion's bed and looks at herself in Marion's mirrors. Jess tries to assemble the policewoman's image in her head . . . curly hair or straight, blonde or brown? Sometimes a face will emerge from nowhere as if it's in one of those paint-with-water books, and for a moment or two Jess will think, yes, that's her, Officer call-me-Jenny Tripp. But then she'll remember that the face she's seeing in fact belonged to Mrs Whittaker, the history teacher, or some girl from Windsor High Jess hardly knew and has no reason at all to remember.

While Jess would like to fill in the cloudy image in a navy-blue peaked hat that is her stepmother, she's not yet ready to plunge her mind into the oil slick of Curvey's Creek, her father, the rabbiter's cottage . . .

It is thanks to Owen that all five of them are now in this train heading for Brisbane and this afternoon will be on a plane bound for Auckland. Yet even that arrival is something Jess isn't willing to think about. Perhaps because she is unable to think beyond the flight itself. Jess has never flown. The prospect terrifies her. She knows it's just like sitting at the movies or in an exceedingly small dining-room while out of the window the world turns into a Tonka toytown. She knows you are brought tiny picnic containers of food and there are movies that can be watched when the topside of clouds become boring. Someone — probably Frank — has described those things.

Jess is scared for a number of reasons that don't include the possibility of crashing. There is the losing-the-tickets fear, the inadvertently-leaving-a-child-behind fear, the fear that all the children may throw up and that one or more may panic and require attention above and beyond that which Jess is able to provide. The first two, at least, are a little irrational since Vicki has asked her friend (Lana — or was it Alleena?) to meet Jess and the kids at the railway station in Brisbane, ferry them to the airport and see them safely onto the plane. Jess had of course protested that it wasn't necessary, but even as she did so she could feel the relief easing and tickling like broken elastic.

Her *real* worry, the big one, is that there will be a moment — perhaps when the door is secured, or when the plane leaves the ground — when fear itself will squeeze the breath from her body. The way it would threaten to when she was a child outside, alone, at night. Or shut in a small room, like in a coffin with the lid hammered closed. Or a cave that is blocked by a landslide. Dying of fright, the way she remembered from dreams.

To wake up panting in a bed and a room she didn't recognise. Not until Owen arrived, looking goofy in his pyjamas and bare feet, and sat down beside the duvet ranges made by Jess's legs. 'What was it?' he would ask in a voice husky from sleep.

And because she could hardly ever remember back into her dream she would tell him it was the landslide again, where she couldn't breathe. And he would say, 'Breathe now. Big. In. Out.' Just as he used to tell them all at school first thing each morning.

Her father. Within twelve hours she would be with them. It was no longer reasonable to keep him out there on the periphery of her consciousness.

He had been right. That was the hard part. And even though Jess's desperate phone call had been a tacit admission of error (a rather large error in that she is now responsible for four other lives besides her own), Owen is entitled to hear Jess say the words. But which words exactly? *I'm sorry* would be easy enough, but given the price of the air tickets plus the extra money he'd sent and the fact that already there wasn't much of that left, *I'm sorry* seems seriously insufficient. Yet *I was wrong* sticks in her throat, even now when she voicelessly tries it out.

*You were right about him.* Yes, she can manage that. Can even, she discovers, get satisfaction from the saying. *You were right about him. He's an arsehole bastard. A hopeless pisshead. A bad-tempered, arrogant prick of a man.*

Even rolling them round in her head, her lips unmoving, Jess feels the words putting iron into her heart. She feels a surge of satisfaction and virtue. It's the kind of feeling that comes from tracking down and removing the source of a stink that has hovered for weeks, unidentified and unlocated. That kind of feeling but, naturally, on a larger scale.

HE'D COLLECTED SHEENAGH on the way to Auckland to meet the plane. Jenny's idea, to ease the meeting. Jenny didn't come. Apart from anything else, the car would be crowded on the way home.

Jess emerged like Snow White with dwarfs at foot and a baby in her arms. Beautiful as Snow White, weary but unmarked. And there were the children; he'd seen photos Jess sent to Sheenagh but those had been of small strangers, discomforting extensions of Ward. Now they were his grandchildren — three of them, anyway — staring at him, talking to him, taking his hand. Owen was enchanted. In their features and expressions glimpses of Corin, of Owen's dead mother, Jess, Sheenagh and Marion would flicker but never surface, like fish in deep water. With relief Owen saw that the presence of the children could forestall forever all need for him and Jess to talk about anything else.

They dropped Sheenagh back at her Hamilton flat and drank tea with her flatmates. On the way out of town Lachie pointed out a playground and Owen stopped. Jess sat the baby down on her rug and she and Owen pushed swings, applauded climbing, scanned slides anxiously (just the thought of it making the heart thud) for imbedded razor blades.

At Te Kuiti they found a McDonalds. 'You shouldn't,' said Jess, 'they eat like horses. Fish and chips'd be cheaper and still a treat.' But Owen wanted to indulge these children, whose faces really did shine at the prospect of playgrounds or french fries in packets. Who were so unlike the children he taught every day.

When he'd got them home those feelings were confirmed. It wasn't just grandfatherly pride. Jess's children were a pleasure to live with, they looked after each other, they lacked the sharp edge of the other children he knew; a selfishness that in recent years he'd seen increasing until its absence in a child became, as now, a cause for amazement.

They had anticipated an invasion, he and Jenny. Had looked, after school on the three days between Jess's call and her arrival, at houses for rent. Not, they'd assured each other, because Jess wasn't welcome to stay as long as she needed, but because children required the security of their own home. Yet now Owen was pleading with Jess to stay longer, make the most of having help with the children, and Jess was refusing. Finally saying to him, '*You* might like having us here, but think about Jenny.'

'She doesn't mind.'

Jess looked at Owen the way she looked at Kathryn with shoes on the wrong feet. 'She says she doesn't. What else can she say!'

JESS STILL HADN'T said her words of daughterly contrition. Not because her recall of Frank's failing was dimming, but because she could never find a suitable moment. The words would be hanging around, awaiting their cue, and Owen would suddenly remember something he'd promised to show the boys or some lesson he hadn't prepared for. Or else he would begin an animated dissertation on a topic so intrinsically boring, even by schoolteacher standards, that it had to be an evasive tactic. Jess had forgotten that this was the way of her family. Declarations not being made because they were too risky. Might prove tactless or hurtful or embarrassing — in fact were almost *bound* to do so.

Living with Frank, Jess had become accustomed to a risky kind of talking. When you got used to it, you came to think it was the norm, and that the Bennington reticence was a whole lot riskier. Frank had never been much constrained by the need for tact, and was possibly not even capable of feeling genuine embarrassment. 'I don't mind telling you,' he would assure strangers as a preface to one of his stories. It was an understatement — he *relished* telling them, no matter what it was. There seemed to be nothing in Frank's head or heart that he couldn't or wouldn't talk about. Possibly to anyone, certainly to Jess.

She remembers the way he would talk about Ruby and baby Ben during those months at the station on the east coast. Both of them squeezed together in his narrow, hard bed, or her narrow, sagging one, and whispering (except for the occasional lucky Friday night when Wi Po and Hans drove off to the pub and Frank had thought up a reason not to join them). Once or twice, as he'd talked of his missing children, his eyes had grown watery

227

— and instantly, Jess had felt that sweet-sour, lemondrop sensation of her own tears welling.

This was not a memory Jess could afford to allow rein. For if Frank had wept over the loss of those two — having only known each of them for less than a year — how would he cope with losing four children?

Owen and Jenny Tripp. There was a time when, reading Marion's bitter letters, Jess had made claims concerning the policewoman. Extravagantly loyal promises such as 'I'll never speak to the bitch' and 'She'll never be part of the family — not so far as I'm concerned'.

But in fact she liked Jenny, who was straightforward, cheerful and full of energy. And she liked the difference she saw in her father, the fact that he now made feeble jokes and wore running shoes and turned up Tracy Chapman on the radio. And had, without hesitation, paid for Jess and the children to come home.

That last required something to be said, yet almost two weeks went by, the words still champing and pacing in Jess's head. Then, finally she cornered Owen alone with his youngest grandchild, playing a xylophone that had belonged to Jess, then Sheenagh, then Corin. He was picking out *Three Blind Mice*, but the low note was loose and just kind of clattered.

They were in Corin's old room, but there was nothing of Corin left there, Jenny had packed up his toys, and pulled down his posters of spaceships and famous rugby players. She had painted the walls an eggshell colour and the shelves were freshly white. She'd told Jess that, when she moved in with Owen, Corin's room looked and smelt as if he was still living there. *Like a museum*, said Jenny. If she hadn't come along it would have stayed that way. She hoped she hadn't done the wrong thing, but in Jenny's opinion people should get on with living.

Jess had realised then that Jenny was asking for Jess's approval, retrospectively. Jess said she thought Jenny was right about getting on with living. She imagined herself walking into Corin's room as-it-was and just the thought of it put her on edge.

Having caught Owen unprepared (*Did you-ever-hear-such a-thing-in-your-life. As . . .*) Jess's considered speeches deserted her. She managed only to blurt: 'Dad, you know all that stuff back then? Frank and all that? I'm sorry.'

Owen sat looking up at her, the xylophone hammer

suspended. He blinked a few times, looking bewildered and slightly embarrassed.

'You can't be sorry,' he said. 'You mustn't. If it hadn't all happened you wouldn't be here with these marvellous kids.'

IT WAS ONLY when he heard himself saying the words that Owen realised the truth of them. He was *grateful* to Jess, this being one of those situations where the end totally justified the means. Assuming, of course, that Jess's life in the intervening years had not been too dreadful. She'd told them it hadn't been. Jenny believed that was just a brave face — Jess protecting Owen and possibly Jess herself) — from the truth.

But, if that was so, surely Owen would be able to tell? Somehow it would show in Jess's face, in the way she spoke and moved? In almost eight years, his elder daughter seemed to have scarcely changed — unlike Sheenagh, whose teenage years had been marked by transformations as unpredictable and unnerving as earthquakes. A brutal life would surely have left its mark? Owen's grandchildren, out-going, lively and good-hearted, could not be the product of a brutal life.

Besides, these days Owen had difficulty with moral judgements. He was a man who had ousted his own wife from their home. A dreadful, shameful thing to have done. Yet if he'd left things the way they were he would have been guilty of wasting lives. His. Jenny's. Possibly Marion's.

At any rate that was one way of looking at it. And who was to say, in such matters, that any one perspective was the right one?

Well, Jenny.

And in Jenny's view Jess's life was a tragedy and a disaster. Even though she had made her escape from Frank, the price was yet to be paid. The burden of raising four children alone would turn Jess into a haggard old woman before she was thirty. Jenny saw this scenario every day in the course of her work — light-fingered children and their exhausted, dull-eyed mothers. The victims of men.

Owen didn't protest, knew that when Jenny talked of men in that tone of voice he was exempted. Instead he'd pointed out that, once Jess and the children were settled in their own place, he and Jenny could have the children on some weekends and during school holidays, thereby easing Jess's load. Jenny had given him a long, steady look, then sighed and said she supposed they should.

It wasn't the first time that Owen had had reason to reflect that Jenny was stronger on theory than on practice. There was, for instance, the matter of Jess and the children's financial support.

They had arrived, of course, with nothing much more than clothes and a few toys. Jenny had advised that Jess should delay applying for a solo parent benefit as long as possible, for once the application was made, Ward would be required to pay maintenance. And there was nothing, said Jenny, like a tug on a man's pocket to launch him into custody battles.

So Owen had undertaken to get them set up in a house and to provide for them during the initial weeks. This would set him back; he was still suffering the effects of matrimonial division of assets, when guilt had made him generous beyond the legal requirement.

But Jenny, it seemed, had anticipated Marion would do the supporting. Owen, having already forked out for airfares etcetera, should inform Marion of her responsibility. Owen flatly refused. The fact that Jess had, come the crunch, turned to him and not her mother still gave him a small euphoric glow.

Jenny could now see Jess and the children costing Owen all the meagre savings that might, in the foreseeable future, have allowed her to leave the force and have babies at least as nice as Jess's. Jenny hadn't said so to Owen, but he read it in the way she sighed and set her face.

THE RENTED HOUSES Jess would be able to afford on a benefit were depressing places on the large-dog side of Windsor. Owen recognised one street as the one where the Green girl had lived. But, without a car — and he certainly couldn't afford to buy her a car — Jess would need to be in town.

Jess, in a hurry to choose, seemed undaunted by ugliness. Her decision was based on proximity to the Windsor West primary school.

There was a bond to pay, plus two weeks' rent in advance. Jenny sent them off to Windsor's super economy second-hand shop and Owen made no protest when Jess chose the cheapest beds and bedding, the cheapest and ugliest table and chairs. The children admired the recycled teddy-bears, the peeling bikes, the battered skateboards and asked for nothing. So Owen had them each choose a toy.

Owen and Jenny felt Jess had made a serious mistake in taking the boy Ben away from his father. They'd tried to point out that legally she had no claim to the child, that technically she had kidnapped him. His father would institute custody battles and use this against her, possibly to win custody of all four children.

Jenny got home from her morning shift while Owen, Jess and the children were still out shopping, and took a call from Ward trying to track Jess down. Jenny pretended astonishment and concern on hearing Jess had gone missing. She believed she'd convinced Ward.

Between them Jenny and Owen decided it was best that Jess should not be told of the phone call. But they did raise with her, once again, the problem of Ben, suggesting ways in which the boy could be returned to his father. Jess had screwed up her face to suggest that what she was hearing was beyond belief. 'He's their brother!'

Owen, shamed, had patted his daughter's arm. 'You're right.'

He saw Jenny give him a cool look that he couldn't readily decipher. Even so, that look was a shock because it was so familiar. It was a Marion kind of look.


THE PHONE HAD acquired a terrible power. Even in silence it drew Frank to it, the receiver leaping into his hand. Their address book had gone with Jess, so he pestered the directory service for the phone numbers of people she knew or had known. Retained, at first, a pretence of casual confusion, but later resorted to grillings and accusations. Eventually, all pride gone, he told them why he was ringing and how badly he missed her.

Sometimes the phone would ring and Frank would run to pick it up, a whinny of hope shivering through his veins, though he almost knew better. Most times it was Monty, though the school rang to see if the boys had come down with something, and a woman rang wanting a dozen pullets, and a man wanting the address of the people who owned the property — which could have been a cause for conjecture and concern if Frank had been in a state to care.

And Kanga Kristofferson rang, returning Frank's call. He offered to come up but Frank said no, there was nothing Kanga could do and Frank would be lousy company. Kanga's wife had walked out on him years before but there was no comparison. She hadn't bothered to take their son and within a week Kanga was saying good riddance and going square-dancing every Wednesday night.

'You reckon she's left for good?' Kanga asked. *Left for good.* Had Jess decided that Frank lay in one direction and good lay in the other?

Frank asked if Kanga had heard from Rumbo McFee recently, and Kanga said, last time he'd heard, Rumbo was on his way to Malaysia to manage a timber mill.

Monty did his best to be of comfort. Once every few days he'd drive up with a crate of dark ale — Frank would write him a cheque for half — and hang around until it was cut. With a few drinks in him Monty would blunder and probe in Frank's private pain like a mother chasing a prickle. But he meant well, poor little bastard.

'You and Jess seemed a perfect couple,' he'd tell Frank. As if the situation was beyond rational belief. As if Jess and the kids had been lured into a spaceship and spirited off for a millennium or two.

'I reckon,' said Monty, the second week, 'she could've gone to one of them refuges.'

'Them whats?' Frank had been only half listening.

'Women's refuges. Don't tell me you never heard of them?'

'I never heard of them,' he said, straight-faced.

'You must've,' pressed Monty. 'Lesbo places, full of radicals and that.'

'That right?' Frank leaned forward. 'Doesn't sound like Jess.' He heard a pleading note in his voice. He'd already had this conversation more than once, with himself and with Helen.

'No,' said Monty after brief thought. 'You're right. M' sister stayed in one, but she's a loose thing, she is. Not like Jess. Jess's got her head screwed on.'

'They've got one in town, have they?' Keeping it casual.

'Don't think so. But then, how d'you know?' They're kind of a secret society, like the Masons, only for women.'

'But just . . . certain kinds of women?' Frank needed to hear Monty saying the words out loud. 'Not,' he prodded, 'say . . . for someone like Del?'

'Del? That'd be the day! Not Jess either — you're right. Not straight-out sort of women like Jess and Del.'

'That's what I reckon,' agreed Frank.

It didn't cheer him up. Eliminating the possibilities wasn't helping him find his family. He had made calls to everyone he could think of, even across the Tasman to Marion, even to the father's house. After each call he'd spend ages sifting those brief and pathetic conversations for give-away pauses or inconsistencies. Could trust no one, except maybe Judy Gordon, but they told him her phone had been disconnected.

Wherever Jess was, he wanted her to be lonely. Lonely enough to want to come home.

Then he got the call about the Torana.

'Are you Frank Ward?'

'I am. Yep, that's me.' Holding his breath.

'Your car is parked outside the Grafton railway station. The key is beneath the back ashtray. Do you want me to repeat that?'

'Hang on,' he said, 'hang on. I don't give a stuff about the bloody car.'

'Grafton railway station. Key beneath back ashtray.'

'Are they all right? Who are you?'

But she'd hung up on him.

He worked on trying to place the voice, even allowing for disguise. Australian, almost for sure. Not his sister Helen. (He'd rung her right at the start. 'When will you learn?' she'd said, automatically holding him responsible.) Not Del's voice. Nor Jody from Tamworth — or was it?

He rang Jody just to be sure. Not her voice. His phone bill would be astronomical, couldn't be helped. Had it been, then, a lesbo radical kind of voice? He rang to consult Monty. Monty admitted to having no first-hand experience in this matter but was happy to speculate. Crouched on the cracked lino with Monty in his ear, Frank yearned for Rumbo, who would've seen the funny side.

There were more important questions. Like — what was the significance of the car? They'd left the country? Jess felt sorry for Frank, alone and carless in the middle of nowhere? Would pity not imply regret?

Monty — loyal, humourless Monty — drove Frank to pick up the car. Up over the ranges, almost right to the coast. The Torana there, just like the woman had said. It was out of gas and the petrol cap was missing.

'Vultures,' said Monty. 'Guess your tyres were too bald to be worth the effort.' When he was younger, Monty recalled, he had an old Rover that crapped out south of Wangaratta. Overnight it was picked clean.

Frank thought of a story to match. It leapt forward in his mind, clamouring for attention, only he couldn't be bothered. On the heels of that story would come the one about Frank and . . . that's right, Jimmy Rider, who pointed out the car behind them crazily veering to avoid a wheel — a regular, upright Holden wheel careering down the hill. Frank's wheel, to be precise. Left rear, until it went AWOL. Or possibly the story about . . .

In the glove box there was a crumpled handkerchief, a chocolate bar wrapper, one fluorescent yellow sock (Kathryn's) and a crumpled automotive repairs receipt from five months ago. On the floor of the back seat there was a marble, a blue plastic dummy with a ravaged teat, half a shoelace, a pink comb with almost all its teeth missing, and one muddy size-four sneaker.

After assembling all these objects on the seat Frank slid in beside them. He could smell regurgitated milk, and something sweeter but less easily defined. He could smell his children.

THE BACK YARD was the worst thing; the corrugated iron fence, the rotary clothesline, the three skulking bushes — Jess couldn't have named these but each was of a species as familiar and inconsequential as freckles. Frank would have known their names, or found them out. He would have crushed the leaves, squashed the berries, sniffed, tasted, consulted strangers and passed his findings on to Jess and the children. And Ben, a small version of his father, would have remembered every last detail, according those dowdy bushes unforeseen importance.

There were a couple more bushes in front of the house and a narrow flower garden where Jess cleared the grass and oxalis. The front garden was open to the street (five large child steps from footpath to front door step — they'd counted with incredulity as Ben stepped them out.) The boys had been bedazzled. A street outside your window, people living right alongside you, a shop you could run to without even getting puffed.

234

'The novelty,' she'd told them, offended by their enthusiasm, 'will wear off.'

The back fence was high. They could see their neighbours' roofs and the top of one back door. Above that the hills looked down on them casting afternoon shade. In the back yard Jess felt crowded. She would tidy the girls and walk to the centre of town, yet still she would feel hemmed in. There was no breathing space here. The hills, the heavy clouds, the familiarity of shops and faces . . . all of this pressed in on her.

The cemetery was a good walk away, up past the domain. Corin's stone had not yet lost its shiny surface. A miniature rose bush beside the headstone, its flowering over, tiny rosehips. It seemed to Jess, had always seemed, that Lachie very much resembled Corin, but no one had yet remarked on this.

Marion had driven her brand-new Mitsubishi up the weekend after they'd moved into Windsor. She stayed at the Paradise Motel and took Jess and the children for drives in the countryside and lunch at a roadside tea-rooms. All the time she would talk to Jess, as if the children didn't know how to talk or had nothing of interest to say, and Jess's efforts to include the kids would go unnoticed. Jess was ashamed that her children's grandmother — the only real grandmother they would ever get to meet — should prove at once so generous and so impolite.

Generous only to a degree. Marion said Jess had done the right thing in asking for Owen's help. 'He's better off than me,' she said.

Owen stayed away that weekend.

The way her parents were about each other made Jess homesick for the farm and Frank. His nastiness was the steam-train kind, thundering and hooting. Dangerous but, in a way, predictable, it fuelled up, it blew, then went on by. The nastiness she sensed about her in Windsor seemed to be woven into life, sneaky as ground glass.

Janine Thomas, who once was Jess's closest friend, came to visit. She brought her eight-month son, and her wedding photos. She had married Peter Chaney, who had once lived down the road from Jess. Janine filled Jess in on who was doing what; some of them people Jess couldn't remember. But after a while she began pretending she did, because Janine had seemed so dismayed, as if Jess's forgetting was an act of betrayal.

Some Jess had no trouble recalling. Leila Samuels lived with a rich old man in Wellington. Gavin Cawley was in Auckland, a trainee doctor. Carol Green had walked naked into the National Bank and been taken down south to a Cherry Farm. Brainbox Linda Quigley was teaching in Uganda. And Wyatt, sad fat Wyatt, had lost weight, and wasn't at all bad looking. He'd started a drama group called the Windsor Players, and was caught in bed with the town clerk's arty but middle-aged wife. 'Mind you,' Janine told Jess, 'that was nothing compared to the talk that went around about you.'

'And look at me now,' said Jess dryly.

Janine took it wrong. 'The guy Pete works with hasn't got a woman, and he's not bad looking. Likes kids.'

'No,' said Jess.

'And there is Ken O'Keefe at Liquorland. His wife died. They've got a little girl.'

'No.'

'He's only twenty-six or so. Doesn't hurt to look.'

All afternoon Jess had been feeling as if she and Janine were shouting to each other across a large paddock and, though the words were clear enough, the significance of them was getting lost in transit.

Jess would like to have seen Judy Gordon. Would like to hear about Lucky and ride Pedro again, but Judy had gone and nobody seemed to know where.


WHEN JENNY IS on duty Owen comes in after school to visit, spend time with the children, give Jess a hand. She's grateful; it had been a shock to realise just how much Frank must have done around the house to make each day fall into place so calmly and with such a sense of purpose. On her own, four children have begun to seem too many.

Yet it's a relief, each time, when her father leaves and she's no longer obliged to pretend to . . . to be okay, to be part of this place, to *exist*.

Back there with Frank, even in the worst times, she'd never felt other than at the centre of life. Now she is barely peripheral. *One day at a time*, she reminds herself in Jenny's voice. But each day she feels a little further away, a little more invisible.

When Owen is around she hears him with Ben or Lachie or Kathryn, explaining, admiring, correcting. Always the schoolteacher, he can't help it, and her kids don't mind, but it makes Jess think of Frank. Of the way he had of talking with the kids — any kid, not just his own — that made them feel *of interest*. Not just kids, either. Frank could make a frog feel significant just by the way he'd step over it.

She tries not to let herself think about Frank, of what he'll be doing or thinking. Tries to not even think of their horses, the foal that was nearly due, the dogs and the chooks and the dopey half-tame roo. But how can she not, when her children talk of them all the time?

She has done the right thing, everyone says so, and she's pleased when they do. She mustn't, she will not, let them down. The police at Grafton, Gloria and Vicki at the refuge, Owen and Jenny . . . When they were staying at the school house Jess had found she could talk to Jenny Tripp more easily than she could to Owen or Marion.

'I just kept hoping he'd give up the booze.'

'Jess, Jess . . . a leopard can't change his spots. Some women just put up with it longer, suffer more, screw their kids up. I've seen it time and again. You did the right thing, kid. Hang on in there.'

More women like Jess and men like Frank would get the message. The future of men and women was riding on Jess's shoulders.

'Put yourself first,' Gloria at the refuge had urged. 'Think of yourself and think of the children.'

But how could she think of the children without thinking of Frank, when so much of him was there within them?

Maybe Owen and Jenny are right and Ben should be with his father. He has become too watchful, too silent. Never asks, as Lachie and Kathryn do, about Frank. Jess tells them — as if she needed to! — that Frank has a drinking problem. But yes, they'll see him again. Someday. And yes, of course he loves them and misses them and thinks about them absolutely all the time.

And she tries to stop her mind from seeing this too clearly. Tries to keep from crying.

In the matter of what to tell the children Jess has been guided by the advice of Jenny, of Gloria and Vicki. This advice transforms Frank into *the abuser* and Jess into *the victim*, a faceless but all-too-familiar pair about whom a great deal is known. Jess initially took comfort from the realisation that her predicament was shared by thousands of women, but now this idea troubles her. She has this sense of her and Frank being viewed through the wrong end of a telescope; they are recognisable but much diminished. If she looks into the lens, Jess can see them for herself — a reduced, convenient image, which contains the truth and yet is not entirely truthful.

HE'D HARDLY USED the car at all, on account of the telephone maybe ringing. Weeks had gone past — six, seven, eight? . . . he no longer counted. Monty had stopped making compassionate visits.

This time, when the phone went, it was Helen again. Somewhere inside she must feel sorry for him, though she'd told him he must have brought it on himself. He was that type, his own worst enemy, always had been. And Helen had known him longer than anyone else.

'I hope you're coming to terms with it,' she told him.

That's how it was supposed to happen, you came to terms. With hurt, with rage, with grief. It was the thing to do.

But Frank was not coming to terms. Each day the enormity of his loss grew a little greater. He'd got thinner, and then he'd got skinny. His jeans billowed beneath his belt and his feet were all dips and sinews.

'Are you getting out and about?' asked Helen. 'You're there when I ring and you shouldn't be. Get out and meet people.'

'GOOD GOD,' DEL said when she opened the door. 'When did you last eat?'

'I cook,' he said, taking offence. 'I'm a pretty decent kind of cook. I've done it for a living now and again.' He'd been hoping for Monty, but Del would do. No sign of their kids, so it must be a school day. Good, Frank didn't feel up to being with kids who'd been friends of his kids.

'I know,' Del was saying, 'I've eaten your bloody cooking. You're a chef. That's not what I asked.' She let the water drain out of the sink and reached for the kettle. A yellow bruise just above her armpit.

'Sit down if you want. You never come and see us anymore. Monty's probably up at the tavern. Or maybe the end pub. Your guess is good as mine.'

238

Frank didn't sit down. 'Haven't been going out much.'

Del plugged in the kettle. 'Still nothing, huh? We had some good times, us and you guys.'

'What I can't figure,' he said, 'is what they'd be living on? Now, you'd know, Del. If they were on Welfare I'd've been asked to pay money by now. Is that right or isn't it?'

'Far as I know,' said Del. 'Far as I know that's how it works, but then I've never . . . I guess it takes a while, you know, to go through. And what if she's gone back home? Things might work different over there.'

For the first time Frank felt sure that, wherever Jess was, Del hadn't been in on it. 'Yeah, I guess. Okay. I look out for his car then?'

'Make you a sandwich?'

'I'll get one at the pub.'

'I'll bet,' she said. Jess would have given him one of those looks. *All your friends are pissheads. Have you thought about that? What does it tell you?*

It told him his friends weren't uptight, miserable, skinflint bastards. That they liked a laugh and they liked a drink and their hearts were in the right place. That's what he always used to tell her. Would say, if Jess knew of just one teetotaller who wasn't a self-righteous, intolerant arsehole he'd like to know the bastard's name. And Jess would say nothing, which proved his point.

Now Frank stands at the bar with its fancy gold hitching rail and scattered beer coasters and watches the barman fill the jug. Inexplicably, his mouth says, 'And a glass of ginger ale.'

Monty can't get over it. 'I said you looked crook, and y'are, right? Ginger ale, shit, you must be coming down with something bubonic.'

While Frank deals with the sickly sweet drink in girlie sips, Monty, his mind set on illness, tells about the time he thought he'd caught mumps when his kids had them, thought his virility had gone completely down the gurgler. Shitting himself about it.

This has reminded Frank of the time Rumbo shot himself in the leg. Monty's heard the story before and every few minutes he says to his drinking mate, whose name Frank's forgotten, 'This is the good bit' or 'I tell you, this fella sure knows how to tell a story.' It's as if Monty is Frank's agent in the yarn business.

'Tell him about delivering the wee fella,' Monty orders.

239

'Delivered his own little girl,' he tells their companion. 'One minute he's trying to get the engine back on its mounts, 'cause it's shaken off and they're on their way . . . Tell him, Frank.'

Frank can't remember when or why he shared around this story that was his and Jess's, and of course the baby's. He shakes his head. And already the drinking mate is telling about an old guy he knew who could tell great stories. Absolute bullshit all of them, but great yarns all the same.

Monty tells a story from Frank's life. He checks details with Frank, and at the end he apologises several times for how poorly he told it. Frank buys another ginger ale. He's thinking already about the phone, which could be ringing, but at the same time he's watching Monty with a kind of fascination.

I'm sitting here, he marvels to himself, drinking ginger ale and watching my mate turn himself into a bloody idiot.

# CHAPTER 21

WYATT'S HAIR FLOPPED, indolent and British, over one eye. He still looked soft, but the slug-like bulk had gone. Features had emerged from beneath the bulging cheeks; downward slanting eyes, pouting lips, an expression of permanent sardonic amusement. He still didn't look like the walking kind.

'I can go on m'own,' Frank had offered, but Wyatt had acted offended. Produced the pack he had specially borrowed, a serious affair with tubing and zips and pockets, and drew attention to Frank's *valise* — a very large shopping bag, open at the top, made of fibrous pink plastic.

From the moment Frank walked out of customs and Crystal set eyes on the bag it had been the cause of much hilarity. So that even now, just thinking about it has Frank grinning — though at the time he couldn't see, damned if he could, what was so funny about a shopping bag.

'Maybe we could find you a nice doctor's bag, a dear little black one.' This was so rich Crystal could barely force the words out.

'A Rawleighs bag,' snorted Debbie. 'Doesn't he look like a Rawleighs man, doesn't he though?'

Frank should have kept himself acquainted with carrier-bag fashions over the last couple of months; he could certainly have done with a laugh or two.

Before they left Auckland he transferred his gear into a canvas bag of Crystal's, with a zip, and PEPSI in large letters on either side. Wyatt had insisted. Never would he have lived it down if someone he knew saw him on the edge of the highway in the company of a cheap pink plastic shopping bag.

Frank would sooner have travelled alone. Two men together put drivers off, and Wyatt belonged to the stand-in-one-spot-and-hold-out-a-thumb brigade, while Frank believed in staying in motion.

On the other hand, he'd spent, God knows, enough time alone in the last few weeks and the longer the journey took the longer Frank got to nurse his faint but irrepressible hope. He knew the odds were against him; if she could cut him out of her life for this long she could cut him out forever. And who would blame her? No one in the whole bloody world. But in this life people got, often enough, that which they didn't deserve. Why not Frank?

And if he didn't, at least he would get to see the kids. Even an hour would be worth it. Ben the thinker, Lachie the talker, Kath the doer. Eve, the baby, still without definition, but only in Frank's mind — already she would be showing her colours, coming out of wraps like a fortune cookie, babies being the kind of lucky dip where everyone wins a prize. Frank wanting more babies, definitely wanting more babies. But this was not, perhaps, an auspicious time for that kind of thinking.

'The first time I ever hitched,' said Wyatt, resting against his pack, 'was out to your place. Bloody near perished.'

'You're certain it was Jess?'

Wyatt gave him a look of pain. The car Frank could hear came over the rise, he straightened up and raised his thumb. The car was full of women and dogs. Frank dropped his thumb and went for his tobacco.

'What? Maybe a million people in Auckland and you chum up with Crystal?'

'Small world.' Wyatt mocking Frank in a fruity theatrical voice, bored with all this. But Frank couldn't get over the thought that a coincidence like that was somehow propitious.

Wyatt had left Windsor after the town clerk — who claimed to have played Foreskin in Wellington Repertory but wasn't even convincing as Eeyore in the summer production — had turned the other players against Wyatt. The town clerk's wife, who could act a bit and appreciated talent, had given Wyatt the price of a ticket to California and the address of her cousin who'd had a walk-on part in *Rocky*. But Wyatt had got no further than Auckland, where he lived well rather briefly before the money ran out. He'd met Crystal when he complained about the undercooked chicken at the Moonshine Café and an astonishingly ugly creature in an apron and peep-toe wedgies had shot out from the kitchen like an ostrich on the attack and compared Wyatt unfavourably to a retarded squid.

Wyatt had yet to convince Crystal that she was made for the stage, although she wouldn't mind being on TV if asked.

'Even then,' said Frank, unable to prise his thoughts from the one remarkable track, 'you could've known Crystal and Debbie for years and the subject of me or Jess just never come up.'

'Oh, you'd've come up, Frank, sooner or later. You're a bit like that story of the fella whose car breaks down outside the lunatic asylum — sooner or later, when people are gathered, your name will come up.'

'That story. I know that story. Did I ever tell you about how I met Ben's mother . . .?'

DEBBIE HAD RUNG Frank straight away. 'Darling heart, brace yourself. I have news.' Debbie knew about heartache because her beautiful Jock had gone back to his wife and not even paid Debbie for his share of the trip to Australia. She'd had to sell the Chrysler to pay off the plastic credit.

As it turned out they did get rides, Wyatt and Frank. Must have been the fancy pack that did it, also Wyatt's prone position at the roadside; people took him for a student or a genuine backpacker.

First ride they got Wyatt played up to it, pretending he couldn't speak English. Frank had to make up a bullshit story about how they'd met up on the road and Frank had felt sorry for him. 'Hamburg,' Wyatt kept croaking from the back seat. 'Hamburg. Ja ja. Hans guten Hamburg.' The driver dropped them north of Huntly and drove on. Frank wasn't hugely amused.

Would make a story, though, this trip. The coincidences, the way Wyatt had turned into someone . . . not exactly likeable, but fairly entertaining. Frank could hear himself telling Jess, could see her laughing. He had stored up a heap of stories for her over the last two months. Two months, four days — it's been that long in calendar time.

When they were dropped off at Te Kuiti, Wyatt complained of a terrible thirst.

'Me too,' said Frank. 'Must be a tea-rooms somewhere.'

Wyatt stopped and stared. 'I thought you were joking. Shitabrick.'

'I'm not stopping you.' Frank jabbed his finger across the road, pubs were easily found. He watched Wyatt trying to decide — company or beer, when anyone knew the two should have gone together. Finally, muttering, he chose to stay with Frank.

Tea in a stainless-steel pot, with another slimmer pot to hold hot water. The stale, intimate smell of old food. Wyatt was unhappy.

'You're kidding yourself, Frank. Stick with this and you're not going to be you.'

'Who will I be?' It was a question Frank had been wrestling with in private.

'You'll be . . . you know, one of them. A wanker, Frank. You'll be a wanker.'

Which was much as Frank suspected. He was betraying all his natural instincts. 'A fish out of water,' he agreed. Saw himself gasping and flapping, his eyes growing opaque.

*Think of the kids, think of Jess, pour the water into the teapot, refill the cup.*


HE CAN SEE in the front window as he walks up the path. Her hairbrush, her fraying blue nightgown on the bed. The jolt of seeing them is like putting your hand on an electric fence. How can that be when the heart is nothing but veins and fat and pulpy red flesh? Medical boffins charting arteries, organs, intestines — all that anatomical crap that keeps the body breathing and shitting — as if that's all there was to it.

The invisible thing that they can't pin down, the bit people have got confused with a palpitating hunk of offal — that's the bit that matters. Only it's not in the boffins' charts and probably never will be.

Love — what does it look like?

Animals know. Children know. So what's the matter with grown-up human beings?

Wyatt gave Frank directions. One day a couple of weeks back Wyatt saw Jess and Kathryn weeding this poor little gesture of a front garden. Saw the boys come home from school. Saw Jess and all the kids come out to stand on the footpath waving goodbye to a bald middle-aged man. Wyatt saw all this from the house across the road, which belonged to the town clerk's daughter and son-in-law who had won a week in Tahiti by sending off the label on a wine bottle. Wyatt and the town clerk's wife used to meet there after the shit had hit the fan and everyone, including the husband, believed the affair was over.

Why has Wyatt come back to Windsor? To see the town clerk's wife? To get more money out of her? None of Frank's business. All the same he thinks, poor bloody woman.

He lets himself quietly through the child-proof netting gate into the back yard, which is just a square of nothing much and clothes hanging limply on the line. He knows those old red jeans, and the Bon Jovi sweatshirt which is Ben's and the blue and green tracksuit which has gone from Ben to Lachie to Kath.

He is trespassing. He is a trespasser on the property of his own family and this is a sad, sad thing. He should step up and knock on the door, but he wants to feel events are happening of their own accord. Also (and this is a thought that has stumbled out of the shadows and won't retreat) if Jess has someone with her — some eager, fresh-faced Windsor bank clerk or stock agent — Frank will need a moment to lance the pain and readjust his face.

He slides Crystal's canvas bag from his shoulder and leaves it on the concrete path. He keeps back from the windows — a face at the glass, especially a face like his, could give someone a nasty fright. He pulls his tobacco from his pocket and crouches beside the small crab-apple tree to roll a smoke. Frank doesn't own a watch, figures it'd be about halfway through this overcast afternoon. He can hear, faintly, voices floating in a syrup of music. Jess in this box of a house soaking her brain in the afternoon soap? In dire need of rescue.

The back door opens and Kathy comes out. She has opened it herself, tall enough now to reach door handles. She doesn't see Frank. She's looking for something, running in small circles.

'No,' she yells. 'No.'

'By the door?' shouts Jess.

Frank finds he's grinning, can't help it. He's in Windsor, in Jess's back yard, hearing her voice.

Kathryn has come across Frank's bag and approaches it in a cautious, mystified fashion. She crouches and tries the zip, looks carefully around the yard.

There's a moment of doubt when she sees Frank. Moment enough for him to think she doesn't know him, already he's faded out of her child memory. But then a smile takes up her face and she runs towards him and he hugs her and hugs her. His hat has tumbled off and he's breathing in the scrubbed-child smell of her hair.

When he finally looks up Jess is standing on the back steps watching them. Her hair is tied, indifferently, behind her neck and she wears a green jersey tucked inside her jeans, and battered woolly slippers. Her face has no expression at all. Nothing to even hint at his chances.

He stands up, putting his hat back on his head. Kathy keeps hold of his hand. He waits, time is nothing.

Jess takes a few wary steps towards him. He realises she's watching for anger.

ANGER, JESS IS thinking, would make it easier. As she steps forward she wills him to be angry and save her from the perils of choice. But this is not the face of an angry man.

She says, 'You're skinny.'

'You too.'

But not like he is. 'What . . .' she begins, but words jam in her throat. She tries again. 'Who's looking after . . .'

'Monty and Del. Staying in the house.'

'Has Angie dropped her foal yet?'

'Any day now.'

'Jed, how's Jed. And Kelly? And the roo — she still around?' So much she needs to know, a thousand questions, it could take all night.

Inside the house, distinct from the TV voices, Eve shouts and rattles the bars of her cot.

Jess rolls her eyes for Frank. 'She's hard case, this one. Come and see.'

Frank follows her into the girls' bedroom. Kathy sits on his shoulders, her chubby arms crushing his hat. Jess is feeling weightless yet clumsy. She's been expecting Frank, yet is unprepared. She wants to reach for his hand. She wants to slap his face and see red welts form. As they pass the basket piled with yesterday's washing, still unsorted, she wants to push it beneath the table out of sight. She sees untidiness everywhere and is ashamed.

Eve enjoys attention, she smiles at Frank. Jess lifts the child out of the cot and hands her to Frank. He stands there draped in daughters, his eyes on Jess. She feels self-conscious.

'How'd you get here?'

'Hitched. Flew then hitched.'

'How'd you know . . . where . . .?'

'Can I put your kettle on?'

''Course. Sorry . . . only I . . . ah . . .'

He carries his daughters into the main room, sits Eve on the floor and swings Kathryn down from his shoulders.

'I use a pot for the water,' she tells him. 'And there's tea bags.' For her father, but she doesn't say so. Jess drops down beside Eve and begins to remove the plastic overpants. She hears water running into the saucepan, she thinks about Bridey, who is the nicest natured of their horses, and good with kids. Still her children talk about Bridey, and the dogs and the kitten that grew. Sometimes Jess has felt such longing for the animals, even the foolish guinea fowls, has found it hard to tell where love for her children ended and love for their animals began, since it was all part of the family they were.

'I don't blame you,' Frank is saying. 'I reckon you did the right thing though it took me a while to come to that conclusion.'

This isn't what Jess is expecting. She has no response.

'I missed you,' he says. 'Missed you more than I even want to talk about. And I missed the kids. I guess the boys are at school? How're they doing.'

'Lachie's okay. Doing fine. Made friends already. Gotta nice teacher. But Ben . . . you'll see.'

'See what?'

'I dunno . . . he's older. Maybe it's just he's been missing you.' Should she have said that? Was it the kind of admission that would be used against her in the custody battles Jenny kept warning about?

He's bending over her now, reaching down his two forefingers for Eve to clutch, raising her to her feet, smiling as she steps out blindly, her face turned up to his. Kathryn, too, is looking up at him, beaming.

'What a kid,' he tells Eve. 'A walk like that could get you press-ganged into the army.' He winks at Kathryn.

Harassing his tea bag with a spoon, Frank tells Jess, 'I've quit drinking.'

It throws Jess on guard. She thinks, cunning old bastard!

'Knew you wouldn't believe me. It's true. Have I ever lied to you? Sober, have I ever lied to you?'

She remembers that this is what he does — uses words to back her into a corner. This time she must find a side-stepping reply.

'I believe you think you've quit.'

He drags the exhausted tea bag from his cup. Squeezes, looks around for somewhere to put it then takes it to the sink and drops it in there with Jess's. 'If I promise you I'll stay off it? Have I ever made a promise and gone back on it?'

Jess hears the question he hasn't quite asked and sees that she is the one with power here. She searches her memory, wants to be fair. 'You never promised anything,' she tells him, bitterness surfacing. 'You wouldn't even admit booze was a problem. Never once admitted that.'

'I do now. I bloody do now.' His voice rising. The two little girls — Kathryn imitating her sister's lumping crawl — stare at him, faces poised to crumple. Frank lowers his voice. 'I'm promising you now that I can stay off it. I will stay off it. With you to help me I can do it. I know I can.'

He's waiting. Jess has the sense of everything shifting and changing. Never before has he allowed her to see the extent of his need for her; and it is a sight so . . . naked, so unexpected and painful that she wants to cover her eyes. Frank has handed Jess the power to tear him apart.

Is that just another sort of cunning? Is he so certain that she would not kick a dog who lies belly up in trust or supplication? Jess clamps her teeth, gets a grip on herself. She does not owe him pity. She will not be manipulated.

'The boys will be out of school very soon,' she tells him. 'You should walk down to meet them. They'll be over the moon.'

Frank, too, she sees from his face. He'll take Kathy with him, so Jess finds the child's jacket and sneakers and gives Frank directions to Windsor West Primary. He doesn't remind her that she has not yet replied to the question he's near enough asked her.

As soon as Frank is out of sight Jess puts Eve in the stroller and almost runs to the phone box. Frank has two blocks to walk to the school but, unless he carries Kathryn, may meet the boys on their way home. Jess must be back before Frank is, back home and resolved.

Yet part of her doesn't give a stuff, wants only to lie about grinning and sighing and giving in. Jess sees things this way; she is drowning and, just like they say, it feels nice and there's a part of her doesn't mind at all, in fact is relieved. But another part of her realises that the serenity is just a part of drowning and must be fought against. This second part of Jess rings her father's house and gets no answer. And the phone book has been torn from its wire so she rings 111 and explains to the voice that answers that it isn't that big an emergency, but she needs to speak to Officer Tripp at the Windsor Police Station and there is no phone book in this booth.

So she is put through and she gabbles to Jenny that Frank has turned up — and yes, she's fine, and no he won't hurt her . . . of course she's sure, he's gone to meet the boys . . . no he won't steal them . . . Jess just *knows* . . . it's not like that, he's totally sober. In fact that, really, is the problem. He's turned teetotal, that's what he says. Promises never to drink again.

Jenny tells Jess to agree to nothing. Jenny can't leave the station right now but she'll be around to support Jess just as soon as she can. Within the half hour. Jenny says drinking is not the real issue; alcohol is only a trigger, a violent man is a violent man, it's in their psyche. 'Be strong,' says Jenny and Jess says, yes, she'll try, but she has to go now.

And she hurries home, tilting the stroller so that Eve gets only two wheel bumps instead of four. She is there before Frank and the children, has time to unload Eve and catch her breath. She remembers that last night she dreamt of Maguilla, one of those anxious dreams she's been having. A steeplechase circuit, and spectators, all of them wearing Frank's hat. A brush jump the stallion could take in a stride but he turned sour on it, stopped dead. Jess felt rigidity, and then was being hurled, shaken, tossed. Landing away from flailing hooves, no real pain but anger. A whip in her hand slashing down on his shoulder as he reared back. Gathering up the reins, raising a foot to the stirrup and seeing her own knee, the way it was shaking.

She got back on again. Even in her dreams. Never had been a horse that threw her and she hadn't got back on; a little wiser, a little meaner, a little heavier on the reins. But you couldn't *not* get back on.

Frank arrives back with kids hanging off him. The baby, hearing their voices drift in before them, gurgles and points. The boys have been asking all the questions that had crowded Jess's head, Frank's replies come up the side path. Bridey is in fine fettle, the pig hasn't been eaten, Sussex Susie still lays her eggs under the sofa if she can find a way in, and there are eight new bantam chicks . . .

They see Jess at the door and the boys fall silent. She smiles at them but still they are uncertain. 'How was school?' she asks, and they mutter and shrug. Frank removes Kathryn from his neck.

Ben takes a big breath, squares his shoulders. 'Are we going home then?'

Jess looks straight away at Frank, then wonders at the extent of her suspiciousness. Of course he hasn't put the boy up to this; he wouldn't have to, and it's not his style.

'Do you want to?' she says.

The boys are nodding wildly, Kathryn too, though maybe just in imitation. They are children and have short memories. Besides, their concern was always for her, she knew that. Jess should never have asked them. She is closing doors. And now they are waiting.

'I guess . . .' Already the kids are jumping about and shouting. It's like Guy Fawkes night. Jess looks at Frank. He's biting his bottom lip, his eyes are watering. She sees his Adam's apple bob. Jess feels colour surge into her, not the pinkness of cheeks but blues, greens, yellows . . . She is no longer invisible.

So Frank was standing there like a pig in shit. Ecstatic. Telling himself that this time life was handing him what he didn't deserve. But he'd make it up, to Jess if not to life, bloody oath he would. And the kids jumping about, chirping like crickets. And Jess's father walks in, came round the path, right in the middle of everything.

Frank saw by Owen's face that he'd got the picture all right. 'You,' he said to Frank. Then he said hello to the kids, how was school?, stuff like that, while Jess and Frank exchanged a look. The kids had picked up the tension and gone all wooden and mumbly.

Owen straightened up and looked at Jess who hung her head. He turned back to Frank. 'They were doing just fine,' he said in a strangled voice. 'Jess, can I have a word?'

'There's no point,' she whispered, still not looking up.

Owen said, 'I can't believe this.' He stepped in front of Frank. 'Why don't you just leave?'

Frank opened his mouth, was about to invite *Have another go at me, why don't you?* but the kids were watching, so he just stuck out his jaw and held his hands behind his back, which said it anyway.

Jess advised in a small firm voice that there was a packet of biscuits in the back of the cupboard and the kids should go inside and have two each. In silence they trooped into the kitchen, each of them touching their mother for comfort as they passed.

The schoolteacher's hands were still at his sides.

'Look,' Frank tried for a calm kind of voice, 'this has really got nothing to do with you.'

Owen shook his head incredulously. 'What kind of a bastard are you?'

At that moment a female copper arrived. Frank took it that she'd come to remove him, pre-arranged by Owen. But how could Owen have known unless Jess had told him? It wasn't until the copper went straight to Jess and put an arm around her as if they were old friends that the penny dropped. Frank decided on politeness, stepped towards her and held out a hand.

'I'm Frank Ward. Don't believe we've met.'

She ignored his hand, her eyes already cutting him down. 'But I know you,' she said. 'I was in the court.'

'Bet you were,' he said. 'Wasting your time.'

'Yes. We should've charged you with arson as well.'

Frank was near to losing his temper. 'Arson! You bastards didn't wanna know. I try and make a statement and no one takes a blind bit of notice. I was an eye witness. Saw the whole bloody fiasco.'

'Saw what?' Onto it, sharp as a bird. But out of the corner of his eye Frank had seen the schoolteacher get a kind of paralysed look, rigid with fear. It told Frank the girlfriend knew nothing about that night and the last thing that the schoolteacher wanted was to have her finding out. Owen was looking at Frank, and for a moment Frank looked back, cool and straight in his eye. Letting him sweat.

'What did you see?' the copper persisted.

'Nothing,' said Frank. 'Not so far as I can remember, it was a fair while ago.'

Owen's face began to unfreeze. Frank looked to Jess for appreciation but she was shoving the kids out the door.

'Fancy that!' The copper was wanting to share her smirk with Owen but his eyes shied away. She looked back to Frank. 'We'd like you to leave,' she said firmly. 'We're here to support Jess and the children. I think you've done them quite enough harm already.'

Jess was holding the door shut. From behind it came delirious giggling. Frank caught Jess's eye and beckoned his fingers — *tell them*. And Jess clapped her hands over her mouth — Frank couldn't believe he was seeing her do this, felt the shock of it like a lash from a stockwhip. Then he saw her hands tremble and realised she had caught a dose of the children's giggles. When he shook his head at her in dismay she bowed her head and let loose a sound that vaguely resembled a sneeze. Frank realised it was all up to him.

'Reckon we're gonna get back together,' he told the copper. He squared his shoulders and took a deep breath. 'I've knocked the booze on the head.'

'Oh yes?' Her voice dripping disbelief. 'How convenient!'

Frank looked anxiously at Jess, who now had herself under control. He wished he could have blocked her ears. Remarks like that could set her thinking, tip the balance against him.

'Hang on,' said Owen out of the blue. 'Give Frank a chance. Seems to me he's a fairly decent kind of fellow.'

Frank couldn't believe he was hearing this stuff. He took off his hat and held it beneath his chin. Owen hadn't finished.

'His kids think he's all right. Perhaps we should leave and let them sort this out on their own?'

The copper was outraged. 'Jess asked me to come!'

The schoolteacher's mouth had got him into trouble.

Frank reached out a hand. 'Thanks,' he offered.

The schoolteacher hesitated fractionally, then gripped Frank's hand in his.

'. . . Dad,' Frank wanted to say. It felt funny enough to be almost worth the risk. But then Jess came back to life.

'I'm sorry, Jenny,' she said in a small voice of shame. 'I didn't want to let you down. I'm so sorry.'

The copper got the dumbfounded look of someone witnessing a major accident. 'You really think it's going to be any different?'

Jess looked briefly at the woman who was her stepmother, and briefly at her father. Then she stared at Frank for a long time.

'Yeah,' she said finally. 'I must. Mustn't I?' And she smiled at Frank with such confidence that he felt certain she was looking far ahead into their future and seeing herself with a top, tea-drinking man.

AT THAT MOMENT, Frank would tell people, *I knew I could stay on the wagon.* 'And here I am,' he might add. But it still didn't make for a great ending. So after a while he cheated a little and had himself saying that *Dad* as he and Owen shook hands. And it worked so much better that, next time they met, Frank made a point of calling Owen 'Dad', so he could end the story there without fabrication.